# THE SILVER TIDE

*John H. Mann*

# J.H.MANN

DARK SPIDER BOOKS

The Silver Tide by J. H. Mann published by Dark Spider Books of 335 Babbacombe Road, Torquay, Devon TQ1 3TB, UK.

ISBN: 978-1-7392953-4-9

Copyright © J.H.Mann 2025. All rights reserved.

No part of this book may be reproduced in any form or by any electronic or mechanical means, including information storage and retrieval systems, without written permissions from the author, except for the use of quotations in a book review.

For permissions: contact@darkspiderbooks.com

This is a work of fiction. Names, characters, places and incidents are the products of the author's imagination or are used fictitiously. Any resemblance to actual persons, living or dead, businesses, companies, events, or locales is entirely coincidental.

Cover by MiblArt

# PRAISE FOR J. H. MANN:

*'J.H.Mann writes compelling fiction set in Cornwall. He transports his readers to rugged coasts and moorlands and introduces us to a range of complex, fascinating characters living in a beautiful but sometimes forbidding part of the world, where even the land itself can be both hostile and benign'*

– Margaret James, Writing Magazine.

*'If you love Cornwall, storms at sea and an engrossing mystery then look no further. J.H.Mann steps straight into the footprints left by Winston Graham and Daphne du Maurier'*

- Cathie Hartigan, author of Notes from the Lost and the bestselling Secret of the Song.

*'J.H.Mann lovingly evokes the Cornish landscape, from the Atlantic coast to the bleak and threatening moors, for his gripping stories'*

– Debi Alper, author of the Nirvana series of thrillers.

*For Nicola*

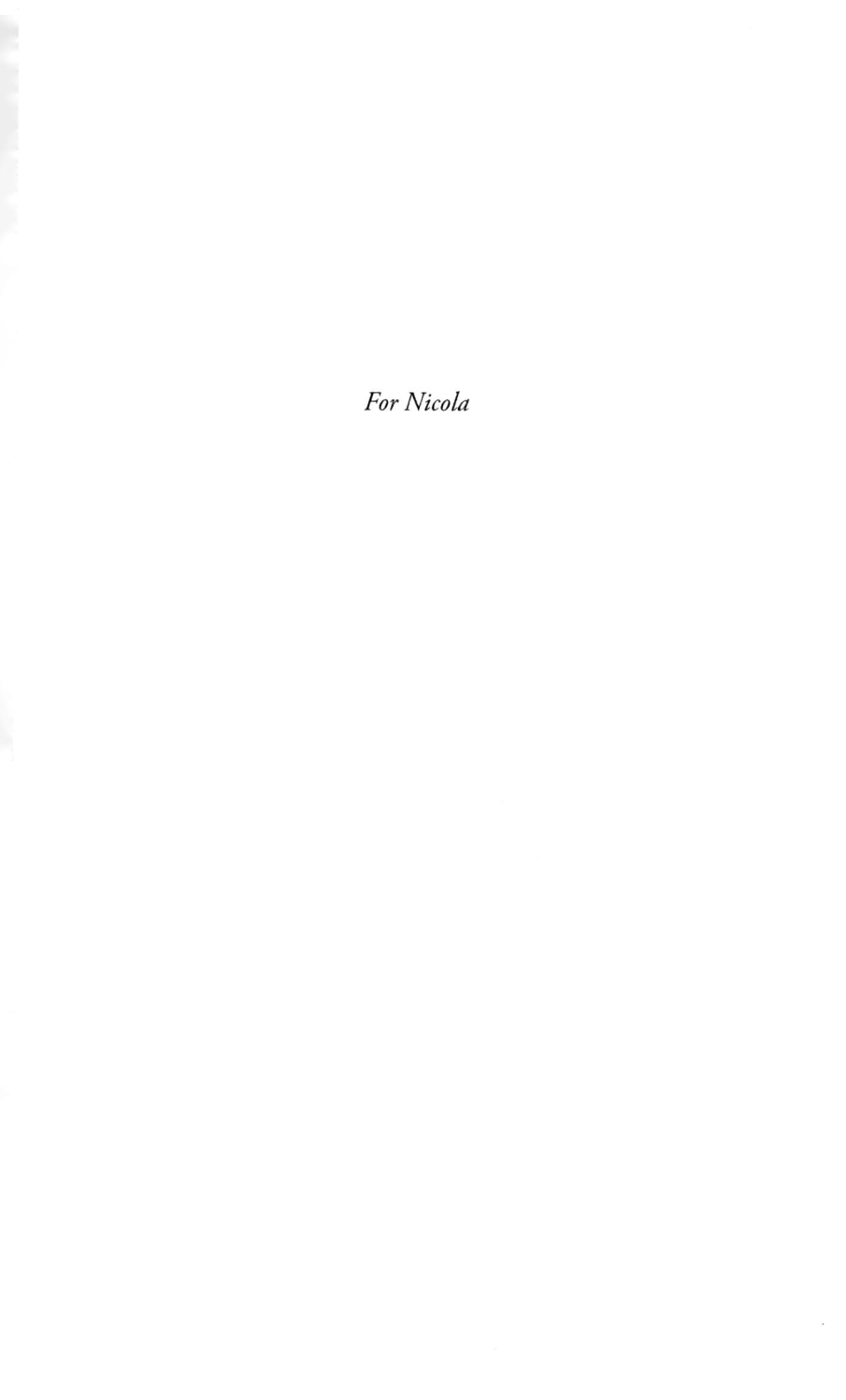

# AUTHOR'S NOTE

In 1874, the life of Margaret Brown, a fisherman's daughter, was changed forever when a summer storm sank her family's fishing boat, killing her father and three brothers. Margaret, standing on the beach with friends and neighbours, was left with the heart-breaking task of pulling their bodies from the sea. As a result of the tragedy, the community's first lifeboat station was established and Margaret threw herself into it fully, helping with many difficult rescues. She did not miss a launch for more than fifty years. *The Silver Tide* is inspired by this brave woman but is a work of fiction and therefore bears no resemblance to Margaret's real life or character. Further details are available at the end of this book.

## ALSO BY J.H.MANN

The Echoing Shore
Hidden Depths

# PROLOGUE

### Cornwall, England 1863

The boy steals out of the fisherman's cottage where he has lived all his twelve years as a hazy sun begins its descent to the horizon. He winces at the click of the latch on the side door and the squeaks and groans of the rusty front gate. A pause, a final glance backwards and then Jowan Bray tiptoes down the lane until there is no chance of the thud of his scuffed boots being heard by his mother. Jowan is a straight-backed, robust lad who already sees himself as a man. He's half a head taller than any boy of his age in St Branok and can outrun any man in the town.

His widowed mother would be furious if only she knew. Norah Bray's abiding vow has been that her son will stay away from fishing. But young Jowan has other ideas as he tramps down St Branok's higgledy-piggledy streets to the quayside in the oilskins once worn by his father. At last he rounds the final corner to stride onto the long breakwater. Built of Tregoning Hill granite, it juts out like a strong, brotherly arm to protect the fishing fleet from the storms that hurl themselves against Cornwall's ragged northern coast.

The harbour is alive with gruff fishermen readying for sea. Jowan slows and scans the organised chaos for the fleet's newest boat. It is easy to pick out. The salt and scum of

Atlantic fishing has yet to take its toll on the jaunty lines of the *Minerva*, a twenty-eight-foot West Cornwall lugger bought for the hefty sum of one hundred and twenty pounds by Solomon Pascoe. Her keel of American elm was laid by a St Ives boatbuilder noted for building by sight alone without any plans.

Jowan breaks into a run when he catches sight of a brawny figure, almost as wide as he is tall. Solomon is well known in St Branok and further afield for his exploits and bountiful catches. He holds the record for the seven-hundred-mile run from the North Sea Fishery. Sixty hours. Some say it will never be broken. Can never be broken. But today there is a flicker of worry in Solomon's weathered grey eyes which cannot be missed even by young Jowan. Solomon's long run of success has deserted him. Of late, his catches have been poor.

A few old salts, content to sit back and swap harbour gossip from the sidelines, insist that the bad luck has been caused by his twenty-one-year-old daughter, Maggie, being allowed to roam on deck when the *Minerva* is readying for sea.

'Weren't so long ago that the women were locked in their houses when the fleet be going out,' one sage, Alfie Cooper, reminds anybody who will listen. He will then often take his battered pipe out of his mouth, point the mouthpiece at the listener and add in a raised tone, 'And St Branok were the better for it, I tell 'ee!'

Superstition runs strong in the fishing town of St Branok, the ancient sea-spirit of Bucca being feared and respected in equal measure.

Jowan jumps up and down, trying to get the attention of Solomon and his three sons. He is ignored and so steps aboard without permission. Kitto, the eldest of the sons, confronts him. 'What in God's name do you think you're doing, boy?'

Jowan juts out his chin and holds his ground. 'Going out?'

Kitto stares down at him with a smirk of superiority. 'What does it look like? We ain't down here just to take the air. Course, we're going to sea.'

'I could be useful. An extra pair of strong hands.'

Kitto chuckles. 'Strong? This is a working boat. For men, not jumped-up kiddies. Sling your hook and get off before I tip you in the briny.'

'You weren't so much older than me when you first went to sea, so I heard.'

'You've got a loose tongue on you, boy –'

A calloused hand on Kitto's shoulder silences him. His father. 'Hold hard, son.' Solomon turns to Jowan. 'How old are you now, lad?'

'Fourteen,' Jowan blusters.

'He ain't nowhere near that age,' butts in a red-faced Kitto.

Jowan corrects himself smoothly. 'Thirteen…nearly.'

A knowing smile cracks Solomon Pascoe's leathery features, raising Jowan's hopes. 'Well, as it happens, we could do with help tonight.'

Maggie, Solomon's daughter, breaks off from handing over provisions to bustle over full of anxiety. 'Norah is dead against Jowan going to sea. You know what happened to his father.'

Solomon pulls a look of irritation. He isn't used to being questioned by his family. 'I know well enough,' he grumbles. 'Every man jack who goes fishing knows the risks. I've sailed these waters for nigh on thirty years and haven't lost a single living soul. This is my boat, girl, and I – and I alone – say who boards her.'

'But he's no more than a boy and Norah made it clear…'

Solomon grunts with disdain. 'To do what then? Grub a living earning eight shillings a week as a farm hand? He's a man near enough with salt water in his blood. He can't cling to his mam's skirts forever.'

With an uneasy eye, Maggie scans the skies scratched with lines of cirrus cloud, a sign that the fine weather of the past two weeks is nearing its end. A breeze is sweeping away the summer heat which has given the fisherfolk bronze complexions – but little else. 'The weather looks set for change,' she says.

Solomon follows her gaze. 'Aye and our luck will change with it.' He stretches his back, sore from heavy fishing duties. 'The pilchers will be back. Sometimes it needs a bit of mixed weather to move them.'

The poor start to the lucrative pilchard season is the talk of St Branok. For a month or more, lookouts along the Cornish coast have scanned the Atlantic in vain for the first signs of the great silver tide. The ocean has been empty of the vast shoals that each summer surge past Wolf Rock before reaching Land's End and sweeping south into Mount's Bay or north past St Ives, Newquay and Padstow. But earlier today a glimmer of hope emerged with a sighting at a nearby headland. The news spread like gorse fire across the towns and villages of the north coast.

But Maggie remains nervous. 'Izzie Rogers reckons that a storm is coming,' she says.

Solomon pauses. 'When did she say that?'

'This morning. There's anger in the sky, she said.'

Solomon shrugs. 'Old Izzie is always prattling on about something and most of it is right nonsense.' He bends to secure a line, impatient to be out at sea where he can catch fish and tackle his mounting debts. 'We need to get going.

The early bird catches the worm. And the early fisherman catches the pilcher.' His features, weathered by a thousand suns and Atlantic breezes, fold into deep creases as he grins. There haven't been so many easy grins of late.

Maggie persists, pushing her luck. 'But maybe a boy like Jowan should go out when the weather is easier?'

'A bit of spray and wind will do the lad no harm. Show him what fishermen are really made of. St Branok men are at their best when out in a gale.'

A snigger comes from Kitto who remains in earshot while fiddling with the hatch covering the fish and net rooms.

Maggie casts a wary eye at her oldest brother. 'Dad, can we talk alone?'

Solomon straightens up to his full height which is barely an inch taller than his daughter. 'Whatever's to be said can be said right here, girl.'

'The boy shouldn't be going tonight,' Maggie hisses. 'Not in rough weather. I promised Norah that we wouldn't encourage him. She says it's a passing phase.'

There are limits even to Solomon's deep patience with his daughter. 'If there was going to be a big blow, we'd have had the warning,' he says, his tone hardening. He points to a landmark on a headland. 'See. No signals. Nothing.' Sure enough, there is no sign of the cone and drum-shaped canvas signals used by the new FitzRoy weather forecasting service to warn of storms. His tone rises. 'These matters don't concern you. The boy needs to learn his trade. And he'll be useful.'

'But –'

'Don't test me.' He gestures with an imperious hand. 'You have home duties a-calling. Leave us men to do the fishing.'

Maggie sighs and clambers off the boat on to the gritty

quayside. 'Too big for 'er blamed boots that one,' Kitto mutters to his father.

Solomon growls a reply. 'She has a good, strong heart and she be your kin, lad, deserving of respect. Since your blessed mother passed two years ago – God rest her soul – she's been the woman of the house and done a fine job of it.'

Young Jowan watches Maggie retreat and wonders if she will tell his mother. If ma finds out, she'll be down the quayside like a shot to haul him home by his ear, despite being inches shorter than her son.

Long minutes pass, time in which Jowan expects his mother to appear in high dudgeon at any moment. He breathes a sigh of relief when the *Minerva* at last quits her quayside berth. The two older Pascoe brothers, Kitto and Logan, pick up long oars and sweep hard to the harbour entrance. Other crews pause to watch them go and then redouble their own efforts.

As so often before, the *Minerva* is the first of the fleet to reach open water. Her main sail is hoisted and sets, slapping in the evening breeze. The wind strengthens, ruffling the ocean. The *Minerva* responds smartly, heeling hard over. With full sails she is a fine sight at sunset, her rounded shape, mast stepped close to the bow, and narrow tall sails highlighting her St Ives origins.

The first saltwater spray splashes in Jowan's face as they round the jagged rocks of Tregloss Point. He senses an urgency amongst the Pascoes. If the silver tide has begun to run at last, St Branok will burst into frenetic life. The first big pilchard catch of the season always brings a carnival atmosphere. There will be a spring in everybody's step and the granite salting houses – known as pilchard palaces – will be full of shrieks and laughter and demands for more salt as the town's girls and women pile up the pilchards on layers of salt for the princely pay of three pence an hour. St Branok thrives on pilchards.

The sheer joy of sailing a lively sea takes Jowan. He chuckles and forgets the confrontation with his mother which will happen when he gets home. That is for later. Much later.

Solomon grins at the boy. 'This is what we were born to, eh lad? Not kicking our heels at home or chewing the fat on the quayside.' He licks salt from his lips and studies an iodine horizon speckled with whitecaps, his voice dropping to a murmur that only Jowan hears. 'In God I trust.'

Solomon eases the tiller over to better catch the rising wind and summons Kitto with a wave of his hand. 'We might be in for some heavy weather. Everything secure?'

Kitto slaps the bulwark. 'This beauty can handle anything the Atlantic throws at us.'

Solomon glances at his eldest son. 'She's a fine vessel, sure enough. But there ain't a fishing boat on this coast that can stand up to the hardest blows the Atlantic can deliver.' He adds with a sigh, 'Anyways, we need the money and some luck. We've not had much of either of late. Hoskin is not a man to be kept waiting.' Solomon's voice turns sombre. Jed Hoskin is his largest creditor, a personage of note in St Branok, known for his wealth and sharp business sense.

'Our bad luck can't last forever,' insists Kitto.

Solomon chews his fleshy lower lip. 'It'll last for as long as the Lord decides.'

Kitto glances over his shoulder. The first of their rivals are emerging from the harbour, red canvas sails, diminished by distance, billowing like handkerchiefs in the breeze. 'And we've got the drop on the rest of the fleet.'

Solomon grunts with satisfaction and then turns to

squint again at the ocean ahead. The *Minerva* ploughs on, shrugging aside the choppy waters slapping at her oak hull. 'Jowan lad, go for'ard and see what you can see with your sharp young eyes.'

Jowan jumps to it with youthful eagerness and is soon in the bow, staring out. He sniffs at a curious oily tang carried on the breeze. As the final rays of daylight break through the gathering clouds, he calls out, his tone high pitched. 'Up ahead. Up ahead. Up ahead. There! I see 'em!'

A swarm hangs above the ocean. Gannets and flocks of screaming gulls are plummeting down to peck at the surface of the sea, which has turned silver, red and purple – as if the ocean is bleeding.

Solomon bellows in exhilaration, 'Get ready!'

The *Minerva* comes alive with movement and strident voices. The main sail is hauled down, leaving only the mizzen flapping in the breeze, and then the nets are shot by willing hands. The boat drifts, trailing a half-mile of netting, with the crew passing the time working handlines to catch dozens of hake, the sharp-toothed predator of the pilchard.

'It's a big one,' Solomon shouts exultantly.

Jowan and the Pascoe brothers work hard, bracing their knees against the bulwarks, hauling in the nets until their arms burn and their breath is harsh. Torrents of sleek, silvery fish spew onto the deck, tails flapping wildly, eyes bright, still full of life.

Hundreds.

Thousands.

Solomon throws back his head and laughs. 'Nobody's going to get a better haul than us Pascoes.'

Jowan is soon exhausted and, though he wouldn't admit it, he is grateful when Solomon urges him to take a rest. The boy settles once again in the bow, watching with envy the strength and power of Kitto hauling in the net hand over hand. The joy of a big catch is infectious. He has never felt so alive, part of something so vital.

He tears his gaze away and stares out over the ocean. Only to blink in disbelief. A dark curtain is racing towards them, shutting out the stars and the moonlight. Even as he watches, it envelopes the distant outline of Gull Rock. And keeps coming.

Young Jowan senses its malevolence.

He mumbles a profanity he has heard Kitto use when Solomon is not in sight and then finds his full voice to point and yell, 'Over there! Over there!'

The crew of the *Minerva* are so consumed by the back-breaking task of hauling in the nets that they fail to hear him.

Jowan tries again but nobody is listening. He glances again at the advancing blackness. Closer now, much closer. Seething. With a line of charging white sea horses at its base. He has seconds. Wading through pilchards and netting, he reaches Solomon and grabs his arm. 'Sir, sir, a storm or summat. Look! Look!'

Solomon's square jaw clenches. 'Squall to port. Brace yourselves, boys.'

He swings the tiller hard over. But the immense catch makes the *Minerva*'s response sluggish as if she is afloat in treacle.

The blast hits the *Minerva* as she's turning. Her mizzen bulges to breaking point. Water pours over the stern, the weight of the huge catch dragging the boat down.

'Cut the nets,' Solomon screams.

Kitto looks on, aghast. 'What? You can't be serious. There's a king's ransom in them.'

'Cut 'em, I tell you –'

A crack like a gunshot sounds out. Something snaps and then the boat is flat on her side, her broken mast splayed in the sea. They hang on for dear life to anything they can lay their hands on.

Jowan loses his grip on the net roller and slides down the stricken boat while scrabbling for a hold. He is thrown overboard to be swept down the side of the *Minerva*, arms flailing, eyes wide with terror, his lips stretched in a gurgling scream.

Plucky vessel that she is, the *Minerva* starts to right herself. Solomon reaches down. 'Jowan, grab hold.'

The boy is hit by a wave, pushed down and then pops up again, gasping for air. Thrashing wildly, he manages to get a hand on the *Minerva*'s side. An iron grip grabs hold of his wrist and, with every ounce of his considerable strength, Solomon starts to haul him back on board the *Minerva*. 'I've got you, boy…'

Another rush of air strikes the *Minerva*, even stronger than before. It whips the surface of the sea into a bubbling cauldron and pushes the boat on to its side again. The lifesaving grip slips and then is lost. A mast crashes down on Jowan's head. The boy drifts away from Solomon's outstretched fingers. He is sucked under again and, when his head bursts clear this time, he is spent. The gap is widening.

Solomon dives into the water. He comes to the surface gasping and strikes out for Jowan but, weighed down by his oilskins and heavy leather thigh boots, cannot reach him.

The *Minerva* settles lower as a torrent of bubbles escapes from her hull. There's no saving her.

Jowan is sucked down and this time no lifesaving hand comes to his aid. He reaches upwards, trying to touch the glittering surface of the ocean, but he is dragged into the depths.

Down.

Down.

# CHAPTER ONE

A blast of wind and rain rattles the windows of the Pascoe family cottage. Maggie looks up from a mop and bucket to peek outside. The sky is darkening. A group of women, some with children, have gathered on a street corner to point and gesticulate out to sea. Maggie can't hear what they are saying though there is no denying the sharp anxiety in their voices. Her first thought is that it is another night of lost fishing, that her father and brothers will soon be home getting under her feet, fretful and dour. Or they might bury themselves in The Mermaid or The Ship for a few hours and come back boisterous from drink.

A gust sweeps a straw bonnet off a woman's head and hurls it up the street. With a shriek of annoyance, she sets off in pursuit. Other loose items follow: a crab pot, a few pages of the West Briton newspaper, even a shawl. The weather is more than troublesome. It's turning malevolent. Her stomach clenches. All her life, she's seen the weather in Cornwall change in a few minutes from sunshine to howling winds and rain. The women outside take shelter in the lee of nearby cottages, their full skirts swelling like the sails of a ship.

Urgent knocking sounds on Maggie's door. She tugs it open to see the diminutive figure of her friend, Norah Bray, clutching a threadbare shawl around her shoulders. Money is tight in the Bray household. Life as a widow with a child is hard. Norah keeps body and soul together by putting her slim fingers to tasks ranging from seamstress to mending fish nets.

Maggie ushers her inside without ado. 'You'll catch your death.'

Norah snatches a breath. 'They're in trouble.'

'Who?'

'All of them. The whole fleet. Out beyond Tregloss.'

Maggie gasps. '*Minerva*'s out there.'

'Are you coming?'

'Where?'

'Down to the waterfront.'

'Why? What in God's name can we do?'

'I don't rightly know, but I'm blamed if I'll hang around up here while St Branok men are dying.'

Maggie grabs her shawl from a hook in the hallway and the mismatched pair, Maggie a head taller than Norah, join a group of women threading their way down the winding streets, some clutching children. More women appear from other streets until a river of humanity is flowing down to the seafront.

They press onwards, their heads tucked low, uncaring of the wind which tugs at their sodden clothes and the rain and hail lashing their faces. On they go. Across the cobbles streaming with water. Down through Ginmouth and its ale houses. Past the empty pilchard palaces, to stare out through sheets of rain at a turbulent sea.

Maggie and Norah push their way through the crowd to stand beside a robust middle-aged woman with iron grey wiry hair.

'Anything?' Maggie asks.

Joan Tehidy talks out of the side of her mouth while

keeping her gaze fixed on the horizon. 'There's nothing. The ocean…it's swallowed them.' There's a catch in her voice. Her features are tight with distress.

A strident voice rings out behind them. 'They've been out in worse.'

Maggie turns to see Rose Pankhurst, the newly wed wife of a fisherman on board the *Prospect*, a lugger like the *Minerva*. A vision of their wedding springs into Maggie's mind: a simple affair but supremely happy. Full of sun and spring flowers. Half of St Branok had turned out for them.

If the St Branok fleet has been out in worse, then Maggie can't remember it. But she stays silent, not wanting to prick this bubble of optimism. The *Minerva* is a stout boat, fashioned by a builder who is one of the best. And there is no more experienced sailor than her father. 'I know this coast like the back of my hand,' he often says with that steady gaze of his. He'll need every ounce of that knowledge and experience now. He might run for cover in a nearby bay or make for St Ives if conditions allow.

The weather worsens. The waiting women are soaked and chilled to the bone, the hems of their long skirts slapping against their ankles. As full darkness descends, a few, the infirm and those with children, head back to their cottages. But most remain to maintain the vigil. If loved ones are battling the storm, then so must they.

'God help me, I hate the sea,' Norah says. 'Thank heavens, I stuck to my promise that I'd never wed another fisherman.' In truth, there have been no shortage of suitors for the fiery young widow but, in a town where fishing runs through the veins of most men, the choice is limited.

There is a parting of the crowd. A tall, eccentric figure, dressed in a claret-coloured coat and long sea boots, moves among them quoting scriptures. Parson Hedrek Kellow raises an arm as if he alone can calm the waters. 'Why are you afraid, oh ye of little faith?' He clasps his hands together. 'Let us find strength in the Lord. Let us pray. Lord God, deliver our fathers, sons and brothers from evil…' His voice rises against the wind. 'When thou passeth through the waters, I will be with thee; and through the rivers, they shall not overflow thee; when thou walkest through fire thou shall not be burned; neither shall the flame kindle upon thee.'

A breathless boy races through the narrow streets and presents himself to Kellow as the parson is finishing his impromptu sermon. 'Been up to the headland, sir. Boats in the distance. They're coming back.'

The murmuring of the crowd builds, tinged with renewed hope. Maggie's heart lifts. Please Lord, bring them home.

With a beneficent smile playing on his lean features, Kellow bends down. He takes the boy's hand but also, Maggie notices, slips him a coin. Kellow's charity takes many forms.

'He'll be expecting a good supper tonight,' a woman says of her man.

'It'll take more than a Cornish storm to drown my Cadan,' says another.

'There they are!' a voice screams. A woman points beyond the beach to a cluster of hazy lights visible near Tregloss Point. Out there are half the menfolk of St Branok.

The wind and driving rain ease. Kellow takes it as a sign. With his familiar limp, he battles his way across the wrinkled, hard sand to the water's edge. 'And Jesus said to the waves: Peace, be still! Then the wind died down, and it was completely calm.'

The crowd follows, hanging on his every word, trusting

in their parson, trusting in God. They line the seething water's edge.

A fresh blast, harder than anything before, assails them, turning the anxious crowd into a huddled mass. Only Kellow remains upright, his claret coat billowed by the storm. Many long minutes pass and when the conditions ease enough for them to look up again, the lights at sea have been swept from the face of the ocean.

'Where are they?' Rose Pankhurst marches into the shallows, ignoring cries from the shore. A frothy wall of water knocks her down. She clambers to her feet only to be pushed down again by a following wave. And by another. The backwash sucks her further out. She splutters a scream.

'I can reach her if we link arms,' Maggie shouts to the women nearest her.

Several women step back a pace, their fear of the ocean insurmountable. But others, including Norah, who detests the Atlantic more than anybody, advance into the surf to stand beside Maggie.

'Link arms. Like this.' Maggie uses Norah's thin arm to show a double grip in which each person holds the wrist of the other. There are grim nods from those around her.

The human chain ploughs into the surf with Maggie at its head. A towering wave crashes into them, knocking Maggie off her feet. Her grip on Norah – her lifeline – slips. Her fingers dig into Norah's flesh. A grunt of pain escapes Norah's lips but her hold remains firm. Maggie finds her feet. On she goes, with sea water stinging her eyes and streaming down her face and the roar of surf in her ears. The surging ocean rises to her neck. Her feet lose contact with the sand as the undertow drags her out. She glances back to see a chain of women, her only link to the shore, standing in varying depths of water, their dresses sodden and heavy.

She kicks her feet and goes deeper, searching among the froth and the spume for the young woman. Where is she? At last, she spies a body in the trough of a wave thundering towards the shore.

A push of water moves the body tantalisingly close. Maggie stretches out with her long, strong arm. The gap lessens to a foot. Becomes six inches. Then grows to two feet as the backwash from a wave pulls the body away.

She reaches again, stretching her arm to its limit. They're struck by another wall of water. Norah, too, is knocked down this time. For the first time her grip weakens and Maggie slips her hand free.

'Maggie!'

Maggie ignores Norah's anguished cry, paddling out with one hand while reaching for the young woman with the other. Her frantic fingers grip the lace on a sleeve. She pulls the floppy body towards her and turns it face up. The woman's skin is white and waxy. Her eyes are closed, her mouth hanging open. Can she still be alive?

A wave pushes them closer to the shore. Norah's outstretched hand comes within reach again. Hands lock together.

Relief is writ large on Norah's face. 'Back…pull us back…take us in,' she yells.

The women heave. Muscles and ligaments are strained to the limit. They make slow, swaying progress. One foot after another. Maggie is soon standing on sand in waist-deep water. With all her remaining strength she hauls the body clear of the surf and passes it to willing hands.

By the time she and Norah stagger ashore, Rose

Pankhurst has been laid out on the beach. Parson Kellow is bent over her.

Maggie edges closer.

'Call the doctor,' somebody says. 'Call Lander.'

'By the time he gets his sozzled soul down here she'll be long gone.'

'Poor lass. Only just wed.'

'We have a man of the cloth to deliver the last rites at least.'

Kellow is doing nothing of the sort. He is pressing down on the woman's chest, pushing the life out of her. The crowd looks on with a mixture of shock and bemusement but reluctant to question the clergyman.

'Sir, what…' a woman starts to say.

Kellow waves her away.

And then miracle upon miracles, Rose convulses, water erupts from her mouth, her lungs drag in a heavy breath, her eyes flutter open.

'Oh, my Lord,' says somebody.

A woman crosses herself. ''Tis the work of the Lord.'

'Or the Devil,' somebody whispers.

Kellow rises with Rose in his long arms. 'The Lord is with us this day. We need to get her to Dr Lander.'

Two quay labourers drag a barrow down to the water's edge and the young woman is placed on board as gently as possible, her head lolling to one side. The barrow is last seen being hauled up the beach and then into the maze of alleyways in the direction of the doctor's residence.

A hand falls on Maggie's shoulder. She swings around to see a fiery-eyed Norah pointing an accusing finger at her. 'That was a stupid thing to do, Maggie. By rights you should have been swept away.'

Maggie freezes. 'What?'

'You slipped my hand. Deliberately.'

'I couldn't leave her to die.'

'Are you trying to kill yourself –'

Norah's words are cut short by a shout nearby.

'Boats! There!'

A shaft of moonlight reveals a gaggle of luggers battling to reach the safety of the harbour. Even at a distance they're a pitiful sight with broken masts and tangled rigging.

A small group of boats splits from the sorry remainder. 'They're making a run for the beach,' somebody shouts.

'They'll never make it over the sand bar,' says another.

'The waves are too big.'

A breaker catches two of the boats and upends them. Shrieks and cries of despair come from the huddled mass of humanity on the seashore.

'They're all going to die.'

A clutch of boats struggles closer.

Maggie calls out. 'We can make another human chain. Who's with me?' A sea of anxious faces stare at her. Maggie persists. 'We did it once. We can do it again."

Norah comes to stand beside her. 'We can't wait here and let them die,' she implores anybody who will listen. 'Thank the Lord, I don't have a man at sea today, but I'll willingly risk my life for others.'

Guilt tugs at Maggie. Norah doesn't know it but Jowan, her beloved son, is out there with Maggie's father and three brothers. He might already be a floating corpse, eyes staring, mouth hanging open never to speak again. But no, her father would have done everything he could to look after the lad.

She turns to Norah, unable to contain her shame. 'Jowan is –'

Her words are drowned out by enthusiastic shouts as dozens of women step forward, ready to take part in a rescue.

No time for confessions. Not now. Let those come later after they have done all they can for the hardy souls fighting for their lives.

The human chain pays out into the surf with Maggie at its head once more. This time it is much longer. It swings and swerves, expands and contracts in the rip tides and the surf – but remains intact, secured by desperate grips.

Maggie braces herself for a huge wave crested with spume. It lifts her off her feet and then comes crashing down. Surf roars in her ears. Salty water is pushed up her nose and into her mouth. She holds her breath until her lungs feel fit to explode before bursting clear, coughing and spluttering.

She presses on, the sea swirling and churning around her skirt. The next curling mountain of water looms. She ducks and it roars over her head. Her grip on Norah and Norah's grip on her remain strong. She glances back to see her friend's face splattered with spray and froth. Can that be a smile on her face? A weak, uncertain smile perhaps but a smile, nonetheless.

'We can do it, Maggie.' Norah's eyes widen. 'Look out!'

Another deluge dashes them. Again, Maggie ducks down. Again, she holds her breath. And again, as she is reaching her limit, her head pops out of the surf. Blessed air. It has never tasted and felt as good. Undaunted, she pushes on.

Up ahead, an object is being pummelled by the waves. A log perhaps. A piece of wood. No, a body. The body of a man. Splayed. Face down. Swaying in the swell. She grabs a trouser leg and turn's the man's body over. Barely a man, really. More a boy. But not Jowan, thank heavens. The lad's skin is alabaster white. His eyes are closed. But his purpling lips move. A whisper of breath emerges.

'He's alive,' Maggie screams.

'Thanks be…' Norah's words are smothered by a mouthful of ocean. The human chain drags the boy ashore until able to hand him over to a group of women and elderly men standing in the shallows. Another life saved.

The success spurs on the rescuers. More women join the chain. Maggie ventures ever deeper. Now she is beyond the surf line and no longer having to contend with crashing waves but rather the rounded mountains of water surging towards the land.

Exhausted fishermen, clinging to the remains of a spar, thrash their way to the shore. Maggie grabs the arm of one of them. A grizzled veteran. He mouths short, staccato sentences between breaths. 'Our boat…she's gone…went down like a stone. One minute she was there…and the next.' He gasps several deep breaths.

Maggie, Norah and several other women help him and the others out of the surf and within a few minutes the entire crew of the lugger *Inigo* are shivering on the shoreline with thick woollen blankets wrapped around their hunched shoulders. Maggie kneels beside the shaking veteran. She knows him. Tensie, so called because he was the tenth son of his family, is a friend of her father's. He is muttering. 'Never seen nothing like it. The storm hammered us.'

'How many boats are in trouble?'

'Dozens. Half the fleet. We saw more than a few go down – pushed towards the rocks. We tried to help but then started taking on water real fast.'

Maggie catches her breath. 'Did you see the *Minerva*?'

'She was a bit ahead of us, away from the rocks.'

'Do you think…?'

Tensie stares down, unwilling to look Maggie in the eye.

'If anybody found a way out, it would be your da. There's no better fisherman on the north coast.'

The desperate rescue operation continues at a frenetic pace. More fishermen are recovered, many dead, others clinging to life. Maggie, Norah and the others work until they are shivering wrecks and their arms are red raw. But not for a moment do they rest.

Another shriek is heard further down the beach. 'Over here!'

A knot of bedraggled women, including Maggie and Norah, rush to where more bodies have been washed up on the water's edge. Maggie reaches for the nearest corpse and turns it over.

Kitto.

Her brother.

Oh God, please no!

They haul him out of the water and lay him on the sand. Maggie holds his head in her hands. Where is Parson Kellow? He must repeat the miracle he managed earlier – whether by the Lord or the Devil, she doesn't care a jot. But he is at the far end of the beach performing the last rites.

'Get the parson,' she yells. Kneeling in the sand and with bunched fists and head thrown back she begs for deliverance.

Kellow limps over as quickly as he can followed by an entourage of women. Maggie looks up with bleary eyes. 'Father…can you do anything?'

Kellow's thin face is stretched in a rictus of remorse. 'Stand aside.' He examines Kitto. Carries out the curious pressing down on the chest action that yielded such spectacular results earlier. But there is no eruption of life in the inert figure this time. With a sigh, he places a light hand on Maggie's shoulder.

Looks into her eyes. 'I'm sorry. Kitto…he's gone…to a better place.'

Maggie crumples, her breath coming in sucking gasps. The world spins around her.

Norah hugs her hard. Maggie hugs her back, even tighter. Tears well. 'The *Minerva* is lost…the whole of my family…gone.'

'We don't know that. Not for sure. Kitto might have been washed overboard. Your da knows the ways of the sea better than anyone.'

Maggie knows this is a sop to ease her agony. But still she's grateful.

A shout comes from the nearby quayside. A group of tattered luggers, loaded with the crews of other boats, have battled their way to the safety of the harbour. Maggie, Norah, Kellow and several others hasten over there as quickly as the soft sand of the beach will allow.

Please God, let the *Minerva* be among them.

Maggie's hopes rise as she climbs the short flight of steps up to the quay. More boats have made it than she expected, their crews shattered and broken but blessedly alive.

Her frantic gaze sweeps the sad remains of the St Branok fishing fleet. And then sweeps it again. Her father's boat is not there.

A body is lifted with care onto the quay. Smaller than the rest. Not a man, more a boy. Parson Kellow pushes his way through the milling crowd for a closer look. He crouches down, exchanges a few words with a robust fisherman, shakes his head and then limps over to Norah.

Maggie stumbles towards them. No. No. No.

Kellow takes both of Norah's hands in a soft and gentle grip, a sad compassion portrayed in his lean face as he gazes into her eyes. She stares back, her petite features screwed up in puzzlement.

He gulps and then says, 'My child, I have terrible, tragic news.'

# CHAPTER TWO

Maggie's world has turned silent and still. She sits slumped on the stairs of her family's cottage, head in hands. The storm abated during the night, leaving a numbing desolation in its wake. All the usual St Branok sounds of wheels on cobbles, children playing, men guffawing and women chatting are absent. The town's heart has been ripped out. The husky tones of her father and the banter of her three brothers will never be heard again. Shortly after daybreak their bodies – and those of many others – were recovered by search parties amid the remnants of smashed fishing boats.

A knock on the door breaks the suffocating silence. Maggie ignores it. But it persists. She smooths her long skirt and stumbles to the front door, glancing at herself in a mirror as she goes. She barely recognises herself. Eyes puffy and red. Hair tousled. The lines around her eyes deeper. She's aged ten years in a day. Maggie wipes away the trails of her tears, sucks a deep breath and tugs open the front door. A rich, morning light floods into the hallway. Shielding her eyes against the glare, she stares up at the tall figure who casts a long shadow on the slate slabs of her cottage.

'Father…'

Parson Kellow shuffles uncertainly on the doorstep, fingering a brimless hat. 'May I come in, Maggie?'

The caustic tang of bile fills Maggie's mouth. She doesn't trust herself to speak. Only a groan escapes. She steps aside as a signal for the parson to enter. Once inside, he places his soft hands on her shoulders. 'I am so sorry for your loss, child.'

His touch brings her voice back to life. 'My whole family dead. Why? Why? Why? We're a God-fearing family. St Branok is a God-fearing town .'

The parson mutters condolences.

Maggie clenches her jaw. ' We've done nothing to deserve all this.'

'All of us have sinned and fallen short of the glory of God.'

'But why us?' She's not going to let Kellow off so easily this time.

'Nobody is promised a life free from pain and sorrow. Even Jesus wept. The Lord commands us to be strong and courageous. He will wipe away every tear from our eyes. The Lord is our rock and fortress where we might take refuge. Believe in Him, child. Cast your cares on the Lord and He will sustain you.' His voice rises as if delivering another of his celebrated sermons.

Maggie takes a deep breath and makes a determined attempt to pull herself together. 'You performed a miracle with Rose Pankhurst, Father. You brought her back to life on the beach when she was most certainly dead. I have never seen anything like it.'

'Yes, quite remarkable. It is a procedure tried by a medical friend of mine at the Royal Free Hospital in London with some success though not yet formally recognised. The Lord guided my hand, I believe.'

'Rose has you to thank for her life.' She dredges up the

best smile she can manage at the resolute but obviously weary parson. 'Can I offer you a tea?'

'That would be wonderful… if it is no inconvenience.'

Maggie goes to the cottage's small kitchen with Kellow in tow, valiantly trying to fill the heavy silence with a semblance of small talk.

The old routines soothe her. The water is boiled, the tea brewed. Maggie leads the way into the cottage's modest sitting room. Kellow, keen to rest his sore left leg, takes a seat near the window, her father's. She imagines Solomon Pascoe tamping his pipe, sucking mightily and with satisfaction, holding forth on some issue of the day. Her vision darkens, her throat tightens as she takes her own familiar seat near the fireplace. She grips the arms of the chair until the spasm passes.

Kellow studies her with soft eyes. 'You shouldn't be alone, child. Do you have relatives who could provide respite?'

Maggie gulps and shakes her head. 'There's no one.'

Kellow rubs his forehead, tries another tack. 'Your friend, Norah, is also alone and grieving the loss of a loved one. You could find solace in each other's company.'

'Have you seen her since the storm?'

'I stopped at her home earlier.'

Maggie stares down at the threadbare rug which her father insisted they would replace when funds allowed, rather than look Kellow in the face. 'How is she?' Her grip on the chair tightens again. The tips of her fingers whiten.

'Much like yourself – distraught and questioning. She didn't realise her son was at sea until…until he was brought ashore.' He gulps. 'We prayed together and I believe it helped. She said she felt calmer afterwards. She asked about you.'

'What did you tell her?'

'I explained that I was on my way to pay you a visit. She would welcome your company, I'm sure.'

'Thank you but no. I don't think I can.'

'Shall we pray together?' Without waiting for an answer, Kellow kneels on the hard slate floor. He winces as he places weight on his troublesome left knee, swollen by recent rigours.

Maggie feels bound to join him. Kellow places a hand on hers. His palms are butter soft compared to the calloused, rock-hard grip of her father and brothers, which were ridged with thick skin from the relentless grind of fishing.

'Blessed be God, even the Father of our Lord Jesus Christ, the Father of mercies, and the God of all comfort; Who comforteth us in all our tribulation, that we may be able to comfort them which are in any trouble, by the comfort wherewith we ourselves are comforted of God…'

The rise and fall of the parson's strong voice is hypnotic. Maggie closes her eyes and lets her mind wander, unable to believe that her brothers won't come bursting through the front door full of laughter, that she won't have to scold them for not removing their grimy boots or for snatching a piping hot scone from the oven tray. The temptation is to curl up. To give up. To die. What is to become of her? She has no income and few worthwhile skills. Her hands are too large and clumsy for an occupation such as seamstress like Norah.

Kellow's authoritative voice drones on. 'And God shall wipe away all tears from their eyes; and there shall be no more death, neither sorrow, nor crying, neither shall there be any pain: for the former things are passed away.'

How apt. Her family has, indeed, passed away.

The parson concludes with a firm 'Amen' and then raises his greying head to look her in the eye. 'Let me walk with you to Norah's cottage. She'll welcome your company.'

Maggie gets up with the aid of a shaky hand on a table, but her voice is firm enough when she replies, 'I'm sorry. I need to rest. I haven't slept all night.' She takes a deep breath and then adds, 'There should be a meeting in St Branok to talk about what happened.'

'A public meeting you mean?'

'Yes, for the whole town.'

Kellow sighs. 'It will reopen the wounds of the tragedy, I fear.'

'But if all of St Branok is involved, we might be able to agree a path which would help prevent a future disaster. If this tragedy has taught us anything, it is that things need to change. We owe it to those who have perished.'

Kellow nods, persuaded. 'I'll make enquiries, see if there is support for such an audience.'

The parson makes a final attempt to encourage Maggie to visit Norah, but Maggie's mind is set and so he departs alone down the lane with a wave of his brimless hat and an assurance that he will call again. Does she need anything? No, no, she will manage, thank you. With only her mouth to feed, the provisions in her larder will last for a week or longer.

Gripping the windowsill, she watches until he has limped out of sight and then – with a pounding headache – drags herself upstairs to her bedroom. It is in the eaves of the cottage with a view down the coast and of slopes of gorse, bracken and grass. To reach it she needs to pass the large bedroom shared by her brothers. This time yesterday it had reverberated to bellowing laughter, exclamations of minor annoyance and, yes, even a whispered profanity or two when their father was out of earshot. Now it is echoingly silent and seemingly much larger.

Reaching the refuge of her own room, she collapses on

the bed, more exhausted than if she had hauled a hogshead of pilchards up from the quayside. She wonders if she has the strength and any reason to rise again.

# CHAPTER THREE

Maggie is roused many hours later. Assertive knocking on her front door breaks her fitful doze. Quitting the soft temptations of her bed, she scurries to the window in her father's room which overlooks the front of the cottage. A petite figure is waiting.

Norah.

A second bout of knocking ensues, louder than before. Can she bring herself to answer it? As Maggie hesitates at the window, Norah looks up and glimpses her friend.

She holds up a slim hand and calls out. 'Maggie!'

No choice now.

Norah stumbles into the hallway as the unlocked door judders open. The two women hug even more fiercely than they did at the beach. It brings warm sensations Maggie has not felt since her mother died after a lengthy illness. The Pascoe family was a loving household right enough, but that love was expressed in the respect of her father and her brothers' banter and jokes rather than any physical contact.

'Oh Maggie, why us?' says Norah.

'I asked Parson Kellow that very question.'

'What did he say?'

'He quoted from the Bible, said we're all sinners and that nobody can be immune from grief.'

'First my husband and now my son. In truth it has tested my faith. Why would a merciful God allow such tragedies?'

Maggie ushers her friend through to the kitchen. 'Who knows what part we all play in the grand scheme of things?'

Norah clenches her little fists. 'Now you're sounding like the parson. Jowan should never have been at sea. I told him. Begged him, I did. But he was like his da with a mind of his own.' She hesitates, thoughtful. 'He must have found a boat which was willing to take him on board. He's a strong boy, stronger than some men.'

Norah still talks about her beloved son as if he is alive. Fresh guilt stings Maggie. Why in God's name didn't she do more to stop Jowan going aboard? She quells the guilt with practicality. 'Have you drunk or eaten anything today?'

'I'm not hungry.'

'Have you?'

'Well…no.'

'I haven't either. We both should.'

'I couldn't eat a scrap.'

'You must. We both must.'

Norah licks her full lips. 'You're right. But not pilchers. I never want to see another of those cursed fish ever again.'

'You'll be needing to get well away from St Branok then. Near enough every soul in this town lives or dies by the pilchard.' She adds before Norah argues otherwise, 'I have some fresh eggs and taters from Denzel's Farm.'

'That'll be lovely.'

The two friends busy themselves in the kitchen, desperate to absorb themselves in simple tasks. 'Have you thought about what you will do now?' says Norah gesturing around the cottage as she washes grey Cornish earth from golden potatoes. 'You can't stay rattling around in this place.'

'It's too early…I…I can't even think about it…not yet.' Maggie's gaze follows the gesture. Across the kitchen to the hallway and beyond to the sitting room, now becoming dim in the half-light of evening. The family home has never felt large, her boisterous brothers making the place cramped at times. But now the place seems as cavernous as a cathedral.

'Do you have money?'

'Not much.'

'Your da was a canny operator. He'll have made provision. And you read and write beautifully. Perhaps the parson could find a place for you at the school. Or what about seamstressing? It has stood me in good stead. I could teach you.'

'You're very kind, but I don't have the fingers for such delicate work.' She holds up her hands for inspection.

Norah glances at them. 'Well, there are other possibilities.'

Maggie moves away to light lamps and bring some warmth to the cottage. Flames splutter to life, creating a golden glow on the ground floor and tainting the air with the musky smell of burning pilchard oil. She returns to the kitchen to find Norah serving up two platefuls of eggs with rich yellow yolks and potatoes. The sight of it provokes Maggie's first pangs of hunger of the day. They eat in silence at the solid kitchen table. Maggie fingers a small crevice in the wood carved by one of her brothers. Logan had gouged at it week after week, slowly expanding the hole, only to get a wallop from his father when the misdemeanour was discovered. The memory brings her closer to him.

Sated, they retire with mugs of tea to the sitting room where Maggie takes her usual place and Norah curls up like a demure cat in Solomon Pascoe's armchair. They talk in short exchanges between long moments of silence as night closes in.

Maggie fetches a Bible from her father's bedroom and reads out a passage from Romans on sufferings and future glory. Norah half listens and then says, 'Parson Kellow would have us believe that our all our solutions are in the Bible but where was God when good men and boys were dying?'

Maggie closes the Bible softly. She has no answer. And neither, she suspects, does the Bible. At least not one she can believe.

A weariness, engendered by grief, overwhelms them. Blessed oblivion falls like a curtain. Maggie wakes with a start to stare with bleary eyes at a snoozing Norah. A hollow feeling of dread tingles through her which for a moment she cannot identify. Then it all comes flooding back. The loss. The agony. The hopelessness. If only it was a nightmare which could be forgotten in the merciful light of day.

Norah blinks. Her delicate features register confusion at her surroundings and then twist into a bleak acceptance as she, too, comes to terms with the harsh new reality. She glances out the window. 'I'd best be getting home,' she says as she uncurls herself.

Maggie takes her hand. 'It's late. Don't go. I can make a bed up.'

'I wouldn't want to put you to any trouble.'

'It's no trouble, no trouble at all. It'll be a kindness to both of us.'

A tear tracks the contours of Norah's gaunt face. She brushes it away. 'If you're sure.'

Maggie snuffs out all but one of the flickering lamps which she carries upstairs.

She visits her brothers' room. To be struck once again by its silent expanse, the beds neatly made by Maggie after her brothers, grabbing caps and pulling on long sea boots, raced out in pursuit of their father who was already striding down the hill. There are the small, personal items: Kitto's harmonica which he played often and badly, Logan's wooden carvings of ships, Ben's books which attracted the derision of his older brothers.

'You're welcome to sleep in here,' Maggie ventures.

Norah's emerald eyes sweep the room. 'Thank you. But it doesn't seem right somehow.'

'There's my dad's room.'

Norah shakes her head. 'Perhaps it would be best for me to go home.'

'No, stay. Please.'

'Could I share your room?'

'It's tiny.'

Norah places her hands on her waist. 'I'm tiny.'

They trudge up the narrow stairs to her room in the attic. Few outside Maggie's family have ever visited the box-like space with a single window. The fluttering light of her lamp reaches into the corners, illuminating the sparse contents – a single bed, a side table, a chair and a small wardrobe, roughly made by her father a few years earlier. And, of course, a Bible and a few other books that she shared with Ben.

'There's more than enough space for little me,' Norah says. The room feels stuffy and airless in the warmth of a summer night.

Maggie slips the latch on the window. Cool air filters in. 'I've got one of the best views in St Branok,' she says pointing outside to a now peaceful scene lit by a three-quarter moon. 'There. Look. The lighthouse at Trevose Head.' In the distance, two lights, one set high and the other lower, are visible to sharp eyes.

Norah, standing on tiptoe, murmurs polite agreement

and then walks over to the bed to sit down. 'I could sleep here. With you.' She looks up at Maggie. 'I can fit in most things.'

Maggie rummages around in the bottom of her wardrobe. 'I have a nightgown about the right size for you.' She hands Norah the neatly pressed garment. 'It was mine when I was a child.'

Norah holds it up, a sceptical expression on her features. 'Thank you. I'll give it a try.'

Maggie does a final round to check everything is secure. When she returns Norah has changed into the white nightdress. It hangs off her like a sack, emphasising her child-like proportions. She gives a nervous little laugh. 'I feel lost in this.'

She slips into bed and, holding the sheet under her chin, watches Maggie as she pulls on her own nightdress. Maggie faces away as she changes, self-conscious of her body. Nobody has seen the milky white skin of her back since her mother. Her body is strong and robust, perhaps too strong and robust for the young men of the town.

At last, she joins Norah. The bed feels cramped for two people, even one as small-boned as Norah. The two women lie side by side, contemplating the ceiling. Outside, an owl hoots and a distant dog barks. The cottage usually echoes to small and not-so-small sounds throughout the night – her father snoring, Kitto pissing or puking the aftermath of a night at The Mermaid in the gutter outside.

'I thought I didn't want company tonight but now that you're here I'm so very glad not to be alone,' Maggie says at last.

# CHAPTER FOUR

The full tragedy of the event which comes to be called the Great Gale of '63 unfolds in the following days and weeks. Seventy-one St Branok fishermen lost. Forty-two wives widowed. Thirty-one families left without fathers and with no income. Fifteen fishing boats sunk. Another twenty damaged. St Branok has suffered a mortal blow.

Parson Kellow has never been busier. He visits the bereaved tirelessly, arranges parcels of food for those most in need, administers funerals and, on Sundays high in his pulpit, preaches fiery sermons of redemption and hope. 'The Lord is nigh unto them that are of a broken heart; and saveth such as be of a contrite spirit,' he thunders to sombre audiences that have never been bigger. 'My flesh and my heart faileth, but God is the strength of my heart and my portion forever.'

Maggie sits at the back of the congregation, gripping a Bible like it is a life raft. Norah doesn't attend.

Kellow places a gentle hand on Maggie's shoulder as she arrives for Sunday service, twenty-three days after the storm that took her family. As always, she is one of the first. He regards her with caring eyes. 'How are you, child?'

'I am coping, thank you, Father.'

Kellow glances around. 'I was hoping we could talk after the service. Perhaps you could stay for a few minutes?'

'Of course.' She always has time. Her days are filled with no more than the preparation of scant meals, prayer and long, empty hours of sorrow. She's lost weight. At home, she stares into the hallway mirror at a haunted face, asking the same questions over and over again, 'Why me? Why us?' Sometimes she whispers it. Sometimes she screams it. There is nobody to hear.

When the church has emptied and the crowd drifted away, its heavy mood lightened by a rousing service, Kellow approaches, his eyes bright.

'Wonderful service, Father,' Maggie says for want of anything better.

'Thank you. I felt truly inspired today. In times of trouble when we are tested, Revelation offers some of the most poignant guidance.' He takes a deep breath and then with relish repeats a few of the quotations he thundered from the pulpit. 'For the lamb which is in the midst of the throne shall feed them and shall lead them unto living fountains of waters: and God shall wipe away all tears from their eyes.'

Maggie waits for his fresh burst of enthusiasm to subside. 'You wanted to speak to me, Father?'

'Yes, yes, indeed. I was hoping we could speak about your good friend.'

'Norah?'

'Yes.'

A twinge of uneasiness flicks through Maggie's stomach. 'About?'

'I could not help but notice her recent absence from the church. Is she ill, do you know?'

'She is well enough…physically at least.'

Kellow gently ushers Maggie away from the remaining churchgoers congregated outside the church. They stop in the shade of an ancient oak tree. He says, 'I fear Norah is struggling with her faith. There have been reports…' His voice trails away as he becomes uncharacteristically tongue-tied. He licks his lips and then gushes, 'For he that wavereth is like a wave of the sea driven with the wind and tossed.'

Maggie stares at Kellow. 'Reports of what?'

Kellow's ruddy complexion colours. 'Of…of indiscretions.'

'Who from?'

Kellow waves away the question. 'Several sources. I am deeply concerned. For her soul and her reputation, you understand.'

Maggie recalls some of her recent encounters with Norah. Her dearest friend has been rising late and her appearance has become dishevelled. 'Have you been able to visit her recently, Father?' She softens her tone to add, 'I'm sure you've been very busy.'

'I have tried to see her. Several times. But she's either not at home or chooses not to answer the door. I suspect the latter. I was hoping that with your help…'

'Anything. Anything at all.'

'We could visit together perhaps. She is more likely to answer the door to a friend, a good friend like yourself.'

'When?'

'Why not now? There is no time like the present.' Kellow's anxious look is replaced by a sudden smile. 'I have some news which will be of interest to you both. Welcome news.'

They stride up the cobbled road to Norah's little cottage after Kellow has delivered a few final warming words to a clutch of his adoring parishioners.

'I am pleased to see you attending my services so

regularly,' Kellow ventures as they walk. 'All things are possible for one who believes.'

Maggie conceals raging doubts with a murmur of agreement. They have crept up on her in recent days but she's not ready to share them with the parson. 'You said you had news?' she says after a short silence.

'Yes, indeed. But let us wait until we are with Norah and…I am able to…catch my breath and rest my leg.' He pauses, wheezing. 'You must excuse me. My limbs are not what they were. Long life is said to bring wisdom and understanding but also infirmity.' They meander up the hill at a more moderate pace with the parson greeting passers-by in his affable, easygoing manner. Everybody in St Branok knows him.

Norah's cottage shows no sign of life as it comes into sight when they turn into Squeeze Belly Lane. The front gate squeaks on rusty hinges, the salty coastal air and lack of maintenance having taken their toll. Maggie knocks on the door and she and Kellow shuffle on the doorstep. When there is no answer, Maggie tries the door. It's unlocked. They step tentatively into the dimly lit hallway.

She listens for a few seconds but hears nothing. 'Norah, Norah, are you there?'

A scuffling sound comes from somewhere. Rats? They're the scourge of St Branok. Maggie makes her way upstairs, leaving Kellow to pace up and down the hallway while levelling a critical gaze at dusty surfaces.

Norah is face down on the bed, her auburn hair tousled, obviously wearing clothing from the previous night. A bottle sits on a bedside table still holding a few drops of a clear liquid. Maggie sniffs at it. Gin. The cheapest kind.

She shakes Norah's shoulder. 'Norah, Norah. Wake up!'

Norah blinks open a bleary eye. 'Maggie, what the…?

'Parson Kellow is downstairs.'

Norah's almond-shaped eyes widen. 'Why?'

'To see you. He thinks you're trying to avoid him.'

'Jesus Christ!' Norah swings her legs over the side of the bed, holding her head in her hands. She groans. 'What can an old windbag like him ever do apart from blow hot air?'

Now is not the time for Maggie to remind her friend of Parson Kellow's innumerable good works. He is the power behind many ventures which have made the hard, grinding life of St Branok a tad easier, including the local school and the harvest festival. 'At least see him.'

'I can't.'

'Please.'

'I'm not ready.'

Maggie places a gentle hand on Norah's shoulder. 'Please. For me.'

'Give me a few minutes,' Norah mutters.

Maggie returns downstairs to find Kellow staring up the staircase with a grim expression. He has heard every word. 'It is as I feared,' he whispers while they wait. 'Satan exploits our weaknesses.'

Norah has performed a minor miracle and succeeded in looking presentable by the time she eases herself down the narrow staircase with a steadying hand on one wall. 'Father, to what do I owe this pleasure?'

Kellow bows. 'Mrs Bray, thank you for taking the time to see me. I have been hoping to speak to you properly for quite a while.' The tone is mildly accusatory.

Norah stares, defiant. Maggie breaks the awkward silence. 'Norah, perhaps I could make tea for us all while Parson Kellow and yourself talk in the sitting room?'

Kellow manages a weak smile. 'An excellent idea. It was a rewarding but long service today. I'm parched, I must confess.'

Norah swallows hard, nods.

Striding as purposefully as his limp will allow, Kellow heads into the sitting room as if he's leading a congregation. Maggie hears him enthusing about plans for the harvest festival as she busies herself with the tea-making. The voices become muffled. The sitting room door has been closed. It is difficult to hear what is being said, though she can tell the parson is still doing most of the talking. She catches half sentences.

'Trust in the Lord…the one who endures to the end will be saved,' she hears Kellow intone, his deeper voice droning on for long periods, punctuated by terse responses from Norah.

As Maggie carries a tray through to the sitting room, Norah's voice rises. 'If God has deserted me, then I will desert him. No loving God would have taken away my beautiful son.' She gulps and then adds, 'Or Maggie's father and brothers.' Her thin cheeks redden as she realises Maggie is standing in the doorway.

Kellow reaches out and seizes Norah's hand. 'Take heart. All of us are tested in our lives. The Bible tells us that Jesus wept at the death of his friend, Lazarus. Deuteronomy says that our God is a merciful God. He will not leave you or destroy you or forget the covenant with your fathers that he swore to them.'

Norah's eyes brim. 'Jowan was my son, my only son. Your *merciful* God took my husband five years ago and now he takes my son. How in heaven's name can he be merciful?'

Maggie places the tray on a nearby table. An awkward Kellow greets the arrival of the hot drink as if it is nectar. 'Ah, excellent. I've been praying for this.' There is another deafening silence while they all sip their tea. Kellow sighs. 'A fine brew,' he says, while studying a frowning Norah over the rim of his cup.

Maggie sets down her own tea. 'You mentioned that you had good news, Father?'

'Yes, indeed. I have been successful in arranging a public meeting on Friday evening to discuss the tragedy. To see what can be done.'

'Who is attending?'

Kellow rattles through a list of St Branok citizens including Jed Hoskin, the wealthiest self-made man in the town, and Nathaniel Narracott, a pencil-thin lawyer with a pale face rarely touched by the Cornish sun. 'Mr Hoskin has kindly offered one of his large storehouses on the quayside as a meeting place.'

'Can anybody go?' says Maggie.

Kellow pulls an uncertain look. 'It will be mainly the menfolk of the town but yes, I suppose so.'

Norah's eyes spark with anger. 'What good will it do? We are slamming the door after the horse has bolted. Our men are dead. The sea will keep taking us. More husbands, fathers, sons and brothers will die. It lures us out with promises of riches and then delivers death. God can't protect the righteous, it would seem.'

Kellow wipes a damp forehead. 'We are all open to the temptation of despair. We must not blame God for our trials. We should thank him whatever our situation.' He sighs and then with a grim smile says, 'It makes demons mad when we thank God.'

Maggie's heart thuds faster. 'I want to attend that meeting.'

# CHAPTER FIVE

On a warm, late summer evening, the cobbles of the town resound to the thud of boots and strident male conversation. Maggie joins the throng with Norah, who has had a last-minute change of heart and agreed to accompany her to the public meeting after all.

The atmosphere of the storehouse is already hot and thick with the whiff of pilchard oil burning in the lamps. Doors are left open to allow a flow of air. Some of the men pause their conversations to glance at the two women, their gazes resting longer on Norah. Maggie and Norah slip through the gathering crowd and make their way to a makeshift stage. The rickety appearance hints at it having been built in haste.

Standing behind a long table on the stage is Jed Hoskin, a man to be reckoned with in St Branok though his stature is unremarkable. Hoskin is of average height, in his late thirties, starting to run to fat, his flashy clothes betraying his desire to distance himself from his humble quayside beginnings. Flecks of grey streak his thick, dark beard and a top hat conceals his receding hairline. He is talking with Parson Kellow, making assertive chopping gestures as he delivers a point in his usual brusque, forthright tone. Kellow is holding the King James Bible that accompanies him everywhere. To the left of Hoskin is the grave figure of Nathaniel Narracott, who has established himself as the local man to go to for legal matters.

Maggie edges closer to better hear the conversation between Hoskin and Kellow. 'Feelings are running high. We should ensure that the meeting remains orderly,' Kellow is saying.

With his narrow blue eyes, Hoskin gazes across at the gathering masses. 'You've no need for concern, Reverend. I have strong men here tonight who are well used to dealing with any manner of disturbance.'

Maggie turns to see several of Hoskin's hefty henchmen posted strategically at the entrances to the building with arms crossed and cold, watchful expressions.

Kellow looks down from the stage to lock eyes with the giant George Moyle, once a noted rabble-rouser, who has inveigled his way into Hoskin's inner circle and now accompanies him everywhere. Moyle has dull grey eyes which rarely reveal his thoughts. More indicative of his mood is the puckered scar on his left cheek which turns livid when he is angry or excited. Tonight the scar is crimson, but his eyes remain the colour of ditchwater.

Kellow looks concerned. 'I hope we can rely on your men to act with restraint, Mr Hoskin.' He nods at Maggie and Norah. 'There are women here. St Branok has had more than enough upset in recent times.'

Hoskin wipes his glistening forehead with a silk handkerchief. 'This is not a place for womenfolk, but rest assured, Reverend, my men will do all that is necessary to ensure order. They will not be the instigators of any violence but, if disturbances arise, they will fight fire with fire.'

Kellow taps his Bible. 'The teachings instruct us to do good to all people, Mr Hoskin. We should all be mindful of that.'

Hoskin taps the table, unwittingly – or perhaps wittingly – mimicking the parson. 'Of course, but it is the book of Exodus, I believe, which invites us to take an eye for an eye and a tooth for a tooth. Unruly behaviour requires a stern response.'

'People are upset but there is no reason to think that they will descend to violence.'

The conversation between the two men rumbles on for a few more minutes before petering out, leaving both looking disgruntled.

The storehouse is full to overflowing, the press of people forcing Maggie and Norah forward. The crowd comprises stout fishermen with luxuriant beards, a variety of local traders and a few other women, mainly wives and mothers of the lost. A myriad of voices, punctuated by shouts and coughs, echo through the stuffy atmosphere. Maggie wipes a cotton handkerchief across her clammy forehead.

Parson Kellow stands and with arms raised silences most of the chattering masses, though a few at the back of the room continue whispering. 'Friends, thank you for coming tonight. It is many years since our community has suffered the sort of tragedy which befell us a few weeks ago. To those who have suffered loss, our hearts go out to you. We are with you. We are one community.' He clasps his hands together. 'I invite you to join me in a minute's silence in respect of those who have been taken from us.'

A murmur of appreciation ripples across the crowd. Heads are bowed and a hush descends, broken only by an occasional cough. When Kellow starts speaking again a rush of blood warms Maggie's cheeks as she senses eyes looking in her direction. Nobody has suffered more than she has. She is careful to keep her gaze on the tall figure of the parson, who is pointing to the two men standing next to him on the stage. 'Mr Hoskin has generously offered to act as chairman for this meeting, while Mr Narracott will be keeping a record of the proceedings and any actions agreed.' He makes a sweeping gesture. 'Mr Hoskin, the stage is yours.'

Hoskin pulls at his beard. He looks hot in his long dark coat, double-breasted waistcoat and pointed boots. A patina of sweat glints on his face despite his best efforts with the handkerchief. For long seconds, he stands with hands on hips, surveying his expectant audience, daring anybody to speak.

'You all know me to be a man of action, a man who gets things done,' he says at last. 'What has happened is a tragedy. Some have blamed it on the waves which wash our shores, saying we should turn our backs on the sea. They are fools. The sea provides our livelihood. It gives us everything we need. We live on it and by it. Without fish this town would be nothing. It wouldn't exist.' He holds up a fist and then thunders, 'Brave St Branok men will never shy away from the sea.' His reward is a tumult of cheering and clapping. Hoskin knows how to stir an audience.

At the back of the room, a tall man raises a hand. He is smartly dressed and has an upright military bearing. 'Why didn't we get any warning of the storm? Why weren't the storm signals put out?'

Hoskin makes a deprecating sweep of his hand. 'Most men in this room will know what I think of FitzRoy's blamed new weather service. It's a muddled contrivance which is not to be trusted. We should rely on the ways that have stood us in good stead for generations. I ask you, how can a panjandrum tucked away in London know the sea and sky around here better than our own fine fishermen? The man's a huckster, peddling myths and snake oil.'

Murmurs, some in agreement, others against, echo through the building. Hoskin waits until they subside and then carries on. 'Now as I was saying…'

The man shoves up his hand again and when Hoskin ignores him, calls out, 'And yet other fishing towns and villages did get the warning and most fishermen didn't go to sea. Why didn't the warning reach a God-fearing town like St Branok?'

A stout, older woman nearby joins in. 'Yes, why weren't we told like others? We should have been warned.'

The murmuring in the crowd grows. Hoskin raises his voice. 'FitzRoy's reports are nothing more than an advisory service. They lack rigour and have not been properly tested.'

The man shouts, 'We should find out why the warning never reached us. There should be an inquiry. A *full* inquiry. By the authorities.'

Hoskin's eyes flare with anger and his shouted reply is infused with spittle. 'My good sir, you are disrupting an important meeting which should be looking forward, not back. If you refuse to desist, I'll be forced to –'

The questioner pushes his way forward. He is not a young man but sprightly and forceful enough. 'Questions need to be answered. We shouldn't rest until we have answers.' An angry buzz in the crowd is gathering momentum.

Hoskin's gaze finds the menacing George Moyle. The two men exchange knowing looks. Moyle performs the slightest of nods and then disappears into the crowd heading for the man who has spoken out. There are the sounds of a scuffle and then the man is bundled out of the hall by Moyle and another of Hoskin's bruisers, still yelling, 'Let go of me. I should be free to speak. We need answers. Men have died – '

'Wait here,' says Maggie to Norah. 'I want to speak to that man.'

She pushes through the packed audience. The crowd has turned restive. Private discussions break out among groups, competing with the speakers on the stage. The anger of the ejected man has broken the surface of an uneasy calm, ripped open a wound.

The journey to the doorway proves long and difficult. Many men stand aside but a few stare at Maggie and remain unmoving, forcing her to slip sideways through small gaps. 'Excuse me, I need to get by, please.'

She passes through the final line of men at the back of the hall, and bursts out into the warm night, sucking in blessed fresh air. It has grown fully dark since she entered and St Branok's streets are lit by glowing lamps in the cottage windows.

Of the angry man who sparked the furore, there is no sign. Maggie strides up Crantock Street. Two women slouch on a street corner. She approaches them. 'Excuse me, have you seen an older man, smartly dressed, pass this way? He left the big meeting at the quayside a few moments ago.'

In the half-light, she sees the women properly for the first time. They return her look with cynical stares, their faces heavy with powder.

The older woman steps forward, a sneer twisting her glossy lips. 'If a man of means passed this way, luv, then he wouldn't have gone no further.' She throws a glance at her companion. 'We'd have found a way of keeping him amused wouldn't we, Vi?'

The younger woman moves out of the shadows. She's young, barely older than Maggie, though the make-up adds ten years. Her smile is less of a sneer, more genuine. 'I did see a man in the distance a few minutes ago. He stopped at the corner and went up Tregloss Street.'

'Thank you. Thank you so much.' Maggie leaves with a grateful smile.

'I hope you get your man,' the older woman calls out. She is still chuckling as Maggie enters Tregloss Street and then walks quickly uphill, her gaze searching the gloom. Tregloss Street is wider and better cobbled than most St Branok streets, the houses and cottages larger and better kept. If he lives here, he is a man of worth.

A figure in dark clothes emerges from a side street. Maggie hurries towards him. 'Excuse me, excuse me, sir.'

The man looks up in the process of lighting a pipe, the flare from a match illuminating youthful, unlined features. It's not the man she is looking for. This one is stockier and much younger. 'Oh, I'm sorry. I thought you were somebody else.'

He grins. 'How might I be of service, ma'am?'

'Have you seen anybody walk this way? An older man, well-dressed?'

He shakes his head. 'No. Nobody. This part of town is deserted.'

'Everybody is at the public meeting.'

'The Parson Kellow gathering you mean?'

'Yes. The man spoke at the event but left in a rush. I was hoping to talk with him.'

The young man finishes lighting his pipe. He seems a cut above most men in St Branok. And he looks familiar. 'I'm not sure it's a good idea for a fine young woman like yourself to be tramping the streets alone at night.'

'I need to get back to the meeting.' Maggie steps away. 'If you'll excuse me.'

'I'm going that way. I'll walk with you.'

'And how can I be so sure that *you* are to be trusted?'

He falls into step with her whether she likes it or not. 'I'm the skipper of the *Eliza Jayne*, as fair a lugger as you will find in these waters. I'm well known in St Branok.'

The *Eliza Jayne*. Of course. 'Thank you, Mr Treloare. But I can fend for myself.'

He grins. 'Ah, you know my name? So my reputation goes before me. Then you will know me as an honest and reputable fellow. Please call me Jack. And you are?'

Maggie ignores the question. 'I thought the *Eliza* was owned by Jed Hoskin?'

He frowns. 'I hold a minority share.'

'Why aren't you at the meeting? I understood all the fishermen were going.'

'It'll be a talking shop. Nothing worthwhile will be decided.' There's a condescending tone in his manner which Maggie finds irritating.

'You are very sure of yourself,' she says. 'How can anything get any better if we don't get together and talk about it?'

He sucks hard on his pipe, giving himself time for thought. 'You might be right at that. Perhaps I should be less of a cynic. Perhaps I should go and put in my two penn'orth.' He continues walking with her.

Maggie quickens her pace, hoping this unwanted companion will take a hint. 'I have a friend who is expecting me,' she says. It does nothing to deter the irritating Mr Treloare.

The meeting is still in full swing when they arrive at the Hoskin warehouse.

Jack glances around. 'Where is your friend?'

'Near the front of the stage. It's a nightmare getting through the crowd. It takes ages.'

'Follow me,' he says.

Jack takes off through the crowd with Maggie close behind. Unlike her, he has no difficulty working his way through the masses. There are nods of respect and even hearty slaps on the shoulder as he eases his way through. Jack Treloare is a popular fellow.

Hoskin is taking questions from the floor as they reach Norah. She is waving her hand for attention, but it is lost in the much taller men standing near her. Hoskin's gaze passes over her to a portly gentleman with an extravagant curling moustache. 'Tom, what say you?'

Norah pulls an exasperated expression when she sees Maggie. 'I've been trying to speak for ages.' She lowers her hand. Her gaze turns to Jack whose attention is focused on the stage. 'How did you find Jack Treloare?' she whispers out of the side of her mouth.

'I happened across him outside,' Maggie hisses. 'He insisted on accompanying me.'

'He's welcome to insist as much as he likes as far as I'm concerned,' says Norah with a mischievous grin.

Their exchange is cut short by the portly gentleman saying there should be a memorial to honour those who have sacrificed their lives. 'And there should be a fund for those most in need,' he adds. 'It is the honourable thing to do.'

Hoskin nods. 'Wise words, Tom. Wise words. It so happens I have a parcel of land near the quayside ideal for a memorial.' He pauses. 'I need not remind any man in this building that the fishing has not been easy for much of this year.' He allows murmurings of agreement and then adds, 'But I am willing to contribute to a fund for those most in need because of this tragedy. Nobody can accuse Jed Hoskin of standing by while St Branok innocents starve.' A thundering round of applause greets his announcement.

Norah resorts to shouting. 'Memorials and charity are all very well but what about taking action to prevent further deaths?'

'What action can be taken?' says a tall man behind her. 'Our men are strong. They know this coast better than any living soul. And our boats are tried and trusted and built of the stoutest timber. The sea gives and it takes. While men go to sea there will always be fatalities. The old ways have stood us in good stead for generations.'

Maggie butts in, her voice high pitched. 'The old ways aren't always the best. I lost my whole family!'

Hoskin pulls a patronising smile. 'You're emotional, my dear, and I can understand why after what you've been through.'

'Yes, I'm emotional and with good reason. Young men – men in their prime with wives and children and mothers and fathers – have died and for what? For a few fish.'

Hoskin's eyes turn icy though the glimmer of a smirk remains on his lips. 'To feed and clothe their families, my dear. That is why those men were out there. That is why our men risk their lives every day: to put food on the table for their loved ones.'

A man further back calls out, 'Women shouldn't have been allowed at this meeting. We need strong, rational talk, not the spouting of bereaved women.'

Maggie clenches her fists. She pushes through to reach the stairs to the stage, a hot and heady anger overtaking her. Gathering the folds of her long skirt, she starts to climb the stairs.

George Moyle grabs her arm. 'You're not going up there, luv. That space is reserved for –'

Maggie shrugs off his grip. 'I'll go where I want.'

Moyle's ditchwater eyes flicker. 'You'll go where I tell you.'

'I want to speak. I have a right to speak.'

A hand the size of a shovel clamps on Maggie's arm again. She pulls away and shoves Moyle hard, harder than she intended. Surprise flashes across his heavy features. He stumbles back down the stairs, only saving himself by grabbing hold of the edge of the stage.

'Damn her!' he bellows.

'What the…' Jed Hoskin strides over.

But Parson Kellow cuts in front of him to usher Maggie on to the stage. 'Let her speak. She's suffered more than anybody in St Branok.'

His words go unheard. There are shouts and yells all over the building, some in favour of Maggie speaking, others against a woman being allowed to address the crowd from the stage.

'Silence! Silence!' Kellow yells at the top of his voice, imperiously holding up his hands. The furore dies.

Kellow repeats his insistence in strong but measured tones that Maggie should be given the chance to speak. He casts a benevolent gaze at her. 'The stage is yours.' He whispers out of the corner of his mouth, 'Be quick. Their patience is short.'

Maggie turns to be confronted with a sea of faces, some angry, others curious and perplexed. She gathers herself, takes a deep breath. 'St Branok should have its own lifeboat.'

Hoskin sighs with scepticism. 'I doubt the powers that be would ever agree to it. The cost would be considerable.'

'And what price should we put on the lives of our husbands and sons and brothers?' It's Norah, yelling from the front of the audience.

Maggie's defiance and determination grow. 'There has been a lifeboat station at St Ives for more than twenty years and Newquay has taken delivery of the *Joshua*,' she shouts. 'Why in heaven's name should we not have one in St Branok?'

Hoskin shakes his head in a deprecating manner as if he alone has all the answers. 'Both are bigger. St Branok is barely a town.'

Another voice calls out above the hubbub. Jack Treloare. Three strides take him up on to the stage. 'The lifeboat proposal makes sense. It's worth a try at least. St Branok has one of the largest fishing fleets in Cornwall. And we are close to the main shipping routes. Look at what happened to the *Copenhagen*. If a lifeboat had been closer, more than fifty lives might have been saved that night. God rest their souls.'

Hoskin gives Jack a poisonous glare as support spreads across the room. Minds stretch back to the wild night five years ago when the state-of-the-art steamship *Copenhagen*, en route to Dublin with a cargo of brandy and tea, foundered off The Moules and sunk within the hour, her iron belly ripped open. Hoskin had led a party of his followers down to the shoreline at first light, ostensibly to rescue any survivors. They reported finding no survivors but did return with five carriage-loads of brandy barrels which melted into the streets and ale houses of St Branok.

Kellow leans forward. 'It is a proposal worth exploring. A letter of enquiry to the Royal National Lifeboat Institution would be a start.' He turns to the hunched figure of Narracott, the lawyer. 'Perhaps we could entrust your good offices with this task?'

Narracott glances at Hoskin who nods grudging approval. 'I will prepare a draft for Mr Hoskin's perusal.' He scratches a note with his steel-nibbed pen.

Jed Hoskin dredges up a watery smile. 'Thank you, Mr Narracott. It is worth a try, I suppose.'

The meeting drags on for a few more minutes and then Hoskin calls a halt to proceedings and Kellow, in warm tones, thanks everybody for attending. The crowd disperses noisily, the rowdiest to the local alehouses.

Maggie finds Norah and they prepare to leave.

Norah pats Maggie on the shoulder. 'Well done. You told them.'

'It seemed blessedly obvious,' says Maggie. She glances around for her unlikely ally. Jack is nearby, vigorously making a point to a group of swarthy fishermen who are nodding in agreement.

'It was an *obvious* idea which you alone suggested,' points out Norah.

They follow the flow of people heading outside. The building is emptying as quickly as a contraband bottle of brandy downed by thirsty St Branok fishermen.

Maggie suppresses a sigh. She should be satisfied at her minor victory, but she feels only drained and exhausted and needing her bed.

# CHAPTER SIX

Jack and Parson Kellow seem good friends. They fall in step with Maggie and Norah as they trudge up the hill.

'A hearty well done to you, Maggie,' Jack says. 'That's the closest I've seen to George Moyle being dumped on his arse!' He glances sheepishly at Kellow. 'If you'll excuse my words, Father.'

Despite her best efforts to prevent it, Maggie feels Jack's ebullience seeping into her.

'And she put roly-poly Jed Hoskin in his place too.' Norah giggles.

Maggie fingers her arm. It is sore.

Norah notices her wince. 'Is it bruised?'

'Nothing serious. I've done worse in the kitchen.'

'I have a herbal remedy at home. Come back to my place.'

Maggie smiles with gratitude. 'Thank you so much.' Where would she be without Norah? Where would Norah be without her? They've become intertwined by tragedy. The greatest friendships are forged in adversity, so they say.

Parson Kellow looks concerned. 'Moyle is a scoundrel and a bully. Always has been. Why Hoskin employs him, heaven only knows.'

'Talk of the devil,' says Jack.

They all turn to see the daunting figure of George Moyle shoving his way through the crowd towards them. A couple of urchins – grubby little boys of eight or nine – get in his way and are swatted aside like flies.

A red-faced Kellow steps in front of him. 'Mr Moyle, you hurt this woman.' He points to Maggie. 'I think an apology is in order.'

'She was causing a disturbance. Got what she deserved. Excuse me, Father.' He steps past Kellow to confront Jack who is a hand shorter than Moyle. 'Mr 'oskin wants to see you.'

'I'm busy with friends, George, as you can see.'

'Mr 'oskin said *now!*'

'Well, I'm otherwise engaged *now*,' says Jack, his tone still light.

Moyle grinds his teeth. 'So, you're refusing to see 'im?'

'Not refusing. Just not now. Tell Mr Hoskin I'll call on him in the morning,' he says, emphasising the *H*.

Moyle seems oblivious of the slight. 'It doesn't do to keep Mr 'oskin waiting.'

Jack turns away without further comment.

Moyle growls an insult and then storms off, still muttering. This time the two urchins are quick to get out of his way.

Kellow watches him go. 'A nasty bit of work. And he's dangerous. I heard talk of him cracking open the heads of a couple of fishermen who crossed him last year. You'd do well not to make an enemy of him, Mr Treloare.'

Jack adjusts his coat. 'I'm well capable of looking after myself, but thank you for the advice.' He yawns, and consults his fob watch. 'It is getting late and I had an early start before dawn today.' He tips his hat to Norah and Maggie. 'I bid you goodnight, ladies. Hopefully, we'll meet again very soon.'

Maggie, Norah and Kellow meander up the lane with Kellow, as ever, doing most of the talking. 'I fear that Mr Treloare is sailing into troubled waters if he's going to antagonise bruisers like Moyle. The man never forgets an insult, real or imagined.' He turns to Maggie. 'But well done, child. I am increasingly of the belief that a lifeboat station is an excellent proposal.'

The compliments warm Maggie's cheeks though when she speaks she finds the strong voice she used on stage has deserted her. 'Hoskin didn't like it very much,' she says.

Kellow murmurs agreement. 'Mr Hoskin rarely likes anything that's not proposed by him.' He hesitates and when he speaks again his voice has turned bitter. 'I ask you, the arrogance of the man – did you hear him? Quoting the Bible to me of all people!'

'He runs St Branok these days,' says Maggie.

'He has a finger in numerous pies. Nobody can doubt the success of his business ventures, but it is his soul I am more concerned about. All of us will be judged equally at the gates, no matter how many fishing boats we own.'

At the rusty gate to Norah's cottage, Kellow says farewell and limps off into the night with a final wave.

'He's a good man,' says Maggie.

'He is, indeed. Come away in. I'll make up that poultice. It'll help to draw the bruise out of your sore arm.' Norah ushers Maggie into the kitchen and clatters around in various cupboards, pulling out jars, bottles and glasses.

Maggie watches with interest. 'What are you making?'

'An old recipe from my great-grandmother. She had a cottage full of herbs and remedies. The locals would often visit her for help rather than waste their time and money with the local doctor. She was accused of being a witch by a woman who thought she was having an affair with the stupid bitch's husband.'

'Oh, my goodness, what happened to her?'

Norah chuckles. 'She lived until she was nigh on a hundred. I remember visiting Great-Granny as a child many times. She showed me this recipe for bruises after I'd hurt my knee and I've never forgotten it.'

'What was she like?'

'A lovely old soul. She had a remedy for everything. My ma said I'm very much like her. She had green eyes. Like me. And she was tiny. Even smaller than me.'

Norah pours hefty slugs of a colourless liquid into two glasses. 'Here's something pretty magical. Drink this. You'll feel better for it.'

'What is it?'

'Try it and see what you think.'

Maggie lifts it tentatively to her lips. A sharp tang reaches her nostrils which she cannot place at first. 'It smells like…'

'You're not supposed to sip it. Down the hatch in one go. Go on!'

With a helping hand from Norah, the glass is upended and the pungent liquid cascades down Maggie's throat. She coughs and holds a hand to her mouth to stop the drink coming back up. 'Oh, my goodness. What in heaven's name is it?'

Norah giggles. 'A local concoction. Made by a farmer friend of mine.' Norah has no shortage of male friends who have misplaced hopes of something more.

Maggie is horrified. 'I don't drink…' Her voice fades as she realises that is no longer true. On one night of desperation, she downed half a flagon of rough cider from her father's store and passed out until the following morning to wake surrounded by puke.

Norah swigs back her own glass of the mysterious liquid and then places leaves of sage on a chopping board. She presses them with a rolling pin and then drops them in a saucepan before grabbing another bottle. 'Now for some vinegar,' she says. She adds the vinegar to the sage in the saucepan and boils it for a few minutes, removes the sage leaves and forms them into a compress which she places on Maggie's sore arm when it has cooled.

Maggie relaxes and enjoys the feeling of somebody tending her, of the gentle touch of Norah's slim, dexterous fingers.

'What now?'

'We leave the compress in place for at least thirty minutes.' Norah picks up the mystery bottle again and applies two more hefty doses to the two glasses. 'And we have a little more of this whilst we're waiting.'

Maggie knocks it back, willing to journey into oblivion.

# CHAPTER SEVEN

On a moody September morning of high winds and torrential rain, Maggie, hunched in a shawl, trudges down streaming cobbled streets to the law firm of Narracott and Tremayne in Crantock Street. The front door, swelled by the recent rains, requires a shove. It judders open to reveal a wizened clerk at a desk scratching his pen across a buff-coloured envelope.

He pauses to look up through thick spectacles. 'How might I help you, madam?'

Maggie shakes the rain from her shawl. 'I have an appointment with Mr Narracott…Miss Margaret Pascoe.'

The clerk ruffles through the papers on his desk. At last, he finds a note filled with spidery handwriting. 'Ah yes, please follow me.' He leads the way up a narrow staircase and then taps on a rickety door at the top. After no response, he knocks again a little louder.

A voice on the other side of the door rings out in an irritated tone. 'What is it?'

'Your eleven o'clock is here, sir.'

'Well, don't loiter out there. Bring her in.'

The door squeaks open. The thin form of Nathaniel Narracott, curved like a farmer's sickle, is bent over an expansive desk buried in papers and files.

He snaps shut a ledger and beckons. 'Come. Come. Take

a seat.' He nods to his clerk. 'Albert, if you would be so kind as to assist our guest.'

The clerk hastens forward to pull out the chair smoothly.

Maggie settles herself as best she can on the unforgiving hard wood of the chair. Mr Narracott clearly doesn't believe in mollycoddling his clients, though she doubts the likes of Jed Hoskin endure such discomfort. No doubt he is received in more amenable surroundings. Her gaze falls on two easy chairs next to a log fire smouldering in the grate, giving enough warmth to ease the unseasonable chill.

Narracott takes a file from the pile on his desk and passes it over to his deferential clerk. 'Ensure you prepare these papers this morning. An associate of Mr Hoskin will be collecting them at three o'clock prompt.'

The clerk seizes the paperwork with the eagerness of a seagull snatching a pilchard and places it under his arm. 'Of course, sir. I will have everything ready.'

Narracott flutters a hand at the door. 'You may leave us.'

The clerk bows. 'Thank you, sir. Oh dear…' A ream of papers slips from the file and floats down to land on the floor. The clerk drops to his knees to snatch them up. 'I'm so sorry, sir.'

The lawyer drums his fingers on his desk while the clerk rummages around on the floor. At last, the wayward documents have been rounded up and with further bowing gestures, the obsequious Albert retreats to the stairs.

The door closes as softly as its ill-fitting construction will allow and the sound of footsteps fade. Narracott's droning voice begins again while he is rifling through the file in front of him. 'Miss Pascoe, let me tender my sincere condolences for your loss. A terrible affair, most terrible.'

Maggie's grip on the arms of the chair tightens. It is

strange how a simple expression of sympathy prompts all the hurt to bubble up again.

Narracott looks up from his papers. He steeples his fingers. 'In such testing times, we can all take strength from the Lord.'

Maggie finds her voice, though it is a pale version of her usual forthright tones. 'Parson Kellow has been a tower of strength. He is a wonderful man. I don't know where I would have been without him.' She lapses into anguished silence.

Narracott manages a watery smile. 'Quite so, where would we all be without Parson Kellow leading us in the paths of righteousness, eh?' His smile fades. He coughs. His voice turns clipped. 'And now to business. I have spent a not inconsiderable time examining the ah…somewhat complex details of your late father's estate. He was a wonderful fisherman by all accounts but, if I might be so bold, record-keeping was not his strong suit.' He ruffles through a pile of papers. 'I regret to say there are extensive debts and creditors who will need to be satisfied. Your father borrowed heavily when he purchased a new fishing boat…' – he flips a page – '…the *Minerva*, I believe.'

He descends into legal jargon, full of clauses and sub clauses, indemnities and insolvencies.

She interrupts. 'Will I be able to keep my home?'

Narracott utters a hollow laugh. 'Good Lord, no. I'm afraid there's no chance of that, no chance whatsoever.'

'But it's my home. It's where I have always lived. All I have ever known.'

'And a valuable asset which will need to be relinquished in order to settle your father's substantial commitments.'

'So, what am I left with?'

'When all debts and arrears have been settled in full, I

believe you will have…' He consults the papers strewn in front of him again before quoting a pitifully small sum.

'What is to become of me? Where will I live?' Maggie's chest heaves.

'Do you have relatives nearby who can assist?'

Lost for words again, Maggie resorts to shaking her head.

Narracott stares at her, expecting her to say something more. At last, he says, 'I have taken the liberty of consulting with your father's principal creditor. He is a merciful man who doesn't want to cause undue hardship, but he has a charge on the property in question and is entitled to take possession if debts go unpaid. Taking account of your circumstances and the considerable sums involved, he is willing to wait two weeks.'

'Is…is that all?'

'You have a *full* two weeks to make alternative arrangements. The offer is more than generous. My client is willing to write off a modicum of the debt if the process can be completed promptly and without fuss. He is within his rights to take possession immediately and to press for full recompense. But he has no wish to see an upstanding woman like yourself in a debtors' prison. The conditions are harsh and, as you will be aware, imprisonment is indefinite until the debt is repaid.'

'Who is the client in question? If I can explain my situation to him in person, he might perhaps grant more time.'

'The debt is owed to a firm called Pendrudgen Holdings.'

'Who owns it?'

Narracott's pale face turns stony. 'Client confidentiality prevents me from revealing personal details. I have discussed this unfortunate situation with the owner at some length and he has been clear that this is his best offer.'

'But he might reconsider when I have personally explained my predicament.'

'I would advise against it. He is a busy man, not known for changing his course once he has set it.'

'Is it Mr Hoskin?'

A twinge of annoyance spasms across the lawyer's face. 'I believe I have made myself clear. I really cannot say.'

Maggie clutches the edge of the desk, giddy. 'It is him, isn't it?'

'Madam, please do not test my goodwill any further. If you persist, I will have no alternative than to –'

His words are cut short as Maggie leans forward, clutching her stomach. A surge of bile rushes up her throat and splats onto Narracott's desk. Pin pricks of light cloud her vision.

She is vaguely aware of Narracott staring at her with disgust.

He strides over to the door and wrenches it open. 'Albert…Albert…Albert, come up here. I need you. Now!'

There is the pounding of running footsteps on the bare stairs. 'Sir, how…?'

'Get over here. Miss Pascoe has been taken unwell.'

'Shall I call Dr Lander, sir?'

'Just get a cloth. Clear up this…this abominable mess.'

Narracott bends over Maggie. 'Miss Pascoe, can you speak?'

Maggie feels Narracott's bony claw of a hand on her shoulder. She leans back. Her spinning world steadies. The nausea passes.

The clerk returns with a cloth and a bowl of water and sets to work. Too vigorously for Narracott. The water mixes with the puke to create a miasmic pool which reaches out to touch the corner of a sheaf of papers. 'For God's sake, be careful,' snarls Narracott. 'I have valuable papers on this desk. Of great import!'

At last, the clerk's efforts pay off and a semblance of order is restored. Narracott examines his fob watch. 'I have another appointment. If there is nothing further I can assist you with?'

Maggie blinks back tears. 'No…I…I…' Her voice fades away.

Narracott opens a file on his desk. 'In which case I bid you good day.' He turns to the clerk. 'Albert, be so good as to escort Miss Pascoe to the front door.' He forces a supercilious smile and then says with finality, 'Good day, madam.'

Maggie stumbles down the narrow stairs. The clerk offers her a helping hand but only succeeds in getting in her way. It is a minor miracle they don't arrive at the bottom of the stairs in a tangle of broken limbs.

Maggie takes a deep breath, gathers herself and then steps outside to find, typical of Cornwall, that the weather has taken a dramatic turn. The rain has been replaced by sunlight glinting off the wet cobbled streets. St Branok life rattles on in its usual vibrant, chaotic manner. Maggie pauses to stare as if she is seeing it all for the first time. She is part of it and yet not part of it. Her place in St Branok, once so set and assured, no longer exists. She has been cut loose, a drifting sliver of flotsam in a sea of change, at the mercy of men like Narracott and Hoskin. Men in tall hats stride to appointments, ragged boys push and pull trailers, shouting and guffawing, mothers cradle babies in their arms while out on some domestic duty. Everybody has a purpose. Everybody has a home. Everybody has their place in the community, no matter how low it might be.

Everybody but her. What is she going to do? What can she do?

# CHAPTER EIGHT

Tregloss Point rears up in all its raw, craggy beauty as Maggie, braving clothes still damp from the morning's downpour, makes her way up the muddy path later the same day. Her ankle-length boots and the hem of her skirt are soon sodden. She doesn't care a jot. Seagulls shriek overhead. Whatever happens to her, whatever poverty she might endure, this place will remain as unchanging and solid as the granite on which it stands.

She plods past clumps of fading white and blue coastal flowers which once thrived in the joy of spring and the heat of summer and then takes a left-hand path down to a haphazard hut made of shipwreck timbers, bleached by the Cornish sun and incessant winds. Parson Kellow is outside stretched out on a chair with paper and pen in his lap. His eyes are closed, his breath is slow and rhythmic. He's fallen asleep.

She sits down on a rock nearby. It is easy to see why Kellow built a hut here as a quiet refuge away from his church duties. It has a magnificent view along the ragged coast to distant, treacherous rocks and is protected from the prevailing south westerlies by a nearby ridge.

The pastor wakes with a start at a polite cough from Maggie. 'Ah, Maggie. I hadn't expected a visitor on this pleasant afternoon.'

'I needed some fresh air and somebody to talk to. I called at The Vicarage and your housekeeper said you would be here. I'm sorry. If this is not the right time…'

Kellow waves away her concerns . 'Please don't feel you have intruded. In truth, I have stayed here too long already. I need to get back to prepare for evensong.'

'Why do you come out here? It's a long walk and your knee…'

Kellow rubs his leg. The trouser leg around the left knee is stretched and tight. 'The day I am unable to come out here will be a grim day indeed. No matter the weather, it brings me peace. Here, I can transcend the everyday.'

'It's a magnificent view.'

'It is indeed. To quote Ecclesiastes, "He hath made everything beautiful in his time: also he hath set the world in their heart, so that no man can find out the work that God maketh from the beginning to the end."' Kellow sighs. 'Here, I am more creative than I will ever be chanting sermons in a pulpit.'

Maggie shakes her head. 'Your sermons are powerful and give us all hope. People come from miles around.' She bites her lip and then says in a rush, 'I need your help, Father.'

Kellow's forehead creases with concern. 'You look troubled, child.'

'I am going to lose everything. In two weeks, I'll be forced out of my home. I have nowhere to go, nowhere at all.'

Kellow's eyes widen. 'Why? How? Your father was a shrewd fisherman. A substantial inheritance awaits you, surely.'

'He was in debt to Jed Hoskin.'

Kellow nods ruefully. 'It seems that everybody in St Branok is in debt to Mr Hoskin. These days he holds our community in the palm of his hand.'

'I saw Mr Narracott, the lawyer, today. He made the full desperation of my situation very clear to me. In truth, I have little more than the clothes I stand up in. I was threatened with debtors' prison. Almost everything will have to be sold and I will be forced out of the family home within two weeks.'

Kellow clenches his jaw. 'Outrageous! Hoskin is a bully who surrounds himself with brutes like George Moyle and shifty weasels like Narracott.'

'So why do you work with him for events like the public meeting?'

'I do it for the good of the people. The community needs to see its leaders united, rather than squabbling like rats in a sack. Hoskin has done some good with his ambitious plans in St Branok. But nobody should be in any doubt of the sort of person he really is. We got a glimpse of the darker side of him and his cronies at the public meeting.'

'Who was that poor man who was thrown out? I hope he wasn't hurt.'

'Ah yes, Jago Rosevear. A widower. Quite a seaman in his day. Captained oceangoing tea clippers. He lost his only son in the storm. He is devastated by the loss.'

'Was there any truth to his claim that the storm warnings were not put out in St Branok whilst they were used elsewhere?'

Kellow licks his lips and then speaks slowly. 'It is an accusation I have heard others mention.'

'Where does he live?'

'Away from the coast. In Rejerrah.' Kellow gathers his writing paraphernalia and then hauls himself into a standing position, favouring his good leg. 'Time for me to get back. I have duties requiring my attention.'

Maggie slips in beside him and together they amble down

a path. She offers Kellow a hand on a slippery section, but he waves it away. 'I am not an invalid yet!'

'I had hopes that you might petition Mr Hoskin for at least a delay on my eviction. I have nowhere to go.'

Kellow shakes his head. 'Regrettably, the likes of Hoskin and Narracott take little notice of me these days.'

'But you have influence.'

Kellow sighs. 'I will do everything in my power to help but I doubt they will listen to an old man such as I.' He reaches out to place a hand on Maggie's shoulder in empathy but also to help him over a slippery patch. 'What about your friend, Norah? She must have a spare room. I'm sure she would welcome your agreeable company.'

'Norah's been wonderful, but she has many concerns of her own. I wouldn't want to be a burden.'

'A good friend loveth at all times, my dear. In thick and in thin. She can be your rock and you hers.'

They amble onwards with Kellow murmuring in soothing tones. On reaching a crossroads full of puddles from the morning rains, Kellow goes in the direction of The Vicarage while Maggie heads to the bustle of the quayside.

Maggie raises her hand. 'Thank you, Father. Thank you so much for finding time for me this afternoon. You have helped me gather myself, to set my world in order.'

'If I can help you find the right path, then an old man will be happy.' He hesitates. A godly fire flares in his eyes. 'And you will find your way. I know it. I see in you a strength I rarely see. Believe in the Lord, child. All things are possible for one who believes.'

She watches him go, limping along the path, an esteemed figure full of contradictions. Resolute but vulnerable. At times, compassionate and, at others, harsh and unyielding.

When she reaches the quayside, the first fishing boats are coming ashore. It has been a good day. One of the best. God-given. The boats are running low in the water with heavy loads. Clouds of squawking gulls circle and there is a spark of excitement and banter on the quayside. In recent weeks, the fishing has never been better. But many of the fishermen who would have benefited are not here to see it. The Atlantic has played the cruellest of tricks.

# CHAPTER NINE

Norah's emerald eyes brighten with a mischievous light. 'So, you were sick all over Narracott's desk?'

Maggie giggles for the first time. 'I couldn't hold it back. I felt terrible.'

'Don't worry. Narracott got what he deserved.' She chuckles. 'I'd love to have seen his self-satisfied face when it all splashed on his desk and spread towards his precious legal papers.' Norah's face turns serious. 'But a paltry two weeks to get out of your cottage. That's terrible. What will you do?'

'Parson Kellow has agreed to intercede on my behalf and ask if Jed Hoskin will make any concessions.' She sighs. 'He's less than hopeful though.'

'If anybody can get Jed Hoskin to think again it will be the parson. Whatever happens, you are very welcome to stay here until you find your feet again.'

'I don't want to be a burden. You have your own problems.'

'You'll be company. When I sit alone, the evenings are very long.'

'Thank you so much. I'll get work as soon as I can.'

Norah takes Maggie's hand. 'You will always be welcome here.'

'But what can I do for work?' Maggie groans. 'I'm no

good at anything apart from scrubbing, hauling and cleaning.'

Norah leans forward and hugs Maggie. When she speaks again her tone is scolding. 'Why put yourself down? Nobody works harder than you. I'll ask around. If worst comes to worst, there's Hoskin's pilchard palace down on the quayside. It's hard work but pays a shilling a shift and it's rarely been busier.'

'I'll give anything a try.'

There's a brief silence before Maggie says, 'I've been thinking about that gentleman at the public meeting who said St Branok didn't get the storm warning. The parson gave me his name. He's a former sea captain of high reputation, called Jago Rosevear. He lives out of town, near Rejerrah. His son died in the storm. I'm going to visit him to find out more.'

Norah's eyebrows crease. 'It's a mystery right enough. When are you going?'

'Tomorrow morning. There's no point in delaying.'

'I'll come. I want to find out the truth every bit as much as you.' Norah purses her lips. 'There's blood on the hands of whoever failed to put out the warning signals.' She catches her breath. 'I miss my Jowan so much. I can't believe he's gone. I keep thinking I can still hear him.' She glances around her tiny cottage with bleary eyes. 'I'll make tea for us both. I was hoping to chat with you about another matter.'

Maggie sits while Norah bustles about clattering saucepans. The kitchen is tiny but warm and homely. A doll's house fit for a doll.

Norah passes Maggie a chipped cup. 'So, what do you want to ask me?' Maggie says as she takes a first sip. The brew is weak, the tea leaves having been used before.

'It's about Jowan.' Norah's features screw in anguish. 'I've been asking around, trying to find out which boat Jowan went aboard on the day of the storm.'

The familiar sucking guilt seeps through Maggie's stomach. 'Why? What difference does it make?'

'They shouldn't have allowed him aboard. He was a boy for God's sake. They risked his life. They killed him. I want to find out who it was.'

The surface of Maggie's tea ripples as her hand trembles. She places the cup on the table. 'Whoever it was is most probably dead themselves. I am sure they would have done everything they could to save him.'

Norah stares at her unconvinced. 'I need to find out what happened if only to set my mind at rest. To know who he was with and how he died. It's the not knowing that is the worst thing.' She sucks a deep breath. 'I hope he died with friends. Not alone out there in those terrible seas.' She leans forward onto the table, her head in her hands.

Maggie puts a strong arm around her friend's heaving shoulders. 'Norah…Norah…we need to put all this behind us. To start again…to…'

Norah's flushed, tear-streaked face emerges from her hands. 'But it's not behind us, is it? It's all still with us, the whole thing. You're being thrown out of your home and we've both been left without a family.' She shakes her head. 'You want to find out what happened as much as I do. If not, why are you going to Captain Rosevear's tomorrow?'

Maggie is caught in a trap of her own making. Her aim in visiting Captain Rosevear is different though. 'Not putting out the storm warning signs was serious neglect which cost many lives. It's a crime. The person responsible should face justice.'

Norah thumps her fist on the table. 'Isn't taking a twelve-year-old boy to sea in stormy weather, without the approval of his mother, a crime?'

Maggie wilts in the heat of her friend's glare. 'I'm sure they…whoever it was…didn't mean to…to risk his life. Jowan was a wonderful boy, but he could be headstrong. You told me so. He might even have sneaked aboard without the skipper knowing.'

Norah's beauty is eclipsed by a pinched expression. 'Somebody knew, somebody was responsible.'

'And what would you do if the person who allowed him aboard was still alive?'

Norah hesitates, the knuckles of her clenched fist whitening. 'I'm not sure. But I'd…I'd do something.' Her tone eases. 'I'm sorry, Maggie, I'm not trying to get at you. You've suffered as much as I have. I'm wrong to bother you with all this, you with your own cares and worries.'

Maggie's hand swamps Norah's fist. 'I'm glad that you feel able to talk about it with me.'

'I mentioned it only because one of the old salts told me he saw Jowan on the South Quay and your da often brought *Minerva* alongside there. I wondered if you'd seen anything?'

Maggie's stomach clenches. 'No, nothing. I didn't go down to the quay that day. I had too much to do about the house.' There's a rush of panic in her voice. One lie is leading to another. She glances at Norah. Has her friend read the deceit in her face?

Norah seems oblivious. 'I'm sorry I had to ask. I wondered…that's all…just wondered.'

'If I could help, I would.' Another lie.

'I know. Of course, you would. Anyway, I'll keep asking around. Somebody will have seen something.'

Maggie picks up her tea. It's stone cold. She gulps it down and rises. 'I must get back to the house. I have so many things to do.'

Norah walks with her to the front door. 'So would you like to stay here for the next few weeks?'

'You're more than kind but, as I say, I wouldn't want to be any trouble.'

'You won't be.' She gazes into Maggie's eyes. 'Please say yes.'

Maggie pauses at the door, desperate to be away. 'Well, yes, thank you, thank you so much.'

Norah takes hold of both of Maggie's hands in a fond farewell. 'We'll always be friends. Always.' She smiles. 'We need to stick together.'

Maggie trudges home, her head down. The walk seems so much longer today. A sapping guilt sucks at her strength. She has lied and been deceitful. To her best friend, of all people.

If Norah ever finds out the truth…

# CHAPTER TEN

The next day, the walk out to the captain's home in Rejerrah starts soon after breakfast with the two friends laughing and joking as if on a leisurely stroll. By midday, the mood turns more serious. They are following a rocky lane which passes through woods, dips down sharp descents and then up breathtaking climbs. Robust Maggie tackles the swooping terrain with her usual stoicism, but Norah soon struggles to keep up, her slim but much shorter legs working nineteen to the dozen. At least the weather has turned out benevolent.

Norah plonks herself down on a boulder with a groan to rub her tired feet. 'It's all very well for you with your long legs,' she groans to Maggie. She plods over to a tinkling stream nearby and bends to take sips of water from her cupped hands. 'How much further do you think?'

Maggie hesitates to get her bearings. The twists and turns of the route have been confusing. She points to a hill bathed in golden sunlight. 'We're almost there. I think Rejerrah is amongst woods over there.'

'Is it still that far?' says Norah in weary disbelief.

'Are you ready to go on?' says Maggie, fighting to hide her impatience. Having welcomed Norah's company at the outset, she now wonders whether it would have been better to go alone. It would have been quicker.

'Give me a few moments more,' says Norah.

A local farmer, leading a weary chestnut nag hauling a cart load of parsnips, comes into view. Like the horse, the cart looks past its best, the left wheel squeaking and squealing rhythmically. The farmer tips his wide-brimmed straw hat to them as he passes. 'A good afternoon to you, ladies.'

Norah gives the red-cheeked farmer a dazzling smile. It works as it does with most of the opposite sex and he cracks a smile back.

'Sir, are you heading to Rejerrah?' she asks.

The farmer nods, his expression kindly. 'That I am, young miss.'

'We're visiting Captain Rosevear. You might have heard of him,' says Maggie. 'Is his house far?'

'Not far. That way. In Treamble Valley.' He studies them more closely. 'I'd heard the captain was seeking to fill a vacancy in his kitchen.'

'We're not kitchen maids,' says Norah, her voice edged with indignation.

'No offence intended, missy. I thought that two fine young ladies like yourselves…' His voice trails away.

Norah rests a hand on the cart. 'Sir, might we trouble you for the smallest of favours?'

The farmer's smile broadens. 'How might I be of assistance?'

'We've been walking since early from St Branok. Would you be kind enough to allow us to take the weight off our pins and sit on the back of your cart? Just until we're over the next hill, you understand.'

The farmer looks dubiously at the parsnips piled into the cart. 'If you can find room.'

'We will. We will. Thank you so much.'

Norah jumps daintily aboard. Maggie clambers up beside her. They set off and make jolting, bone-jarring progress.

A formidable hill is summited, and the farmer pulls into the side to point out a large house below nestling among trees. 'Captain Rosevear's property. Trecarn Manor. As fair as anything you'll see in this valley. I'll be carrying on along the ridge so this is where I must say goodbye.'

Even from a distance the three-storey building is impressive, adorned with towers, turrets and dormers, stained glass and decorative woodwork, and surrounded by sweeping lawns. Captain Rosevear is a man of means.

The farmer tips his hat and goes squeakily on his way along a muddy, pock-marked path.

Maggie and Norah trudge down a narrow lane, damp from the autumn rains, and after a few bends arrive at the cast iron gates of Rosevear's manor house. The imposing gates are open with nobody in sight. A gravel driveway is bordered by tall thin poplars. The house slides into view as they round a bend.

Breath hisses from Maggie's lips. 'Heavens above. It's beautiful.'

The dark front door is dominated by a brass knocker shaped like the tail of a whale. Maggie raises the knocker and lets it fall back. It crashes against the door. The two young women stifle giggles.

There is the sound of movement on the other side of the door and then a stocky man, immaculately dressed, with long, greying sideburns and curious, wild eyebrows appears. He regards them critically. 'Can I help you?'

Maggie gulps down her giggle. 'I…we… we were wondering –'

'The position was filled last week.'

'We're here to see Captain Rosevear,' says an assertive Norah.

The wild eyebrows rise. 'Captain Rosevear?'

'Yes, he does live here, doesn't he?'

'Captain Rosevear is indeed the gentleman of the residence.'

Maggie joins in. 'Well, we need to see him.'

His cool gaze switches from Norah to Maggie. 'And what might I ask is your business with the captain?'

'It concerns the recent public meeting in St Branok to discuss the storm disaster,' says Maggie.

Those magnificent eyebrows crease together in disapproval. 'A rowdy affair, by all accounts.'

'Captain Rosevear expressed his concerns at the meeting. We would very much like to talk to him,' says Maggie.

'You see we, too, have questions about what happened,' chips in Norah. 'My young son died in the storm and Maggie here lost her father and three brothers. We understand that Captain Rosevear also suffered a bereavement – his son, I believe.'

The man's expression eases. 'A terrible tragedy. I will see if Captain Rosevear is available for visitors. Who might I say is calling?'

'Miss Margaret Pascoe and Mrs Norah Bray, of St Branok,' says Norah.

He ushers them into the hallway. 'Wait here please.' He disappears down a darkened corridor.

Norah chuckles. 'Miss Margaret Pascoe and Mrs Norah Bray call for afternoon tea,' she whispers, making a dainty crook of her small finger.

Maggie shushes her with a finger to her lips. 'I'm nervous.'

She gazes around in awe. A wide, elegant staircase curves upwards to a galleried landing.

Norah frowns. 'Why?'

'He's worth a packet.'

'So what? He's a man with the wants and needs of any man.'

'But the house…it's so beautiful.'

Norah shrugs. 'It's worth a pretty penny, I'll grant you, but I've seen grander.'

'Where?' says Maggie in disbelief.

'Morwenstowe.'

'Lord and Lady Kendall's place? Next, you'll be telling me that her ladyship invited you up there.'

Norah looks affronted. 'I'm as good as her hoity-toity ladyship any day and I bet his lordship would have a sight more fun with me than with her.'

Maggie pulls a sceptical expression. 'Have you really been up to Morwenstowe?'

'Yes, of course.'

'But not at the invitation of Lord and Lady Kendall, I'll be bound.'

'I have a cousin, Polly, who works in the kitchens,' Norah confesses at last.

Mr Wild Eyebrows reappears after a few minutes with a smile on his lips. 'Captain Rosevear will be pleased to receive you in the sitting room. If you'll be so good as to follow me.'

They walk down a panelled corridor to arrive in a spacious room warmed by a crackling log fire. A tall man is standing at a bay sash window with his hands clasped behind his back.

Mr Eyebrows coughs. 'Sir, the two young ladies we discussed.'

The man turns to reveal a fulsome smile. 'Ah yes, thank you, Jenkins.' His gracious gaze rests on his guests. There is a bruise on his left cheek and his left eye is bloodshot. 'So, ladies, you have come all the way from St Branok?'

Maggie steps forward. 'Yes, we walked, sir. We felt it was important to speak with you after the disturbance at the meeting.'

Captain Rosevear gestures to a chaise longue. 'Please, take a seat. You must be thirsty after such a wearying journey. Jenkins, some tea and cakes for our visitors?'

Maggie perches on the edge of the chaise longue. It looks expensive. 'We lost family in the storm, my father and my three brothers and Norah's only son.'

Sadness seeps into the creases of the old man's eyes. 'I am so sorry to hear of your loss. The death of my son has taken its toll on me, I must confess.' His voice cracks. 'I blame myself.'

'Why?' says Maggie. 'None of us could have known what was going to happen.'

Captain Rosevear sighs. 'I indulged him too much, I fear. He had a friend on the fishing boats and he insisted on going. I assumed that in time he would see sense. I had hopes of him becoming an officer on an oceangoing ship. It is a rewarding career and the big clippers are magnificent vessels.' He shakes his head. 'The impetuosity of youth. I should never have allowed it. Never.'

'My son went without my permission,' says Norah, bitterness in her voice. 'I've been trying to find out which boat he was on, but nobody seems to know.'

Heat suffuses Maggie's cheeks. She licks her lips, not trusting herself to speak.

Fortunately, Jenkins arrives at that moment with a full

tray. 'I took the liberty, sir, of asking Mrs Hennessy to run up some sandwiches as well as cake and tea. Cheese, cress and lettuce.'

'Excellent. Where would I be without yourself and Mrs Hennessy, eh?'

Maggie and Norah lick their lips at the selection of triangular sandwiches and hearty slices of cherry cake, neatly placed next to delicate china cups and a formidable tea pot. A thick slice of bread and a wedge of cheese had sufficed for breakfast.

Rosevear watches them with mild amusement. 'Do not stand on ceremony. Please help yourself, ladies.'

Maggie picks two sandwiches. She'd like to take more. Norah chooses one and nibbles it daintily.

Captain Rosevear sighs. 'We live through our children, do we not? They are our future. I always thought that this…' – he gestures round him – '…all this would one day be Edgar's, whatever path he chose.' His voice drops to a whisper. 'And now I have nobody. My world is empty. And all *this* is of no value.'

'You said at the meeting that there should have been a storm warning?' says Maggie, swallowing her sandwich.

Captain Rosevear nods. 'I have made enquiries with my seagoing contacts and it appears that everywhere along the Cornish coast got the warning – apart from St Branok. The telegraph station at Penzance confirmed that it received a warning from FitzRoy in London and that the alert was passed on to all local stations. Only St Branok failed to put out the signals.'

'In heavens name, why?' says Maggie.

The captain shrugs. 'Parts of FitzRoy's new service are still developing. In most regards it is excellent, but it doesn't yet always operate as smoothly as it should in some of the more remote areas.'

'What do you plan to do?' says Norah.

'What can I do? I am not a young man and, in truth, I am not in the best of health. I have made the authorities aware of my concerns. No doubt they will carry out their own investigations.'

The conversation moves on to a more general discussion about the dangers of seafaring. Sandwiches and cake are consumed at a steady pace in keeping with the refinements of the surroundings. Eventually, Maggie achieves that pleasant state of being full but not bloated. She glances out the window at the lengthening shadows and realises the lateness of the hour. It is well into the afternoon and the autumn day is nearing its end. If they are not to face the prospect of walking home after dark, they will need to leave immediately.

'I'm afraid we must be going,' she says. 'It will be dark soon.'

Concern sweeps Captain Rosevear's aged features. 'I'm so sorry. I have kept you good people far too long. The days draw in so much earlier at this time of year. And, since the passing of my beloved wife, it is a long time since I had the pleasure of female company.'

Norah smiles coyly. 'We have enjoyed our afternoon with you, sir, but it is a lengthy walk back to St Branok and, as it is, we won't get back until after nightfall.'

The captain's eyes widen. 'Walk? I wouldn't hear of it. There are any number of vagabonds and miscreants on lonely roads after dark. No, please take my carriage. You'll be home in half the time.' He rises eagerly from his chair. 'Indeed, it will be an honour to take you myself.'

'We couldn't put you to so much trouble,' says Maggie and receives a sharp nudge from Norah.

The captain's blood is up. 'Nonsense! It'll be a pleasure to spend more time in your delightful company.' His smile rests on Norah. 'And it is the very least I can do having wasted so much of your day on an old seaman's yarns.' He pulls a cord and a distant tinkle is heard.

Norah pulls her most beguiling smile. 'I would love to hear more of your memories. You have a wonderful house.' She reaches up but stops short of touching the captain's battered cheek. 'That looks a horrible bruise, Captain.'

Captain Rosevear blinks his creased eyes. 'A scratch, nothing more, from one of Hoskin's bully boys. An ignoramus called Moyle. In my youth, the oaf would have bitten off more than he could chew, I can tell you. I've met sailors who would have that fool for breakfast.'

Maggie feels an unwanted spare part as the captain and Norah stare into each other's eyes.

The bubble bursts when Jenkins arrives. 'You called, sir?'

The captain issues clear instructions with a commanding voice which must have stood him in good stead on the high seas. The carriage is to be made ready for a journey into St Branok.

They pass the time with small talk as they make ready to leave. On the driveway is an elegant four-wheel carriage with a calash retractable roof, drawn by a finely muscled black horse, snorting steam in the cool of the late afternoon. Captain Rosevear clambers into the coachman's seat and takes the reins, while Maggie and Norah settle in the back, exchanging grins.

'I could get used to this,' whispers Norah as Captain Rosevear cracks the whip and they rumble down the gravelled driveway at pace, heading for the open road.

The homeward journey takes a fraction of the time of their outward slog and there is still a smear of light in the sky as they pull up outside Maggie's home. A jolly Captain Rosevear offers to drop Norah at her own home, but Norah declines and steps down with Maggie.

'I couldn't put you to the trouble, Captain,' she says.

'It is no trouble,' he says to Norah with a twinkle in his aged eye.

Norah curtseys. 'You're more than kind, sir, but I need to help my dear friend with some pressing chores.'

When the carriage has clattered out of sight the two women retire to the kitchen with raised spirits. Maggie glances around her plain but immaculate kitchen. 'What chores were you planning to do here?'

Norah sweeps an imaginary speck of dust from a work surface. 'I wasn't going to let a gentleman like Captain Rosevear see my hovel, not after tea and cake at Trecarn Manor.'

Norah sits down at the table. 'He's lonely,' she says thoughtfully. 'He could do with a good woman in his life.'

'He seems to be well looked after already. Those cakes and sandwiches were delicious.'

Norah's lips twitch. 'That fusty old butler Jenkins and Mrs Hennessy can't do everything for him. He needs a woman to keep his old bones warm at night.'

'He isn't that sort of man,' says Maggie, a little shocked.

Norah grins slyly. 'Every man is that sort of man. It's natural. But gentlemen like Captain Rosevear are careful to hide their simmering emotions until the time is right.'

Maggie can't stop her own mouth creasing into a smirk. 'So, you've got designs on Captain Rosevear, have you?'

'I could do worse.' Norah's voice fades as her imagination

surges. 'Norah Rosevear, the lady of Trecarn Manor. It has a certain ring, don't you think?'

'It's curious,' says Maggie, filling the kettle to make tea.

'What's so curious?'

'A man who has spent his life at sea living in a house far from the coast. I'd have expected him to live in a clifftop villa looking out over the Atlantic.'

'He's probably had his fill of the ocean,' says Norah. 'Especially now he's lost his only son.' She pauses and then adds, 'Like me.'

Maggie turns the conversation to the questions rattling around in her head since the meeting with the captain. 'It was interesting what he said about the storm signals. Every fishing community received the warning except St Branok. Why?'

'Somebody failed in their duty?'

Maggie runs a finger down a thin bladed knife used for filleting fish. 'I don't know but when I find out…'

# CHAPTER ELEVEN

Maggie and Norah revive themselves with a few tots of brandy before retiring to Maggie's box bedroom. Her father had a stash and, since the passing of his wife, kept it well stocked.

They soon fall into a long, dreamless sleep with Maggie sprawled on one side of the bed and Norah curled in the other. They are woken the following day by insistent knocking on the front door. Maggie surfaces with a heavy head to a day of strong breezes and intense sunshine. The sun is well up. It's late. She makes her way to her father's bedroom where she can look out on whoever is knocking.

It could be a debt collector or bailiff sent by Nathaniel Narracott or Jed Hoskin to settle arrears. Her old life of certainty seems a lifetime ago. But, no, it is the kindly figure of Parson Kellow, dressed in his familiar crimson coat, sea boots and fisherman's smock.

'Be with you shortly, Father,' she calls out from the open window and then withdraws before Kellow can see she is still in her night clothes. Whatever will he think?

She rushes back to the box room and shakes awake a tousled Norah. 'Parson Kellow…Parson Kellow.'

'What about him?' murmurs Norah. She had glugged more brandy than Maggie.

'He's here. Outside.' Maggie slips out of her nightclothes

and wrestles her way into stays and a dress. After pushing and pulling, brushing and refining, she glances into a mirror, declares herself presentable and clatters down the stairs, leaving Norah still sprawled in bed, uncaring whether the visitor is a vagrant or the emperor of Austria.

A gentle cough and shuffle of feet indicates that Parson Kellow is waiting patiently. Maggie smooths down the front of her skirt and then hauls open the door.

'Father…a most pleasant surprise.'

Kellow tips his hat. 'Miss Pascoe. Good day to you. I have news. Perhaps we could talk?'

Maggie's hopes rise. Has Kellow been successful in negotiating a stay of execution with Jed Hoskin and she'll be able to stay in her home a little longer?

'Tea, Father?' Is there anything else she can offer? No, the cupboard is bare, the last slices of home-made Hevva cake having been consumed the previous evening between swigs of brandy when she and Norah returned from Trecarn Manor with optimism enflaming their appetites. It's a poor reception compared to Captain Rosevear's lavish offering.

The Parson pulls a kindly smile. 'A tea would be most welcome.'

Maggie directs Kellow into the sitting room. The room is cold with an empty grate. How different to when her father and brothers still lived. Then, the sitting room had a perpetual fire on chill autumn and winter days, well stocked with Welsh coal. 'Better still, come into the kitchen. It'll be warmer there,' she says.

Kellow settles at the kitchen table, once so busy with the banter of strident male voices.

'You said you had news?' prompts Maggie as she fills the kettle.

'Ah yes, well, we have movement on the proposal – your proposal – for a lifeboat station in St Branok.

Maggie forgets her heavy head. 'What's happened?'

'The Royal National Lifeboat Institution has responded most promptly to our letter. It is to send a working party to our town to discuss the proposal and to evaluate possible locations.'

'That's wonderful. Who will meet them?'

Kellow reels off a list of names that includes himself, the ebullient and at times annoying Jack Treloare and, of course, Jed Hoskin and the lawyer Nathaniel Narracott.

Maggie's mood rises despite it not being the reprieve from Jed Hoskin she was hoping for. A lifeboat for St Branok will save many lives. 'I want to attend the meeting if it is appropriate for me to do so.'

Kellow's wide mouth droops at the corners. 'I suggested that very thing, but Mr Hoskin felt that, after the furore at the public meeting, a frank discussion between men of influence and expertise was the most appropriate course.'

'Why? Who can talk about the tragedy which has befallen us better than me? I have lost everything.' Her voice is stifled by her tight throat.

'I agree but Mr Hoskin ruled it was a meeting for measured discussions, rather than…ah hum…unbridled emotion. Mr Narracott supported the view. There will be practical facts to consider on funding, possible locations, administration and much more. Hard pragmatism is essential. Naturally, I will be happy to convey your thoughts and concerns to the committee.' Recognising a lost cause, Maggie gives it up. 'Did you manage to speak to Mr Hoskin about my home?' Now there is a hint of desperation in her voice.

Kellow licks his lips, his discomfort obvious. 'I did…I

did. Regrettably, he remains adamant that, in view of the considerable sums involved, he needs to take prompt action to recover the outstanding debt. Of course, I made the case as strongly as I could, but Mr Hoskin is not a man to change course.'

'A man of his means, why can't he wait a little longer? The fishing has been plentiful in recent weeks. He must be raking it in.' Maggie pours water into the pot, her hand trembling. 'He's throwing me out of my home.'

A gentle hand comes to rest on her shoulder. 'There, there, child. Do not despair. Have confidence in the Lord with all your heart. In all thy ways think on him, and he will direct your steps.'

'When is the meeting?' A voice pipes up from the doorway and then Norah appears, having performed another minor miracle with her appearance since Maggie left her tousled form sprawled in bed a few minutes earlier. Maggie marvels at the transformation.

'At ten in the morning on Thursday next,' says Kellow. 'The party will meet at the church hall, tour possible locations and return to debate the details. Judging by the tone of the institution's letter, it sounds more than hopeful.'

He captivates them with stories of recent lifeboat rescues elsewhere in Cornwall before supping the final dregs of his tea. 'Ladies, I must bid you adieu. I have a busy day ahead. There are services to prepare for and, sadly, I have received a request to attend the Monkton family home. I fear dear Edith Monkton is not long for this world.'

Maggie imagines the good-humoured face of Edith Monkton. She'd passed her in the street only two weeks previous and the stocky woman had seemed as robust as usual. 'Oh my, poor Edith. She'll be a great loss to St Branok.'

Kellow nods. 'A fine woman. She has ten grandchildren.'

'It has come on so suddenly. You don't think it's a resurgence of the typhus, Father?' says Maggie. The evil of typhoid swept St Branok ten years earlier and is still feared. If it isn't the sea killing off St Branok's citizens, it is diseases like typhoid and cholera. Maggie wonders what transgressions have been committed by the local community to bring the wrath of the Lord down on their heads so many times.

Kellow shakes his head as he limps to the front door. 'Thankfully, no. Dr Lander believes it to be a palsy. Distressing but not contagious. A course of bloodletting failed to provide a cure.'

He disappears down the street to one of the grubbier parts of town with a final wave. Maggie turns to Norah, her face bleak.

Her friend is quick to read the signs. She grimaces. 'So, the parson couldn't get Jed Hoskin to change his mind?

'He refused to budge an inch. Said he needed the money.'

'What? Jed Hoskin?' says Norah, her tone rising. 'The man's got bags of money.'

'The parson tried his best.'

'He *says* he tried his best,' says Norah. 'It's no secret that even Parson Kellow owes Hoskin money.'

'That's mouthy local gossip. They dislike each other but they hide it for the sake of the local community.'

'Like or dislike has nothing to do with it. Mark my words, the new vicarage must have cost Kellow a pretty penny. If he needed money, then Jed Hoskin is the most likely local source. A shrewd businessman like Jed doesn't care who he lends money to so long as he's going to get it back with interest. It'd be good business for him.'

'Anyway, what difference does it make if the parson does owe money?'

Norah pulls a knowing smirk. 'He'll be less inclined to rub a man up the wrong way to whom he owes a wedge of debt.'

Maggie sucks air. 'The parson was my last hope.'

A cheeky glint sparks in Norah's eyes. 'I might pay a visit to Hoskin myself. I bet I could persuade him.'

'You? What can you do that a personage of the standing of Hedrek Kellow can't?'

Norah runs her hands down the curves of her body. 'Hoskin did a bit of gawking at me at the public meeting. I think he liked what he saw.'

'He's a businessman through and through.'

Norah chuckles. 'Businessmen have balls.'

Maggie has warmth in her cheeks at the bawdy turn of the conversation. 'I couldn't ask you to do that. It will put you in his debt.'

'I know what I'm doing. And it'll be fun.' She brushes a lock of auburn hair from her emerald eyes. 'I have a mind to pay him a call before dark today.'

# CHAPTER TWELVE

Norah's visit to Jed Hoskin fails. Or so it appears at first.

'He was charming right enough,' she tells Maggie the following day while sipping more tea in the kitchen of the Pascoe cottage. 'But he insisted that he needs possession of your home to settle other debts.'

Maggie pulls a sad smile. 'At least you tried. I can't thank you enough.'

'Oh, I haven't quite given up yet,' says Norah with her pixie grin.

'What do you mean? You said he refused to budge.'

'For now, yes. But Jed has extended me an invitation for when he returns from business up county.'

'Why?'

Norah grins. 'You don't know much about men, do you?'

Maggie is irked by the assumption of her naivety. 'I lived in a house full of them.'

'I don't mean brothers and fathers. Men like Jed Hoskin must be worked on. They need to be tempted and flattered. Important men like to be told they are important. When you put ideas in their head you have to make them think it is *their* idea. It takes time. Jed is going to treat me to afternoon tea the day after tomorrow at the Regent. I will renew my endeavours then.'

'I hate to think you're putting yourself to all this trouble.'

'Truth to tell, I'm enjoying myself. Don't give up yet.'

Despite Norah's optimism, Maggie prepares for her impending departure from her lifelong home. She trawls through cupboards and drawers, putting the clothes and possessions of her father and brothers into piles. Often, she will pick up a smock and hold it to her face while tears flow and her body convulses, as she smells one of her beloved brothers, particularly Ben, the youngest. The desolation grips her like a vice, leaving her so distraught at times that she can do nothing more than lie in her box bedroom and stare up at the shadowy ceiling. Cobwebs have been spun in the corners. She lacks the will to clean them. Soon it will all be gone. Unless Norah can perform a miracle. But it is hard to imagine even her beguiling friend persuading steely Jed Hoskin to change his mind.

The same questions rattle through her over and over again. What has she done to deserve this? Why her? Why her family? How will she make ends meet? How will she survive?

She seeks out her family's most personal items, the few that she will be able to take with her to Norah's cottage – her father's pipe, Kitto's harmonica, Logan's wood carving of a young woman praying, a few of Ben's favourite books. Only the most valued items can be kept. She sells some items for paltry sums to neighbours and passing traders. Impaled on their own hook of desperation, they drive hard bargains.

Like her life, the weather is turning colder and more uncertain by the day. The south-westerlies strengthen. Surges of water explode against the jagged coast, pushing high up coves, sending clouds of spray over St Branok's formidable harbour wall. Occasionally, Maggie will look up from a task to see rivulets of rain cascading down the windows of her cottage. Winter is coming.

She visits Norah on the morning of her friend's second meeting with Jed Hoskin. Norah is primped and prepared, wearing a low-cut deep green dress of silk and delicate lace that Maggie has never seen before.

Norah poses in front of her. 'What do you think?'

'You look wonderful. Where in heaven's name did you get that dress?'

Norah swivels in front of the mirror with a critical look in her eye. 'A lady I did some seamstress work for. It was a gift. She was taller and wider than me, so I have made adjustments.' She places her hands on her waist. 'And now it fits just so.' She pauses and then, looking pleased with herself, says, 'If this doesn't turn Jed Hoskin's head, then he truly has a heart of Cornish granite.'

'You're not going to walk through town like *that*?'

'Jed is sending his carriage.'

Maggie raises her eyebrows. 'You must have made quite an impression last time.'

'That's nothing compared to the impression I will make this time.'

They laugh in unison. There is a tinkle of mischief in Norah's laugh.

The clatter of hooves on cobbles sounds outside. The two women peek through the window. A sleek black carriage, pulled by two straining black horses, comes to a smart halt. An immaculately turned-out driver hops down and trots over to fling open the carriage door to reveal a bulky form in a tweed jacket and matching waistcoat and trousers. Jed Hoskin. Dressed up to the nines. He descends the steps, strides imperiously over to the front of the cottage and raps on the door.

Norah's eyes turn panicky. 'It's best you're not seen here. Jed might think we've been conniving and colluding. Wait here until we've gone and then slip out the side gate.'

Maggie hides in the kitchen. Through a crack in the doorway, she sees Norah open the front door.

Jed sweeps off his top hat and bows, his fleshy lips twisted in a leer. 'Your carriage awaits, ma'am.'

A grinning Norah curtseys. 'Thank you, Mr Hoskin.'

'Jedediah, please.'

The front door bangs closed and Maggie rushes forward to peep through the front window. The couple, for that is what they now seem to be, step over to the carriage. The epitome of gallantry, Hoskin sees Norah aboard before clambering up himself. Maggie hears him say, 'I was thinking that before partaking of afternoon tea we could go for a drive. Take the air and see the sights.'

When the carriage has rattled away, Maggie lets herself out of the side gate and heads in the direction of town to collect a few provisions still within reach of her shrinking budget. On her way home with a basket half-full of essentials, she spies a familiar figure striding up the lane. Jack Treloare. Even from a distance she can see he is his usual effervescent self, greeting passers-by, exchanging gossip with traders, his tanned face split by that ever-present wide grin.

Maggie can't help but feel irritated by his easy-going confidence. She doesn't have the strength today to engage with his jolly banter. A dressmaker's shop off to the left offers her a way out. She reaches for the door handle and pulls. It refuses to budge. She pushes. Same result. She feigns interest in a shimmering ballgown in the window.

'Mrs Chegwin always closes for luncheon between one o'clock and two,' a voice says behind her.

She turns red-faced to see Jack, arms folded, leaning against a wall.

Maggie feels herself shrinking in the glare of his smile. 'Yes…yes, of course. I hadn't realised how late it is. I'll come back later.'

Her retreat is blocked by Jack moving to stand in the centre of the path. His smile continues to blaze. 'A new dress, is it?'

'I'd heard that Mrs Chegwin had taken a new delivery of satin.' In truth, her knowledge of Mrs Chegwin's deliveries is precisely nil, but it is the best her imagination can stretch to in the heat of the moment. A dress of any description is well beyond her means.

'A sapphire blue would suit you well. It would match your eyes.'

Maggie searches for some smart words in reply. But finds none. A man like Jack Treloare taking interest in her eyes and imagining her in a blue dress is disconcerting. Unlike Norah, the attentions of the male sex are alien to her. Passing glances perhaps but nothing more.

She gulps, certain she's making a fool of herself, and tries to slip past. 'If you'll excuse me, Mr Treloare, I am exceedingly busy.'

They face each other, staring into each other's eyes. His are hazel brown. He is not as tall as she thought, her gaze only two or three inches lower than his.

At last, he steps to one side. 'Where are you going?'

'Home,' slips from her lips.

He falls into step with her without being invited.

'It is a bonny day for a stroll,' he says. 'Especially when a man has charming company.'

Maggie speeds up. Jack stays alongside, the pace easy for

him, the conversation more challenging. His attempt at discussing the latest dress fashions soon founders, due to Maggie's shaky grasp of the subject. The latest Truro gossip and the news that a ball is to be held at the Assembly Rooms also sink without trace. Silence falls.

Maggie takes pity on him. 'I am told that a working party from the institution will be visiting soon to discuss the lifeboat proposal.'

Jack seizes on it. 'Aye, and not before time. I have been invited to attend. If we can persuade the institution, it will be a huge step forward for St Branok.'

'Surely, the case for a station is obvious.'

'Not as obvious as we would hope, I fear. Funding will be an issue and we are by no means the only community on the north coast pressing for a lifeboat.'

'It's hard to believe that anybody has a stronger case than us. We have lost so many over the years. Has any thought been given to where such a station would be located?'

'The town beach, next to the quayside, is the obvious choice. Jed Hoskin has said he could make a patch of land available on a peppercorn rent at the bottom of St George's Hill.'

Maggie halts to make a point. 'But it has its limitations. My father insisted that that stretch of coast could be a problem when the tide's pushing and the wind's hammering from the northwest. He always insisted that the quay should have been built on the north shore.'

Jack shakes his head. 'Most of the time the south side is best. It's the easiest way to get out of the bay.'

'But the lifeboat will often be launching in bad weather, and the worst weather and the biggest seas come from the northwest.'

Jack gazes at her with a glimmer of amusement in his eyes. 'And when was the last time you went to sea?'

'I have had a taste of the Atlantic,' she says in a firm voice.

'I hadn't realised you were such an expert. So where, in your *expert view*, is a suitable location on the north side?' His tone is teasing.

'Trencreek Cove.'

'Get on, you're joking.'

'It's the best protected. You of all people – an experienced fisherman – would realise I am talking the truth.'

Jack chews his lip. When he next speaks, there is a new measure of respect in his tone. 'You should come to the meeting with the institution.'

'Parson Kellow suggested it, but Jed Hoskin refused.'

Jack stares. 'In God's name, why?'

'He said it was a meeting for straight-talking sense, not ranting emotional women.' She can't help sounding bitter.

They start walking again. Jack sighs. 'Jed Hoskin can be a right arse at times.' He colours and apologises for his choice of words.

'You're in his employ, are you not?'

Jack demurs. He clicks open the wicker gate leading to Maggie's home and holds it open for her. 'Not precisely. Jed is the majority shareholder in my boat but that doesn't stop him being…what I said. He's a successful businessman, sure enough. And credit to him, he's created a business from nothing. Made himself one of the richest men south of Wadebridge. But who has he got to share it with, eh?' He pauses with a twinkle in his eye. 'Apart from George Moyle.'

Maggie can't help chuckling as she pictures Jed Hoskin's huge shadow, accompanying him everywhere. Jack can be annoying, but also funny and perceptive.

Maggie slips through the gate. 'In any event, Jed Hoskin doesn't want me at the meeting and he's not going to change his mind.'

'I'll invite you.'

'I doubt you're allowed to.'

'I can and with good reason. You've got some capital ideas worth exploring. Nobody knew this coast better than your father. The Pascoe boats were the most successful in St Branok since anybody can remember.'

Maggie opens the front door and steps inside. 'I'm not my father.' She murmurs after a hesitation, 'Sometimes I wish I were.'

Jack lingers on the doorstep. 'Well, I'm pleased you are not your father, much as I admired him. But it sounds as if he passed on his shrewd sense to you.'

Maggie pauses. Maybe she can add something of value. She's spent her life with a man revered for his fishing skills and coastal seamanship. Perhaps sprinklings of her father's rough and ready magic have settled on her shoulders. And the thought of putting Jed Hoskin's fleshy nose out of joint is appealing. 'If I did come, where should I go and when?'

'I'll call at nine-thirty on Thursday morning. We can walk down together.'

'Thank you. You're very kind.' She closes the door. She isn't going to invite Jack in. Not yet. Her final glimpse is of him pulling a look of disappointment and then concealing it with a grin.

# CHAPTER THIRTEEN

Maggie gazes out of her kitchen window at the soft, purple dusk, looking for Norah. Surely, her friend has completed working her considerable charms by now. Could she achieve the impossible and make the headstrong Hoskin, known for his intransigence and general bloody mindedness, change his mind? If anybody can turn the head of the opposite sex, it is the mischievous Norah.

The final vestiges of daylight fade. Waiting patiently is not for Maggie. She finds an activity to pass the time – a hard scrub of the kitchen's slate floor. She works the mop hard, pushing it into every corner and crevice until the slate has been buffed to a dull grey sheen in the lamplight.

After a final flurry of vigorous strokes, Maggie stands there, leaning on her mop, breathing hard. But there is still no sign of Norah. It doesn't augur well. If Norah had good news, wouldn't she have burst in by now with a triumphant grin on her face?

Maggie has to find out. She grabs her shawl from the hook in the hallway, pulls it closely around her shoulders and heads out into the chill autumn night. Stars are twinkling in a clear sky. A light breeze carries the sound of waves crashing on the shoreline. She shivers. It's going to be a cold night, the coldest of the autumn so far. Most people are already in their homes, warming themselves in front of a fire or settling down for supper. It is the one part of the waking day when many can relax. It was always a special time of day for her family: her father settled in his armchair with a pipe reading *The West Briton* newspaper, her brothers japing and laughing, snatching a wedge of cheese despite Maggie's entreaties for them not to do so.

She turns the final corner. Norah's cottage, unlike most of the properties nearby, is in darkness. So, Norah is not yet back. Or she has gone to bed early. In which case, she won't want to be disturbed.

Maggie trudges back home, her legs aching. Tiredness is starting to take her. Her head and limbs are heavy. She forces herself to eat the remaining chunk of a Stargazy pie and then heads for her tiny bedroom, slipping with haste past her father's and her brothers' bedrooms. Their powerful presence haunts these rooms especially strongly at night.

The night is sleepless and long. She tosses and turns, desperate for oblivion. But blessed sleep refuses to oblige. By the time a grey dawn seeps on to the horizon her night clothes are clammy with sweat. Maggie clambers out of bed, gathers herself while sipping a piping hot tea, and then passes the time with a few minor chores before returning to Norah's cottage. Her need to know has gathered momentum during the night.

Norah has developed a habit of sleeping late but today she is up and about. Maggie sees her through a window bustling about her tiny cottage. There is a joyful enthusiasm in her brisk movements. She sees Maggie and gives her a wave. The time with Jed Hoskin must have gone well. Is there hope?

Norah opens the front door wide, a curve on her lips and a glint in her eyes. 'I was coming up to see you this morning.'

'How went it?'

'Well…in fact, better than well. I had a wonderful afternoon.' Norah ushers Maggie into the kitchen. 'Come and have a tea and I'll tell you all about it. Jed took me on a tour. I hadn't realised he owned so much. He's got warehouses and salting cellars everywhere, even in Padstow and Newlyn, and a majority share in many of the St Branok fishing boats. He's bought land to the east for his country estate which he says will be the grandest in the parish.'

'He's set on becoming the lord of the manor,' says Maggie when Norah's gushing description dries up.

'He deserves it. He's worked so hard. If Cornwall had more people like Jed Hoskin, it would be a better place.'

'You had afternoon tea?'

'It was wonderful. Put Captain Rosevear's into the shade. I felt quite the lady.' Norah swishes her skirts in an imaginary dance and places her hands on her tiny waist. 'I'll need to be more careful if I indulge in many more afternoon spreads.'

'Did Jed agree to let me stay in the house?'

Norah's self-satisfaction dims. 'He agreed to give you more time.'

'How long?'

'A further two weeks.'

'Thank you so much.' Maggie hesitates, searching for words that don't sound ungrateful. 'In truth, I'd hoped for more.'

There is a flush to Norah's delicate cheeks. 'Jed explained it all to me. Your father died owing a substantial amount of money. He'd been in difficulties for some time, but Jed held back, doing as much as he could to help out.'

'Might he reconsider, do you think?'

Norah shakes her head. 'If I push any harder, Jed's the sort of man who will dig in his heels.'

Maggie raises a hand to her mouth to hide her desperation. Her final hope of saving the family home has been extinguished.

Norah pulls out a chair at the kitchen table. 'You're pale. Take the weight off your feet. There I was gabbling on about my wonderful afternoon without a thought for you.'

Maggie settles with her head in her hands. 'I slept barely at all last night. I kept wondering about…' – she pauses to stop her voice running away from her – '…what is to become of me.'

Norah places a gentle hand on Maggie's shoulder 'We're friends. I'll never let you down. Never. Don't forget there is always room for you here.'

'Yes, you've been more than kind.' Maggie rises. 'Actually, would you mind if I don't have that tea? There is so much to do at home before I leave.'

With a final wave, Maggie starts the short journey back to her home. *Her* home. But not for much longer.

# CHAPTER FOURTEEN

Thursday dawns bright and clear. An orange sun is peeping over the top of distant hills. A ray of sunlight slips through a crack between the thin curtains to fall on Maggie's face. She wakes, blinking and consults her father's old fob watch, placed with care on the small table by her bed the previous night. Thank heavens, he never took it to sea. Come what may she will never part with it.

Jack Treloare will be here within the hour. She needs to throw off the numbing depression which has gripped her. She prepares for his arrival with some urgency. Her smartest day clothes are pressed into service: a high-neck blouse, a long blue skirt – not quite the 'sapphire blue' that Jack had in mind but close enough – and a small, buckled belt, emphasising the slenderness of her waist. Not as slender as Norah's, of course. It could never be as slender even if she was in the workhouse. Maggie's broader frame lacks the graceful femininity of Norah but then so do most of the women in St Branok who typically turn stocky after their first birth and relentless domestic duties take their toll. Trim and presentable is the best that she can hope for, she decides. She is still fussing with her hair when there is a knock on the door. There is jauntiness to its rat-a-tat beat. It can only be Jack Treloare.

As ever, he is grinning as she opens the door. Maggie

can't help smiling back. Jack's grins are infectious. He is dressed smartly, but not flashily, in a black frock coat with a full collar and broad lapels and doeskin trousers.

'Mr Treloare.'

He sweeps his top hat off his head and performs a deep, theatrical bow. 'At your service, ma'am. Ready to accompany the enchanting Miss Pascoe to the ball.'

Maggie is too nervous to join in the joke. Keeping a straight face, she beckons him into the hallway.

'I have taken the liberty of arranging Shanks's pony,' says Jack. 'A stroll in this weather will be energising.'

While Jack waits in the hallway, Maggie grabs her shawl and, for good luck, pins a silver filigree brooch from her most beloved mother on the blouse above her left breast.

They step outside.

'Might I compliment you on your appearance today, ma'am.' Jack offers Maggie his arm. Maggie ignores the gesture and starts walking down the hill, leaving Jack standing there in bemusement. He hastens to catch her up. Men pushing barrows or carrying loads acknowledge Jack with a nod or a tip of their hat, some with a hearty, 'G'day to you, Mr Treloare.' Jack gestures amiably in return, wishing them well and, on occasion, pausing to engage in light chat. He is careful to always introduce Maggie.

Maggie is aware of glances in her direction from passers-by, men and women. There is a questioning look in the eyes of the women and a fleeting hint of appreciation in the eyes of the men, whose gazes rest longer before slipping from her face to her waist. The trouble she has taken today has been worthwhile. Despite her robust sensible nature, she indulges in a flight of fantasy. They are a couple – respectable, married – taking the air or attending church on a sunny Sunday morning. Perhaps with a child, a well-dressed but mischievous boy or girl.

The church hall comes into view. A clutch of men are gathered outside. Jed Hoskin and Parson Kellow seem to have drawn a truce for the time being and are engaged in an enthusiastic discussion full of bonhomie with two men she doesn't recognise. George Moyle is standing to the side, watchful with those dead eyes of his but taking no part.

Kellow greets Jack with a smile and a wave, his grey eyes widening when he also sees Maggie. 'Ah, Jack and er…Maggie, welcome. Let me introduce you to Mr Lanyard and Captain Beauregard, two representatives of the institution, who have generously given their time today to explore the proposal of a lifeboat in St Branok.'

Captain Beauregard is a man of some presence, cut from the same cloth as Captain Rosevear, nearly as tall as George Moyle, with long, greying sideburns merging into an imperial moustache. There is a twinkle in his seadog eyes which doubtless have admired many a curvature, whether it be the horizon or of the female variety. 'I had no idea we would be graced with such delightful company today,' he says with a smile at Maggie.

They engage in formal pleasantries. Hoskin retreats a few yards to consult in whispered tones with his tame lawyer, Nathaniel Narracott. Maggie hears snatches of their conversation.

'What's *she* doing here? Who invited her?' Hoskin hisses.

Narracott's tone is defensive. 'Not me, Mr Hoskin. Not me at all. It appears to have been Treloare.'

Hoskin grinds his teeth. 'What in the devil's name is Jack playing at? My instructions were clear: do nothing to encourage that woman.'

'Oh, they were clear, absolutely clear, Mr Hoskin,' Narracott assures him.

Maggie gulps down a rising nervousness. Perhaps she shouldn't have accepted Jack's invitation. Her stomach, more tightly waisted than ever before, tingles with anxiety.

More snatches of Hoskin's outrage reach her ears, most of it indecipherable though she hears him mutter to Moyle, 'Get Jack over here.'

Moyle strides over to Jack who is discussing St Branok's latest disaster at sea with Captain Beauregard. Moyle lays one of his huge hands on Jack's shoulder and says 'Mr 'oskin wants to speak to you.'

Jack looks up at him in surprise. 'What? Now?'

'Yes, now.'

Jack turns back to the captain. 'If you would be so kind as to excuse me for a moment, sir.'

Captain Beauregard nods. 'It's been a pleasure speaking with you, Mr Treloare. Hopefully, we'll have time later to continue our conversation.'

'Indeed.' Jack walks over to Hoskin with Moyle's paw still resting on his shoulder like a jailer taking a villain into custody. Kellow takes up the empty space left by Jack and, for Captain Beauregard's benefit, launches into a lively appreciation of the growth of the institution. By all accounts, it is going from strength to strength, establishing new lifeboat stations every year. Maggie stands to one side, keeping an ear open for the conversation between Jack and Hoskin behind her.

'What in God's name is *she* doing here?' Hoskin asks Jack with the subtlety of a sledgehammer.

'She has some excellent ideas which I felt were worth sharing with the institution.'

'Excellent ideas about what? The latest bodices and crinolines?'

'She has more seafaring knowledge than you might expect, learned from her father.'

Maggie clenches her fist as she hears Hoskin say, 'Damn her father. Is there no end to the Pascoe clan?'

'Her father was one of the most successful fishermen in these parts for many a year.'

'This is a serious business meeting, not a soirée at the Assembly Rooms. You're a good fisherman, Jack, and I cut you a lot of slack. But you'd be wise not to push my patience too far.'

'Jed, do me credit. Miss Pascoe has some proposals, based on her father's expertise, that merit consideration.'

'Her father was a loose cannon, a chancer and a drinker who got lucky in the early days. But it caught up with him in the end. And *she* instigated most of the trouble at the public meeting. She's a rabble rouser, like her father. If she'd been a man, I'd have instructed George to turf her out that night like the other troublemakers.'

The thin voice of Narracott chimes in. 'Yes, I have heard many an unsavoury story about the Pascoes, Kitto in particular.'

'She lost everything in that storm…her whole family.' Jack is holding his ground, but he's outnumbered.

Fury rises within Maggie as Hoskin continues talking in condescending tones about Solomon Pascoe. She doesn't recognise the portrait of her father painted by Hoskin. He had always been respectful of the sea and its many moods, and his boats were always shipshape. *Minerva* was the best boat in the St Branok fishing fleet bar none, better than some of Hoskin's older vessels which swill sea water in their leaky bellies.

Maggie's heard enough. She disengages herself from conversation with an admiring Captain Beauregard and steps over to the cluster of men.

Hoskin is spewing more claptrap when he sees her coming. '…if we are to get the support of the institution, then we need to remain business –' He pauses, a smirk on his face. 'Miss Pascoe…'

'How dare you speak about my father like that.'

Hoskin licks his fleshy lips. 'I spake true enough.'

'You thought so little of my father and yet you loaned him a considerable sum for the *Minerva*. At exorbitant rates, I might add. If my father is…was as unreliable as you say, it doesn't say much for your business sense.'

A short, chubby man who Maggie doesn't recognise strides forward. 'Please, please, we need to show a united front to the institution if we are to get anywhere at all with our proposals.'

Hoskin snarls. 'I've said my piece. If it is felt that this woman can bring some value to the meeting, then so be it. I for one think it's a mistake.' He casts a murderous stare at Jack. 'I'll hold you responsible for any disturbances.'

Murmuring platitudes, Kellow leads them indoors and everyone takes their places at a long table in an anteroom which looks out on a cemetery that has grown significantly in recent years. The institution men are at one end of the table, Hoskin and Narracott are at the other and the rest are in the middle.

The parson welcomes them all and a formal introduction of all those present takes place. The short, chubby man turns out to be the local commander of the coastguard, Cubert Dawe. Maggie looks on him with interest, a question fluttering in her mind. He stands to survey the assembled group with steady brown eyes, his hands resting on the shiny tabletop. There is a natural authority about him. Another retired seaman.

'St Branok has never had a greater need for a lifeboat,' he says. 'The fishing fleet has doubled in the last ten years. Countless boats have been wrecked. Hundreds of fine seamen have died. The nearest lifeboat – at Padstow – takes two hours to reach St Branok waters even in the most benign conditions. In this modern age, such a situation is intolerable. How long will the shattered remnants of our fishing fleet be allowed to wash up on our shores?'

As he talks, there is a nodding of heads around the room and murmurings in support. The two institution men listen intently, their gazes fixed on the speaker. The shorter man takes notes. Captain Beauregard asks occasional questions to clarify and confirm points made.

Jed Hoskin stands to add his own two penn'orth, emphasising the import of fishing to the local community. 'Mr Narracott will confirm that I put forward the proposal of a lifeboat after careful consideration. Our brave fishermen risk their lives in the most dangerous of waters to harvest the sea's riches. We owe it to them and their families to do everything we can to keep them safe.'

Maggie stares at Hoskin in disbelief, scarcely able to believe that Hoskin is passing off the lifeboat proposal as his own. But she holds her tongue. This is not the time or place for an argument.

Jack adds, 'Consideration should also be given to the fact that we are close to major shipping lanes.' There is a further nodding of heads around the room.

Captain Beauregard then speaks, looking solemn. 'Gentlemen, you have made a powerful case for a lifeboat in

St Branok, but so can other communities. In assessing the viability of any new project, we must consider funding. I recently met with a community in West Wales which is a little further advanced with its proposals. We estimated that a lifeboat station built to the required specifications would cost about one hundred and thirty pounds and I would anticipate a similar cost here in St Branok.'

Hoskin holds up a hand. 'What support could we expect from the institution?'

'If the case for a lifeboat is successful, the institution will fund the lifeboat and the boathouse and provide expertise and advice on specifications and training for the crew. The remainder of the costs, including any land needed, usually comes from the local community. Fortuitously, there might be an opportunity to use a lifeboat at Holyhead which is to be replaced. She is six years old, seaworthy and strong. The boat is to be taken out of service for improvements at a fraction of the cost of a new lifeboat.'

Kellow leans forward, exuding grim determination. 'Whatever the cost, it is a small price to pay in return for lives saved. We have a duty under God. The cost of not taking action is far worse.'

His fiery words are greeted with further murmurings and nods. Maggie senses strong agreement. St Branok will have its lifeboat, come hell or high water.

'Of course, we must also consider location,' says Captain Beauregard. 'Perhaps now is the time to visit the locations you have proposed – the town beach and the harbour, I understand?'

Jack Treloare holds up a hand. 'There is also a third possible site which has merit.' He gestures at Maggie, sitting on his left. 'Miss Pascoe has proposed Trencreek Cove. It is well protected in the worst weather.'

Maggie jumps in, eager to argue her case. 'Yes…yes, my father, Solomon Pascoe, a well-known local fisherman, said it was the safest place in a storm, well protected on three sides.'

Hoskin smirks. 'It's a long way to Trencreek. We're all grateful for Miss Pascoe's interest, I'm sure. And I for one have sympathy for her tragic circumstances, but she knows little of –'

Beauregard cuts him short, his hand raised. 'By coincidence, Mr Lanyard and I engaged in conversation with a number of experienced fishermen at a local inn last night and several of them suggested this cove as a possible location.'

Hoskin pulls an expression of irritation. 'The rigour of your enquiries do you credit, sir. But I'm afraid some of our local fishermen have a reputation for shooting their mouths off when they have ale swilling in their bellies.'

Captain Beauregard's seagoing eyes turn icy. 'I recognise when a man is sober, Mr Hoskin. The proposal merits consideration. We will include it in our surveying.' He stands. 'Gentlemen…and lady' – he nods at Maggie – 'thank you for your time today. There is already no doubt in my mind that a lifeboat is needed in St Branok, most sorely needed. It's a question of location and funding but we note your confidence in gathering the necessary local support. Our report will provide more detail on the sums required and the proposed site.' He nods at Jack. 'Mr Treloare, perhaps you would be so good as to accompany us on our surveying of the various sites?'

Jack dips his head in acceptance. 'It would be a pleasure, Captain.'

Captain Beauregard looks across the table. 'And, of course, you, Mr Dawe, Mr Hoskin and Parson Kellow.'

As the small party prepares to leave with Beauregard at its head, Maggie takes advantage of a pause to place a hand on Cubert Dawe's arm. 'Sir, a moment of your time, please.'

Dawe regards her with a smile. 'How might I be of service?'

'I wanted to ask you about the new FitzRoy weather service.'

'What do you wish to know?'

'How does it work?'

'It is straightforward enough. FitzRoy and his assistants in London assemble weather reports from telegraph stations around the country, such as Penzance and Plymouth. They analyse the results and then send their forecasts back to the telegraph stations which then relay this information to local sites. If severe weather is believed to be imminent, then, as you will have seen, warning signals – lanterns at night, canvas shapes in daylight – are used to advise local fishermen. It is early days, though already demonstrating its worth. FitzRoy is an admirable fellow. He accompanied the renowned naturalist Charles Darwin on his researches on *HMS Beagle*. I have had the honour and pleasure of meeting him once in London.'

Maggie frowns. 'And yet, when the great storm came this summer, St Branok was not warned.'

Dawe studies her. 'That is regrettably correct, so I understand.'

'Did any other fishing communities in your area not receive the alert?'

Dawe takes a deep breath. 'It was a tragedy for St Branok alone.'

'Do you know why?'

'Enquiries have been made. It seems that the person responsible for putting out the required signals for St Branok failed in his duties.'

Dawe hesitates, bites his lip and then says, 'Drink is the root cause, I fear. The man had a strong liking for gin and other intoxicants, so we have been led to believe. There are reports of him being seen worse for wear outside The Mermaid prior to the storm.'

'Who is he?'

'A retired fisherman called Clement Thomas. He was paid to maintain and put out the warning signs when required.'

Maggie clenches her jaw. 'The man has blood on his hands. Has he been interviewed?'

'Regretfully, not. He has disappeared with his tail between his legs. The man has a lot to answer for. No doubt the full force of the law will fall on his head when he breaks cover. If it was down to me, I'd have the fool strung up.'

'Where does he live?'

Dawe pauses again before saying, 'Somewhere in Uppertown, I believe.' He glances over at the small party which is ready to leave. The institution men are looking over expectantly. 'I'm required elsewhere. Please accept my most sincere condolences. To suffer the loss of one beloved person is tragedy enough, but to lose your whole family in a day….it is beyond words.'

There's a quaver in Maggie's voice as she thanks Cubert Dawe for his time.

The inspection party sets off and Maggie watches them go, her mind dwelling on the old salt who failed to put out the storm warning signs. If not for his stupidity and neglect, her father, brothers and many other St Branok fishermen would still be alive.

# CHAPTER FIFTEEN

Uppertown is a messy, tight-knit community of St Branok's poorest residents who grub a living by fair means or foul, usually foul if its reputation is to be believed. Cob huts with patchwork roofs crowd its narrow streets. Only a fresh south-westerly from the Atlantic purges them of a persistent, rank odour. Downpours turn them into cesspits of scum and waste.

Maggie steps around the puddles. She is pleased she went home and changed out of her smartest day clothes before coming here. The hem of her beautiful blue skirt would now be caked with filth and, in any event, would look ridiculously out of place in streets inhabited by scrawny children in rags, dour men and pinch-faced women. A gaunt man with a sack slung over his shoulder shuffles past. He takes no interest in her and continues down the hill.

A middle-aged woman, humming tunelessly, is beating wet clothes on a slab of rock outside her home while two raggedy young urchins throw stones at a scraggy dog nearby. They pause to stare at Maggie with wide eyes, emphasised by their filthy faces. Maggie smiles at them. They don't smile back.

Maggie hails the woman who looks like the sort of gossipy person who knows everybody. 'Excuse me. Excuse me.'

The woman looks up, still clutching the clothes she is

washing, wariness flickering in her tired eyes. Strangers only venture into Uppertown when necessity demands.

Maggie delivers the most reassuring smile she can manage. 'I was hoping…could you tell me where Clement Thomas lives?'

'Who wants to know?'

'Me. Only me.'

'And who's me?'

'Maggie Pascoe. My father is…was a fisherman. Solomon Pascoe. You might have heard of him or his fishing boat, the *Minerva*.'

The woman's hard look softens. 'I knew Solomon Pascoe. Everybody knew him. A good man 'e was.'

'He and my brothers all died in the storm.'

'A tragedy. I feel right sorry for you, girl.' The woman points to a shadowy side street. 'Old Clemo lives down there, fourth house on the right. Not that there's been much sight of him recent like. A few people have been up here looking for him.'

'Who?'

The woman shrugs. 'Official types …and a few others.'

Maggie strides onward. 'Thank you.'

'God bless you, girl.' The woman returns to her washing.

Clement Thomas's home is in a sorry state, even by the impoverished standards of Uppertown. Slate tiles are missing from the roof and there has been a ham-fisted effort to fill a hole in the wall with straw and mud. A spiral of sooty smoke from a pipe indicates there is somebody at home. Maggie's hopes rise. She knocks on a flaking, poorly fitting pine door.

No answer.

She tries again. A little harder.

Still no answer.

Hearing a rustle of movement inside, she calls out. 'Hello…hello…hello.'

Nothing.

Her tone rises. And keeps rising. 'Hello, I'm looking for Clement Thomas.'

Women dressed in tatty, workaday gowns and aprons emerge from nearby houses to find out what the fuss is about.

A young woman next door, cradling a grizzling baby, says, 'You won't find Clemo around here. He's long gone. Vanished. Left Nessa, his missus in a right old lather. No money. Nothing. She bin living off the charity of others.'

'Is Nessa at home now?'

'She ain't answering to no strangers. There've been any number of folks up here snooping around and not one of them got a peep out of her.'

'I want to speak to her for a few minutes. A few questions. That's all. I don't want to cause her any harm. My whole family…was lost in the recent storm.' Maggie catches her breath. What has befallen her family is still too raw to be told clearly and cleanly. She talks in spasms of snatched words.

The young woman passes the baby to an older woman who has also emerged from the house and then steps over to hammer on Nessa's door. 'Nessa, Nessa, a young girl be 'ere to see yer. Right important it is. Nessa. Nessa. Open this blamed door or so help me I'll kick it down.'

A curmudgeonly, cracked voice sounds on the other side of the door. 'I ain't opening the door to no stranger. Tell 'er to go away and leave an old woman in peace. Leave me alone.'

'Please,' Maggie calls out. 'A few minutes, that's all.'

The door judders open to reveal a bent crone with iron grey hair, wrapped in a threadbare shawl. She looks up at

Maggie who towers over her more than a head taller. 'Me 'usband ain't 'ere if that's what yer asking.'

'Where did he go?'

Nessa Thomas shrugs bowed shoulders. 'No idea. And who are you anyways?'

'I'm Maggie Pascoe. I live down the hill in St Branok. When did he leave?'

'The night after that there blamed storm. Went off without a by-your-leave and didn't come back. Left me in a right old dither. Hardly a ha'penny to call me own. It comes to summat when a woman of my age has to rely on the kindness of neighbours.'

Maggie fishes out of her purse one of her few precious coins, a sixpence – almost half a day's wages for some. It glimmers in the light. 'Can I ask you a few more questions? It'd be worth your while.'

At the sight of the coin, Nessa's eyes also glimmer. She shuffles aside. 'You better come in, I s'pose. Don't want to be standing on the doorstep where half of Uppertown can hear yer.'

The inside of Nessa Thomas's home is a picture of abject poverty: a single room with rough slate floor tiles, a table, a couple of chairs and a bed. A lifetime of work, of struggle, have been rewarded with this. A smouldering fire takes an edge off the cold. A mangy grey cat is curled up nearby.

'Times been hard of late.' Nessa coughs, a harsh, raw cough. 'It wasn't always like this. Clem was a right good fisherman in his day, but fishing's a young man's game.'

Maggie places the sixpence on the table in full sight but keeps a finger on it. 'So, he had to stop?'

Nessa eyes it hungrily. 'That's about the size of it. He got too rickety for crawling around on fishing boats. But Jed

Hoskin looked after him. He's a gentleman, that man. Grew up like the rest of us, he did. And now look at him, king of St Branok.'

'How did Jed help?'

'He put in a word with the right people. Got him the job of maintaining and putting out the storm warning signals for St Branok. Clem got a shilling a shout. It kept our heads above water.'

'So, why didn't he put out the warning signals for the recent storm?'

'I don't know nothing about that. That was Clem's business.'

'I heard that he was in The Mermaid.'

Nessa's eyes darken. 'What of it?'

'Some people have been saying that your husband was a heavy drinker, that he was unreliable and failed in his duty.'

'That's a lie! He liked a jar like the next man, but he was no drunk. Took his duties serious. Always did. He'd been doing it for a year. Never missed a call-out.'

'What did he say after the storm?'

'He didn't say nothing.'

'Nothing at all?'

'Just said that, didn't I?' Nessa clenches her spidery hands. 'Are you going to give me the money or not?'

'Yes, when you have answered a few more questions. So, what was he like when you last saw him?'

Nessa glances at the coin again. 'Upset. He kept pacing up and down with his head in his hands. I thought it was because folks he'd shipped with had died. But a few days after he'd gone, more and more angry folks began turning up here, demanding to see him. Called him a murderer. Said he should be strung up, that he'd neglected his duty.'

'Did he say when he would return?'

Nessa shakes her head. 'He walked out that there door and never came back.'

'Do you have any idea where he might be?'

Nessa grits her teeth. 'No, and even if I did, I wouldn't be telling the likes of people round here.'

'Do you have a picture of Clem?'

The old woman shakes her head. 'Do I look like the sort of person who can waste money on pictures?'

'What does he look like?'

'You can't miss him. The left side of Clem's face was stoved-in in an accident on the quayside when he was a lad. It left his face lop-sided.'

Maggie has a sudden memory of an elderly disfigured man who often hung around the quayside when the fleet was readying for sea. 'I think I remember him,' she says and at last passes over the coveted sixpence. The old lady snatches it up with a swiftness belying her age.

Nessa hobbles to her rickety front door and holds it open. 'You've had yer money's worth, missy. I ain't telling no more.' She adds hastily, 'And there ain't no more to tell, anyways. What's done be done.'

Maggie wishes she had more coins to loosen the old woman's tongue though she has already given far more than she can afford. She steps outside, followed by the cat which slinks down a shadowy side street.

The nosy neighbour confronts her. 'Did she help?'

Maggie pauses, unsure what to share. 'She says Clem walked out and never returned.' A thought strikes her. 'Did you see him on the night he disappeared?'

'Nah.'

'Do you know where he might be staying?'

'He has an older sister, I do believe.'

Maggie licks her lips. At last she is getting somewhere. 'Do you know her name or where she lives?'

'Nah. She's not local.' She pauses and then adds, 'Clem was a strange fella at times but all these rumours about him not doing his duty don't seem right to me. My da fished with him and said he was a good man.'

'Was he a heavy drinker?'

'No more'n the next man.'

'Well, thank you.' Maggie walks off down the street with the eyes of the neighbour burning into her back. Relief sweeps over her when she quits the rank filth of Uppertown.

A fresh Atlantic breeze, dry for a change, blows away Uppertown's fetid tang as she crests a rise and heads down toward the harbourside. St Branok is sprawled serenely in front of her, giving little clue as to the hive of industry it has become. She sucks in deeply, thankful for the purity of the ocean breeze. It clears her mind as well as her nose and sets her thinking sensibly.

What can she be sure about? She knows that the storm alert didn't happen for St Branok and that the man responsible for putting out the signs was old Clement Thomas who has, not surprisingly, vanished. The easy answer is that he is an unreliable drunkard. Except it is too convenient and doesn't fit with people who knew him. His wife might have viewed his wrongdoings with rose-tinted glasses but his neighbour?

Clem Thomas – a man with blood on his hands? Or a useful scapegoat? And where is he hiding?

# CHAPTER SIXTEEN

Triumph is writ large on Norah's face when she turns up at Maggie's home the following day.

'I have exciting news,' she says after letting herself in by the side door and finding Maggie in the kitchen.

Maggie pauses from scrubbing a persistent stain on the wash basin. 'What is it?'

'Would you like to work at Morwenstowe?'

'Lord Kendall's estate?'

'The very same. It would give you a place to live until you find your feet.'

'What could I do there?'

'Polly, my cousin who works in the kitchens there, says they have a vacancy for a kitchen maid. You'd pick it up in no time. She's happy to put in a good word for you.'

Maggie hugs her friend while avoiding placing her mucky hands on Norah's dress, a new one by the look of it, no doubt funded by Hoskin. 'Oh Norah, where would I be without you?'

'So, are you interested?'

'Yes…yes, most definitely yes.'

There's a twinkle in Norah's eyes as she says, 'Actually, I have already said yes and my cousin has mentioned your situation to the cook, Mrs Penrose, who has suggested an interview on Tuesday morning.'

'Thank you…thank you so much.'

The twinkle in Norah's eyes turns mischievous. 'I hear you've been spending time with Jack Treloare.'

Maggie turns away to deal with the stain. Conveniently, it means Norah can't see the flush in her cheeks. 'Who has been saying it?'

'Jed told me. He wasn't best pleased at you turning up yesterday morning arm-in-arm with Jack for the meeting with the lifeboat men. He's going to have it out with Jack, says you shouldn't have been allowed to interfere.'

'I wasn't arm-in-arm with Jack,' Maggie says with an edge of irritation, adding in a softer tone, 'I hope I haven't caused Jack problems.'

'Nothing serious. Jack's too canny a fisherman for Jed to stop doing business with him. Jed knows which side his bread is buttered.'

'Why oh why does Jed hate me so much? I've never done anything against him.' Maggie sighs. Life is tough enough without having a person of the standing of Jed Hoskin sniping at her.

'He doesn't hate you. He's just suspicious, what with you being a Pascoe and all. Him and your da never got on and, after the public meeting, he thinks you're putting your nose in where it's not wanted.'

Maggie finds herself gripping the washbasin. 'I have a right. My whole family died.'

'And my son,' says Norah, her voice suddenly heavy.

Maggie stays staring at the washbasin, unwilling to show her face, which she feels sure must be ridden with guilt. 'I have learned quite a lot more. A retired fishermen called Clement Thomas was supposed to put out the storm warning signals, but it is claimed he was too drunk to do so.'

'He has a lot to answer for.'

'Unfortunately, he's now disappeared but I spoke to his wife yesterday. She lives in Uppertown.'

Norah's eyes narrow. 'What did she say?'

'Something's not right,' Maggie says through gritted teeth.

'Of course, it's not right. Honest fishermen's lives were thrown away because that stupid old soak was three sheets to the wind.'

'It's more than that.'

'What more can there be?'

Maggie at last feels strong enough to look her friend in the eye. She turns. 'I don't believe Clem Thomas was drunk like some folks say. Being a fisherman himself, he took the storm warnings seriously.'

'Is this what his wife says?' Norah raises an eyebrow.

'Yes.'

'Some wives can only see the good in their men. I knew a woman whose husband beat her black and blue every Friday night, but she'd never hear a word against him. Not a word. Thought he was God's gift.'

'A neighbour also said he was no drunkard.'

'What difference does it make how drunk he was? He failed – failed us all and good men died as a result.'

Maggie shakes her head. 'I don't believe that's the whole truth.'

'What else can there be?'

'I...I'm not sure...' Maggie's voice fades. She turns the conversation to more positive matters. 'Thank you so much for finding the opportunity at Morwenstowe. I'll always be grateful.'

They share a brew of tea, the last of a fine Darjeeling which Maggie can no longer afford. After a final hug, she waves Norah on her way.

For the first time since the Great Gale, Maggie's hopes are rising. A new opportunity has arisen from the most unlikely of places: the much-vaunted Morwenstowe estate. Kitchen maid will be a huge fall from her position as the daughter of St Branok's most esteemed fisherman. But it will provide security at a time when she yearns for certainty and stability.

# CHAPTER SEVENTEEN

On a blustery Tuesday morning, Maggie makes light of the three-mile walk from St Branok to the country estate of Lord and Lady Kendall, hope of a new life easing her steps. She shelters under trees from downpours interspersed with spells of bright sunshine. The deluge finds its way past her bonnet and thick shawl to trickle down her neck and she is chilled and damp – but still optimistic – when Morwenstowe at last hoves into sight.

Gothic pinnacles peep above the tall and slender Cornish Elm trees, standing to attention along the curving, gravelled driveway. She trudges on, past puddles and over a carpet of golden-brown leaves dislodged by the gusts of the previous night.

Soon, Morwenstowe is visible in all its opulent glory, exuding power and unimaginable wealth. Maggie halts in wonder. Despite its proximity to St Branok, she is seeing it for the first time. Fluted columns and snarling gargoyles adorn the entrance. Mullioned windows give the impression that the front of the building is a wall of glass. Elegant parkland, far more extensive than Captain Rosevear's property at Rejerrah, stretches down to a river and manmade lake surrounded by willow, elm and oak. It is a world away from the last place she visited – the downtrodden hovels of Uppertown or, indeed, the rest of St Branok. Surely, this cannot be the home of an ordinary mortal but of an extraordinary being with the world at their feet. Who can have anything. Do anything.

Maggie feels small and inconsequential in the presence of this imposing seat of power. Shyness sweeps her as she meekly approaches a man in his thirties, dressed impeccably in a coat with a turned-up collar, cravat and crisp white shirt. He is slouched on a wall out of sight of the main entrance.

'Excuse me, sir, I have an appointment with Mrs Penrose – for a vacancy. Where might I find her?'

He contemplates her with a sneer. 'The new kitchen maid, eh? Follow me.' He strides off at pace and, when Maggie falls behind, turns round to say, 'Step lively, girl. Don't dally! I haven't got all day.'

Maggie is hustled past neatly trimmed bushes to a side door where she descends stairs into the bowels of the great building – along shadowy corridors, reeking with the tang of substances used for cleaning and polishing. The metallic clatter of pots and pans sounds up ahead. At last, they reach a large kitchen, filled with the warm aroma of baking.

'Stay here,' the man tells Maggie before striding off into the kitchen. And so Maggie waits in the corridor, licking her lips, her hands clasped in front of her. Through a crack in the doorway, she glimpses the man approach a roly-poly woman in a printed gown and lace collar who is using a linen cloth to take a hot tray out of an oven. A pleated cap sits on her grey, wiry hair, tied up in a bun.

'Mrs Penrose, a girl's here to see yer. The kitchen maid you were talking about.'

'Where is she?'

'Out in the corridor.'

Mrs Penrose places the tray on a surface. 'Well, don't

leave her standing out there, Mr Jarvis. Make yourself useful and take her into the hall where we can talk properly.' She raises her voice. 'I'll be with you in a moment, dearie.'

Mr Jarvis returns to Maggie, looking irked by Mrs Penrose's reprimand. 'Come on.' He leads her deeper into the maze of corridors to a large room with a long table at its centre. 'Stay here and don't touch anything,' he commands and then strides away. Maggie sits at the table to wait, glancing around, chewing her lower lip.

Mrs Penrose appears after a few minutes, her broad features dripping with perspiration. 'No need to be nervous, dear. We're all friends here.'

Maggie twists her hands in her lap. 'I…I have never been in a house like this before and I think I must have upset Mr Jarvis.'

'Oh, don't take any notice of him, dearie. Got ideas above his station has that man. He's a footman, nothing more.' She studies Maggie with curiosity. 'You're Norah Bray's friend, aren't you?'

'Yes, she's a wonderful friend.'

Mrs Penrose sits next to her. 'She's been through a lot, that girl. To lose her husband and now her son. And you? You lost your father?'

Maggie nods. 'My father and my three brothers all died in the storm. And I have nowhere to live.'

Mrs Penrose pats the back of Maggie's hand. 'You'll find a way, a new way. And that could be at Morwenstowe.' Her voice turns businesslike. 'We work hard here. There's a lot to do. You'll be on your feet the best part of fourteen hours a day. It's a long day but not as stretching as some. I hear talk of eighteen hours at an estate in Devon.'

'I'm sure I can manage. I kept house for my family after my mother died, did all the cooking and the cleaning.'

Mrs Penrose casts an appraising eye over Maggie's broad shoulders and robust physique. 'Well, you look like you'll be able to cope with the demands. Polly, Norah's cousin, has settled in well here. Meek as a mouse she was at first and now quite the chatterbox.'

The talk moves onto the details of the job. At last, Mrs Penrose smiles and says, 'I think you'll do well here. It's half a day off a week, your food and lodging are included, and you get eleven pounds a year. The job is yours if you want it.'

'I do. Thank you. When can I start?'

'The sooner the better. His lordship is planning a banquet next week for some duke or other and we'll need all the help we can get.'

The warmth and hope in Maggie grow. She is introduced to Polly, a slight girl barely taller than Norah. The family resemblance is obvious. 'The two of you will be sharing a room,' says Mrs Penrose, placing a hand on Polly's shoulder. 'Polly's a good girl. Hard-working.' The two girls smile broadly at each other.

'Have you completed your duties?' Mrs Penrose asks Polly.

'Nearly, Mrs Penrose.'

'Well, get on with it, child. Those pots won't clean themselves.'

'Yes, Mrs Penrose.' Polly bustles away with a light step.

Mrs Penrose regards Maggie with a benevolent gaze. 'You've a fair walk home. We can't let you go without summat to eat and drink.'

Maggie is soon tucking into a thick slice of cheese and the heel of a fresh loaf. The warm bread and cheese are delicious. If this is a sign of food at Morwenstowe, she won't go hungry.

There is a cheeriness in her mood when Maggie heads for home. Morwenstowe offers her the chance of a new life and a new start. Not the sort of life she imagined a few months ago – that life is gone forever – but a new start, nonetheless.

# CHAPTER EIGHTEEN

'My old life is over,' Maggie mutters to herself as she wanders through the family house for the last time, her thoughts sombre. She will never return here. Her father's battered wood and leather case is in the hallway, filled with the clothes and possessions she is taking to Morwenstowe. The remains of her former life are contained in a single case.

Every room sparks memories. She pauses on the threshold of each, determined to capture every detail: the kitchen where her mother bustled about cooking and cleaning; the sitting room where her mother and father would settle of an evening in companionable silence, her father sucking his pipe, her mother darning a sock; the big bedroom where her brothers laughed, shouted and japed endlessly; her own small bedroom, set in the eaves, with its special view of the coast. All now Jed Hoskin's property.

For the thousandth time, she thinks of old Clem Thomas. If he had put out the storm-warning signals, would it have made any difference? Would her father have still insisted on going to sea on that fateful day? No, she decides. Her father would never have risked the lives of his beloved sons. So Clem Thomas killed her family – and many others.

From an upstairs bedroom window, she spies Norah coming up the street. It sparks a fresh pang of guilt about

Jowan. Could she have done more to stop him going aboard? She had tried. Oh yes, she had tried but there was no moving her father. The knowledge that she hasn't been honest with Norah, that she hasn't told her the whole truth, is gnawing away at her. Would they still be friends if Norah knew that her beloved son had died aboard the *Minerva* and that Maggie had stood on the quayside and watched him go?

Norah calls out. 'Are you ready?'

'Yes…yes, I'll be down in a moment.' Without thinking, Maggie wipes away a smear on a wall mirror. A young woman stares back at her. Not beautiful by the tightly corseted feminine standards of the age but forthright and interesting. Interesting enough to attract more than a passing glance from the esteemed Jack Treloare, though there has been no sign of him since the meeting with the lifeboat institution men. He will have been busy. Or perhaps Jed Hoskin has frightened him away.

Coincidentally, as Maggie trudges down the stairs for the final time, her friend says, 'Has Jack been around of late?'

Maggie sucks in her lower lip. ''No, there's been no sign of him.'

Norah smiles. 'Jack liked you, liked you a lot. But he's a busy man. He'll come sniffing around again soon enough, you'll see. Once a man like Jack gets a liking for a girl, he doesn't give up.'

'There are lots of women who would set their cap at Jack, prettier girls with better prospects.'

Norah stares at her as if she has gone mad. 'Why do you put yourself down so? It's no good telling a man that he can find a better woman elsewhere. Make him work for your affections. Believe me, men love the chase.'

'It's going to be more difficult to stay in touch once I'm

out at Morwenstowe,' says Maggie. 'And I only get half a day off a week.'

There's a cunning gleam in Norah's eyes. 'Don't fret. Absence makes the heart grow fonder. If he's interested enough, he'll find a way. Have you told him you are living out at Morwenstowe?'

Maggie nods. 'I sent him a letter but heard nothing back. I think Jed Hoskin has put him off. Hoskin hates us Pascoes...' She adds, 'And I'm the only one left.'

Norah's smooth forehead creases. 'If he hated you, he'd never have agreed to the extension.'

'He offered it because you persuaded him.'

'Jed's not as bad as some folks say. A lot of people in this town and further away have him to thank for giving them a good living.'

'Are you falling for him?' Maggie says, staring at her friend.

Norah chuckles. 'I don't fall for any man. They fall for me.' She sniffs. 'There are worse men than Jed to hook up with in the county. He's got everything he needs in his business. Now he needs a good wife and a family to fill his big new house. It's going to be right cold and empty if it's only him and a few servants rattling around in there.'

Outside, a clatter of hooves rings out. Maggie opens the front door, expecting it to be Kellow's small buggy. The parson has offered to take Maggie out to Morwenstowe. But no, it is a much grander vehicle.

'Whoa!' The driver comes to a halt with a firm tug on the reins and a pull of the long brake lever. The two black, glistening horses, fine examples of their breed, snort and stamp impatiently, their breath misting in the damp autumnal air.

'It's Jed Hoskin's carriage,' says Norah in surprise.

The scrawny figure of Nathaniel Narracott, the lawyer, slips out of the back seat. George Moyle towers behind.

The cadaverous lawyer advances towards them, clutching a ledger, with the usual glint of cold disdain in his eyes. Maggie's stomach somersaults.

He smiles at Norah. 'Mrs Bray, a pleasure as always.' He regards Maggie with an infinitely colder look. 'Your preparations for departure are complete, I trust?'

'You're early,' Maggie manages when she has cleared a catch in her throat. 'I thought…I had a few more hours.'

Narracott's fingers whiten as they tighten on the ledger. 'You have been given more than enough time to get your affairs in order. Mr Hoskin's instructions are clear: you are required to vacate the property today. Hand over the keys and be on your way.'

Maggie turns to go back inside the house. 'I still have a few items to collect.'

She is held back by one of Moyle's meaty paws on her shoulder.

'Your time has run out, Miss Pascoe,' Narracott says. 'Mr Hoskin's been more than generous. The building and everything it contains is now his property. Anything removed will be treated as theft and, if you venture back inside, it will be deemed as trespass. If you fail to comply, I will have no hesitation in bringing the full authority of the law to bear.'

Maggie shrugs off Moyle's heavy hand. 'There are family possessions – my mother's brooch, her necklace – they mean everything to me.'

'You had yer chance, luv,' says Moyle. He grabs her again, pulls her back. Maggie wriggles out of his grasp, slips and falls to the ground. Muddy water oozes through her skirt, wetting her knees. The palms of her hands are grazed and bruised. Blood seeps from the palm of her right hand. Moyle's hand grabs her arm, hauls her onto her feet like she is a rag doll.

Norah glares daggers at the lawyer. 'Restrain your dog, Mr Narracott! Make no mistake, Mr Hoskin will hear of this.'

A laughing Moyle, encouraged by the women's protestations, grabs Maggie by the waist and pulls her closer. 'You're a wild little thing, luv. You need a man to keep you in check.'

Narracott pulls an expression of discomfort. 'Get off her, Moyle. This is not the place for a scene.' He glances around. The furore has caused women to emerge from nearby houses, one with a baby on her hip and another clutching a dish cloth. They watch silently, concerned but reluctant to interfere in Hoskin business.

Moyle releases Maggie with an inane grin on his face. She scrambles away.

Norah turns back to Narracott, her eyes blazing. 'I hold you personally responsible for this, Mr Narracott. For letting this animal…' – she nods at Moyle whose grin has turned to a smirk – '…loose on a vulnerable young woman.'

Narracott's pale grey eyes narrow. 'Miss Pascoe was uncooperative. She ignored our express instructions to leave the property. Mr Moyle was merely trying to restrain her. To prevent her from committing theft and trespass.'

Norah advances on Narracott. 'She was collecting a few valued family keepsakes before leaving the home she has lived in all her life.'

Uncertainty flickers across Narracott's face. 'Mr Hoskin is a man of compassion. In the circumstances, I am willing to permit Miss Pascoe to keep her mother's brooch and necklace. Where are they?'

'In a cupboard in my father's bedroom on the first floor,' says Maggie.

Narracott turns to his mountainous sidekick. 'Moyle, fetch them so that we can clear up this matter and make progress without further delay.'

Moyle disappears inside and reappears with the brooch and the necklace. He hands them over to Maggie with a snigger. A link on the necklace is broken. She stares at Moyle. Her head is thumping. 'What have you done?'

'It fell apart in me 'ands,' says Moyle with a snigger.

'You did it deliberately.'

'Don't talk daft, woman. It's old.'

Narracott steps forward. 'We need to get on. There are many arrangements to be made. We have potential purchasers of the contents which will help to defray some of the Pascoe debts.' He holds out his hand. 'The keys, Miss Pascoe, the keys. Hand them over, please.'

A smaller carriage appears. Parson Kellow's buggy at last. Unfortunately, the driver is not the parson himself, but a red-faced little man called Mr Ellis who is in the parson's employ at the vicarage. Norah leads a trembling Maggie over to the carriage. 'Come on, let's get out of here.'

Maggie resists. 'My case. It's in the hallway.'

Narracott blocks her return to the house. 'Moyle, fetch her case.'

Moyle strides inside and reappears carrying the case as if it is as light as a feather. He dumps it next to Kellow's buggy. Mr Ellis jumps down and, puffing and straining as if it has suddenly grown much heavier, lifts it on to the rear of the carriage as Maggie and Norah climb aboard.

With a flick of a whip, the buggy sets off at a brisk trot down the road, heading towards Morwenstowe. Maggie slumps in the seat, staring straight ahead with bleary eyes, unable to bring herself to look back one last time.

Her home is gone.

# CHAPTER NINETEEN

Maggie's nerves are still jangling by the time she arrives at Morwenstowe. She alights from the parson's carriage and says a heartfelt goodbye to her friend, who will return to St Branok with the carriage, as a sweating Mr Ellis places the trunk at her feet. A young maid called Tess takes Maggie to the kitchen which, unlike the previous visit, is seething with bustle and industry. A blast of hot air from an open oven warms their faces as Mrs Penrose, perspiring mightily, issues curt instructions to a team of women of varying ages, who are tending boiling pots, hot ovens and cutting vegetables. Women in lace caps hustle back and forth, each a cog in a much larger machine.

Mrs Penrose looks up from whisking the contents of a bowl. 'You've come at a busy time. Her ladyship is entertaining guests tonight and so it's all hands to the pumps as you fisherfolk might say.' She regards the dried mud on Maggie's skirt with a quizzical look. 'What in heaven's name happened to you, girl?'

Heat washes through Maggie's cheeks. 'I'm sorry. I was knocked down.'

Mrs Penrose's double chin sags in shock. 'Oh my goodness. By a carriage?'

'By a beast of man called George Moyle.'

The cook's expression softens in sympathy. 'I've heard of

Moyle. He's an animal. One of our maids had an unfortunate encounter with him.' She clenches her jowly jaw. 'Anyways, you need to tidy yourself up. There is a clean set of more appropriate clothing in your room –' She halts in mid-sentence.

Indeed, the whole kitchen freezes. A tall, fair-haired woman in her thirties has appeared. As tall as Maggie. A vision of elegance in silks and brocade. The new arrival walks into the room in a rustle of skirts and with the poise of the titled.

Lady Kendall.

'Mrs Penrose, I'd like to discuss tonight's menu.'

Mrs Penrose looks irked. 'I thought it had all been agreed, ma'am. Preparations are well underway.'

'Perhaps we should reconsider the dessert. Two of my guests, Miss Harper and Mrs Shapps, have sensitive palates.'

'What do you suggest?'

'Something a little lighter. A gateau aux pommes?

Hands on hips, the cook looks rebellious. 'As always, we will do our best but at this stage it's all very – '

Lady Kendall claps her hands, oblivious to her cook's protest. 'Excellent. You really are a wonder, Mrs Penrose.' Cool blue eyes sweep around the room. They settle on Maggie and her muddied skirt. 'And who do we have here?'

Maggie dips in a curtsey. Her stomach tingles. 'Miss Margaret Pascoe, new kitchen maid, ma'am. I…I had an accident.'

Lady Kendall looks her up and down. 'So I see. What happened?'

Maggie wishes she could sink into the ground. 'I fell, ma'am.'

A flustered Mrs Penrose intervenes. 'She's just arrived. We were sending her off for a clean set of clothes before she commences her duties.'

Lady Kendall's gaze appears warm and friendly. 'Pascoe. I recall the name. You are from St Branok, yes?'

'Indeed, ma'am. My family has lived there for generations.'

'Fishermen?'

'They were, yes.'

'Were?'

'My father, Solomon Pascoe, and my three brothers were lost in the summer storm, ma'am.'

Lady Kendall holds an immaculately manicured hand to her mouth. 'Oh, my goodness. How terrible. What remains of your family?'

'There's only me now, ma'am.'

'And your home?'

'Gone, ma'am.'

Lady Kendall sighs with empathy. 'Well, I am pleased we have been able to offer you a position, Miss Pascoe. Rest assured that we look after our own here at Morwenstowe. Don't we, Mrs Penrose?'

Mrs Penrose's mutinous expression softens. 'We do indeed…we do indeed.'

Lady Kendall turns to go but then pauses. 'Your father was a wonderful seaman by all accounts, quite the hero. We must talk again. When you feel ready, I'd be pleased to hear more about him and the rest of your family.'

And with that her ladyship is gone in a whisper of swishing petticoats.

Mrs Penrose rumbles discontentment. 'Pah! Gateau aux pommes indeed! If her ladyship wanted a gateau aux pommes for her precious friends, she should have said yesterday. She changes her mind like the wind. The last Lady Kendall wouldn't have done it. Nor would she have turned up in the kitchen unannounced. Without a by your leave. And that's as it should be. By rights, them upstairs should stay upstairs and leave arrangements to us down here, let us get on with our jobs.'

The hiatus is over. The kitchen returns to industry. Polly appears, fresh from her endeavours elsewhere, and exchanges grins with Norah.

'Ah Polly,' says Mrs Penrose. 'Here at last. Be so good as to take Maggie to your room and help her get ready.' She turns to Maggie. 'Polly will show you the run of the house.'

Maggie smiles at the flaxen-haired girl. 'I'm sure we'll be great friends.'

Mrs Penrose waves Polly away. 'Well, don't hang around here, girl. I need you both back within the hour. There's no end of work to be done.'

Polly leads the way down a darkened corridor, pointing out rooms as they go. 'That be the back parlour…there be the front parlour…and that's the scullery.'

So many rooms. So many nooks and crannies. 'I'll never find my way around this place,' says Maggie, only half-joking.

'You'll soon get the hang of it,' Polly assures her as she paces onward.

Finally, they arrive at a small room in the depths of the building, similar in size to her bedroom at home, except that it has none of the sunny aura of her attic room. A slit window at head height, with a view of an inner courtyard, provides the room's only natural light. Two single beds, separated by a small table, take up much of the space at one end of the room. Her new home.

'It's a cosy room,' Polly says, 'unless a cold wind blows down from the north, and the bed is comfortable. Mine's the one on the left.'

'How long have you been here?' says Maggie.

Polly sits down on her bed. 'Two year now. I've been happy. Mrs Penrose works us hard, but she's fair.'

'Lady Kendall seems nice.'

'She ain't the first Lady Kendall, you know,' Polly says, her brown eyes bright with gossip.

'Oh, what happened?'

'The first Lady Kendall died quite a few year back. Lord Kendall wasted no time in finding a new wife. Keen to find an heir, he was. And she's done that alright – a boy, Jasper, and a girl, Charlotte.'

'So, her ladyship is younger than the first Lady Kendall?'

'A lot younger. Twenty year, at least. She has her own ideas about the place of women in society.'

Polly relates a variety of stories, some of them mildly scandalous – none of which involve the virtuous Lady Kendall – as she helps Maggie into her crisp new kitchen maid's outfit. Quiet little Polly can be quite a gossip. Doubtless she will reveal much more about the workings of Morwenstowe and its inhabitants in the weeks ahead, though much of it appears to be no better than hearsay.

Polly tugs Maggie's clothing this way and that before standing back with a critical eye to pronounce her 'shipshape'.

# CHAPTER TWENTY

All week, Maggie is kept busy scouring floors, cleaning plates and preparing food at the beck and call of Mrs Penrose. She has slotted neatly into being a minor cog in the great machine and the demanding Mrs Penrose appears satisfied with her endeavours.

On her first half day off work, Maggie braves the first real cold snap to walk the winding road into St Branok. The harsh turn of the weather does nothing to deter her. These few hours each week when she escapes her duties at Morwenstowe are too precious to be wasted.

As Maggie crests a rise, she hears the roar of the Atlantic and feels its invigorating breeze for the first time in a week. The ocean unleashes a surge of emotions and memories. Despite all the pain it has caused, it raises her spirits and she ups her pace. The sea is part of her. It surges in her veins as it did in those of her father and brothers. No matter how much time she spends at Morwenstowe, however many friends she makes there, it can never replace the salty, tangy welcome of St Branok, her lifelong home. If she'd been born a man, she would most certainly have gone to sea.

Curious eyes gaze at her and then flick away as she nears Norah's home. In St Branok, she remains a subject of interest.

Even by the harsh standards of the fishing town, the extent of her loss is without parallel.

Norah flings open the front door when she sees her coming and embraces her in a hug. 'Lord in heaven, if you aren't a sight for sore eyes. How are you? You look well. Are the staff at Morwenstowe treating you right? I've heard from Polly that Mrs Penrose can be a bit of a tartar.'

'Mrs Penrose won't tolerate any slackness but if you work hard, she'll see you right.'

'And the work is suiting you?'

'It's long hours but no harder than home. I'm sharing a room with Polly. We get on well.' Maggie takes Norah's hands. 'But I've missed you, missed you so much.' And she's missed the hustle and bustle of the close community of St Branok, reeking of fish and the oozing detritus of the modern age.

Norah tightens her own grip. 'And I you. Promise me you'll come and visit whenever you get the chance.'

'I will. I will.' Maggie holds up a bag of ginger biscuits. 'I've brought these for you. Baked this morning.'

Norah sniffs the delightful aroma. 'Hmmm, lovely. We'll have some with tea.'

The friends chat happily, laughing at old stories. The biscuits taste every bit as good as they smell and the two women are soon groaning at having eaten too many.

'Have you heard anything from Jack?' says Norah, her eyes full of that mischievous glint when talking about matters of the heart.

'I've been much too busy to think about Jack,' blusters Maggie. In truth, she has thought about him every day.

'You should write to him again. Tell him when you have an afternoon off.'

'It's a long way out to Morwenstowe.'

'He can ride out there in no time.'

Maggie stores away the thought. Perhaps she'll write to him this evening when she gets back to Morwenstowe.

'I'd like your opinion,' says Norah.

'About what?'

'Come on, I'll show you.'

She skips upstairs like an exuberant child with Maggie in tow. From a wardrobe in the bedroom, she carefully pulls out a thing of beauty, a dress of shimmering green rustling silk.

Maggie catches her breath. 'Oh my, it's beautiful. Where did you get it?' This shimmering construction of silk and lace was surely beyond the powers of any dressmaker in St Branok.

Norah holds up the dress in front of her. 'Where do you think?'

Maggie snatches from her mind the one dressmaker of repute in St Branok. 'Mrs Chegwin?'

'No, of course not,' says Norah, clearly affronted by the suggestion. 'Jed took me into Truro. He's invited me to a ball at the Assembly Rooms in Truro next week.' Norah's eyes blaze. She sways this way and that in a pretend dance.

'I've never been.'

'Neither have I.'

Norah's elation is contagious. Maggie has a vision of elegant men in ruffles and women in shimmering silks wafting around a ballroom, a race apart from the hardy, desperate souls grubbing a living in the slimy back streets of St Branok. The gap between her and Norah is widening. Norah is moving up in the world while Maggie languishes as a kitchen maid. She is happy for her friend but with the scheming Jed Hoskin?

Maggie fingers the fine material, imagining what it would be like to feel it against her skin. 'And Jed is paying for this?'

'He insisted on it. It's turned out to be an excellent fishing season, after all. Jed's boats have been coming ashore loaded to the gunwales and, with the new connections to London, the prices have never been better.'

Maggie turns to practical matters. 'Can you dance?'

'Of course.'

'I mean the sort of dancing they'll do at the Assembly Rooms.'

'I'll manage,' says Norah, defensively. 'Jed has been showing me.'

Maggie frowns. Burly Jed Hoskin doing anything elegant is hard to imagine, no matter how many dresses he buys or manor houses he builds.

'What's wrong?' says Norah, brow creased in confusion.

'Our lives have changed so much. There's you thinking about what to wear to a ball and there's me thinking about scrubbing floors at Morwenstowe.'

Maggie's sombre tone quells Norah's delight. She lays out the dress on her bed with great care. 'You'll come through this. Things will get better. You have a new home.'

'I still can't believe that I'll never see Dad and Kitto and Ben and Logan ever again. I…I keep thinking they'll suddenly appear.' Maggie's voice falters.

'That day changed all our lives. Jed has promised to try to find that drunken oaf Clem Thomas who let us all down and when he does, he'll have him strung up. And if he doesn't string him up, then I will.'

'Has nobody seen him?'

'It's like he's been swept off the face of the earth. But Jed's been putting out feelers. He knows a lot of people. The old fool might have been seen in Truro.'

'I was told by a neighbour that he has an older sister who lives away, but I have no idea where. It could well be Truro.'

'What's her name?'

Maggie shakes her head slowly. 'I don't even have a Christian name.'

It's getting dusk when Maggie waves goodbye to Norah and starts the journey back to Morwenstowe, later than she planned. The musty tang of autumn leaves fills the cold night air. Time has run away from the two friends, lost in reminiscences and the simple delight of each other's company. The little time they have together made those few hours especially precious. Maggie's mind is full, swinging between hope and loss, sadness and joy. Uppermost in her mind is Clem Thomas. Is he hiding out in Truro? It sounds possible. If she could speak with him, she might at last find out the full truth as to why he didn't put out the storm warning signs. But how to find him, that is the question. She has neither the time nor the resources.

A possible answer occurs in the shape of Jack Treloare. He must visit Truro often. He could make enquiries on the quayside while going about his business. Fugitive or not, an old salt like Clem Thomas wouldn't be able to stay away from the boats and his lop-sided features are memorable. It would give her another reason to write to Jack. Catch two mackerel with one hook, as her father used to say.

At last, she spies lights streaming from the windows of Morwenstowe gleaming through the trees. Her home. For now, at least.

She slips in through a side door and goes straight to her room, intent on writing that letter to Jack. The rhythm of the house is slower this evening, footsteps less urgent, voices more relaxed. The Kendalls are out for the evening, dining at a neighbouring house. Polly is stretched out on her bed, dozing. Maggie's arrival wakes her. She looks up with a smile. 'I was wondering what'd happened to you.'

Maggie forages through her few belongings to find her father's much-admired fountain pen, ink and a sheet of precious paper. She places them carefully on the small side table next to her bed and then bends to her task, much to the interest of Polly. Her mind is full of what to say and how to phrase it. She wants to sound friendly but not intimate, to convey the warmth she sensed between them when they last met without gushing. Brevity is key. Jack is a busy man who will value succinctness. So much to convey in one short letter.

Finally, she writes. *'Dear Jack, I trust you are faring well with your fishing endeavours since my last letter. I have it on good authority that it has been an excellent season for pilchards…'*

Maggie pauses. An excellent season for pilchards? Is that what she really wants to say? She takes a new sheet of her precious paper and starts again.

*'Dear Jack, I trust you are faring well with your fishing endeavours. I am settling in at Morwenstowe. The work is busy and demanding but my fellow servants are friendly and generous. My half day off each week – on Wednesday afternoon – allows me the free time to visit my friends in St Branok. I wonder if I might trouble you with a favour when you are next in Truro…'*

The words begin to flow as her pen slides across the paper. Writing unlocks something in her mind and the words come freely and naturally.

Polly's eyes never leave the sweeping pen. 'Your writing is beautiful,' she whispers in awe.

'It's simple enough when you know how.'

'My da didn't hold with such things. Called it stuff and nonsense.'

'I was lucky. My father insisted we all learn to read and write. He said it was essential in the modern world and that one day everybody would be able to do so.'

Polly chuckles. 'That's a mad thought.'

'Why?'

'Ordinary folk don't have the time to go around writing letters and whatnot.'

'Would you like to?'

Polly sighs. 'I don't think I've got the brains for such highfalutin stuff.'

'But you would like to try?'

'I s'pose so…'

Maggie picks out one of her treasured books from her case and hands it to Polly, who holds it with reverence. 'I could teach you to read this.'

Polly flips through the pages, her eyes as wide as saucers from Morwenstowe's capacious kitchens. 'What? No, I could never read nothing like that.'

'You could. If you stuck at it. It would take a while.'

Polly strokes the embossed cover. 'What's it about?' she says at last.

'It's about the life of a heroic woman called *Jane Eyre*. It was written by a woman, Charlotte Brontë. You'd love it. I could read the start for you tomorrow.'

Polly nods, breathless. 'Why not now?'

'First I must finish my letter.'

'Who are you writing to?'

'To Mr Jack Treloare, the skipper of a fishing boat in St Branok, the *Eliza Jayne*.'

Polly's small mouth turns up in a smile. 'Is he your beau?'

'He's a friend, a friend who I am hoping will be able to help me.'

With a gleam in her eyes, Polly says, 'But he's a single gent, yes?'

'He's not married. He's a busy man with numerous important duties to perform.'

Polly chuckles and says in a Norah-like way, 'Every man has time for…'

Maggie squirms. 'We're friends. Nothing more.'

Polly is relentless. 'But you like him?'

'His character is…' She pauses before settling on, '…agreeable.'

'Is he a good looker?'

'I…I really couldn't say.'

Polly looks smug. 'You like him. I can tell.' She nods. 'He sounds right nice.'

'Do you have anybody?'

Polly turns coy. 'Mr Jarvis has walked out with me a few times.'

Maggie pictures the footman she met when she first arrived at Morwenstowe. A little too full of his own importance for her liking but no doubt he has a more charming side. Polly has a knack for putting people at their ease.

Maggie finishes her letter, still watched by a rapt Polly, and then puts it to one side for sending in the morning.

The small bedroom is cold this evening. Shivering, she quickly changes into her nightclothes and then dives beneath the bed sheets, heavy with a damp chill. Polly blows out the bedside candle and they lie in the dark in their respective beds, chatting in a desultory fashion until blessed sleep claims them. Another busy day tomorrow looms. It will start before sunrise and finish long after dark when dinner has been prepared for Lord and Lady Kendall.

In the meantime, Maggie's letter will be winging its way to Jack.

# CHAPTER TWENTY-ONE

Weeks pass with no response from Jack Treloare. Each day Maggie waits for the arrival of the post with tingling expectation. To be left disconsolate. She searches for a reason. Perhaps he's been at sea. Perhaps he has been unwell. Perhaps Jed Hoskin has warned him off. Or perhaps he has no lasting interest in her and she was nothing more than a passing amusement to be discarded when Jack moved on to richer fishing grounds. Her expectation subsides and then shrinks to nothing.

At least she is settling in well at Morwenstowe. She soon knows all the staff, most of whom are welcoming. The exception is Mr Jarvis, the footman, whom she treats with care, sensing a devious side to his nature. What Polly sees in him, apart from his fine clothes, she fails to understand. The most senior figures among the household staff, Mr Henderson, the butler, and Mrs Hicks, the housekeeper, are almost as aloof as the Kendalls and Maggie has few direct dealings with them, taking her day-to-day instructions from Mrs Penrose, who runs the kitchen as her own personal fiefdom. Mr Henderson is a tall, sombre man of well over six feet with an expansive girth to match. Mrs Hicks is an anxious woman of little patience, also tall though thin as a stiletto.

Polly is the person to whom Maggie grows closest. As

autumn tightens its grip on the landscape, leaving the fields and hedges heavy with morning dew, their relationship grows warmer by the day. The reading and writing lessons go well. Polly proves an attentive learner, her initial hesitation and uncertainty replaced by a growing confidence as she writes her first words, her tongue sticking out of the corner of her mouth. *Jane Eyre* inspires her. She listens with an open mouth as Maggie reads to her by the flickering light of the bedside candle at the end of a long day, and, in the final moments before sleep, she rails at the iniquities of the cruel Aunt Reed. By the time they reach the three-quarter mark in the story, Polly is reading sections to Maggie, haltingly at first but soon with more fluidity.

It's not long before this new-found passion for literature causes trouble. Mrs Penrose is scathing when, during a lull in the working day, she finds Polly and Maggie in a quiet corner with their heads buried in *The Personal History of David Copperfield*, a work of the renowned author Charles Dickens.

'What's all this nonsense?' Mrs Penrose demands, staring down at them with her floury hands on her hips.

Both girls jump up, red-faced. Polly holds out the book. 'Reading, Mrs Penrose.'

Mrs Penrose snatches the book and flips through the pages with illiterate eyes. 'What reason do you have to read? You shouldn't be wasting your time with this nonsense, Polly. You have duties to perform.'

Polly stands her ground. 'It were only five minutes, while we were having a short break.'

Mrs Penrose shuts the book with a thunderous clap. 'What's the good of filling your head with all this tripe. I've a strong mind to –' Her voice fades as the whisper of rustling skirts sounds behind her. Lady Kendall is on one of her fact-finding tours. She glides into the room with a questioning look on her delicate features. 'Goodness me, what is all this? Quite a commotion.'

Mrs Penrose holds up her hands, still holding the book. 'Tis nothing, ma'am. A minor matter.'

The weighty tome catches Lady Kendall's eye. 'Charles Dickens…Mrs Penrose, I had no idea.'

'Not me. I don't have time for such stuff and nonsense. 'Tis Polly here.'

She hands the book to Lady Kendall who turns a few pages with dainty fingers before staring at Polly with a new respect. 'And you're reading this, Polly?'

Polly curtseys. 'Yes, ma'am. 'Tis a right good story.'

'When did you learn to read and where did the book come from?'

Polly nods at Maggie. 'Maggie here taught me, ma'am. The book's hers. She started reading it to me and now…' – her cheeks flush with triumph – '… I'm reading it.'

The Kendall gaze falls on Maggie. 'I little suspected we had such prodigious teaching talents in our midst.'

Mrs Penrose butts in. 'I've warned them to stick to their duties, ma'am. I'm not sure all…' – she waves a hand in a deprecatory fashion – '…this here claptrap is good for their minds.'

'Let's not be too harsh with them, Mrs Penrose. Learning is the essence of modern civilisation.' She hands the book to Polly and turns back to Maggie. 'And what do you make of *David Copperfield*?'

'A wonderful book, ma'am.'

'Yes, this Charles Dickens fellow is quite the writer. He is the talk of London, so I hear. But I'm surprised you have the time for such an extensive work.'

'Quite,' mutters Mrs Penrose with an accusing gleam in her eye. 'Neglecting their duties they be.'

'A few minutes a day, ma'am. No more. By candlelight. When we're ready for bed,' says Maggie.

Lady Kendall's eyes take on a zealot's gleam. 'Commendable. Make no mistake, the world is changing. We are stepping into a bright new era of emancipation in which we will throw off the shackles of the past. Young women like yourselves could be at the forefront of change.' She pauses, catches her breath. 'I host a…ah literary group on Friday afternoons. How would you feel about attending this week? I'm sure my friends would be delighted to hear of your thoughts on *David Copperfield*. You could read a short section if you wish.'

A stunned silence is broken by Maggie sucking in a breath. 'It would be an honour, ma'am, but I'm not sure any thoughts I have would be of value to your friends.'

Lady Kendall beams at her. 'There's no need to be nervous. We are a small group of friends who get together to discuss literature and a few other matters.'

'If you're sure, ma'am.'

Her ladyship turns to her head cook, a cool smile playing on her lips. 'I trust the absence of Miss Pascoe for a short time on Friday will not disrupt your kitchen routines too severely, Mrs Penrose?'

Mrs Penrose's jaw clenches. 'I suppose we'll manage, ma'am.'

'Excellent.' She claps her hands. 'Miss Pascoe, be so good as to present yourself at the sitting room at two o'clock on Friday and I'll introduce you to the other ladies. They'll be delighted to meet you.'

Lady Kendall departs in a swish and swirl of skirts,

leaving behind an atmosphere of excitement, confusion and, on the part of Mrs Penrose, resentment. 'Get back to work,' the stern-faced cook says. 'The work won't get done when you're wasting your time with that there David Copperhead.'

'Yes, ma'am,' Maggie and Polly chant in unison, unable to hide grins.

Mrs Penrose wags a finger. 'Don't get ideas above your station. The age of emanci…emancipagan isn't going to arrive any time soon for the likes of us.'

The rest of the afternoon is frenetic. Mrs Penrose works them hard, and they flop into bed at the end of the day. But Polly's new-found enthusiasm for literature is not to be denied. 'Read me a few more pages of *David Copperfield*,' she says, stifling a yawn.

Maggie starts reading. With tired eyes, she makes a few mistakes that Polly with a hint of glee points out. Her mind is everywhere but in that tiny bedroom. Opportunities are emerging.

# CHAPTER TWENTY-TWO

Maggie prepares for the Friday afternoon meeting with excitement and a degree of trepidation. At two o'clock precisely, wearing her best blouse and her favourite blue skirt she taps on the tall double doors of Morwenstowe's majestic sitting room. A maid opens the door and then ushers her inside. Maggie enters, clutching a copy of *David Copperfield* in her clammy right hand. A smiling Lady Kendall comes forward to greet her. 'Thank you so much for coming.'

Maggie is introduced to three immaculately dressed women and a man who are sat in armchairs, forming a semi-circle. They are drinking tea in delicate china cups and gazing at her with interest. The male participant is none other than Parson Hedrek Kellow. The smiles all around help quell her tingling stomach.

'Please take a seat.' Lady Kendall directs Maggie to a vacant chair next to her own. 'Tea?'

Maggie sits. 'Thank you, ma'am.'

The maid pours the tea into an elegant cup seemingly so delicate it would shatter at the merest tap. Maggie takes quick, nervous sips, barely tasting it, squirming inside at being the subject of so many interested eyes.

Lady Kendall speaks in warm tones. 'Miss Pascoe is a recent addition to our household after falling on difficult times. She was left with nothing, through no fault of her own, but is finding a new life for herself here at Morwenstowe. She is a person of learning, a young woman of resilience who epitomises our modern age. Her father was one of the finest fishermen of his generation.' Her ladyship turns to Maggie. 'Would you be willing to tell your story?'

Maggie's heart is pounding, her mouth is dry. She believed she had been invited to discuss a book not her own tribulations. 'I…I…'

Her ladyship places a gentle hand on her arm. 'Please, you are among friends here.'

'I will do my best, ma'am.' Maggie starts, hesitantly at first. Nobody interrupts. The only other sound is the occasional gasp as Maggie reaches the most traumatic elements of her story. Cups of tea are allowed to grow cold. 'And now I am here with a chance to start afresh,' she finishes with the bravest smile she can manage.

The conversation about the tragedy rattles on for a little longer and then, thankfully, moves on to the work of the esteemed author Charles Dickens and his novel, *David Copperfield*. Maggie's confidence gathers momentum. She enthuses about the prose and then reads a short passage.

'Beautifully read,' says a smiling Lady Kendall. The ancient clock in the hallway strikes five. It is the trigger for a rush of exclamations and comments about time having flown. The attendees rise and depart with earnest wishes of goodwill. Their warmest smiles are reserved for Maggie.

Elegant carriages convey them away at a brisk pace. They disappear down Morwenstowe's long, sweeping driveway in a flurry of grit and spray with the carriage drivers cracking their whips and urging on their steeds. Of the guests, only Parson Kellow remains.

Lady Kendall takes Maggie's hands. Compassion floods her eyes. 'Parson Kellow is waiting for me to discuss an urgent parish matter, but I wanted to say that I'm so pleased you were able to join our meeting today. You are a fine example for women everywhere. You have enthused us with your determination and perseverance.'

'Thank you for inviting me, ma'am. Truth to tell, I was nervous beforehand, but your friends were very welcoming.'

'They're good people.' She lowers her voice in conspiratorial fashion. 'And, in truth, we are more than a group for idle afternoon chatter. Much more.' Her eyes take on a purposeful gleam. 'It is time for ordinary people to make their voices heard. To make this world a better place than it is today. Not just in Cornwall, but across the country. There is a growing demand for all to have the common elementary right to have the Vote. People like yourself can be the torchbearers of a new movement. I have high hopes for you.'

Maggie gulps. 'I'm an ordinary person, ma'am, trying to make my way in the world.'

Her insistence of modesty only serves to strengthen Lady Kendall's belief in her. 'It is ordinary people who can change the world. She hesitates as if wrestling with an inner uncertainty before saying, 'After your magnificent reading today, I wanted to ask a favour of you.'

'Anything ma'am. Anything at all.' What favour could a kitchen maid bestow on a woman of Lady Kendall's standing?

'Jasper, my son, is having difficulty with his reading. Nothing his tutor does seems to work. He is a good-hearted boy but…' – she searches for the right words – '…difficult at times. You have done such a wonderful job with young Polly's reading I was hoping some of your magic might work for my son.'

'I'm no teacher, ma'am. I've never had any training or anything. Perhaps Parson Kellow would be better to assist? I understand the new school he has established at the chapel in St Branok is doing well.'

Lady Kendall waves away the suggestion with an expression of mild irritation. 'The parson is a busy man, and, in truth, I was hoping that a younger person's touch might make all the difference.' Her warm smile returns. 'I was thinking a short session…to start with at least."

Maggie bows her head. 'If you think I can be of any help…'

'Excellent. Please present yourself here at eleven o'clock on Monday morning. I'll arrange with Mrs Penrose for you to be released from your kitchen duties for a brief period.'

'Thank you, ma'am.' They walk into the hallway to find Parson Kellow regarding a painting of a stern-faced gentleman with an icy gaze.

Lady Kendall says to Maggie, 'Run along. Don't let me delay you from your duties.'

As Maggie trips away, she hears Lady Kendall explain that the portrait is of her husband's grandfather.

'Ah yes, I see a likeness in Lord Kendall.'

Her ladyship chuckles. 'Not too much, I hope. By all accounts, he was a noted philanderer who came close to wiping out the family fortune with an addiction to the roulette wheel.'

Maggie descends into the depths of the building and makes her way to her small bedroom to change into her workaday maid's clothing. On returning to the kitchen to find it empty she looks through a window to glimpse Parson Kellow getting ready to leave in his single-horse buggy. A thought strikes her and she slips out of a side door and approaches the parson.

Kellow looks up when he hears her approach. 'Well, well, well, Maggie, the young woman of the hour, I hadn't expected to see you again today.'

Maggie catches her breath. 'I was wondering if you'd seen Jack Treloare recently.'

'Mr Treloare? No, I can't say I have. He's been away of late, pressing the case for a lifeboat for St Branok, I believe.'

Maggie's hopes rise. So, Jack's failure to respond might have a laudable reason. 'And how is our petition for a lifeboat faring?'

'There have been favourable noises from the institution. And I am pleased to say that prospective local benefactors have come forward to offer help, one in particular.'

'Might I ask who?'

Kellow hesitates and then says, 'Well, I don't suppose it can do any harm. It will be public knowledge soon enough. Mr Hoskin has stepped forward with an offer which is more than generous. I must admit, I have had my doubts about him and his methods of doing business, but I cannot fault his beneficent involvement in this project. The man has deep pockets and he's willing to dig into them for the good of St Branok.'

'So, Jed Hoskin is willing to fund the project?'

'Not the whole project, but a substantial amount, including the donation of an appropriate piece of land. He has one condition.'

'What is that?'

A flicker of discomfort sweeps Kellow's face. 'I fear I've said too much. But the truth will be out soon enough, and it is eminently praiseworthy. Mr Hoskin is requesting that the new lifeboat be named after one of the victims of the summer storm.'

Maggie's thoughts fly to her father. Could Hoskin find it in his hard heart to make such a gesture? No, of course, it cannot be him. The suggestion that Hoskin would ever fund a boat with the Pascoe name on it is beyond absurd.

Kellow beams. 'Mr Hoskin is insisting that the new boat be called the *Jowan Bray*.'

# CHAPTER TWENTY-THREE

When Maggie is excused for her session with Jasper at a busy time for the kitchen, there are dark mutterings from Mrs Penrose about 'upstarts not knowing their place' and 'maids being allowed to neglect their duties'. The young kitchen maid changes into her best day clothes and then goes to the sitting room where Lady Kendall is waiting. Her ladyship notes the book tucked under Maggie's arm. 'There is no need to bring your own book. We have plenty here.'

Maggie hands her a copy of *The Three Musketeers*. 'This is an exhilarating read, ma'am. It's a novel by a Frenchman which has been translated into English.'

Lady Kendall opens the front page. 'Oh, my goodness, French you say?'

'It's a fine adventure which I believe your son will enjoy.'

Her ladyship chuckles, a touch nervously. 'I hope you're not planning to fill Jasper's head with stories of revolution and bloodshed.'

Maggie licks her lips. 'It is a story of comradeship and honour. I happened to see Jasper outside yesterday and noted he was play-acting as a swordsman.'

'The things which please my son aren't always ones of

which I would approve.' She bites her lip. 'But anything that encourages his reading is to be welcomed. Follow me.' She leads Maggie out of the sitting room.

'It was my youngest brother Ben's favourite book, ma'am,' Maggie says as they walk.

They stop at a closed door at the end of a long corridor. A man's raised voice can be heard on the other side. 'If you do that one more time, I'll –'

Lady Kendall eases open the door to reveal an angry man in his late fifties in a small room with shelves of books covering one wall. He is wearing a rumpled dark suit and his grey hair is tousled. At a desk, a fair-haired, slim boy with many of the aristocratic features of Lady Kendall is staring back at him defiantly.

The tutor's voice moderates as he realises he has an audience. 'Ah, Lady Kendall. Your arrival is timely.'

He huffs with irritation. 'I regret to say that Jasper is being his usual wayward self this morning. He refuses to listen to me.'

Lady Kendall's admonishment of her son is mild. 'Jasper, how many times have I told you to pay attention to Mr Gilbert?'

The boy fidgets in his seat. 'It's boring. *He's* boring.'

Lady Kendall bestows an icy stare on her son that would freeze oceans but is treated with indifference by young Jasper. 'You are rude and impertinent. I will speak to you later.' She turns to the tutor. 'Mr Gilbert, I can only apologise for my son's rudeness. Rest assured he will receive a strong talking to later.'

Mr Gilbert nods. 'Nothing more than youthful exuberance I'm sure, ma'am, easily quelled by a touch of the birch.'

Lady Kendall's eyes flash in anger. 'A strong hand doesn't

always require use of the cane, Mr Gilbert.' There is an awkward pause and then she gestures at Maggie. 'In any event, this is the young lady I spoke to you about, Miss Margaret Pascoe. I would commend her to you.'

The tutor fixes Maggie with a condescending eye. 'A pleasure, Miss Pascoe. Her ladyship speaks highly of you. Your formidable teaching rivals Socrates so I have been led to believe.' He grins at his own weak joke and then says, 'You are…somewhat younger than I expected. I look forward to seeing your formidable powers bestowed on our boisterous young heir.'

The idea of Mr Gilbert watching coldly from the shadows while she engages with the boy fills Maggie with dread. 'I was hoping that I would be able to spend half an hour alone with Jasper.'

The tutor smirks. 'Please don't hold back on my account. I'll sit here quiet as a church mouse. You won't know I'm here.' Clearly, he's going nowhere.

But Lady Kendall has other ideas. She holds the door open. 'Mr Gilbert, this gives us an excellent opportunity to talk about Jasper's future schooling. His Lordship and I have been considering Winchester. I'd be grateful for your view. Perhaps we could discuss it in the drawing room over tea.'

They disappear down the corridor, Mr Gilbert, himself a former Eton scholar, espousing the merits of that formidable establishment. Maggie is left alone with Jasper. She hands him *The Three Musketeers*. 'I've brought a book that I think you will like.'

Jasper examines it suspiciously. 'Books are boring. What's it about?'

'It's about adventure, swordsmanship and four great friends in France.'

The boy flips a few pages and then hands it back to her. 'Read to me,' he commands.

Maggie purses her lips in irritation. 'I was hoping you would read to me. Can you read?'

Jasper studies the book more closely, clearly enticed. 'Of course, I can read,' he huffs.

Maggie gestures for the boy to sit. 'Good. Then let us begin.'

The half hour passes all too quickly for both tutor and pupil. The sound of footsteps and talking reaches their ears. 'I have my doubts about French novels,' the droning voice of Mr Gilbert is heard to say. 'The French are a volatile nation, prone to excessive emotion and, as we have seen only too recently, mindless butchery.'

'The British have not been without their own revolutions,' Lady Kendall points out.

'A long time ago,' Mr Gilbert assures her. 'Thankfully, we saw the error of our ways and sense and reason were restored within a few years.'

'The brutality of revolution is to be deplored, of course, but sometimes change is necessary if mankind is to advance.'

The door opens and in step Lady Kendall and Mr Gilbert, their furrowed brows hinting at a strained relationship.

Lady Kendall's expression brightens at the sight of Maggie and Jasper sitting together with their heads buried in *The Three Musketeers*. 'How went it?'

'It went well…I think.' Maggie glances at a bright-eyed Jasper.

He nods vehemently. 'I want more.'

Lady Kendall gazes benevolently at her son. 'Well, perhaps we have a scholar in our midst after all. If Miss Pascoe is willing, further readings might be possible.'

'I'd be delighted, ma'am,' says Maggie. She turns to Jasper. 'You read well.'

Petulance flashes across the youngster's cherubic face. 'Why do we have to stop now?'

'Because, young man, you are due a lesson in arithmetic,' says Lady Kendall.

Jasper bursts into a fit of pique. 'When can I have Miss Pascoe again?' He jumps up and down. 'When… when… when?'

Lady Kendall turns to the tutor. 'I'm sure we can squeeze in another half hour in the near future. Can't we, Mr Gilbert?'

Mr Gilbert's eyes narrow. 'I find it is important to keep the young mind focused on serious, diligent learning and we have much to cover –'

Lady Kendall's stare turns glassy. 'Quite so, but I'm sure a further half hour can be carved out of your busy schedule?'

He nods the most grudging of nods. 'As you wish, ma'am.'

She turns to Maggie. 'Thank you, Miss Pascoe. You have performed wonders in a remarkably short space of time. Don't let us delay you from resuming your kitchen duties. Mrs Penrose is very busy today.'

Maggie curtseys. 'I am pleased to be of service. It has been a pleasure listening to Jasper.' She gathers her skirts and heads downstairs with a tingle of excitement pulsing through her. After so much uncertainty and pain, a brighter future must lie ahead.

# CHAPTER TWENTY-FOUR

The familiar Atlantic gales recede and for a time the immaculate parklands of Morwenstowe are coated in a fragile, glimmering sheen of hoar frost. Shrubs and trees still holding their berries attract redwings, fieldfares and waxwings. The days fly by in a whirl of heavy kitchen duties which prove all consuming, both physically and mentally. At the end of each day, Maggie lays her weary head on a cold pillow and, after a short reading, succumbs to deep sleep.

A second reading session for Jasper is arranged and then a third, much to the chagrin of Mr Gilbert who whinges about 'insidious undercurrents' apparent in *The Three Musketeers*. The boy is spoilt, but he is bright and a quick learner. Occasionally, Maggie takes a momentary respite from mopping a floor or scrubbing a pot to watch Jasper playing outside with two pieces of wood nailed together as a sword, fighting imagined enemies.

A letter arrives from Jack Treloare. At last. Maggie rips it open with nervous fingers and bated breath. The letter is succinct and businesslike. It apologises for the 'tardiness' of his reply and explains that he has been 'up country' making arrangements for the new St Branok lifeboat, plans for which are well advanced. A date for a celebratory event marking the arrival of the new boat has been proposed – Wednesday

December 16, 1863. The letter concludes, 'I have asked for you to be invited as a guest of honour and hope in earnest you will be granted time away from your duties at Morwenstowe to attend.'

Maggie's heart leaps. A new era for St Branok and its fishing community – and she will be there to see it. *If* she can get the day off. At Morwenstowe, a full day off is rare. She bypasses the harassed Mrs Penrose and takes the opportunity of a brief encounter with Lady Kendall after her third session with Jasper, which went especially well.

'Ma'am, I have been invited to an event marking the arrival of the new St Branok lifeboat,' she says, expecting resistance. 'I was hoping…I…I would forego my pay.'

Lady Kendall interrupts. 'Of course, you must attend. And, in the circumstances, there is no need for you to give up your pay, my dear.'

Maggie's hopes surge. 'Thank you, ma'am, thank you.'

'Your patience with Jasper has worked miracles.' She lowers her tone a notch. 'I suspect even Mr Gilbert has perceived an improvement though he is reluctant to acknowledge it. Jasper's eyes light up whenever he sees you. I am thinking that we should arrange a few more reading sessions.'

Maggie bows her head and whispers further thanks.

Lady Kendall regards her benignly. 'Excellent.' She pauses, her eyes sweeping down Maggie's clothes. 'What clothes do you have apart from your beautiful blue skirt and blouse?'

'Not much, ma'am. I was able to only bring a few of my most treasured items when I left my home and came here.'

'Well, we must secure you a few more.'

'Yes, ma'am. Thank you.'

'There will be a little less time for your kitchen duties, but I doubt that will be of too much concern for you.'

The suggestion of less cleaning and hard scrubbing is welcome though a measure of uncertainty still ripples through Maggie. 'I'd be delighted but Mrs Penrose will have concerns.'

'I'll deal with Mrs Penrose,' her ladyship says with a steely glint in her eye.

'She relies on me a great deal.'

'I know. You're a good worker. But there are others who can help take up the slack. Your friend Polly, for example.'

'I don't want to be a burden on others.'

'You won't be. Rest assured we have a large enough staff to cover the few hours you'll be unavailable.' Lady Kendall's tone hardens. 'Most staff would jump at a chance like this.'

Maggie pulls a nervous smile. 'I would love to have this opportunity.'

'Well, you'd better get along then. As you say, Mrs Penrose will be needing you.'

Maggie changes into her maid's clothing and then returns to the bustle of the kitchen in a state of euphoria. Lady Kendall has presented her with a wonderful chance.

Mrs Penrose, Polly and the other kitchen maids are slaving at hot ovens when she arrives.

The cook's cheeks are flushed but her look is cold. 'Ah, you're back at last. I was thinking you'd disappeared for the rest of the day.'

Maggie pulls on an apron. 'Lady Kendall wanted to speak to me afterwards. It was important.'

'And what could be so important between her ladyship and one of my kitchen maids that I don't know about?'

'It was about reading sessions with Jasper.' Maggie's voice trails away.

Mrs Penrose nods. 'Ah yes, I'd heard that Mr Gilbert was less than content with interference in the boy's studies. He was going to raise it with Lord Kendall.' She places a hand on Maggie's shoulder in an attempt to appear sympathetic. 'You did the best you could, girl. But the thought of a kitchen maid tutoring the heir to the Kendall estate…well, it's plain daft, isn't it. It's misguided, it is. And cruel. Gives a person ideas above their station, it does. I'm surprised a learned woman like her ladyship ever contemplated such an irregular state of affairs.'

Maggie's bile rises at the sight of Mrs Penrose's smug expression. 'She wants me to take more sessions.'

The cook's face drops in shock. 'What?'

'Yes…yes…more sessions. They have been very successful.'

Mrs Penrose emits an exasperated huffing sound. 'Why have I been told nothing about this? How's the kitchen supposed to manage when staff are off gallivanting?'

'Her ladyship said she would be speaking with you and that arrangements would be made to cover the short periods I'm away.'

Mrs Penrose switches from exasperation to outrage. 'It'll mean more work for the rest of us,' she says loudly so that the rest of the kitchen staff can hear. 'Her ladyship will be hearing from me on this matter. I sometimes wonder if her ladyship appreciates the work involved in the smooth running of a modern kitchen.'

Maggie bites her lip. 'I don't want to create extra work for anybody.'

Mrs Penrose stares at her. 'You'd be wise to remember who you're speaking to, girl.'

'I'm…I'm sorry.'

'Well, don't just stand there. You've got work to do. There's any number of dirty pots needing some elbow grease.'

'Yes, Mrs Penrose.'

'And I 'spect them to be gleaming by the time you've finished.' She returns to kneading a slab of dough in a vigorous manner that emphasises her many frustrations.

With her head down, Maggie sets to scrubbing a pile of blackened pots. She's making friends at Morwenstowe. Important friends.

But also attracting enemies.

# CHAPTER TWENTY-FIVE

Maggie halts on the road outside Norah's house. It has an empty and unused air. No smoke from the chimney. Windows closed. Rooms dark. She knocks on the door, softly at first, then louder. Nothing. Her mood darkens. Her treasured afternoon off, so much anticipated, has been sacrificed for a wasted journey.

A greying head pops out of the small cottage next door. 'If you're looking for Norah, she's out.'

'When will she be back?'

'No idea. That swank, Hoskin, turned up in a carriage with all his trumped-up airs and graces and they went off. Into town, I think.'

'Could you tell her I called?'

'If I see her. But she's not at home so much these days. Too good for the likes of us, she is. Spends most of her time with that new man of hers.'

On the doorstep, Maggie ponders her next move. She's desperate to see Norah. Less keen on running into Hoskin. Still, she's come this far. And walking straight back to Morwenstowe to spend the rest of the day in her small, shadowy room is unappealing. The other staff, including Polly, will be far too busy to engage in idle chatter.

After a few moments of uncertainty, she walks down the

hill into town. The sights and sounds of St Branok in full flow assault her senses. The clatter of hooves and carriages. The shouts of tradesmen. The rumble of wagons. The tang of fish. Always the tang of fish. Everywhere. With the exception of the demanding Mrs Penrose, Morwenstowe is an oasis of quiet in comparison. St Branok remains Maggie's true home – will always be her home, for all its filth and desperation. The ghosts of her father, mother and brothers are still here, their faces glimpsed at every corner, on every street.

As she rounds a bend into Crantock Street, a diminutive, hourglass figure emerges from Gadsby's, the ironmongers. Norah. Beautifully dressed in a high-necked blouse and a full embroidered skirt of a daring length which allows the occasional glimpse of ankle. She's every inch the lady these days. Maggie, in her regular day clothes, feels like a wallflower by comparison. Of Jed Hoskin, there is no sign. Thank heavens.

'Norah!'

Her friend looks up and beams. 'Maggie! What are you doing here? It's wonderful to see you.'

'I came into town hoping to find you. It's been so long.'

'Too long,' says Norah.

'One of your neighbours said you'd gone off with Jed Hoskin.'

'I did. But Jed gets bored with the shopping. Told me to get what I want and put it on his account.' Her voice is gleeful. The years of endless scrimping and saving are over for her, but Hoskin's limitless resources remain a novelty.

Maggie glances around. 'Where is he?'

Norah sighs. 'In The Mermaid. For business. I'm to call on him when I've finished. You've arrived at just the right time. I need to pop into Chegwin's for a new dress. Please come along. I could do with a second pair of eyes. I swear Mrs Chegwin would sell me a sack if she thought she could make money out of it.'

'Another dress?' Maggie can't help sounding incredulous.

Norah chuckles. 'A lady can never have too many dresses. In any event, Lord and Lady Kendall are planning a social event at Morwenstowe and Jed's been invited. For the first time. He wants to have an elegant lady on his arm.'

Maggie smiles. An invitation from Lord and Lady Kendall, no less. Hoskin is at last getting the opportunity to climb the social ladder that he has craved. And Norah is bathing in the glory.

'If I can be of help, then I'd love to accompany you to Chegwin's,' she says.

The shop is one of the few islands of affluence in a town devoted to the feast or famine vagaries of the fishing industry. A glance through the windows is the closest most of the wretches grubbing a living in St Branok get to sampling its wares.

Norah steps through the door with the authority of one who has visited many times and is sure of a warm welcome. Maggie follows tentatively. Mrs Chegwin is quick to leave another customer in the care of her assistant and bustles over. 'Mrs Bray, it's a pleasure, as always, to see you.'

They exchange smiles and pleasantries like old friends. 'I have everything ready for the fitting,' says Mrs Chegwin, leading them into the darkened inner sanctum.

The fitting turns out to be a lengthy affair. Norah revels in the fuss and attention. She chats endlessly with Mrs Chegwin about fabrics and styles, bodices and necklines. 'The low neckline is very much in vogue in London,' Mrs Chegwin says.

Maggie sits to one side, responding with stumbled answers on the odd occasion she is asked her opinion, an onlooker rather than a participant.

When Mrs Chegwin disappears into another room to fetch more fabric samples, Norah turns to Maggie, her face gleeful. 'I understand Jed in a way that many people don't. He's not as brusque and unfeeling as people say.' There is a tremor in her voice. 'Times are changing. It's businessmen like Jed who are starting to run this country. Jed owns more land than Lord Kendall.'

Maggie's mouth falls open. 'How do you know?'

'He told me. He recently bought a parcel of land around Wistman's Wood from the Kendall Estate.' She pauses and then says with delight, 'And Jed is funding most of the new lifeboat. Money talks these days. The gentry no longer have everything their own way. Jed's the real power in this town, not the highfalutin Kendalls. He insisted that the new boat be named after Jowan. And when Jed sets his mind to something there's no arguing with him. He's a man who knows his own mind.'

The dressmaking session comes to an end. Any number of fabrics have been appraised, precise measurements taken. Norah's ultra slim waist is no longer as it once was. The good life with Jed Hoskin is changing her. But Norah looks the better for it. Her once-gaunt face is plumped by a little more flesh.

They head out into Crantock Street with the profuse thanks and well wishes of Mrs Chegwin echoing in their ears.

'Did Jed get anywhere with finding out where Clem Thomas might be hiding out?' says Maggie.

Norah swallows. 'I asked him several times.'

'And what did he say?'

'He's a very busy man.'

'So, he hasn't come up with anything of value?'

'Not yet.'

'He's had several weeks.' Maggie can't help sounding impatient.

Norah purses her lips. 'Why don't you come down to The Mermaid with me now and ask him yourself?'

A pang of anxiety ripples through Maggie at the thought of encountering Hoskin again. 'I can't. He hates me.'

Norah tsks. 'Jed's a softie when you get to know him.'

'To you perhaps, but not to others.'

The lit windows of The Mermaid hove into view. Norah beckons her forward. 'Come on. He won't bite your head off.'

Maggie hesitates. 'I…I'm not sure.'

'It's safe enough,' says Norah with a beckoning gesture.

They enter a fuggy, male world of smoke, hearty laughter and the tang of intoxicating liquors. A couple of gaudily dressed women are draped over two local tradesmen. Maggie recognises them as the women she met on the street corner on the night of the public meeting.

She senses eyes lingering on her and comes to a halt. 'I really don't think…'

Norah waves a dismissive hand. 'There's nothing to worry about. You're my guest. Jed has a share in The Mermaid.'

She leads Maggie through the bustling main bar to where the giant George Moyle is leaning against a wall with his arms crossed. He tips his hat when he sees Norah. 'Mrs Bray. Mr 'oskin is in the back room in a meeting, but he said for you to go straight through when you got 'ere.'

Moyle steps in front of Maggie. 'But not you.' His dead eyes linger on Maggie's curves.

'She's with me, George,' says Norah in a firm tone.

Moyle steps aside, licking his lips. 'If you say so.'

The rumble of intense discussion can be heard on the other side of a flaking door. Hoskin's strident voice is unmistakable.

Norah opens the door without knocking. Hoskin, flanked by three middle-aged men, is thumping his fleshy fist on a long table which runs the length of the room.

'The London market is the future. They'll pay top prices. Much more than down here. Stop kicking your heels on the quayside and get your goddamned boats out on the water –' Jed halts in the middle of a tirade when he sees Norah. He grins. 'Ah, here's a sight for sore eyes.' His expression hardens when he spies Maggie. 'What's she doing here?'

'Maggie helped me with the dress at Chegwin's.'

Hoskin's sour look sweetens. 'Did you get everything you needed?'

'Yes, I think so. Mrs Chegwin's selection of lace is limited.'

'We should have shopped in Truro.'

'I like to give the trade to local people, where possible,' says Norah.

Hoskin turns to one of the men he has been ranting at, a perspiring, balding individual. 'Hear that? Wise words. Look after your local people and they'll look after you. Charity begins at home, so they say.'

'Yes, Mr Hoskin,' the balding man mutters.

'Have we finished here?' says Hoskin, his tone turning impatient.

'You've made yer wishes very clear, Mr Hoskin. Rest assured –'

Hoskin waves him away. 'Yes, yes, now I have other matters which require my attention.'

The men file out, leaving Hoskin, Norah and Maggie in the room.

Norah delivers the coquettish smile she does so well. 'You'll love the new dress.' She gestures at Maggie, bringing her into the conversation. 'Maggie has a good eye. She was very helpful in my selections.'

'You'll be the belle of the ball at the Kendalls, I'm sure,' murmurs Hoskin, his gaze never leaving Norah.

'Maggie has a question to ask you, Jed.'

Hoskin drags his gaze away from Norah to regard Maggie. 'What?'

'I wondered if you had heard anything of the whereabouts of Clement Thomas.'

Hoskin's face turns stony. 'Why should I have done?'

Norah intervenes. 'We talked about it, dearest. Don't you remember? A few weeks ago. You said you would make enquiries.'

Hoskin's eyes flicker in irritation. 'And I did. I did. There's been talk of him being seen in Truro.'

'Where in Truro?' says Maggie.

'On the quay and other places.'

'What other places?'

'A few drinking houses.'

'Which ones?' Maggie is relentless.

'The Fortune, The Spar and such like.' His tone rises. 'They weren't what you might call reliable, no more than passing glances. Clem Thomas was a silly old fool and a drunkard who failed to do his duty and has now run off to escape justice. He could be anywhere.'

Maggie clenches her jaw. 'If he was as much of a drunkard as you say, why in heaven's name was he ever employed to put out the storm warning?'

'Why ask me?'

'Clem Thomas's wife told me that it was you who got him the job.'

Hoskin bangs the table. 'What has the world come to, eh? It comes to something when a gentleman of my standing – a man who has helped build this town – is accused by the likes of a busybody nobody like you.'

Maggie's stomach roils but she stands her ground. 'You haven't answered the question.'

'And I don't plan to answer questions from…' – his lip curls in contempt as he looks her up and down – '…a kitchen maid.'

'I might be a kitchen maid, but I still have the right to find out the truth. My whole family – '

'Your family were an unruly crew who took risks. It was bound to catch up with them in the end. Truth to tell, St Branok is best off without their kind.'

Maggie just manages to stay her hand from delivering a hearty slap to Hoskin's perspiring features. 'Answer the question. Why did you put a man who you say is a drunkard in charge of the storm warnings?'

Hoskin explodes. 'You don't have the goddamned right to ask me anything!'

'Why won't you answer? What are you hiding?'

A trickle of frothy spittle dribbles on to Hoskin's beard. 'You're a fine one to talk, you are. You. With your own secrets.'

Maggie stares. 'What secrets?'

'You know very well what secrets. Why haven't you told Norah about young Jowan, her son, eh? Why haven't you told her that?'

'Told her what?'

Hoskin sneers, back on the front foot. 'It's not for me to break up old friends but you've asked for it. Why didn't you tell Norah that her son died aboard the *Minerva*, your father's boat?'

A thumping headache is building in Maggie's head. 'I've no idea what you…'

Hoskin's expression turns triumphant. 'I've been asking around the quayside about that day of the storm, trying to find out what happened to the lad because Norah kept asking me, bless her soul. And do you know what every man jack of them said?'

Maggie gulps, her mouth dry.

Hoskin puffs out his chest. 'They told me that Jowan went aboard the *Minerva* that day, that the Pascoes invited him aboard and that you were there and saw it all. Why haven't you told Norah any of that, eh? Why?'

Maggie's forehead feels fit to explode. The truth floods out of her. 'I begged my father not to take him. I begged him, I begged him, but he wouldn't listen.'

Norah grabs Maggie's arm. 'What's Jed talking about?'

Maggie sees a terrible hurt in the depths of her friend's eyes. Her eyes brim with tears. No more deceptions. No more lies. 'I'm sorry…so sorry, Norah. I would have told you, should have told you but I didn't know how, couldn't find a way and the longer it went on –'

Norah tightens her grip on Maggie's arm. 'You knew… you knew all along. You lied to me. Your family killed my boy, my beautiful boy. You could've stopped them.'

'I couldn't. Honestly, I couldn't. My father was a law unto himself. He didn't take orders from anybody.'

'How many times did I tell you that I never wanted Jowan to go to sea? How many? How many?'

'It was my dad. I couldn't go against him.'

'My wonderful son is gone. Dead. Your da killed him. And you helped. You bitch!' Norah lashes out, delivering a stinging slap to Maggie's cheek.

'I'm sorry, so sorry. If you only knew how many times I've hated myself for what happened.'

Norah's beauty has been transformed into a pinched, twisted mask of pure hate. 'May your soul go to damnation for what you have done. You lousy bitch…you bitch.' She strikes out with her hand again.

Maggie parries it. 'Please, don't hate me.' She tries to take Norah's slim shoulders, but her friend shrugs her away, stronger than she appears. 'Get off me! I never want to see you again, never want to talk to you again.' She points a finger. 'You'll pay for this. Murderer!'

Maggie turns and runs away with Norah's hate and spite ringing in her ears.

# CHAPTER TWENTY-SIX

The bustling Mrs Penrose has become ever more critical of Maggie's work. She was always a stickler for detail but now she finds fault where no fault exists. Maggie works hard to satisfy her. However much she tries, there is always something that is not right, not good enough. Or is it a figment of her fevered imagination? Her guilty conscience? She takes heart from her sessions with Jasper. They lift her, at times, lowly spirits.

After another reading with the boy, Maggie returns downstairs, to be confronted by a stony-faced Mrs Penrose. 'Back at last, eh? You took your time, I must say.'

Maggie stares at her. 'Her ladyship wanted to speak to me.'

'What about?'

'She thanked me for helping with her son.'

The cook harrumphs disdain. 'Idle chit chat with her ladyship never got no kitchen cleaned. You're getting too big for your boots, girl.'

'I changed clothes and came straight here.'

Mrs Penrose points with an accusing finger. 'Don't give me no cheek and no lies. And don't dawdle there like a lummox. You've got real work to complete. There are any number of pots and saucepans which need scrubbing. I told Polly to put them aside for your special attention. You can't expect the poor girl to be doing everything whilst you be off gallivanting. Remember, pride comes afore a fall, my girl.'

The rest of the day is spent in a whirl of kitchen duties. Many long hours later, Maggie flops into her cold bed. Polly is already there. 'Not reading tonight?' she ventures.

Polly sighs. 'I'm too tired. Mrs Penrose has got me doing your duties when you're off with Jasper. She says somebody must do them. And it's got to be me.'

Maggie feels fresh guilt mounting. 'Lady Kendall told me that the duties would be shared.'

'Mrs Penrose says there's nobody else.'

'I'm sorry. I never meant…'

'It must be right easy doing a bit of reading with that boy in a nice warm room whilst the rest of us skin our knees scrubbing floors and the like.' Bitterness has crept into Polly's voice.

'I didn't ask Lady Kendall to give me these extra duties. She asked me.'

'Ask her to stop then. Tell her you're too busy with proper work. Mrs Penrose says it's not your place.'

Maggie grits her teeth. 'I can't do that.'

'Oh yes, you could. You're a kitchen maid, not a teacher.' Polly sits up and points at Maggie. 'You think you're too good for us all, don't you?'

'It's not that. I enjoy working with Jasper and I think he enjoys being with me. Jasper's reading has improved.'

Polly grunts disbelief. 'You're twisting the truth, doing it for your own ends.'

The conversation comes to an end, leaving an awkward silence. Polly's breathing soon turns steady and deep, but Maggie can't get to sleep despite her tiredness.

The well of goodwill she drank from when she first came to Morwenstowe is being poisoned.

# CHAPTER TWENTY-SEVEN

Maggie arrives promptly for her next reading with Jasper. It is eleven o'clock on a Tuesday morning and the session is due to start, but there is no sign of either Lady Kendall or Jasper. She waits patiently, clasping her hands behind her back while staring out of the ornate windows at Morwenstowe's elegant grounds, carpeted with a light covering of white after snow flurries overnight. A brisk wind is chivvying the remaining clouds westward, leaving a blue sky and a dazzling sun. It has rarely looked more beautiful.

The door opens behind her and a grim-faced Mr Gilbert strides into the room. Maggie's mouth hangs open in surprise. Something is wrong. 'Good morning, Mr Gilbert. Where is Jasper? I was expecting to see him.'

Mr Gilbert glares. 'The lesson – if it can be called such – has been cancelled.'

'Is Jasper unwell?'

'Jasper is well enough, but he is deeply upset.'

Maggie freezes. 'Upset?'

'Something of value has gone missing since your last meeting with him.'

'What?'

'A fob watch. Of significant worth, but, more importantly, a treasured gift from his late grandfather.'

'A simple case of it having been mislaid, surely.' Maggie

imagines a cursory search finding it tucked behind a sofa or under a rug. 'I remember the item. I'd be happy to help search for it.'

Mr Gilbert snorts with derision. 'Yes, I am sure you do. There is no need. A search has already been undertaken – regretfully, without any success.'

'It must be here somewhere.'

'Of course, it is.' Mr Gilbert's expression is as cold as Bodmin Moor on a January day.

Disquiet tingles in Maggie's stomach. 'Where is Jasper?'

'With his mother. Distraught, as you might imagine.'

'If I'm not needed, I'll return to my duties in the kitchen.'

Mr Gilbert blocks her path. 'You need to remain here until the search has been completed.'

'You said that a search had already been undertaken and that nothing had been found.'

'And now the search is being widened.'

'To where?'

'To the rest of the house – staff quarters, the kitchens and the like.'

The tingle turns to prickling. 'Why?'

'Lady Kendall wishes to cover all possibilities.'

'You can't be saying…'

'I am merely making the point that it is best to ensure all possibilities are investigated. The sooner the watch is found the better for all concerned.'

Maggie gulps. 'But why do I have to stay here?'

'All staff have been asked to wait under supervision until the search is complete. Most are in the servants' hall.'

'And it is suspected that one of the staff might be responsible?'

'It is a regrettable possibility.'

An uneasy silence falls between them. They wait. And wait. Mr Gilbert gestures to a chair. 'Sit, if you wish.'

'I'm fine standing.' Maggie walks to the window to stare outside. The red breast of a robin is bobbing about in the snow, hunting for scraps. She watches it without her usual enjoyment of seeing nature. The late autumn has been hard, with spells of cold, interspersed with snow and sleet which have turned the muddy paths into quagmires. The robin flies off with a twig. Maggie turns to Mr Gilbert who has taken his own advice and is seated, a foot tapping on the carpet. He is not as relaxed as he might wish to appear.

'How much longer?' she ventures at last.

'I have absolutely no idea.' He gazes into space.

'You can't expect me to stay here forever.'

'Everybody will remain where they are for as long as it takes.'

'You can't hold me here.'

'I have been asked to *ensure* you remain here.'

Maggie sighs.

At last, the door opens. Mrs Hicks, the housekeeper, bursts in, her habitual edginess even more pronounced than usual. 'It has been found. The watch has been found,' she says. There is a tension in her voice. She glares at Maggie.

Maggie's hands go to her mouth. 'Oh, thank goodness.' She starts towards the door.

Mrs Hicks glares at her. 'Mr Henderson will be here shortly. You must wait.'

Maggie halts, alarm jangling through her. 'Why? I thought you said –'

The rotund figure of Mr Henderson marches into the room. He regards Maggie with utter contempt. 'Miss Pascoe, your post at Morwenstowe is terminated forthwith.'

'W...Why?'

Henderson holds up his hand to show Jasper's watch. It catches the sunlight and dazzles as if it has a light of its own. 'I think you understand perfectly well. This most treasured item was found in *your* room, hidden amongst *your* possessions.'

Maggie gasps in shock. 'That's...that's not possible. I certainly didn't put it there.'

Mr Henderson's fleshy upper lip curls in disgust. 'Even now you deny it?'

'Of course.'

'So how did it get there?'

'I have no idea, no idea at all.' Maggie flounders for an innocent explanation. 'Perhaps it became attached to my clothing. Or...or perhaps Jasper –'

Mrs Hicks butts in, her tone strident. 'How dare you! How dare you accuse Lord and Lady Kendall's son of acting improperly.'

'I'm not accusing him of anything. I'm saying that the watch must somehow have become caught on my dress.'

'Enough!' thunders Mr Henderson. 'Is there no limit to your brazen lying? The watch was discovered hidden in one of your books. You are a thief and a liar. If it was down to me, I would report the matter to the authorities and let you face the full tilt of the law. But Lady Kendall, being of an exceedingly generous nature, has decided against such a course of action.'

Maggie's mind is racing. How could the watch have ended up among her possessions? It made no sense. 'Where is Lady Kendall? I want to see her, to explain.'

'There is nothing for you to explain. The facts are plain for all to see. Lady Kendall has asked me to deal with the matter. This distasteful episode has left her deeply, most deeply disappointed. I have promised her ladyship that you will be gone from Morwenstowe before the day is out.' He points to the door. 'I will accompany you to your room where you will gather your possessions and leave immediately.'

A terrible pressure is booming behind Maggie's eyes. 'Please. I must see her.'

'Lady Kendall wants nothing more to do with you. You will have no further opportunity to wheedle your way into her affections or take advantage of her generosity.'

'Can I at least say goodbye to Jasper?'

Mr Henderson huffs in fury. 'You will go nowhere near that innocent boy. If you refuse to leave forthwith, I will have you thrown out, with or without your possessions.' He pushes her towards the door.

Mr Gilbert watches her go with a smug expression on his face.

Maggie is marched at pace to her room, a condemned prisoner heading for the gallows, her mind spinning at this shocking turn of events. Mr Henderson waits impatiently as she gathers her few possessions. It doesn't take long.

As she hefts her case down a long corridor with Mr Henderson in close attendance, though not offering any help, she comes across Polly.

The little maid stares at her in shock. 'I…I thought you'd left,' she stammers.

'I'm leaving now.'

'Where will you go?'

'I have no idea.' Maggie gathers herself. 'I'll find something. I left you some of my books, *Jane Eyre* and the like. It's best that you have them.' Maggie manages a grim smile. 'Your reading has progressed so much and, in truth, they are too heavy for me to carry any distance.'

'I couldn't. Not after…They mean so much to you.'

'At least hold them for me for safekeeping.'

Polly looks as if she is about to burst into tears. 'I'll take good care of them. And when you're set up, you can have them back.'

'Thank you. In the meantime, enjoy them.'

'I dunno if I can read them without you around.'

'Of course, you can.'

Mr Henderson coughs. 'Back to your duties, Polly,' he says firmly.

'Yes, sir.' Polly retreats down the corridor, glancing back several times until she is out of sight.

Maggie is escorted by the butler to a rear entrance. On the way, she passes the servants' hall. A small knot of servants are gathered there, deep in animated conversation. They pause to watch her – some with curiosity, others with disdain. 'Talk o' the devil,' somebody whispers. They've been gossiping. About her. Everybody knows.

With a final sneer, footman Jarvis holds the door open for Maggie as she stumbles outside. The cold takes her breath away. A sunny morning is turning grey with sleet likely. The door slams behind her. She pauses to glance back at the majestic house, full of warmth and certainty, and then pulls a wool shawl around her shoulders to head down the sweeping driveway.

Her life at Morwenstowe has been ripped apart in a few unbelievable hours. She has nowhere to go. And nobody to go to.

# CHAPTER TWENTY-EIGHT

Dusk comes all too soon on this short winter day. Maggie trudges on, head down. Away from Morwenstowe. To what or to where she has no idea. The hem of her skirt is soon saturated. The chill nips at her throat and fingers. Raindrops drip from trees and bushes. She looks up. The sky is clearing again. Stars are beginning to twinkle. A freezing night is taking hold.

Where to go? St Branok is the only possibility. But who might offer her sanctuary when she gets there? Not Norah. The cold seeps into her, making the journey seem so much longer. Her arm is aching from the burden of her carrying case. Thank heavens, she left most of her books in the safekeeping of Polly. For the umpteenth time, she switches the handle of the case from one hand to the other.

Rounding the corner of a country lane with high hedgerows, she spies the first welcoming lights of cottages. The outskirts of St Branok. In each of these, there will be preparations for supper, a good fire and the prospect of a quiet evening in a chair before retiring to a warm bed. But there is no place for her in any of them. Down the hill she goes towards the seafront.

Laughter and cheers take her attention as she nears the quayside. The Mermaid Inn. As vibrant and bawdy as ever. It has rooms available. For a few coins. A few coins which she doesn't have. Perhaps she could throw herself on the mercy of the pub landlord. Tom Southcott has a knack of finding a place for lost girls in his establishment. He's always on the lookout for serving maids. They wiggle their way between tables to deliver frothy pints. A forced kiss from drunken lips, a muscular arm around their waist, a grasping hand on their bottom as they bend to pick up empty glasses from a table – for some, the desperate and the penniless, an acceptable price to pay. But not Maggie. At least, not yet.

A group of men are gathered on a corner, talking in low tones. They turn in her direction and study her with unconcealed interest. One of them approaches, a mountain of a man. The light falls on his face, highlighting a livid scar on his cheek. Bullyboy Moyle. His mouth curls into a leer. 'You've got a nerve turning up 'ere again.'

Maggie pulls herself up to her full height, as tall as many men but barely reaching the broad, stubbled chin of Moyle. 'I will go where I please. I haven't done anything wrong.'

Moyle's dull eyes register a rare flicker of excitement. 'You ain't got Norah Bray to protect you no more. She hates you. For what you've done. For the lies.'

'Leave me alone.' Maggie tries to step past, heading anywhere out of the reach of Moyle.

He blocks her path. 'If you're looking for a warm bed fer the night, I can oblige.'

Maggie slips to one side, closer to The Mermaid. There's safety in numbers, even if those numbers are the bawdy clientele of The Mermaid. 'Let me pass.'

Moyle chuckles. 'Maybe. Maybe not.'

'I'll shout for help.'

'Shout all you like, luv. Nobody's interested in scum like you.' His gaze falls to Maggie's case. 'What's in there?'

'A few items. I…I am delivering them to a friend.'

'That's a lie for a start. You ain't got no friends in this town. Not anymore.' He reaches out to snatch the case from her. 'Let's have a gander then.'

Maggie holds on. 'Get your hands off. It's mine.'

He pulls harder. With both hands. 'You're a strong 'un, ain't yer.'

'Let go!' She slips in the mud and slime of the street, ending up on her side.

Moyle's chuckle becomes a full-blown laugh. 'Miss high and mighty Pascoe, down in the shit where she belongs.'

The other men look on, their expressions ranging from interest to concern, but nobody interferes. Then a stocky man, another of Hoskin's henchmen, emerges from The Mermaid and strides over. 'George, Mr Hoskin wants to see you.'

Moyle pauses. 'I'll be there in a minute. Got some business of me own to sort out first.' He winks at the group of onlookers, who bay rowdy laughs.

The stocky man is unamused. 'Mr Hoskin says *now*.'

Moyle drops the case with obvious reluctance. He points a thick finger at Maggie. 'I'll catch up with you later,' he says before striding inside.

Scuttling away, Maggie shelters as best she can beside a wall, blowing hot breath on her freezing fingers. Her desperation is rising. The Mermaid with its ribald humour and customers with wayward hands is becoming more acceptable by the moment. Heaven help her. The thought prompts a flash of inspiration. The church. Of course, the church.

She starts walking again – constant movement helps to ward off the cold – heading uphill. 'My doors are always open.

The church is a sanctuary,' Parson Kellow is fond of telling his parishioners. The church's flagstones will be as cold as ice on a night such as this, but the windows will be shut tight and she will be out of a chilling Atlantic breeze which is growing in strength. It will do. It will have to.

Disappointment awaits. The church's doors are barred. The heavens open with hard rain. The torrent cascades off the roof onto the sodden ground below, leaving the stone path slick and shiny. Maggie huddles in the church's small porch. Where now? Not back to the corner where the devilish George Moyle awaits. She won't be so lucky next time. The thought of what Moyle might do to her if he got her alone is beyond terrifying.

If only Parson Kellow was here. That prompts another idea. The Vicarage. Of course. The kindly Kellow will not turn her away on a night such as this. He will find a place for her. And then, in the morning, having rested, she will be able to decide on her next move with a clear head and, hopefully, a full stomach.

Her mind made up she takes a road out to the Tregloss headland. It is wide enough for a carriage, but slippery and full of puddles from the recent rains. Maggie splashes through them, the hauling of her case becoming more painful by the moment. Her arms and shoulders are burning. The palm of her right hand has been rubbed raw. She is cold, thirsty and ravenous. Not far. Nearly there. A vision of Kellow's warm smile and a welcoming fire propels her onward.

A pounding hissing to her left signals that the Atlantic is pushing hard against the coast, driven by a storm far out to sea. Thunderous waves hurl themselves against rocks, disappearing in explosions of surf. Maggie glances out to a black horizon and whispers a silent prayer for any unfortunate souls out there tonight. May the Lord have mercy on them.

A half-moon slides out from behind clouds driven by the wind and a shaft of pale light picks out the gates of Kellow's home. Maggie breathes a sigh of relief and stumbles down the driveway. The building with its soaring chimneys looms up in front of her, a jagged shadow. There are no lights. Is the clergyman abed early? Or is he away perhaps for the evening, or even for the night? Please God, no. She cannot lug that infernal case any further.

A brass knocker shaped as a cross stands proud on the front door. Maggie puts down her case and picks up the knocker with both hands – it's even heavier than she expected – and delivers a firm rat-a-tat-tat which echoes through the silent house.

She waits, shuffling on the doorstep to keep warm.

Nothing.

She picks up the knocker again and this time hammers it against the door with all her strength.

Still nothing.

Maggie pushes against the door. Of course, it is locked.

She calls out, her tone rising in desperation. 'Hello, hello, is anybody there? Help me. Please help me.'

Silence.

The downstairs windows are firmly closed, discouraging any thoughts of prising them open. What now? Return to St Branok and throw herself on the mercy of landlord Tom at The Mermaid? No, Moyle will be waiting.

She cannot lug her case an inch further. She looks around for shelter. The Vicarage's neat porch is next to useless, swept as it is by the sea breeze. Sopping wet, she crouches against a stone wall, shivers pulsating through her body. Her mind is blank. She's going to die on Parson Kellow's doorstep. The sinking of the *Minerva* will have killed her as well. Like her father. Like her brothers.

Long minutes pass. She whispers a prayer. 'For I know the plans I have for you, declares the Lord, plans to prosper you and not to harm you, plans to give you hope and a future.'

She will not give up, never give up while there is breath in her body. After a time, she feels strong enough to get to her feet and, knees aching, she follows the narrow path towards the headland, having dumped her case in the most sheltered part of the porch. The going is treacherous in the dark, but she carries on, clambering up a short flight of steps, reduced to all fours on one slippery section. George Moyle and Jed Hoskin would love to see her now. How they would laugh.

Parson Kellow's haphazard hut of bleached driftwood comes into view. Maggie slips the latch and gratefully steps into the darkness, sniffing at a pungent odour not dispelled by the ocean breezes. Two woollen rugs are rolled up in a corner. She closes the hut's door and spreads one on the floor. The sound of the sea and the wind settle to a distant thunder. By touch and smell she searches for anything to eat. Nothing. Not even a dried biscuit. She pulls the second rug up to her chin and then, thank heavens, finds a cushion for her weary head. It will do. It will have to. She must survive until daybreak.

# CHAPTER TWENTY-NINE

Screeching gulls wake Maggie. She finds herself in a cold, grey world, mercifully free of the demons and giants conjured in her dreams. From gaps between the hut's timbers, thin shafts of light spear the darkness. Other sounds prick her consciousness: a whistling, blustery breeze, the pounding of waves on cliffs far below, a steady thudding in her head.

She sits up, the harsh memories of yesterday flooding back. The accusations. The disgrace. The hatred of some. The smugness of others. Her body comes to life. Slowly. Creakily. Painfully. Her clothes are still damp from the previous day's rains. Pangs of hunger and thirst strike her afresh. She has drunk and eaten nothing since being thrown out of Morwenstowe the previous day. A fresh search for food with the aid of daylight reveals a pouch of tobacco. She chews and sucks on it, grateful for the earthy taste, any taste.

A noise outside shatters her fragile demeanour. Not seagulls. Not the wind. Or the sea. Human. A cough. She sits there, listening hard, holding her breath, halfway through a chew.

The door squeals open to reveal a tall, thin silhouette. Maggie sighs relief through trembling lips. Not one of her enemies, of which there now seem so many, but a friend.

Parson Kellow.

Thank the Lord.

He pauses on the threshold. 'Who's there? Who's there?'

His eyes widen as they adjust to the gloom. 'Maggie? Maggie Pascoe?'

He steps inside with an outstretched, caring hand. 'My child, what in heaven's name are you doing here?' He adds in disbelief, 'Don't tell me you spent the night in my hut? Why are you not at Morwenstowe?'

Maggie scrambles up, shame gripping her. So, this is what she has descended to. She takes the deepest of gulps. 'I was thrown out yesterday.'

Kellow's jaw drops. 'In God's name, why?

'There was a mistake…a misunderstanding over a watch.' Her guilt grows even though she has no reason to feel guilty.

Kellow's gaze hardens. 'What happened? The watch went missing?'

'They said I'd taken it, stolen it. But I didn't. I'd never do such a thing. I'd never steal.'

Kellow nods. 'Have you eaten?'

Maggie licks her lips. 'Not since early yesterday.'

'Come down to The Vicarage, child. Doubtless I'll be able to prevail upon Mrs Ellis's good offices to arrange a late breakfast. And while you're eating, we can talk.'

They step carefully down the path with Kellow regularly warning of its slick and slippery surface. Despite his limp, he offers Maggie his hand on a steep section. 'Be careful. This path can be so treacherous in wet weather. I assume the case I found outside my front door is yours?'

'Yes, I couldn't carry it any further. I knocked on your door last night but there was no answer.'

'Regretfully, the house was empty. I was out late last night supping with Dr Lander and my housekeepers, Mr and

Mrs Ellis, took the opportunity to visit Mrs Ellis's mother, who's been poorly of late. Your case was a source of some puzzlement when I returned. I rose early this morning determined to solve the mystery. I noticed fresh footprints in the mud heading out to the headland and feared the worst, I have to confess.'

'I wouldn't do anything like that,' Maggie assures him.

'You would not be the first to succumb to your sorrows on Tregloss Point. Thank the Lord, you were safe and sound in my cosy little hut.'

It felt anything but cosy last night with the wind whistling through the cracks in its haphazard timbers, but Maggie is genuinely grateful when she says, 'It saved my life.'

They round a rocky promontory and catch a glimpse of The Vicarage. Warmth and civilisation beckon. Wispy smoke spirals from two of the building's soaring chimneys to be whipped away inland by the breeze.

The Vicarage, built by Kellow a few years earlier, is his strength and his weakness. The fine and elaborate building boosted his standing in the community and further afield but resulted, so it is said, in him taking a substantial loan from the hawkish Jed Hoskin. And Hoskin never does anything without payback.

As they step into the hallway, Maggie glances down at her blue skirt, a birthday present from her oh-so-proud father two years ago. Yesterday it had been pristine. She'd been given no time to change it during her ejection from Morwenstowe. Now dried mud and slime conceals its lustre. There is a rip at the side from the scuffle with Moyle.

Her cheeks flush. 'I must be a dreadful sight. Is there somewhere I could wash and change into clean clothes?'

Kellow's grey eyes study her with sympathy. 'Of

course…of course, I am forgetting my manners.' He ushers her into a sitting room. 'Wait here. I'll find somebody to show you to a room.' He disappears down a darkened corridor shouting, 'Mrs Ellis, Mrs Ellis.'

Maggie slumps on a cushioned chair, marvelling at its softness after the hard, chill night in the hut, but then remembers the dampness of her skirt and immediately stands up again. She does her best to brush the damp and dirt away and then passes the time taking her first proper look at the interior of Kellow's residence. The building's timbers still have the smell and creak of newness. It's a fine property for a man who espouses the virtues of a simple, contented God-fearing life.

Kellow reappears with a stout woman of later years. 'Mrs Ellis will show you to a bedroom where you can change. Come down when you are ready, and we can eat and talk.'

Mrs Ellis leads the way to a pleasant first floor room with a view down the valley to St Branok. 'I'll get you a bowl of water and ask my husband to fetch your case,' she says and then strides away.

The little red-faced man who drove the carriage that took Maggie out to Morwenstowe when she was evicted from the family home appears a few minutes later huffing and puffing with the case. 'The parson requests the pleasure of your company in the sitting room, miss,' he says before leaving, closing the door behind him.

Driven by a raging hunger and thirst, Maggie completes the necessary repair work to her appearance in a few frantic minutes. Having washed away the sheen of filth on her face and most of the mud under her cracked and broken fingernails and untangled her hair by means of vigorous action with her hairbrush, she slips into a fresh skirt and a high-necked blouse adorned with the brooch which belonged to her mother.

Downstairs, she finds Kellow reading from a Bible in the sitting room, his round spectacles perched on the end of his nose. He looks up as Maggie draws close. 'Goodness me, can this be the lost soul I encountered on the headland this morning?' he says with a playful gleam in his eye. He points to a tray on a table nearby which is loaded with bread, ham and eggs, an elegant teapot, cups and a jug of milk. 'Mrs Ellis has done us proud. A veritable feast.'

A soft 'thank you' slips from Maggie's hungry lips.

Kellow pours the tea. 'Well, tuck in. Please don't hold back on my account. We can talk when you are refreshed.'

The food disappears at a pace that would usually be considered unseemly. The parson chats about the weather, the fishing and assorted items of local gossip. A notorious criminal has been apprehended on the moor and will soon be going before the Bodmin Assizes. 'A desperate fellow, by all accounts,' Kellow says as he pours a third cup of tea for Maggie. 'It will be the rope for him, I'm sure.' He crosses himself. 'May Almighty God have mercy on his soul.'

'You have been so kind, Father,' Maggie says when her full stomach is stretching against her undergarments. Truth be told, she has eaten a little too much.

Kellow regards her with compassion. 'You look much improved. It's good to see colour returning to your cheeks. So, what happened at Morwenstowe? You were wrongly accused of the theft of a watch?' He takes her hand. 'Please tell me the truth. I am not here to judge you. We are all sinners with cause to repent.'

Maggie recounts in quivering, halting fashion the full story: the discovery of the watch amongst her possessions, her flight from Morwenstowe, her desperation to find somewhere to stay and then her encounter with Moyle at The Mermaid.

Kellow purses his lips. 'Why a man of the standing of Mr Hoskin tolerates Moyle is beyond me. Hoskin should be made aware of his actions.'

'I doubt Jed Hoskin will care. He has a terrible hatred for me.'

Kellow's eyebrows crease. 'Why?'

'In truth, I don't fully understand the extent of his loathing. He and my father were rivals but not sworn enemies.'

'There must be a reason. Hoskin never does anything without a reason.'

'It stems from the public meeting. He says I've been poking my nose in where it isn't wanted.'

'And have you?'

'I'm determined to find out why there was no warning of the storm that killed my family. Unfortunately, the man responsible, Clement Thomas, is nowhere to be found.'

'I know and, in the circumstances, I am not at all surprised. He has questions to answer. And no doubt when he is found, they *will* be answered in a courthouse.' He pauses in thought. 'The fishing community is tight knit. Old Clem worked on one of Hoskin's boats for many years.'

'I believe there is much more to this than simply an old man neglecting his duty. And I have a right to know the truth!' Maggie's outburst is stronger than she intended.

Kellow nods. 'Mrs Ellis recalls Clement very well as a fine young man in his youth. But, if he is innocent, why hasn't he remained to answer the accusations?'

'He'll be scared, I expect.'

Kellow sits back in his chair. 'Questions remain unanswered, but I would question if you – as a vulnerable young woman – are in the best position to uncover the truth. Perhaps your enquiries are best left to others.'

'Who?'

'The authorities and the like. Is there anybody you can stay with tonight?'

'My friends are few and far between these days and, as you are aware, I have no relatives.'

'Your friend Norah Bray would be happy to help.'

Maggie shakes her head sadly. 'We are no longer friends. There was an argument.'

'About what, pray?'

'Norah discovered that her son was aboard my father's boat when he died and that I knew about it.' She sucks a breath. 'I should have told her the truth, but I could never find the right moment.'

'Friendship comes to the fore in times of need. You were such good friends. Surely, a reconciliation is possible.'

'I don't think so. Norah believes I should have stopped Jowan going aboard. But I tried…my father insisted.'

Kellow exudes sympathy. 'It is a tragedy when good friendships are prised apart.' He pauses in thought and then says, 'There is space here at The Vicarage while you recuperate and, as soon as I get the opportunity, I will speak to Lady Kendall on your behalf to ensure that your good name is restored. She trusts my judgement, I believe. In the meantime, your company on winter evenings will be welcome.' He lowers his voice. 'Mr and Mrs Ellis are redoubtable folk but somewhat lacking in the art of finer conversation.' He glances at a clock and then rises. 'Please excuse me. I have duties to perform. My parishioners need me.'

'I am indebted to you, sir. For your kindness. I hope my presence here won't cause you any…ah difficulties.

'My housekeepers keep themselves to themselves. I'm sure we can rely on their discretion. I will ask Mrs Ellis to prepare a room for your stay. I would advise you to rest today after your recent trials.'

Maggie stays seated in the sitting room long after the parson has left, dozing at times when weariness takes her. Under his patronage, she at last feels safe. Even the malign Moyle wouldn't dare to threaten her here. She walks to the window to stare down at the cliffs and the grey ocean beyond. The weather is improving. Pale sunlight is at last breaking through heavy clouds. She can see part of St Branok harbour and the ground above it where old Clement Thomas should have put out the storm signals on the eve of the disaster.

She will discover the truth. Whatever it takes. She owes it to her father, to her brothers, to Norah's son and every other soul who died on that fateful day.

# CHAPTER THIRTY

It is another day before Maggie gets the chance to have a proper conversation with the 'redoubtable' Mrs Ellis, a pleasant, God-fearing woman but, as Kellow indicated, one of few words to anybody but her husband to whom she says plenty, often in chiding tones.

The housekeeper bustles in with a pot of afternoon tea when Maggie, on Kellow's recommendation, is reading John Bunyan's *The Pilgrim's Progress* and feeling a kinship with its troubled main character, Christian. 'I thought you could do with a brew to wet your whistle, miss,' she says, placing the tray on a table before turning to go.

Maggie puts down the book. 'Thank you, Mrs Ellis. You're very thoughtful. Do you have a moment? I was hoping to speak with you.'

Mrs Ellis halts, a questioning look on her broad features. 'How can I be of service?

'I wanted to…to thank you for helping to make me so welcome…and…and to…' Maggie flounders for the right words.

'A right pleasure, miss. You've been through a lot, so I hear. I can't imagine what it would be like to lose all your loved ones.' Her voice dies away, her cheeks colour. 'I'm sorry. I have no wish to reawaken painful memories.'

'It was a terrible day. Not just for me but for many others as well. I can't help thinking that they might all still be alive if only Clement Thomas had put out the warnings.' She hesitates and then takes the plunge, 'The parson tells me that you know Clement.'

Mrs Ellis's smile fades. 'Clem? I ain't seen him for ages.'

Maggie tries to lighten the conversation with her own smile. 'He said you remember him as an honourable man in his youth.'

The creases on Mrs Ellis's forehead ease. 'Oh aye, he were careful, thoughtful like. Not a rabble rouser like some of the young men.'

'And now nobody seems to have any idea where he's gone.'

Mrs Ellis purses her lips. There is a long moment of silence between the two women. At last Maggie says, 'I was hoping to contact him. I wondered if you might know of anybody close to him?'

'There's his wife in Uppertown, though it's not a district I'd commend to an upstanding young woman like yourself.'

'Yes, I've met her. She said she hasn't heard hide nor hair. He has a sister? In Truro?'

Mrs Ellis turns away. 'I don't recall a sister. If that's all, I have a loaf in the oven.'

Maggie is not ready to let the matter drop. 'Who else might be close to him? I merely want to find out what happened.'

Mrs Ellis pauses at the door. 'Nessa, his wife, worked at Jed Hoskin's pilchard palace in Ginmouth for many a year. They had any number of friends there.'

'Anybody in particular?'

'Nessa was close with Ellie Wilkins. Ellie's old man worked on the same boat as Clem. They were best friends.'

'What's his name?'

'Tristan Wilkins.'

'Does Ellie still work there?'

She shrugs. 'I think so. I must get back…that loaf.'

Maggie watches her go. A visit to Ginmouth is in the offing to try to find Ellie Wilkins or anybody else who will admit to knowing Clem Thomas. And, of all places, it will involve stepping across the threshold of one of Jed Hoskin's establishments.

# CHAPTER THIRTY-ONE

A scene of organised chaos greets Maggie when she makes her way into St Branok the following day with a scarf covering the lower half of her face. She pauses on the quayside where a crowd has gathered to see the landing of what might be the last big pilchard catch of the year. The Atlantic has never been more generous, the season starting late but running on much longer until the second half of November. Hoskin must be a happy man. And a wealthier one.

Maggie slips through the crowd to get a better view. It is a scene she has seen more times than she can remember in her twenty-one years but the energy and exuberance of such an occasion never ceases to enthrall her.

On the quay, men armed with big wooden shovels, standing up to their knees in writhing fish, are hurling quantities of the great silver tide into hand barrows which are then raced along a narrow path through the masses to Hoskin's salt cellar, or pilchard palace, as it is known locally. A smudge-faced urchin runs beside the barrows, striking their edges with a long cane. When a gaggle of ragged children dash in to snatch as many fish as they can from the barrows, they suffer a sharp stroke from the urchin's cane across their little hands. It does nothing to put them off. They dash in again and again, howling with pain at the strike of the cane but undeterred.

Maggie follows the barrows to Ginmouth, revelling in the air of joyous industry which prevails in St Branok today. If only her father and brothers could see this. Hoskin's pilchard palace is seething with activity. She tries to stop a few people to ask if they can direct her to Ellie Wilkins, but they shrug her off, caught up in the fever of the moment. She finds a wrinkled old man leaning against the outside wall of the salting house with a swaddled baby in his arms.

Maggie approaches him with the most engaging smile she can manage. 'A beautiful baby,' she says.

The old timer smiles back. 'Me granddaughter,' he says with pride.

'Where is her mother?'

'Daughter's inside, earning her thruppence an hour.'

'I'm looking for Ellie Wilkins.'

The old man's eyes brighten. 'I know Ellie. She's also in there.'

'I need to speak to her.'

'She won't have no time speaking right now. Yer'll need to wait.'

'It's important. Can you show me where she is?'

The baby starts crying, her small face screwed up in anguish. The commotion around the pilchard palace drowns out most of her cries. The old man tries to rock her to sleep, but the wailing continues. 'Yer've gone and woke her up again,' the old man says. 'I only just got her off to sleep.'

The suggestion that amidst the commotion of the pilchard palace it is Maggie's voice which has disturbed the infant is absurd, but she confines herself to saying, 'I can hold her. I might be able to get her back to sleep. A woman's touch…'

No second asking is needed. The old man hands over the wailing bundle with a haste indicating he is nearing the end of his patience. 'Her name be Clarissa,' he volunteers while heaving a sigh of relief.

Maggie cradles the baby feeling more nervous than she lets on. She's a woman right enough, but her experience of babies is limited. A miracle occurs. The crying ceases. The cherubic little face turns smooth and untroubled.

'You did it. Hats off to you, girl. You be a natural,' says the old man looking brighter. 'What brings you down here wanting to speak to Ellie?'

'I'm Maggie Pascoe. My father and brothers used to fish out of St Branok aboard the lugger *Minerva*.'

'I remember your family and the boat. She was a fine vessel. And your da was a fine man.'

'Are you a fisherman?

'I was 'til I had to retire because of rickety knees. Now all I'm good for is chewing the fat with the old salts down at the harbour and looking after m'daughter's babe when she's earning the pennies.'

Maggie takes a leap. 'Do you know Clement Thomas?'

'Old Clem? I know him well enough to pass the time of day. We never worked together or nothing, but I often saw him on the quayside.'

'What's he like?'

'A good 'un. You can always rely on Clem.'

'You've heard, I suppose, that he failed to put out the warning signs before the summer storm?'

The old salt shrugs. 'Course I have. Everybody's talking about it. Gossip spreads like wildfire in this town.'

'They say he was drunk, that he neglected his duty.'

'And I don't believe a word of it. Clem was always reliable.'

'Why do you think he's disappeared?'

'He's scared. Anybody would be. There was talk of him being strung up in the town square.'

'Where might he be, do you think?' Maggie does her best, with limited success, to ask the question in as relaxed a manner as possible.

The old man's eyes turn shrewd. 'Is that why you want to talk to Ellie?'

'Yes, it is. I was told she is a good friend of the family. I merely want to speak to Clem. Nobody else need be involved.' Her voice deepens as she gives way to her grief. 'I…I want to…I need to… know the truth. My family died in that storm, my whole family. My father and my brothers. And the more I learn about what happened, the more I think there is more to all this than meets the eye and that Clement Thomas might be a victim of injustice, that he is not the rogue some people are making him out to be.'

The old man nods with sympathy. 'I heard it said that he'd been whisked off somewhere secret until the hue and cry had died down.'

'Whisked off? By whom?'

'Now there's a tale and a half. It was said that…' His voice fades. He is looking over Maggie's shoulder. She turns to see George Moyle barging his way through the crowd, staring straight at her, his gaping mouth curved in triumph. He has her cornered on Hoskin land.

A sucking panic grips her. She looks for a way out, passes the baby back to the old man – miraculously, without disturbing its serenity – and then after a hasty 'thank you', slips into the mayhem and stench of the pilchard palace. Everywhere there is movement and noise. Ahead is a mound of fish and a mass of brownish salt. Further ahead, women of every age, from girls to old crones, are building a mass of pilchards, twenty feet long by four feet wide and already three feet high. There is singing, there is squabbling, there is laughter, there are shrill screams for 'more fish' and 'more salt.'

A young woman strides past. Maggie tries to stop her. 'Excuse me, please.' The woman pushes her away.

Maggie sees a small, plump woman she knows. 'Becca Hammett, isn't it? Is there a side door or back door out of here?'

Mention of her name halts the woman in her tracks. 'Maggie? I ain't seen you for months.'

'I need to get out of here. I'm being chased.' Maggie's voice is high-pitched, panicky. Empathy flashes in the woman's eyes. 'Why? What you been and gone and done?'

'George Moyle is after me.'

'Moyle? There's a brute if ever there was one.' Becca takes a deep breath. 'Don't you worry, girl. We know how to deal with the likes of George Moyle. Wait here.' She snags the attention of a group of women and Maggie is the subject of snatched glances.

Becca beckons Maggie. 'Follow me, m'dear,' she says. And then she is away, wending her curves through the teeming masses, with Maggie doing her best to keep up. Moyle is held up by the group of women. They are remonstrating with him. He tries to shove his way through. There is a shriek. A fair-haired girl falls to the floor, clutching her ankle. The women round on Moyle, shouting, holding their ground, emboldened by their numbers. Moyle thunders abuse but is forced to stop. In the confined space of the pilchard palace, his size is working against him, like a big ship trying to manoeuvre in St Branok harbour. Maggie plunges onwards. She has gained vital seconds.

Past the reeking mass of pilchards she goes, through more

frantic activity. Her guide stops at a side door. 'This'll get you out to an alleyway which leads on to Crantock Street. You better get going. Rachel and the rest of the girls won't be able to hold up Moyle for long.'

'Thank you, thank you so much.'

'It's a right pleasure to put a spoke in Moyle's wheel. None of us like him.'

'If he'd caught me, I dread to think what might have happened.'

Becca grimaces and gives Maggie a gentle push. 'I know exactly what would've happened. Best of luck. Don't hang around. Get going.'

Maggie races away down the slimy alleyway. The tang of fish has been replaced by the ripe stink of human habitation. Shit. Urine. Mouldering garbage. There is a commotion behind her. She glances back to see Moyle forcing his way past a girl with a dog. He has bludgeoned his way through the women in the pilchard palace and is taking huge strides towards her, mouthing obscenities under his breath. The scar on his cheek is livid.

Maggie slips on the cobbles, twists a knee and then staggers towards the safety of busier streets. The safety is illusory. She stumbles out into Crantock Street to the stares of passers-by who give her a wide berth. Where now? The church, of course. Parson Kellow will hopefully be there. But it is more than half a mile away.

She starts running as fast as her skirts and her breathing allow. Nowhere near fast enough when a striding giant like Moyle is in pursuit. Down the street. Past an ironmongers. Around a corner. She glances back again and stumbles into a person ambling in the opposite direction.

'Oh, I'm sorry, so sorry.'

'I've had worse encounters.' A friendly voice. A familiar voice. A firm hand steadies her.

Jack Treloare.

The fickle hand of fate is on her side for a change.

'Mr Treloare. Thank heavens.'

'Now that's the warmest welcome I've had for many a day.' Jack looks her up and down. 'You seem in a hurry.'

'Moyle…George Moyle is chasing me.'

On cue, a huge figure sprints around the corner, red-faced and gasping for breath. Jack strides forward. Moyle comes to a halt a few feet away.

The giant points a thick, accusing finger. 'That woman… she's a thief, a liar and a trespasser.'

Maggie steps forward to stand beside Jack. 'I am not!'

Moyle sneers. 'You were kicked out of Morwenstowe for thieving.'

'I didn't steal anything. I was wrongly accused.'

'And what were you doing at Mr 'oskin's salting cellar? Up to mischief, I'll bet.'

'I went there to see a friend.'

'You went there to nose around, to cause trouble.'

Maggie grits her teeth. 'I visited to ask about Clement Thomas. To try to find out what happened to him.'

'That old fool ain't your concern.'

'My family might still be alive if it wasn't for him.' Her wavering voice strengthens. 'When the authorities find him, they'll uncover the truth about what happened.'

'You're a stupid little fool, messing with things that don't concern you.' Moyle turns to Jack. 'If you'll take my advice, you'll have nothing to do with her. She's trouble. Mr 'oskin said –'

'Who I choose as friends is my concern, not Jed Hoskin's.'

Moyle balls a fist in a clench that would shatter oak but confines himself to: 'Mr 'oskin won't like it, won't like it at all.'

'If Mr Hoskin has concerns, he can raise them with me in person. In the meantime, Miss Pascoe and I will be taking tea together at the Regent.'

The livid scar on Moyle's cheek twitches. 'You want to mind your step, Jack. Mr 'oskin's patience with you is running low.'

'Keep your advice to yourself, Moyle.' An insouciant Jack turns to Maggie, offering his arm. 'If I might have the pleasure.'

They step past a bemused Moyle to head up the street in the direction of the Regent Hotel. When Moyle is out of sight, Jack laughs. 'I didn't get the chance to ask but if you do have time for tea, it would be a huge pleasure.'

Maggie glances down at her clothes which remain remarkably clean. 'That's very kind of you.' She has escaped George Moyle's clumsy clutches but for how long?

# CHAPTER THIRTY-TWO

The Regent is a newly established hotel in St Branok, which once existed as a gloomy public house called the Royal Oak. A red-haired beauty called Mrs Hewitt came down from London a few years earlier and wasted no time in turning it from a drinking establishment into a place of genteel refinement. She is a woman of determination and not insignificant means. Her London ideas have been welcomed by most and dismay by a few, most notably the old soaks who once frequented the Royal Oak.

When Jack and Maggie arrive, the Regent is busy with a more refined clientele than the Royal Oak could ever have hoped to attract. St Branok's small but growing aspiring classes are coming to the hotel in ever-larger numbers with mid-morning and afternoon high tea proving popular.

The impressive Mrs Hewitt hastens over. Her smile is warm and appraising. She rests a hand on Jack's arm. They are clearly friends. The hand remains there for long seconds. So more than friends. 'Jack, as always it is a pleasure to see you back in town. I have it on good authority that your vigorous nature is turning heads.' When Jack appears tongue-tied, she adds, 'With preparations for the new lifeboat.'

'Yes…yes, it has been time-consuming and at times challenging but rewarding all the same.'

'You are to be congratulated. Your endeavours will benefit generations to come. I trust that the powers that be will ensure your unstinting work is suitably acknowledged.'

'It is reward enough for me to know that lives will be saved.'

'Admirably said.' Her gaze rests graciously on him for several seconds and then slides over to Maggie. 'Jack, you're forgetting your manners. You haven't introduced me.'

Jack recovers a measure of his usual nonchalance. He turns with a grin. 'Forgive me. Let me introduce a good friend – Miss Margaret Pascoe.'

Mrs Hewitt subjects Maggie to a shrewd gaze which spreads into a smile. 'I hear you gave Jed Hoskin a run for his money at the public meeting.' Her smile turns mischievous. 'A strong woman – just what a young rake like Jack needs to keep him in check.' She turns on her elegant heels. 'Let me show you to a table.'

They are ushered to a table for two laid with bone-handled silverware. It is in a favourable location, next to a window which looks across the town beach to the Atlantic beyond. More proof, if proof be needed, that Jack is a valued client. When Mrs Hewitt has hastened away to deal with other guests, Maggie and Jack chat about minor matters until a waitress brings tea and an assortment of delicate sandwiches. The presence of Mrs Hewitt has stilted Jack's usual easy flow of conversation. He compensates by polishing off a cucumber sandwich in two bites and then says, 'So, what was all that fuss with George Moyle?'

'It was more than a fuss. If he'd got his hands on me…' Her voice fades as she runs out of words to describe the horrors of a close encounter with Hoskin's mountainous sidekick.

'What made him so angry?'

'I visited Jed Hoskin's salting cellar in Ginmouth today hoping to see a woman who knew Clement Thomas well. I thought she might have an idea where he is hiding and be willing to speak about it. Moyle chased me out.'

Jack sighs softly. She can guess what he's thinking. 'I'm surprised you managed to speak to anybody in that place. It's chaos with people racing here, there and everywhere. I keep well clear when they're busy. What did this woman say?'

'I didn't manage to speak to her, but I did talk to an old acquaintance of Clem's outside. He hinted that someone in St Branok might have helped spirit him away.'

'Who?'

Maggie shrugs. 'I think he had an inkling but wouldn't say. He was scared.'

Jack leans forward. 'I realise you don't want to hear this, Maggie, but isn't it time to forget all this and start afresh? Old Clem will turn up eventually and then he'll have to account for his actions to the authorities.'

'You haven't been through what I've been through.' Her tone rises. She quells it with difficulty. 'I can't give it up and leave it to others,' she whispers. 'His important friends might spirit him away for good and then we'll never get to the truth.' The conversation between the two women on an adjacent table goes in fits and starts. One of them is eavesdropping.

Jack smiles, a little condescendingly, Maggie thinks. 'The quayside is full of gossip and rumour. I don't hold much truck with most of it.'

'Did you make enquiries about Clem in Truro as I requested in my letter?'

Jack nods. 'My time has been short of late, but, yes, I did

speak to a few contacts. Regretfully, my investigations have so far failed to bear fruit.'

'Thank you for trying.' She smiles, keen to move the conversation on to more positive ground. 'So, tell me about the lifeboat. I can't wait to attend the launch event. Everything's ready?'

Jack's eyes brighten with enthusiasm. 'Not quite. There remains work to be done but we are getting there.' He pauses. 'Your suggestion of the boathouse being located at Trencreek Cove unfortunately failed to find favour with all of the committee. It was deemed to be too far from town. After much discussion, the town beach was chosen. Construction of a boathouse is under way as is the task of recruiting a crew. Thankfully, there have been no shortage of volunteers with seafaring experience.' He licks his lips. 'The organising committee have taken the step of offering me the post of coxswain. It is an honour and, of course, I have accepted. You are the first person I have told.'

Maggie claps her hands, happy for him. 'Congratulations!'

'Thank you.'

'But…out there in the worst weather, it will be dangerous.'

'No more than my usual fishing duties. We have a fine vessel built to the latest specifications, the best equipment and the best advice.' He pauses. 'I heard that you are no longer employed at Morwenstowe.'

A hot flush sweeps Maggie's cheeks. 'There was a…a misunderstanding. Parson Kellow stepped in to offer help in my hour of need. I am staying at The Vicarage until I can find my feet.'

'The parson is a generous man. What happened?'

She takes a deep breath and confesses the horror of her

desperate situation. 'I had no choice other than to take refuge in his hut out on the headland.'

Jack stretches out his hand on the table until it is an inch from Maggie's. It goes no further, the gap small but seemingly unbridgeable. 'Kellow's shaky old shambles out at Tregloss Point?'

Maggie nods. She wilts in his questioning gaze to stare at the table, shame gripping her. To have fallen so low.

Jack displays only compassion. 'It must have been an appalling experience in this weather.'

'There was nowhere else. Thank goodness, it was only one night.'

'What about Norah? Why didn't you stay with her? She's a wonderful friend.'

Maggie gulps down a bitter taste. 'Friend no longer, I regret to say.'

Jack's jaw drops. 'In God's name, why? How?'

Once again, she relates the tragic unfolding of events and finishes by saying, 'It is unlikely our friendship will ever be revived.'

'You were such strong companions. She'll come around. Passions ease with time.'

Maggie shakes her head slowly, sadly. 'I doubt it. She will never accept the loss of her son or how he died. She hates me now.'

'What happened at Morwenstowe to make you leave?'

Maggie gathers herself for yet another testing explanation. She seems to be spending most of her conversation with Jack recounting what has gone wrong in her life. 'As I said, it was a misunderstanding.'

Jack frowns. 'How so?'

'A watch, owned by Lord and Lady Kendall's son Jasper,

went missing. The item was found among my belongings in my room.' Maggie cringes. The story sounds more incriminating every time she repeats it.

Jack looks puzzled. 'How in heaven's name did the watch end up in your room?'

She shrugs. 'I have no idea. I suppose it could have become attached to my clothing.' She stops talking, suddenly breathless. The suggestion sounds absurd.

'To be frank, that sounds unlikely,' says Jack. There is an uneasy silence.

'Please believe me, I would never…never…'

Jack shakes his head. 'You misunderstand me. I mean the more probable explanation is that somebody left it there knowing it would be found.'

Maggie sucks in her lower lip. 'I have come to the same regrettable conclusion.'

'Somebody wanted to get you into trouble.'

'But who would be so malicious? I did nothing more than be polite and work hard at Morwenstowe.'

'There must be somebody.'

'Well, Mr Gilbert, Jasper's tutor, disliked me. I helped Jasper with his reading and Mr Gilbert believed I was interfering with the boy's tutoring.' A sense of clutching at straws steals through her.

Jack pours more tea. 'He could have taken the watch when he was with the child.'

Maggie shakes her head. 'But I cannot believe that he felt strongly enough to do such a thing. He was irritated rather than angered by my help for Jasper.'

Jack bites into the last sandwich, chews it slowly in thought and then says, 'I must admit it's hard to believe a tutor would risk his reputation to make trouble for a kitchen maid.' He adds quickly, 'I'm sorry. I meant no offence.'

Maggie smiles ruefully. 'I'm past caring about insults.'

Jack's fingers at last touch hers. A soft touch, barely a touch at all, gone in a trice. But it sends a stab of electricity pulsing through Maggie. 'You have been amazingly brave,' he says. 'So, if not Mr Gilbert, who?'

Maggie pauses to consider the question. Most staff at Morwenstowe were friendly. A few who had spent half a lifetime scraping and scrabbling to achieve a modest position in the Kendall household, were envious of her favoured position with her ladyship. But, surely, none of them were jealous enough to descend to such appalling behaviour.

'There's nobody,' she says at last.

Jack is relentless. 'Who had easy access to your room and your belongings?' Maggie begins to see how he has been so successful with his lifeboat endeavours.

'I shared a room with another maid, called Polly.'

'She must be the most likely suspect. Would she have any reason to wish to get you into trouble? Jealousy perhaps?'

A vision of the slim young Polly creasing her forehead while absorbed in *Jayne Eyre* springs into Maggie's mind. 'It is something I have considered but we grew to be friends,' she says. 'I taught her to read, loaned her my books.'

'You are a generous person, Maggie, perhaps too generous. Some people are not always as grateful for good deeds as you might expect.'

'It was she who helped get me the job at Morwenstowe in the first place.'

'How?'

'She's Norah's cousin. Norah asked her to put in a good word for me.'

Jack studies Maggie over the rim of his cup as he takes another sip of tea. 'But you say you are no longer friends with Norah, that she has become your enemy? Might there be a connection?'

Weariness engulfs Maggie. She has had enough of the endless speculation. 'Jack, you have very kindly invited me to a splendid tea. Don't let's spoil it with endless talk of malicious lies and falsehoods.'

'I apologise. I had hoped this to be a happy occasion.'

Maggie makes a determined effort to change the subject. 'I am told it has been a bumper year for the St Branok fishing industry.'

Jack's usual buoyancy returns. 'That it has. I have rarely seen Jed Hoskin more smug. Fortunes change so fast in the fishing community. At the beginning of the season there was talk that he was on shaky ground, that he'd overstretched himself with his grand new manor house and some unwise investments. And now his cup is full to overflowing.' He adds in a rueful tone, 'It is almost as if the huge catches are recompense for the disaster in the summer.'

'Catches, however plentiful, can never make up for the deaths of good men and boys.' Maggie adds thickly, 'This whole town seems to accept deaths at sea as a price worth paying.'

Jack's tanned features redden. 'Forgive me, Maggie. I didn't intend to make light of such a tragedy, but we fishermen have learned to accept the risks. People here have little choice. How else would many of us make a living? The Cornish tin mining industry is not without its own problems – and its fatalities. Fishing is the future. With better links to Bristol, London and abroad, we have new mouths to feed; mouths who are willing to pay a high price for our catches.'

'How will you manage your lifeboat duties as coxswain of the lifeboat with being a skipper often at sea?'

Jack pulls a look of profound self-assurance. 'Others elsewhere manage it. My situation is not unusual. The lifeboat will usually launch during poor weather when my fishing vessel will be safe in harbour. And, if for any reason, I am not available, there will be others ready to take my place.'

'The arrival of the new lifeboat will be exciting. I'm looking forward to it.'

'Oh aye, a day of much celebration. The whole of St Branok will turn out.' He runs a hand across his chin and then says, 'Who knows, perhaps even old Clem might show his face.'

'Do you think Clement Thomas would dare to appear?'

'There is safety in numbers. And Clem was a St Branok man through and through. Wherever he's gone, he'll have had difficulty staying away. It might be the occasion for him to test the waters for a return.'

Maggie's high tea with Jack is over all too soon. Out in the street, Jack thanks her for a 'nanty narking afternoon'.

Maggie searches his features. The usual light amusement is playing over them. Too often she can't tell whether he is joking or not. 'Nanty narking – is that good or bad?'

He grins. 'It's a phrase I picked up on my travels. It means great fun.'

'Well, I've had a nanty narking afternoon, too, then.'

They both laugh. Jack says at last, 'Might I call on you at The Vicarage when you are free?'

Her stomach tingles. 'Yes, of course. I'm sure Parson Kellow won't object.'

'I will be away for the next few days, but back by Saturday. So, Saturday afternoon?'

'That sounds lovely.'

Maggie heads back to The Vicarage with a lightness in her step. Even the weather is better. It has been dryer of late. Her hair is ruffled by a playful, warmer breeze from the south.

# CHAPTER THIRTY-THREE

Maggie's lighter mood doesn't last long. She is brought crashing to earth by two letters from Jack. The first, little more than a brief message, explains that his visit up country will take longer than anticipated and he is unable to see her on Saturday. She puts it to the back of her mind. These things happen, she tells herself. Jack is a busy man with considerable responsibility. And there is still the lifeboat launch to look forward to.

But then it turns out that she will not be a guest of honour at this most momentous event after all. Jack's second letter a week later is longer and more apologetic. Unfortunately, the committee has settled its guest list and there is no opportunity for additional invitations.

'Is something wrong, my dear?' Parson Kellow ventures when they sup together that evening in silence. 'I couldn't help but notice your happy mood of recent days has dimmed somewhat.'

Maggie toys with her food which in happier moments she eats with gusto. Mrs Ellis is a fine cook and Maggie has a ready appetite. 'I'm sorry. I'm poor company tonight.'

Kellow persists. 'You are never poor company. That letter you received today contained unfortunate news, yes? Please tell me if I am interfering in matters that do not concern me.

I am a clumsy old churchman who sometimes puts his foot in it.'

Maggie puts down her knife and fork. 'In truth, I am disappointed – and a little baffled. Jack wanted me to be among the guests of honour at the lifeboat celebrations, but he has since written saying that such an invitation is not possible.'

Kellow's cheeks flush. 'Jack was presumptuous to invite you without consulting with the organising committee.'

'He sounded so certain.'

Kellow clears his throat. 'The committee expressly agreed that all personal invitees would be agreed by the whole committee.'

'So, the committee voted against my attending?'

Kellow's discomfort deepens. 'Not…not precisely. The committee in its wisdom agreed that personal invitees required unanimous consent. Of course, there is nothing to stop you being part of the many people who will line the streets. It will be a wonderful day for the whole town.'

'So, at least one member of the committee voted against my attendance?'

Kellow contemplates a lamb cutlet on his plate. 'I'm not at liberty to talk about the discussions of the committee. Our meetings are held behind closed doors.'

Maggie senses she has pressed her host too hard. 'I didn't mean to pry. If you say you cannot discuss it, you have good reason, I am sure.' She sighs. 'You have been wonderfully helpful to me. You offered me shelter when nobody else would. I can never thank you enough for your kindness, your compassion.'

Kellow lays down his fork, pushes his plate to one side. 'If I provide more detail, I would appeal to you to never repeat it elsewhere.'

'Of course.'

'Jack spoke strongly in your favour. As did I, of course. And there was much sympathy for your situation from most of the committee members.' He holds up his hands. 'I cannot say anything further.'

Kellow retires to the library for a puff of his pipe and a reading of Isaiah in preparation for a visit to a sick, elderly spinster the following day. Maggie goes to her room, mulling over the committee's decision. She has little doubt who spoke against her.

Jed Hoskin.

# CHAPTER THIRTY-FOUR

The arrival of the lifeboat sparks a surge of expectation and excitement not seen in St Branok for many a year, putting even the first bumper pilchard catch of the season in the shade. Flags are hoisted, bunting is run out and a makeshift stage is built next to the town beach and the new lifeboat house, glistening in the winter sun with its new paint and fresh timbers. But the real star of the show is the lifeboat itself. It stands on the slipway at the front of the boathouse for all to see, bedecked in flags and other finery.

The weather on launch day turns out dry and fine with a gentle breeze. A good omen, some say. As the opening time of midday nears, a large, chattering, happy crowd gathers on the open ground beside the stage. Traders, never ones to let an opportunity pass, have set up stalls and are selling everything from baked potatoes to muffins and tea.

Parson Kellow leads Maggie through the throng to a trestle table on a corner of the street, set up by Mrs Hewitt, of the Regent Hotel, to serve coffee and other enticements. Coffee is a luxury for most. But the air of jollity and Mrs Hewitt's careful pricing ensures that business is brisk. She is most certainly a woman of enterprise. A maid from the hotel is kept busy filling mugs with coffee and selling bread and butter, slices of fruit cake, watercress and ham sandwiches and hardboiled eggs.

The crowd parts deferentially for Kellow.

He turns to Maggie with a smile. 'Can I treat you to a coffee, my dear?'

The sharp tang of coffee reaches Maggie's nostrils. She swallows in expectation of such a luxury. 'Yes, please.'

A steaming mug is passed to her and she sips it with pleasure as the bitter sweetness hits the back of her throat. Among her talents, Mrs Hewitt makes a fine cup of coffee.

Having manoeuvred Maggie into a prime location close to the boathouse and the stage, Kellow announces he is required among the other dignitaries. 'You'll be able to see everything from here. In truth, I'd prefer to be down here myself.' He gestures at the crowd. 'Among my flock.'

Maggie realises these words are intended to soothe any lingering feelings of rejection. Kellow loves a stage, in every sense.

He eases his way through the masses and is soon a member of the small party on the stage, exchanging words with the other special guests who regard the noisy assemblage with benevolent smiles. The exception is Jed Hoskin, his eyes screwed up in that perennial thoughtful expression of his. The rare smiles he delivers are reserved for the diminutive figure at his elbow, dressed in silks and lace. Norah. Their relationship is growing closer. A wedding is in the offing.

Midday nears. The party onstage gathers, though there is no sign of Jack. And then he appears, running a hand through his thick hair to quell an unruly quiff. He climbs up onto the stage and stands next to Mrs Hewitt, who is also a member of the VIP party. Irritation surges through Maggie. The owner of the Regent lost nobody close in the disaster. Why should she be up there, and not Maggie?

The crowd are held back by a line of stout, sour-faced men. Off to her right, stands a giant, a head taller than most. George Moyle is scanning the crowd with those dull eyes of his. Maggie ducks her head when his implacable gaze turns in her direction. For long seconds he stares at her but is unable to do anything more because of the need to remain at his post.

The speeches begin. Hoskin, as chairman of the organising committee, makes a meandering, predictable speech on the need to save lives at sea, thanking the Royal National Lifeboat Institution for its enduring support. Parson Kellow leads a prayer for the boat and its crew, followed by a senior member of the institution and, finally, Jack evokes a lusty cheer from the crowd with hearty comments about his fledgling crew. The crew are brought up on stage to be presented to an admiring crowd – tough, hard men with deep tans, well used to the dangers of the sea, but less comfortable being the centre of attention.

Then it is time for the boat to be launched. Shouts and whistles of support ring out as Norah is brought forward. She hurls a bottle of Champagne, hung on a rope, against the side of the vessel. It breaks into a thousand pieces and the bubbles cascade down the boat's hull, prompting laughs and exclamations. 'I name this vessel the *Jowan Bray*,' she says with a smile tempered by a flicker of sadness in her eyes.

'A grand-looking vessel,' an old salt next to Maggie says.

'About time too,' a woman mutters in response.

The crew and a few robust helpers haul the lifeboat across the sands until she's standing in knee-high water with ripples from a placid Atlantic washing around her. The crowd follow and raise another almighty cheer as the crew take their oars and pull with enthusiasm out to Tregloss Point.

Maggie stays to watch as people drift back to the stalls in the square or to the local watering holes. The memory of that dreadful day not so long ago, holds her there.

The *Jowan Bray* completes a short navigation of the bay and returns to the beach. As Jack jumps ashore, he sees Maggie among the small group of people still watching the lifeboat's progress. He paces over to her with a half-smile. A deep flush, visible even under his tan, washes through his cheeks. 'So, what do you make of St Branok's first lifeboat?'

'She's a fine craft and your crew look as sturdy a group of men as one could wish for.'

'Oh aye, they're a good bunch of lads, brimming with enthusiasm. They've come together well. More training is needed but we'll get there.'

'I'm sure you will.' There is a pause and then she says, 'Well, I will leave you to your duties.' She starts to turn away.

Jack touches her arm. 'Wait! Please. I was hoping to speak with you.'

Maggie waits in expectation.

Jack regards her with anxious eyes. 'I owe you an explanation.'

'No explanation is needed. I understand the situation well enough.'

'I don't think you do.' He huffs a deep breath. 'Typical of me, I jumped the gun when I wrote inviting you to the celebrations as a guest of honour. I…I should have checked with the committee first.'

'I realise it was not of your doing.'

Jack's brown eyes widen. 'How do you know?'

Maggie holds his gaze and then says, 'I know. Jed Hoskin was bound to object to any generosity shown towards me.'

'It would be manifestly wrong of me to discuss…'

Maggie waves a hand in a dismissive gesture. 'There is no need.'

'He insists you are needlessly stirring up dissent over the failure to put out the storm warnings. He is furious.'

'Questions remain unanswered. Clem Thomas wasn't a fool and he wasn't forgetful so why didn't he do his duty?' She glances around at the happy faces around them. 'I was hoping your suggestion that he might turn up for the event today would prove correct. But there has been no sign of him.'

Jack shrugs. 'There are rumours on the quayside of an imminent arrest.'

'There are always rumours on the quayside,' says Maggie, her voice laced with scepticism.

'These appear to be of more substance.' He blinks, looking uncharacteristically nervous. 'I was hoping that I might see you again. There is a private celebration for dignitaries this afternoon at the chapel, but I should be able to get away after an hour or so. I'm sure Cara…Mrs Hewitt would squeeze us in for a table at the Regent.'

Maggie feels obstinacy building inside her. Jack has raised her hopes in so many ways, none of which have materialised. Now it is his turn to find out what it's like to be slighted. 'I have other plans.'

She strides up the beach, irked by Jack's flirtations – she is not an object to be toyed with and then dropped – but also intrigued by the talk of an imminent arrest of Clement Thomas. If the forces of law are gathering around old Clem as Jack claims, then the full truth of what happened on that fateful day may at last come out.

# CHAPTER THIRTY-FIVE

At The Vicarage two days after the lifeboat launch, Maggie answers an urgent rapping on the door to find a boy on the doorstep. The youngster holds a grey cap in his hands, twisting it as if he is trying to wring every drop of moisture from the tatty, stained material.

'Message for Parson Kellow, ma'am. Tis urgent like.'

'What's it about?'

'A body been found, ma'am. Doctor Lander sent me. Asked me to fetch the parson straightaway.'

'Where?'

'Silvery Cove, ma'am.' Silvery Cove is small and sheltered with a reputation for collecting the flotsam and debris of the ocean currents.

'I'll get the parson.'

She doesn't need to. Kellow emerges from the library with a book in hand and spectacles perched on the end of his long nose having heard the commotion on the doorstep.

'A body?' he said. 'Who?'

The boy eases his grip on the cap. 'An old 'un, he be. Found early this morn. Doctor Lander and a few others are down at the cove now.'

Kellow turns to grab a coat.

Maggie touches his arm. 'I'll come with you.'

Kellow's forehead creases. 'This doesn't sound like a place for a young woman.'

'I have seen my share of bodies, including those of my own family.'

'I really don't see…'

But Maggie insists on accompanying the parson. She has a fearful idea who this person might be.

Kellow nods, recognising Maggie's determination. 'Very well. If you must. But I'd ask you to keep your distance. Bodies left to drift in the ocean can be a distressing spectacle. I have seen many more than I would wish.'

Coats are gathered, walking boots found, and they set off with the boy leading the way along the narrow cliffside path at a brisk pace, slipping and sliding on ground made treacherous by the overnight rains. It is a wet and breezy day with the wind howling in the crevices of the cliffs and ruffling the coarse grasses on the headlands. A brief period of early morning sunlight has given way to threatening clouds. The grey ocean is sprinkled with whitecaps.

A heavy downpour forces them to shelter in the lee of a rocky outcrop but as soon as the rain eases, a determined Kellow is on the move again. With his ever-present Bible in his hand, he leads the way, head down, limping only lightly, shoulders hunched into the wind, the occasional encouraging words to his two companions slipping out of his grimly set mouth. They are soon all soaked to the skin. Maggie's long skirts cling to her legs as they stumble onward.

Silvery Cove isn't far as the crow flies, but the rocky path comprises long, steep climbs and difficult descents next to cliffs. Kellow marches onward, seemingly oblivious to the dangers and the foul weather. Maggie watches her every step on the descents while the boy jumps from rock to rock as sure-footed as a mountain goat.

At last, their destination comes into sight. The silver-grey pebbles and sand which gave the cove its name can be seen through curtains of rain.

The boy points. 'There! There they be!'

A knot of people are clustered around something close to the water's edge. A cloud of squealing gulls flap overhead; with its sheltered position attracting so much of the ocean's waste, Silvery Cove provides rich pickings for man and beast alike. Maggie wonders how long they have feasted off this human corpse before it was found.

Kellow ups the pace and they slither and slip down the remainder of the route, crossing a gushing stream, swelled by the downpours.

He turns to the boy as they jump down on the sands and gives him a coin. 'For your trouble, lad. Get home to a warm fire.'

The boy touches the peak of his cap, beaming. 'Thank you kindly, sir.'

A stocky, bearded man approaches carrying a brown leather Gladstone bag. Dr Lander looks haggard. 'Thank you for coming so quickly in this appalling weather, Reverend.'

'A few drops of rain can't be allowed to interfere with the Lord's work or yours,' Kellow says, his face stern.

The doctor points at the body. 'Regrettably, this poor fellow is beyond anything I can do for him. His soul has long since departed.'

Kellow nods. 'How long has he been dead do you think?'
'A couple of days.'
'How did he die?'
'Impossible to tell. There is bruising around his upper

torso and neck and a cut on his wrist which might be related to his death. Poor fellow. He is not a pretty sight.'

'Doubtless I have seen worse,' says Kellow. He strides over to the body, clutching his Bible and bends over the bloated corpse to say a few words.

Steeling herself, Maggie edges closer. The doctor puts a restraining hand on her arm. 'I would advise against getting too near.'

'Who is this poor gentleman?' she says. Her voice sounds strained now she is close enough to see the body in detail. A churning nausea grows within her at the sight of the bloated, rumpled shape which not so long ago had been a living, breathing man. The figure lies there in little more than rags, legs together and arms down by the side, mouth hanging open. Dark sockets are all that remain of his eyes.

Maggie realises Dr Lander is speaking again. 'He was identified by a man who knew him well. It is our fugitive, Clement Thomas.'

# CHAPTER THIRTY-SIX

In the sitting room the following day, Maggie hears the clip-clop of a horse's hooves. She looks out to see a large chestnut mare stamping and snorting in the morning chill. Astride the magnificent animal is Jack. He jumps down and approaches the front door where, in typical Treloare fashion, he proceeds to deliver a hearty rat-a-tat-tat which resounds through the house. Maggie restrains her temptation to rush outside. Let Jack wait. She is irritated by his nature which seems as changeable as the Atlantic itself. While she is dithering, she hears Mrs Ellis answer the door and the ensuing conversation.

'Mr Treloare, I'm afraid the parson is out on his rounds.'

'It's Miss Pascoe I came to see. Might she be available?' He sounds unusually contrite.

Maggie has a splendid vision of Jack standing on the doorstep with cap in hand – like the young lad of the day before. She forces herself to remain seated. When Mrs Ellis announces the arrival of the esteemed Mr Treloare, Maggie's head is buried in a book.

She looks up as if the announcement is a surprise. 'Please show him through.'

Jack appears with not a cap but a tall hat in hand. 'Maggie, I've just heard about old Clement Thomas.'

'I went with the parson to Silvery Cove when the body was discovered.'

His forehead creases. 'In God's name, why?'

She sighs. 'In truth, I feared it might be old Clem.'

He moves closer, within arm's reach. 'Not a sight for a young woman.'

'I have a strong stomach. Women are not the fragile creatures that some men believe.' She shuts the book she is holding with a loud clap to emphasise the point.

Jack's eyes brighten with humour. 'I would never associate fragility with your robust self, ma'am.' And then they darken again. 'There is strong talk in St Branok of him having taken his own life.'

'There are other possibilities.'

'Suicide is the most likely cause. The man was being hunted by the authorities. They were closing in. He would have received a long prison sentence at the least. And no man could be inured to the heavy guilt he would have felt after the storm.'

Maggie takes a deep breath. 'He could have been murdered.'

Jack raises a sceptical eyebrow. 'By whom? And why?

'Revenge. There are any number of people who had a grievance against him after his failure. I was by no means the only person to lose loved ones. It is quite possible that somebody – or some people – learned where he was hiding and took retribution into their own hands.'

Jack shrugs. 'In any event, whichever theory you might believe – and I must confess my own view turns to suicide – his death brings an end to the matter. The poor old fool most probably took his own life and, if not, somebody has exacted the justice he deserved.'

Anger erupts out of Maggie. 'An end to the matter? By no means is it an end for me.'

'Maggie, your feelings remain red raw. I understand that. But there is nothing more to be done –'

'There is yet another possibility.'

'What other possibility could there be?'

Maggie plunges on. 'Somebody might have shut up Clem to save themselves.'

Jack snorts dismissively. 'That is madness!'

'Is it? Clem disappeared with help. So, who helped him? And why? He had few family but for his wife and a sister.'

Jack fiddles with his hat. 'Maggie, hear me. You are becoming obsessed. I knew your father well and please believe me when I say he would hate to see you driven to despair by what happened. He would hope you can start a new life.'

A glob rises in Maggie's throat. A gulp sends it back down again. 'I can't. I can't.'

Silence descends, heavy and awkward. Jack steps closer. 'I came here to raise your spirits, not lower them.' His mouth turns upwards in a gentle smile. 'In truth, I came with an invitation. There is a social event at the Assembly Rooms in Truro two days hence. It is short notice, but I wondered if you might be available. There will be music, food and fine company.' With an apologetic expression, he adds, 'I will not let you down this time.'

'You're very kind, but I'm not sure…'

Mischief flits across Jack's ruddy features. 'Well, I could ask Cara Hewitt, I suppose. She is always excellent company.'

Maggie's voice turns wintry. 'Please feel free to invite whoever you wish.'

Undeterred by such a cool response, Jack persists. 'I have it on good authority that Norah is attending. Perhaps in the convivial atmosphere of a ball the seeds of a reconciliation might be planted?'

Maggie shrugs. 'I doubt whether anything will change her opinion of me.'

'I passed the time of day with her yesterday when meeting Jed.' He pauses, choosing his words carefully. 'I sense that her view has mellowed somewhat. I left her in no doubt that you had been left homeless after the baseless allegations at Morwenstowe and, that if it hadn't been for the parson's generosity, you might well have died.'

'You told her all that?'

'I did. I hope I didn't overstep the mark, but I thought it was vital she understand the extent of your suffering.' He waits a moment, trying to read her inner thoughts, and then says, 'So, will you come?'

'I…I'm not sure.'

Jack steps up his efforts. 'It will be a grand evening and I know we enjoy each other's company, at least I very much enjoy yours.'

Maggie wrestles with the thought. Half the womenfolk of St Branok would jump at the chance of accompanying the dashing Jack Treloare to a ball. And the opportunity – any opportunity – to ease her broken relationship with Norah is hard to resist. At last, a glimmer of a smile breaks through her forlorn features. 'Thank you. In which case, I would love to.'

Jack grins. 'Excellent! You won't regret it.'

He departs, flourishing a carefree wave, and disappears down the drive at a brisk canter, the hooves of his horse throwing up a cloud of spray.

Maggie watches him go, her thoughts in turmoil.

The prospect of an exciting evening with Jack lies ahead, as does the opportunity to thaw her icy relationship with

Norah. But, if Norah is present, Jed Hoskin also won't be far away. The thought of being confronted by him again sends a familiar spasm of dread through her stomach.

# CHAPTER THIRTY-SEVEN

The weather deteriorates over the next two days. Winds strengthen. Heavy clouds bring torrential rain. The Atlantic becomes a swathe of churning grey topped with white froth and spume. The storm warning signals are out on the headland, the duty now performed by another retired fisherman. The St Branok fishing fleet is penned in the harbour. But nothing will stop the ball at the Assembly Rooms.

Jack and Maggie share a carriage with Mr Curnow Teague, a local salt trader, and his wife, Amelia. The carriage splashes and bounces through the puddles. An occasional fat drop of water drips on to the seat next to Jack as torrential rain hammers on the roof. Jack appears not to notice and, during the journey, maintains a desultory conversation with Mr Teague while Maggie and Mrs Teague exchange occasional pleasantries after finding they have little in common. Periods of silence are broken by the thunder of the wheels along the carriageway, the regular crack of a whip and urgings of the coachman, riding up top in a heavy coat and hat, hunched against the wind and the rain.

Mr Teague, a thickset, corpulent man with bushy eyebrows and a receding hairline, takes the opportunity to relate in detail the success of his salt trading company which has flourished in concert with the fishing industry. The demand for salt has never been stronger, he assures Jack. Vast quantities of the mineral are needed for preservation purposes so that the millions of fish can be transported far and wide. Record catches require record quantities of salt, he explains. The talk eventually moves on to the lifeboat.

'A boon for the fishing trade, for sure,' the salt trader observes. 'I hear that you've already been out for a rescue.'

Jack nods. 'A minor matter. We were called to assist a fishing boat which had fallen into difficulties out beyond The Moules. Thankfully, we were able to rescue all the crew and the vessel concerned.'

The trader regards Jack with respect. 'It's long overdue, I hope you don't mind my saying. Mr Hoskin did a considerable service to the community by stumping up much of the funding.'

'Yes, indeed. He has been more than generous. The community owes him a debt.'

Mr Teague makes a wry grin. 'He's got deep pockets, has Jed. Spent a fortune on that newfangled manor house of his.' The trader gulps from a silver metal flask on his hip, wipes the top and then offers it to Jack. 'Your health, sir. May the rich bounty of the sea never stop flowing.'

Jack takes the flask. 'Your health.' His sip of the proffered liquid is so small that Maggie wonders if he took any at all. 'Yes, Jed Hoskin is spreading his wings and has many interests these days. He has purchased three more fishing boats and there is talk of him investing heavily in mining ventures up north.'

'He's fiercely ambitious right enough but he should avoid spreading himself too thin,' Mr Teague observes before sucking again from his flask.

At last, their leaky carriage is clattering through the

cobbled streets of Truro and pulls in at the Assembly Rooms behind a line of carriages. Maggie, Jack and the Teagues wait while the carriages up ahead disgorge their elegantly attired passengers on to the entrance steps. Couples step quickly into the building, some pausing to admire a performance of Silent Night by a bevy of carol singers.

Maggie feels dour by the standards of the socialites who sport finely cut silks in shimmering blues, greens and reds. Mrs Ellis has done her best, but Maggie's limited choice of clothing and her sturdy physique prevents her from looking as svelte as the shining visions who adorn the arms of tailcoated men.

The house orchestra is already in full flow, playing a lively polka as they walk into the main ballroom. Maggie's spirits soar at the vibrancy and the colour. Happy couples move smoothly around the dance floor, seemingly without a care in the world. She studies them with envy and wonder. Her first time at a ball. It is unlike anything she has experienced before. The music. The exquisite gowns. Her wonder is tempered by an uneasy sense of being out of place. She is inches taller than most other women in the room, her clothes smart enough for most circumstances but plain by the exquisite standards of a ball.

Maggie and Jack observe the dancing for a while and then, when a waltz begins, Jack offers her his arm. 'May I have the pleasure, ma'am,' he says with a grin.

Maggie steps back. 'I don't think…'

Maggie's dancing experience stretches no further than fun afternoons with Norah in much happier times in her sitting room when the two women had attempted waltzes and polkas before falling about laughing.

Jack urges her forward. 'You need to follow me. You'll soon get the hang of it.'

Maggie is whisked on to the dance floor by a partner who is not to be denied. 'Relax. Stay with me,' Jack says firmly and Maggie finds herself being whirled around the dance floor. She is tense and awkward but with Jack's guiding hand soon settles into the rhythm of the dance and begins to enjoy it.

A schottische, a slower version of the polka, is next. It is beyond Jack's repertoire. They leave the dance floor with Maggie breathless and exuberant. Norah is standing next to the dance floor with Jed Hoskin who is engrossed in conversation with a portly gentleman. Her expression is neutral with no sign of the pinched-up hate of recent times. Perhaps Jack is right. Perhaps this is indeed an opportunity for a coming together, or the first glimmerings of reconciliation at least.

When Norah starts talking to a group of young women and Hoskin has moved out of sight, Maggie slips away from Jack, who has fallen into a heated discussion on politics with an elderly gentleman. Norah finishes her conversation when she sees Maggie heading in her direction. The two women face each other in a quiet corner, away from the chatter and the music.

'Norah, I was hoping to speak with you.'

Maggie's onetime friend keeps a straight face, but the tone of her voice is amenable enough. 'And, in truth, I was hoping the same. I heard what happened to you. It must have been a frightening time.'

'I was falsely accused of theft.'

'I know,' she murmurs. Her eyes flick sideways.

'I have given it much thought. And come to the regrettable conclusion that somebody left the item, a watch, in my possessions knowing it would be found.'

A spasm of discomfort flashes across Norah's petite features. She purses her lips, says nothing.

After a moment of heavy silence, Maggie continues. 'It

had to be somebody who had easy access to my belongings.' She stares at Norah. 'I suspect they were persuaded by someone who had a grudge.'

Norah glares back at her. 'Perhaps this person of whom you speak had good reason to have a grudge.'

Maggie touches Norah's arm. 'We have both wronged each other. My hope is that we can draw a line under the problems of recent times and at least be cordial.'

Norah blinks. 'I was angry with you.' She clears her throat. 'Not without good reason. But I see now that the real culprit was that old fool, Clement Thomas.' She grits her teeth and then attempts a weak smile. 'And now that he is dead there is no better time to start afresh.'

'Not for Clem's widow. I have no idea how she will manage. She has nothing.'

'Jed has promised he will see her right.'

'His generosity knows few bounds.' Maggie makes little attempt to hide her cynical tone.

Norah rallies in defence of her man. 'Jed is loyal to his own. Even to a drunkard like Clement Thomas. Clem was a fisherman aboard one of Jed's luggers. Once a Hoskin man, always a Hoskin man, he says. He feels he has a responsibility to him and his family.'

Norah's voice fades. Jed Hoskin is approaching. His lips are curled in a smirk more reminiscent of a snarl. 'Miss Pascoe, I'm surprised you dare show your face in genteel society these days.'

'I have no idea what you mean.'

He spits a reply. 'Stealing from Lord and Lady Kendall? I hear you ended up sleeping in a ditch.' He looks Maggie up and down, his round face full of derision. 'Typical Pascoe, only ever fit for the gutter.'

'Jed, not here…please.' Norah puts a restraining hand on Hoskin's arm.

He pats it paternally. His smirk turns benevolent. 'You're right, m'dear. We shouldn't concern ourselves with such unsavoury matters. We have the brightest of futures ahead of us. We should let bygones be bygones. I have it on strong authority that the next dance will be a quadrille. If you'll do me the honour.' With a hand on her trim waist, Hoskin guides Norah to the dance floor where couples are organising themselves in square formations.

Maggie is aware of a person coming up behind her. She turns. Jack. He's smiling. 'Made it up with Norah then?'

She sighs. 'We're making progress, I think. In the fulness of time, we can be friends again.' She bites her lip, watching Norah laugh at a whispered comment from Hoskin. 'Though I'm not sure we can ever be what we were.'

The quadrille is in full flow with couples moving around each other in intricate patterns. Norah is elegant and smooth, Hoskin jerky and awkward. But there is an intimacy between them, Jed beaming at his partner and she smiling coyly.

'Not the most elegant of sights,' Jack murmurs to Maggie, his eyes on Hoskin hauling his bulky frame around the dancefloor to the lively rhythm of Le Pantalon.

'There is room for improvement, though in truth he is better than I expected,' concedes Maggie.

'Norah's persuaded him to take lessons.'

'He is as happy as ever I have seen him.'

Jack nods. 'With good reason.' He glances around. 'Norah has accepted Jed's hand in marriage. He has been pressing for a while and, typical of Jed, he has finally got what he wanted.'

'When will they marry?'

'Soon. Jed says he doesn't want to stand on ceremony. He is talking about an event at his new manor house in the spring, says it's the perfect way to celebrate its completion.'

Maggie watches with trepidation Norah and Hoskin process around the dancefloor. Soon Norah will be living the life of a lady at one of the finest country estates in the county with a man who holds nothing but hate for Maggie.

# CHAPTER THIRTY-EIGHT

The happy evening passes all too quickly. It seems no time before Jack is escorting Maggie down the wide steps of the Assembly Rooms to their carriage where the Teagues are waiting impatiently. The damp corner has, of course, been left for Jack. The ball is still in full swing, but Jack has duties the following morning which cause him to leave earlier than he would like. And Mr Teague, too, is due to have an early start, the arrival of a shipment of salt requiring his supervision.

Their tongues loosened by drink, Maggie and Jack maintain a happy conversation, watched by the other two occupants who stay silent apart from a few brief comments on the unpleasant weather. The rain has stopped, resulting in a welcome end to the steady dripping that accompanied their outward journey. On the open road, the horses break into a canter, urged on by the driver and a blustery tail wind that has strengthened to gale force. Dark clouds, edged with silver moonlight, scud across a sky peppered with stars. They clatter past the dark shadows of trees bent by the wind.

As they near the outskirts of St Branok, the coachman calls out, 'Whoa,' and the thunder of hooves slows.

Jack pulls down the window sash and leans out to shout to the coachman. 'What's wrong?'

'A lantern. Up ahead, sir. Somebody on the road,' says a broad West Cornwall voice from the driver's seat.

The salt trader's wife wakes from a doze, her full cheeks creased with concern. 'Should we not press on? I have heard stories of robberies out on the high road.'

Jack squints into the darkness. 'It's a boy. He's standing in the middle of the road. Unless we are proposing to run him down, then we have little option but to stop.'

Mrs Teague pulls an askance look. 'A boy? At this time of –'

She is cut short by the coachman calling out into the night. 'Come here, lad. What in God's name are you doing out on a night like this?'

'I bin sent to fetch a Mr Jack Treloare, sir. They said he would be returning from Truro about this time.'

Jack leans out further. 'I'm Jack Treloare. What do you want?'

A pale face appears at the window. The boy's shivering, soaked to the skin. 'Me ma sent me, sir. An emergency. Out at sea.'

'Speak up, lad. What sort of emergency?'

'A ship on rocks.' He adds with a sob, 'Me da's on board.'

'Where's your mother?'

'Down at the lifeboat house. They went to your house first, only to be told you were out in Truro but should be back soon. I was told to wait on the Truro Road until you came along.'

Jack opens the carriage door. 'Jump in, lad.' He calls out to the driver. 'To the lifeboat house. As quick as you can.' When the driver grumbles that his horses are tiring, Jack yells, 'Crack on, man, without delay.'

Maggie makes space for the boy to sit beside her and then

wraps her shawl around his thin shoulders. He slumps there, trembling as the carriage gathers a jolting momentum, quicker than before, but not rapid enough for Jack. 'Faster, man, faster.' Jack calls out the window. 'Lives are at stake.'

They trundle down the hill, the wheels clattering on the cobblestones in St Branok and juddering through potholes. The coach lurches as they round a sharp corner, throwing the occupants from side to side like a ship in a storm. The hefty salt trader just prevents himself from ending up in Maggie's lap.

At last, the brick lifeboat house appears out of the darkness. Its folding doors are open and the sharp bow of the boat can be seen in the light of lanterns. A large group of people, primarily women, are waiting. Anxious faces stare up at the carriage and then broaden with relief when they see Jack.

The boy leaps out of the carriage and runs to a stout woman who wraps him in her arms. It's Mrs Tehidy, one of the women who led the attempts to rescue stricken fishermen during the Great Gale.

She approaches at the head of a sea of faces as Jack jumps down on to the road followed by Maggie. 'Mr Treloare, a brig's in trouble. The *Endeavour*. On rocks near Silvery Cove. Bob, ma husband, is aboard.'

Jack freezes. 'That's one of Jed Hoskin's merchant vessels. What's she doing out in this weather?'

Mrs Tehidy's eyes flicker. 'It…it couldn't be helped, sir.'

Jack has no time to ask more questions. 'We'll do everything that we can.'

Goron, a fishing veteran who is the oldest member of the lifeboat crew, grips Jack's arm with a gnarled hand. 'Thank the Lord you got here at last. We've been waiting.'

'Tonight, of all nights, I was at a social event in Truro.'

Maggie scans the faces around her. 'Are all the crew here?'

'Most of 'em,' says Goron. 'They're ready and willing.'

'They'll need to be…on a night like this,' says Jack.

Goron scratches his salt and pepper beard. 'I'm not sure we can launch. Wind's backing to the nor'-west, pushing inshore on an incoming tide. The waves are six footers, worst I've seen in a while.'

Jack narrows his eyes against the wind. 'We've got to try. Let's get her down to the water.'

He disappears into the lifeboat house and emerges minutes later, wearing black oilskins and a sou'wester hat. He tightens the cork lifejacket around his chest and gathers the lifeboat crew. 'A grim night, lads, the worst we've faced so far. But our folk are in danger. They need our help.'

Shouts of support ring out.

'This is what we've trained for,' Jack says with a grin.

The crew and other helpers take their positions at the thick hemp ropes to pull the *Jowan Bray* the short distance to the foaming sea.

'Brace! Heave!' Jack shouts and the four wheels of the carriage on which the *Jowan Bray* rests start turning, grudgingly at first, but then fast. Too fast. Two of the crew fall on the wet, slippery surface, one landing in front of the sliding lifeboat. He tries to wriggle clear. Too late. The carriage runs over his leg. A scream splits the night air.

Jack races forward and kneels beside the stricken crewman whose crumpled face is pale grey in the light of a lantern. 'Don't move, Bill. We'll get you out of there.'

The crewman groans.

Jack calls out to a young woman who is standing horror-struck nearby. 'Get Doctor Lander. It's urgent.'

The woman stays rooted to the spot, staring with wide eyes at the stricken man.

'Go, girl…go,' Jack yells again.

As the woman picks up her skirts and races away, Jack turns to his crew. 'Back! We need to pull her back!' his voice strident and high-pitched.

The crew brace themselves to haul back up the slope. 'One…two…three. Heave, heave, heave,' Jack bellows. The crew's faces are contorted with extreme effort. The lifeboat moves an inch and then stops.

'She ain't moving. We need more help,' a crewman calls out.

Maggie pushes forward. 'I'll help.'

Mrs Tehidy comes to stand beside her. 'And me.'

They are followed by many more women, insisting on playing their part.

Jack forms them into an organised group as best he can. 'For God's sake, stay away from the front of the boat,' he says. 'She might slip forward again.'

Maggie finds a place near the head of the line of people and clamps her hands around the thick hawser. Behind her, women of all ages and sizes are doing the same.

'One…two…three…heave!' Jack shouts again.

The strain is taken up. The hawser becomes as taut as piano wire. Maggie heaves with all her strength, breathing hard. The wind whips at her hair. A fresh downpour breaks out, soaking her to the skin. She slips on the hardstanding, almost falls over but recovers her footing.

'Harder, harder,' Jack yells. 'She's moving. Nearly there…nearly there. Keep going.' His words are snatched away by the cry of the wind.

The boat inches back up the incline. At last, the injured crewman is clear.

'Hold! Hold!' shouts Jack. Goron shoves a block of wood

under the wheels of the lifeboat's carriage, preventing it from sliding down again and those who have done the hauling take a rest, their breathing ragged.

Doctor Lander arrives clutching his sturdy Gladstone bag. He cuts away the trouser around the injury and, after a brief examination, approaches Jack who is standing with Maggie.

'How bad?' Jack says.

'The leg is crushed. Beyond saving. I cannot work here. He must be taken to my surgery.'

A hand barrow is pressed into service to convey the injured man. It judders away, rattling on the bumpy road. Thankfully, the victim has lapsed into semi-consciousness.

A dazed Jack watches them go.

Maggie shakes his shoulder. 'Jack, the rescue. There isn't much time.'

He blinks and pulls himself together. 'Yes…yes.'

A young fisherman offers to take the injured man's place. He confesses scant experience of the lifeboat but insists he is ready and willing. Jack accepts him aboard. He has little choice.

They brace themselves for the backbreaking task of hauling the boat down to the sea.

Maggie insists on keeping her place on the rope. 'It'll be much faster if we all help,' she says.

Mrs Tehidy is similarly resolute. 'We've got men out there who are risking their lives. Husbands. Sons. Time is short if they're going to be saved. We'll stay well clear of the bows.'

'Aye!' Shouts of approval ring out.

Jack nods. This is no time for argument. 'Get ready…heave.'

Again, the lifeboat rumbles down the slipway, this time

at a more measured pace and without mishap. The *Jowan Bray* is hauled off its carriage on to wooden skids which have been run out across the soft sands towards the ocean.

'Go!' yells Jack and the boat slides onwards on its laborious journey. Maggie's hands, though hardened by domestic chores, are soon sore and chafed. The skin breaks leaving the palm of her right hand smeared with blood. She keeps pulling. A skinned palm is a small price to pay if lives can be saved.

Keep going.
Pull.
Pull.

The roar of the surf soon eclipses all other noise. Even Jack's shouts can barely be heard as they inch closer to the water's edge. Away from the shelter of buildings, the full force of the storm hits them. They are slapped by wind and a driving, stinging rain. Streams of water run down Maggie's face. She squints, but not for a moment does she relax her grip on the rope.

The Atlantic is a black amorphous mass ahead. A cold wetness seeps into Maggie's shoes. The first ripples of sea are lapping at her feet.

'We're almost there!' she screams.

Her words provoke a fresh bout of maximum effort. Every ligament, every muscle of every person is strained to the limit. The lifeboat gathers momentum.

The water deepens, creeping up Maggie's legs, the push and pull of the waves against her long skirt becoming stronger. A few hours earlier she had been twirling around a dancefloor to lively music. Now she is fighting for her footing on a storm-swept beach. The water reaches her thigh. The first wave of significance hits her, knocking her back. She rights herself, only to be swept off her feet by another wave. The sea laps at her neck. Her grip on the hawser tightens, despite the agony of her chafed hands, and she hauls herself back into a standing position.

The lifeboat sways to the heave of the ocean as the water lifts her and takes her weight. They battle to hold her bows straight into the waves until the crewmen, who have already taken their positions in the boat, are pulling on their oars and the boat is making headway. Goron takes to the bow to stare into the darkness.

'Brace yourselves!' he bellows.

A wall of water races towards Maggie.

It hits her harder than any blow George Moyle could inflict. She's knocked down and engulfed in a foaming mass which swirls around her. A roaring fills her ears. She clamps her eyes and mouth shut, a feather in a storm.

Her feet scrabble for firm ground but find nothing. The hawser slips from her grasp, and she is swept sideways and pushed down. She fights her way upwards, arms scrabbling, legs kicking. Where is the surface? Her lungs yearn for air.

Can't hold on much longer.

# CHAPTER THIRTY-NINE

Something hard bangs against Maggie's shoulder. She shoves it away. Panic is beginning to take her. Is this the end? The sea will claim her. Like it did her father. Like it did her brothers. And so many others.

No!

Her feet touch sand at last. She finds a footing and her head bursts clear of the sea like a cork from a whisky bottle.

She sucks in blessed air, her breath coming in gasps.

'Look out!' somebody shouts.

Another wave smashes into her, knocks her off her feet again and, though she surfaces more quickly this time, her thrashing feet fail to touch bottom. The lanterns on the water's edge fade into the murky distance. A riptide is pulling her out, sucking her out beyond the surf line. She strikes for land, arms flailing.

Yet another surge of water sweeps her up. On the crest, she spies the lifeboat. Not far off. She gurgles a scream. 'Help! Please help me! Help! Help!'

Old Goron is in the bow with a swinging lantern, his ruddy features highlighted by its glare like a carnival mask. He sees her and points. 'There!' The boat surges towards her.

Maggie waves. She's pushed under again, fights her way back to the surface and gasps another lungful of precious air.

The lifeboat is nowhere to be seen.

She's alone.

Twisting back and forth, she searches for its light.

But sees only mountains of black water. Where… where… where?

She is lost.

*Please God. Not me as well.*

Another mound of water lifts her up and she glimpses a shimmering light, low down in the trough of a wave. The lifeboat rises on a swell and draws nearer.

Goron is leaning over the side, still staring into the darkness with his lantern.

'Help! Help!'

At last, he points. 'There! She's there!'

Jack bellows, 'Pull hard, lads.'

Goron hurls a rope in her direction. She grabs hold and is hauled in closer.

Another rush of water drags her away, but she hangs on to her lifeline. The tug of the rope drags her under. Saltwater pushes its way into her mouth. She bursts clear of the water, spluttering.

Almost there.

Goron reaches down. 'Take my hand!'

Fingers brush against each other before the lifeboat swings away and Maggie loses her desperate grip on the rope.

A kick of her legs, a wild thrashing of her arms brings her up against the boat again.

And then Goron has her wrist in an iron grip and she is clutching him equally hard, her cold fingers clamped in a death hold.

Another hand reaches out from the boat and takes her other arm. Strong arms pluck her from the sea and she lands face down on the deck, sucking air like a freshly landed mackerel.

Jack manages a grin. 'I didn't think we'd be catching mermaids tonight.' With a guiding hand he directs her to the stern of the boat and then hands her a spare life jacket. 'Put this on. It's going to be a right rough ride. No time to drop you off at the shore.'

Willing hands help her to a bench. At the tiller, Jack yells, 'To Silvery Cove. Quick as you can. Pull your arms off, boys.'

Maggie slumps on the hard, wooden bench as the rhythmic creak of oars builds momentum against the elements. The crew put their backs and every other part of their bodies into it. Legs are pumping. Arms are heaving. Breaths come harsh and fast as the boat makes headway. The men are close to their limits.

Jack is urging the crew on to even stronger efforts when his jaw drops and he shouts, 'Hang on…' The lifeboat is upended by a mountain of water, crests the top and then plunges down the other side. Everyone is left sprawling in the bottom of the boat except for Jack who somehow clings on to the tiller and retains a semblance of control.

They drag themselves back on to their seats. The young man who replaced the injured crewman screams out, holding his right arm. 'I can't move it.'

Goron carries out a cursory examination before announcing the lad won't be doing any more pulling tonight.

The boat loses headway, wallowing at the mercy of the waves. Maggie nudges Jack who looks close to despair. 'I can row.' She has to repeat her words before getting a response. 'Jack! Jack!'

'I admire your pluck, Maggie, but it's no job for a woman.'

'I rowed often enough with my dad and brothers. There is nobody else.'

Jack takes a deep gulp. 'Very well. You have your chance.'

Maggie stumbles over and seizes the oar.

'Ready. On the count of three,' shouts Jack. 'Heave!'

Maggie pulls for her life, wincing as the raw flesh of her broken hands grips the wood wetted by salt water. Chafed skin is split. Her grip becomes slippery with blood.

'One…two. Keep in time, boys.' Jack adjusts the boat's bearing, somehow finding a path through the churning turbulence.

Progress is slow and hard. Pain burns in Maggie's chest, back and arms but it is as nothing compared to the agony in her hands. How long can she keep this going? Got to keep going. Got to. She loses herself in the motion of each stroke. One more. One more. Around her, the grunts of the lifeboatmen indicate that they are immersed in their own worlds of pain. The boat rocks back and forth as it makes headway. A deluge of wind and water hits them from the side as they turn to round Tregloss Point. The boat heels to starboard, its gunwale dipping into the water. Spray is hurled into their faces.

'We're going over,' somebody shouts.

Jack pushes the tiller hard over. The alarming angle eases. The boat swings to face back into the wind and ride the incoming waves head on.

'Brace yourselves…another big one,' yells Jack.

Maggie glances behind her to see another mound of black water, topped by spume, looming high above them.

No escape.

The boat rises. And rises.

'Heave…heave…heave,' Jack is shouting.

Maggie hauls on her oar for all she is worth.

Up. Up. Up.

The wave crashes over the bow. Water surges down the length of the boat.

Over the top they go and then race down the other side to hit the trough with a splash. The boat shudders and then begins rising again.

The *Jowan Bray* follows the dark outline of the coast, wallowing and tumbling through huge rollers, at times battling into the wind and at others with the wind and waves pushing at the stern. Jack's hand is clamped on the tiller, steering as safe a course as possible. Another broadside wave could sink them.

In the darkness, the shadow of a jagged headland looms up.

Jack points. 'Nearly there, boys. Keep going.'

Another mountain of water picks them up and pushes them inshore.

'Silvery Cove up ahead,' yells Jack, squinting into the gloom.

'I can't see no ship,' one man says.

Jack studies the dark coastline. 'We will…we will.'

They row into calmer waters in the lee of the headland and then rest on their oars, slumped forward, gasping, warming freezing fingers with hot breath. Jack sends up a green flare from a wooden tube and searches the darkness for a response.

They wait. A faint light glimmers on the far side of Silvery Cove. Maggie jumps up and points, nearly losing her balance and ending up in the sea. She saves herself by grabbing hold of the gunwale and points again. 'There! I saw something…a light…close to the rocks.'

Every member of the crew turns.

'I saw a light,' insists Maggie. 'It was there and then it was gone.'

'The ocean can play the devil's tricks in a storm,' mutters Jack but still he continues staring.

Time is stretched. The wind snatches at the crew's overalls. And then the thunder of distant surf and whistling of the wind is broken by Jack shouting, 'I see her. Not far. Pull, boys! Pull your hearts out! She's aground. Across the other side…not much time.'

Tired arms and sore backs take the weight of the oars but there is a new enthusiasm to their efforts and the lifeboat goes forward with fresh momentum.

They draw closer. 'There are men on deck,' yells Jack. 'They've seen us.' He screams into the storm, 'Hey! Hey! How many are you?'

He repeats his words twice more. At last, a thin voice screams, 'Ten of us left. Two injured. She's breaking up.'

'We're coming for you. Hold hard.' Jack turns back to his crew. 'We'll run a line to them if we can get in closer.'

Goron stares at him as if he has gone mad. 'Jack, this is a treacherous stretch of water. Rocks all around.'

Jack wipes sweat and spray from his forehead. 'Ease her in slow, lads. Keep a sharp look out for rocks. Get ready with the rope.'

The *Jowan Bray* edges closer. 'Rocks to starboard!' somebody shouts.

'We can't get no closer,' yells Goron.

'We'll stand-off here,' says Jack. 'Hold her steady, boys.'

Maggie gets her first proper look at the desperate men on the deck of the stricken two-masted brig, their grim faces given a ghostly pallor by a ray of lunar light as the moon sails into view between scudding clouds.

Goron stands at the front of the lifeboat with loops of rope in his hands. 'Get ready!' he shouts out, whirling the rope above his head before hurling it towards the stricken vessel. It falls short. He mutters a curse and throws again. This time it reaches them, but the surge and swell of the ocean drags it away. A third time the rope is hurled out into the darkness and this time desperate hands clamp hold. It goes taut.

There is a scurrying of shadows on the broken *Endeavour*. A man is carried forward to the side of the boat. One of the injured. The rope is secured under his arms, and he waits at the gunwale for a signal from the lifeboatmen.

'Now!' Jack bellows. 'Now!'

The injured man is lowered into the water and Goron and two other lifeboatmen haul on the rope for all they're worth.

Jack shouts instructions at the top of his voice, his face contorted with anxiety. The man is pulled over the side into the safety of the lifeboat.

He squeals. 'Ma leg!' The leg below the knee is twisted.

Maggie throws a blanket over his trembling shoulders and takes his hand. 'You're safe.'

As if to disprove her assurance, the lifeboat lurches from side to side as it's rocked by another wave. She steadies the rescued man until the wild motion eases.

Another of the *Endeavour*'s crew is hauled to the lifeboat. This man's arm has been crushed. Maggie rips a strip from the hem of her best skirt and uses the material as a tourniquet above the man's elbow. The blood flow eases. The man whispers thanks through trembling lips and shuts his eyes.

More men are dragged aboard. The lifeboat crew settle into a rhythm, each one clear in his task of either manning an oar or hauling men to safety. Three. Four. Five. Six. Seven.

Maggie counts them aboard, making each of them as comfortable as possible in the surging swaying lifeboat.

Only three figures remain on the *Endeavour*. But time is running against them. A wave pushes the lifeboat sideways, close to the rocks. Jack and the oarsmen fight to get their boat back into position. Maggie helps the man with the crushed arm who is drifting in and out of consciousness and in danger of falling overboard. A screeching of breaking timbers causes her to look up. The *Endeavour* is in her death throes, her bow awash.

'She's going down!' Jack shouts.

The remaining three hurl themselves into the water and flail towards the lifeboat, disappearing for long seconds as waves and tides take them. Soon, three heads become two and then two become one. The final head disappears.

'They're gone,' says Jack, his voice heavy with grief. With a hand shielding his eyes, he scans the water one last time, blows the deepest of sighs and then says, 'God rest their souls. Let's get home.'

As the boat turns, a grasping hand emerges Neptune-like from the deep. Maggie reaches out and grabs a thick wrist. 'Here…over here…in the water.'

The hand clutches her own wrist. Maggie is dragged forward until she is leaning over the side, fighting to keep her balance.

Jack grabs her shoulders and hauls her back to safety. A head pops out of the water. Terrified eyes stare at Maggie. Sea water spurts from a gasping mouth. Together, they haul the last man to escape the *Endeavour* aboard. He's a big, muscular man. Maggie pulls with everything she has left. The crewman lands gulping and gasping in the boat and lies there, chest heaving, lips quivering, puking sea water. Maggie, kneeling, settles the man more comfortably.

'I thought I be gone,' he mutters.

'It's a miracle we saved you,' says Maggie, though they still have a rough journey home.

The man's eyes widen at the softness of Maggie's voice. 'A maid! What in God's name are you be doing out here, girl?'

'I helped launch the boat and got caught by the tide.'

'You're a vision of loveliness. What's your name?'

'Maggie. Maggie Pascoe.'

'A Pascoe, eh? I mighta known. I knew your da and your brothers. Hard as Bodmin granite, you Pascoes. Good, hearty men, they were…' A weak smile curls the corners of his mouth. 'And the women too.'

'And who are you?'

'Bob Tehidy, skipper of the *Endeavour*.' He gestures at the shattered hulk of the brig. 'Or what remains of her.'

'I met your wife on the quayside before we left. She was frantic with worry and helped to organise the rescue. She's a formidable woman.'

'Aye, that she is. A good lass, is Joan. Sound as a pound.'

'What were you doing out on a night like this?'

Tehidy purses his lips. 'It was madness. I told Mr Hoskin, told it to him straight I did, but he wouldn't have none of it.'

'Jed Hoskin insisted on you going out in this storm? Why?'

'Best not to ask, girl. We would have made it if the rudder hadn't jammed.' He pauses, wipes a meaty hand across his forehead, closes his eyes, signalling an end to the conversation.

The rhythmic creak of oars resumes, less urgent now. The boat rides over a curling, breaking wave which hurls spray over the men at the front. A hefty crewman from the *Endeavour* has taken over Maggie's oar, leaving her free to tend the injured men and make them as comfortable as possible.

Silvery Cove fades into the distance and after battling into a head wind, they round Tregloss Point. The welcome lights of St Branok shimmer through sheets of rain. The town beach where they launched is visible but it's a seething turmoil of white water. No place to land there.

Jack steers for the harbour. 'Come on, lads! One more big heave and we're home.'

The last push to safety seems to take a lifetime, despite a wind which is now coming from behind. As they manoeuvre through the narrow inlet between the seaweed-encrusted harbour walls, the wild movement of the boat eases and the wind softens.

Safe at last.

Their progress has been monitored from the shore and a multitude is waiting as they tie up alongside the harbour steps. The robust figure of Mrs Tehidy is at the front of the group with Parson Kellow. She waves frantically. 'Thank the Lord. You're alive.' Her husband, clutching his blanket, holds up a shaky hand in acknowledgement.

Parson Kellow rushes to Maggie, his thin features lit by a beaming smile. 'I feared we'd lost you.'

Maggie wrings sea water from her wide skirt. In a ripped, sorry state, it will never see a dance again.

Jack strides over. 'The boys did well tonight, right enough. And Maggie, too. She helped in the rescue. Bob Tehidy has his life to thank her for. Plucked him from the ocean, she did.'

'Be thou plucked up by the root, and be thou planted in the sea, and it should obey you,' Kellow says with a grin. 'Luke 17.'

There is a commotion at the end of the quayside. The crowd parts. A large man appears, towering above all others. Maggie's stomach tightens. George Moyle.

# CHAPTER FORTY

Everybody turns to stare. Not at Moyle but the chubby figure with him. Jed Hoskin. Still wearing the fine attire he sported during his clumsy cavorting at the Truro dance. His face is stretched with fury. It is hard to believe this is the same smug individual who accompanied Norah during a spirited rendition of Le Pantalon.

'Where is he? Where is the miserable bastard?' he shouts, spraying an old salt with spittle.

The old man's jaw drops. 'Where's who?'

'Bob Tehidy, you fool.'

The man points a trembling finger. 'Right over there he be, sir.'

Tehidy is hunched in a blanket with his wife near the quayside steps. He looks up and sees Hoskin and Moyle homing in with thunderous faces. His mouth widens with a gasp. He clutches the arm of his wife. Seeing a man as tough as Tehidy cowed is unnerving.

Hoskin halts, his spittle-infused beard inches from Tehidy. 'Where's my ship?'

'There was nothing we could do, Mr Hoskin, sir. We fought against the wind and tide with everything we had – every man jack of us.'

'So where is she?'

'Lost. On rocks. North o' Silvery Cove.'

Hoskin clenches his jaw. 'And the cargo?'

'Gone to the bottom. All of it. Naught we could do. 'Twas a miracle any of us survived.'

Hoskin shoves a fist in Tehidy's face. 'It would have been better if you hadn't. Damn you!'

At a nod from Hoskin, Moyle steps forward and reaches out for Tehidy but his hand is knocked away by an angry Mrs Tehidy. 'Get your hands off my man.' She faces up to Hoskin. 'Those men went to sea and died. At your bidding. You forced them.'

Hoskin spews words at Bob Tehidy. 'What kind of man are you, Tehidy? No man worth his salt gets his wife to do his talking. Send her home and we'll settle this as men.'

Mrs Tehidy holds her ground. 'I'm not going anywhere. You leave my husband be. He's injured. He's coming home with me.'

Moyle pushes her hard. 'Get out of our way, woman. We've business with your husband, not you.'

Mrs Tehidy is forced back a step, slips on the slippery cobbles and lands on her rump. Onlookers gasp. She jumps up in a trice, eyes blazing, launching a volley of punches at a guffawing Moyle, who fends them off with ease.

Kellow forces his way among them like a referee in a prize fight. 'Mr Hoskin, this is not the time or the place for accusations. This woman is distraught and these men are exhausted. They need medical attention and rest. Save your skirmishes for another time.'

Hoskin bathes him in a look of contempt. 'This is not your concern, Reverend. Stick to Bible-bashing, I'd advise.'

Kellow harrumphs. 'How dare you,' he croaks.

The crowd watches with bemusement. A public spat

between two of St Branok's most prominent citizens was the last thing they were expecting tonight.

Hoskin points at Bob Tehidy, wipes spittle from his beard and thunders, 'Don't think about ever getting a job in this town again.'

'Good men died tonight. Where is your compassion, Mr Hoskin?' Kellow shouts, having found his full voice again.

Hoskin ignores him, addresses Moyle. 'Let's get out of here. There can be a reckoning with that fool Tehidy another time.' He stabs a finger at Tehidy's chest. 'I'm coming for you. Mark my words, your days in St Branok are over.'

The two men stride up the road with Hoskin spitting profanities and Moyle murmuring agreement.

Maggie goes in search of Jack. She finds him securing the lifeboat. He gives a wave and then climbs up the steps to join her. 'The first true test of our new boat,' he says. 'She stood up to it well, a credit to St Branok.'

'The crew were wonderful,' says Maggie.

'Oh aye, I'm mighty pleased with them.' He bites his lip. 'But not all the *Endeavour* crew will be seeing their families again. We should have saved more of them. And we have two lifeboatmen injured, one with a crushed leg and another with a broken arm. That is a failure in my book.'

'Without the lifeboat, all the men aboard the *Endeavour* would have died. You should be proud of your work tonight.'

Jack clenches his jaw. 'How can I be proud when men have died?'

There is no moving him. Maggie moves on. 'Jed Hoskin is furious with Bob Tehidy.'

Jack drops his voice to a whisper. 'I don't doubt it. I heard the *Endeavour* was loaded to the gunwales with contraband.'

'What sort?'

'I've heard rumours…'

'And what do these rumours say?'

Jack glances around. 'Irish whisky. A king's ransom, some say. The loss will hurt even somebody as wealthy as Hoskin.'

# CHAPTER FORTY-ONE

The storm blows itself out early the following day, leaving an aftermath of broken trees and giant waves. At The Vicarage, Maggie wakes a short time after dawn to a firm tap on her bedroom door. She stretches and groans, aching from the extraordinary exertions of the rescue.

'Yes?'

The greying head of Mrs Ellis pops her head round the door. 'Miss, a Mrs Tehidy is here, asking to see you.'

'Joan Tehidy? What does she want at this hour?'

Mrs Ellis shrugs. 'She would not say but insists it is important. She is waiting in the sitting room.'

Maggie jumps from the bed only to stumble and nearly fall as the aches and pains from the previous night's endeavours assert themselves. Muscles and ligaments, sorely tested during the rescue, have tightened up overnight. Her hands are covered in sores and ruckled, blood-stained skin. 'Please tell her I'll be down in a few minutes.'

Mrs Ellis looks on with concern. 'The parson tells me you were involved in great things last night.'

'It was a night I will never forget.'

'The parson said men owe their lives to you.'

A hot flush rises in Maggie's cheeks. 'He is generous, but it is thanks to Mr Treloare and his redoubtable lifeboat crew that lives were saved. I was little more than a passenger. Is the parson downstairs?'

'He set out early to visit the families of crewmen who were aboard the *Endeavour*.' Mrs Ellis pauses and then adds, 'Mrs Tehidy says you saved her husband's life.'

'I was able to help pull him aboard the lifeboat, nothing more.'

Maggie's modesty does little to quell the housekeeper's admiration. 'The seas were mountainous, so I was told.'

An image of huge, curling waves rearing up to consume the lifeboat flashes across Maggie's mind. 'In truth, I've never been so frightened.'

'A soul would have to be mad not to be scared on a night like that. Every man jack of 'em would have been terrified, I'll be bound. Even your Mr Treloare.' She smiles. 'Enough of my prattling. I have things to do and I'm delaying you from getting dressed.' She closes the door softly and the sound of her footsteps fade.

Maggie dresses and goes downstairs to find Mrs Tehidy slumped in a chair in the sitting room. When she sees Maggie, she rises unsteadily as if twenty years older. Maggie is shocked by her pale, exhausted appearance and a deep bruise which has purpled on the older woman's chin and jawline.

'Oh, my goodness, I had no idea you were injured on the quayside last night.'

Mrs Tehidy looks away. 'It weren't on the quay,' she mutters.

Maggie frowns. 'When then?'

'We were making our way back up the hill, Bob and me and our son, Josiah.' She chokes on spittle. 'We took a short cut down Squeeze Belly Lane. It's dark there, not well lit. We were set upon. Three of 'em, there were. Masked, the cowards.'

'Were you robbed?'

Mrs Tehidy shakes her head. 'They didn't take anything.' She gulps again. 'One of them was that brute Moyle, I'm sure of it. Nobody in this town is anywhere near as big as him.'

Maggie takes her hand. 'You look exhausted. Please sit down and let me get you some tea.'

Mrs Tehidy shakes her head. 'I haven't got time. I need to get home to my poor Bob. He was beat up real bad. He's in a right sorry state today. Cuts and bruises all over. He can hardly walk. If some locals hadn't come along, I think Moyle and his bully boys would have killed him. They scarpered when they were disturbed. And young Josiah's not much better. Seeing those men lay into his da, terrified him.'

'What are you going to do?'

Mrs Tehidy shrugs. 'Bob won't be able to work for weeks and Hoskin will make sure nobody offers him a job in this town. We've decided to leave St Branok today. My sister lives up county at Launceston. She's a kind soul and will put us up while my husband regains his health away from Hoskin's poison.'

On an impulse, Maggie hugs her. Her own problems are small by comparison with those of the Tehidys. 'I'm so sorry.'

Mrs Tehidy hugs her back hard, reminding Maggie of the distraught woman's considerable strength. Her fire had seemed unquenchable when helping to haul the lifeboat down to the water's edge.

Mrs Tehidy pulls back. 'I came here because I needed to say summat.'

'There's no need to thank me further. I did what any right-thinking person would -'

'It isn't that though we'll always be grateful for what you did.' She takes a deep breath. 'You've been asking around town about Clement Thomas, haven't you?'

'Yes, he neglected his duty in the summer. He failed to put out the storm warning signals and lives were lost as a result, including my brothers and father. But perhaps you haven't heard, he's dead. His body was washed up on Silvery Cove.'

'Oh, I heard right enough. Gossip spreads like gorse fire in St Branok, as you well know. His wife, Nessa, was distraught terrible like. She's been going around saying some right strange things.'

'I spoke with her. In truth, she was less than forthcoming. I think she knows more about what happened on the day of the Great Gale but won't tell me.'

Mrs Tehidy licks her lips and leans forward. 'Methinks her tongue will be a good deal looser now. She wants to get back at Hoskin. Blames him for getting her husband into trouble. She says…well, it's best you hear it from her.' She clambers up. 'I must be on my way. The sooner we're on the road out of St Branok, the better.'

Maggie accompanies her to the front door. 'You've been so kind coming out here in the circumstances.'

'We owed it to you after last night.' She pauses to gaze into Maggie's eyes. 'I hope you get to the truth and Hoskin and Moyle get their comeuppance. They're murderers. Hoskin has had a grip on this town for far too long.'

'What do you mean, murderers?'

Mrs Tehidy edges away. 'Ask Nessa Thomas. She'll tell you. Best you hear it from her.'

'Thank you. Thank you, so much.' Maggie watches her go, shuffling down the drive, admiring the older woman's tenacity. But a new hope is building within her. After all this time, after all this pain, might she be on the brink of the truth?

Twenty minutes later, the rhythmic thud of a cantering

horse brings her to the front door again. She waits in the porch while Jack brings his steed to a halt and jumps down more carefully than usual. So, even he is feeling the rigours of the previous night.

He regards her with a grin. 'How is our heroine?'

'A little sore but well enough. I could ask the same of you.'

'A few twinges. I'll survive.'

'Your new crew acquitted themselves well. They're a credit to your training. How are your injured crewmen?'

He gulps. 'Bill's leg had to be amputated. Dr Lander says he had no choice. Young Jimmy's arm has been set. He should be back at sea within a couple of months. Young bones heal soon enough.'

'I'm so sorry to hear about Bill. What will he do now?'

'What *can* he do? He won't ever be working aboard the lifeboat or a fishing boat again.' Jack rubs his forehead. 'Tasks will be found for him ashore, but it will be hard. Bill lives for the sea, a fine fisherman, strong as an ox. I am hopeful that funds will be made available from the institution and the people of St Branok to help him in his time of need.' He sighs. 'I…I feel responsible. As coxswain, I should have ensured a safe launch.'

Maggie takes his hand. 'You shouldn't blame yourself. You did everything you could. You were a hero last night. Eight more men would be dead if it wasn't for the efforts of you and your crew.'

Jack pulls a grim smile. 'And you. You were magnificent. If you weren't a woman…' His voice trails away.

'If I wasn't a woman, what?'

He chuckles. 'If you weren't a woman, I'd recruit you for the lifeboat, let you take Bill's place in the crew.'

'So why not? Didn't I prove myself last night?'

Jack shakes his head. 'Impossible.'

'Why is it so impossible?'

'The authorities would never allow it.'

A surge of frustration rises within Maggie. She gulps it down. 'I could still be involved. And I'm not the only one. Many of the wives and daughters are more than eager to play their part.'

'Your willingness is admirable, but I don't see how –'

'In some places women are responsible for launching the lifeboat.'

Jack's face turns thoughtful. 'Yes, there are such cases,' he says slowly.

'So, why not in St Branok? There'd be no shortage of volunteers. And last night we showed we could do it, didn't we?'

'You almost drowned.'

'Nobody – man or woman – could have done better.'

'I'm really not sure…'

'I can do it. I'm sure I can.'

Jack's expression becomes accepting. 'Are you certain?'

Maggie nods, full of enthusiasm. 'Yes, of course.'

'I will speak to the committee.'

The obstructive Jed Hoskin will take some persuading but Maggie presses on, determined to prise open this chink of light. 'I'll gather the names of those wanting to help.'

'We'd need a dozen to be available. And they'd need to be trained. I never want to see a repeat of what happened to poor Bill last night. Not on my watch.' He pauses. 'I passed Mrs Tehidy on the way here. A formidable woman. She could be an excellent volunteer.'

'Unfortunately, that won't be possible. She and her family are leaving St Branok today.'

Jack's tanned brow furrows. 'Why? The Tehidys have lived here all their lives.'

'Jed Hoskin has driven them out. There's nothing here for them anymore. Moyle and his cronies attacked them on their way home last night – under Hoskin's orders, I have little doubt. Bob Tehidy was lucky to get away alive.'

Jack flinches. 'That's appalling. I saw Hoskin this morning. And I have never seen him so angry and agitated. The loss of the *Endeavour* has hit him hard.'

'With his wealth, he can afford to lose one boat.'

'It's not the boat. It's the cargo. He lost a small fortune in Irish whisky. It was supposed to be offloaded well out of the sight of the excise men at Silvery Cove.'

'Surely, even the loss of a huge quantity of whisky can't hurt a man with deep pockets like Hoskin.'

'The talk on the quayside this morning was that he's had a few reverses recently. Some of his ventures up country have not worked out as planned and that country house of his is costing him a fortune.'

'So, what will he do now?'

'Hoskin will lean on those owing him money and, I suspect, he will step up his smuggling.'

A worrisome thought sparks in Maggie's mind. 'Do you owe Hoskin money?'

Jack's broad features turn deadpan. 'I have no particular concerns…'

His prevarication heightens her fears. 'Do you?'

Jack sucks his lower lip. 'Some.'

Maggie wants to shake him hard. 'Why in heaven's name would you allow yourself to get in debt to such a man?'

'I had no choice. The lifeboat preparations have taken far more of my time than I expected and the *Eliza Jayne* needed a re-fit.' He winces. 'Almost every person worth his salt in St Branok owes Hoskin money. Even Parson Kellow.'

She groans. 'Oh Jack!'

'It is all under control,' he says in a faltering fashion which hints at it being anything other than under control. 'Do not fear. I'll manage.'

There is little to be gained from pursuing the subject further. Maggie moves on. 'Mrs Tehidy said Clement Thomas's wife is devastated by her husband's death and might now be willing to answer my questions.'

Jack looks askance. 'About the summer storm?' He sighs. 'Maggie, can't you let that be? Clem is gone. It's over. Whatever secrets he held died with him.'

'Not for me. I want to know. I *need* to know. And Nessa Thomas has some of the answers.' She adds in a softer tone, 'I was hoping you might accompany me.'

'I'm not sure I approve of bothering a destitute old woman in her time of grief.'

'I will go alone, if necessary.' Maggie's tone chills.

He puffs concern. 'Uppertown is no place for a respectable young woman alone.'

'Don't treat me as a naive fool, Jack. I've been there before.'

Jack stares at Maggie. 'I suppose I have little alternative.' A fleeting smile slips across his face. 'I will escort you on one condition.'

'Which is?' says Maggie warily.

'That afterwards you do me the honour of taking tea with me at the Regent again.'

Maggie laughs. 'Tea at Mrs Hewitt's is a harsh price to

pay but, yes, I will be delighted to come with you. If you can afford it.'

'The day I can't afford to take an admirable young woman for afternoon tea is the day I take to robbery out on the Bodmin high road.'

'You shouldn't joke about such things. No shortage of highwaymen have swung at the gallows.'

He looks into her eyes.

A shiver tingles through Maggie. 'Jack…'

He leans closer.

She pushes him away without understanding why. 'Jack… no…not here…please.'

Jack steps away. He looks crestfallen. 'I am sorry. It was presumptuous of me, but I thought we had grown much closer of late.'

'We have. You took me by surprise, that's all.'

Jack's expression turns rueful. 'Not all surprises should be rejected.'

'There might be people watching.'

'Who? Mr and Mrs Ellis? They're quiet people who stay away from the gossip.'

They exchange a few more words, their conversation awkward and stilted. Jack consults his watch. 'I have duties to perform at the quayside this morning, but I will return at one o'clock with my buggy, and we can go find Clement Thomas's poor widow and see what she knows.'

Jack takes the reins of his mount, Betsy, climbs into the saddle and, with a dig of his heels, heads back to St Branok. Maggie waves him goodbye, her mind awash with conflicting thoughts and emotions. Jack's rejected kiss has put a barrier between them. Why in heaven's name did she stop him?

# CHAPTER FORTY-TWO

A snorting Betsy pulls the little buggy up through St Branok with Jack's steady words of encouragement urging her on. Maggie is sitting quietly beside him, the forthcoming meeting with Nessa Thomas dominating her thoughts. The old woman will doubtless be distraught. Maggie is anxious not to cause Nessa an ounce of extra pain whilst nevertheless hoping that the full truth will come out at last.

The hill eases and they build speed without putting too much strain on Betsy. By the time they enter the mucky streets of Uppertown, Jack has cajoled the horse into a good clip. Women pause to watch the buggy clatter by. Carriages are rare in Uppertown, most residents relying on handbarrows and the proverbial Shanks's pony.

Nessa Thomas's hovel comes into sight as they round a corner.

They come to a juddering halt. Maggie looks at Jack who is still seated with the reins in his hand. 'Mrs Thomas will be more forthcoming if I talk to her alone. Perhaps you could wait here?'

Jack nods. 'Yes, it's for the best. Anyway, possessions have a habit of disappearing in this district.' He pulls one of his amiable grins. 'I'm nearby if you need me.'

Maggie raps on the front door, softly at first and then

with more force. The hovel remains silent with no sign of life. She peeks in at windows, sees nothing, and so calls out. 'Nessa. Nessa Thomas. It's Maggie Pascoe. I was hoping to speak with you. Please…'

A rasping cough sounds from within and the door creaks open. Maggie steps back a pace. Nessa Thomas slumps there, a sad image of a human being, even more bowed than before by a hefty weight on her shoulders.

Maggie makes a tentative start on the few words she has rehearsed during the morning. 'Nessa, I was so sorry to hear about Clement. A tragedy…'

The old woman butts in, a defiant glint sparking in her rheumy eyes. 'Did Joan Tehidy send you?'

'Yes, yes, she did. She said you might be willing to talk to me again.'

Nessa clenches her jaw. 'That I am.' She glances over Maggie's shoulder to where Jack is waiting with Betsy and the buggy. 'You've come in style this time.'

'A friend offered to bring me.'

'Well, come along in. No point in us freezing on the doorstep.' Maggie is ushered inside.

The hovel looks dirtier, more unkempt than her previous visit.

Nessa Thomas directs Maggie to a shabby chair. 'Please sit. Tea?'

'You're very kind but I'm fine, thank you.'

The old woman pulls up a chair. 'I'm sorry, m'dear, that I was so off when we last met. You deserved better. I was protecting Clem, you see. I thought the fuss would die down in time and that he could return. But…but he ain't ever coming back.' Her voice cracks. She pulls out a rag from the pocket of her skirt and blows her nose. 'What I be trying to say is that I meant you no harm. I was scared for me husband, you see. But now he's dead…and the manner of his passing…that changes everything.'

Maggie takes the old woman's withered hand. The wrinkled papery skin is cold to the touch. Nessa Thomas allows it to remain in Maggie's young hands, her creased eyes brimming. After a difficult pause, Maggie says, 'Whatever your husband might have done – or did not do – I am so sorry for your loss.'

Nessa sniffs. 'All our lives we were together, through thick and thin. Clem took a shine to me in the winter of twenty-two. A harsh, cold winter it was, but I didn't feel it and didn't care. I was young and in love and could turn a few heads back in them days. We were married in the spring down at the old church at Treduggan. The bluebells were out in the woodlands and hedgerows. Clem picked a bunch of primroses for me. He wasn't the best looker – the injury to his face when he were a lad saw to that – but he had a kind, warm heart. Any number of people turned out to wish us well…the Bolithos, the Jagos, the Tangyes, the Rowes…all gone now.' The old lady stares sightlessly at a grimy wall, lost in memories of a time when the world was younger and brighter.

Maggie tries to fill the silence. 'You have many happy stories, I'm sure.' She bites her lip. 'Memories are all I have left of my family.'

Her host wipes her nose again with the rag and then fixes Maggie with a determined glare. 'Clement was a good man. He's not to blame for what happened last year. He wanted to do his duty that night.'

'But he didn't put out the storm warnings. It was his job –'

The old woman butts in. 'He would have done if he could.'

'So why didn't he?'

'Jed Hoskin interfered.'

Maggie sits forward on her seat. 'Hoskin? Why?'

'He said it was a false alarm. The fleet needed to go to sea. Honest men's livelihoods depended on it and families needed food on the table. A month earlier, Clement had put out the storm signals all right and proper, but that storm never came and a day's fishing was lost. Hoskin was furious. He said FitzRoy's weather forecasting was a sham and not to be trusted.'

'Did Hoskin come here?'

Nessa sneers. 'A man like Hoskin wouldn't be seen dead in Uppertown. When Clem went to put out the storm signs, Hoskin and that brute of his, George Moyle, were waiting for him.'

'Did Hoskin bribe him?'

Nessa Thomas's eyes slide to one side. 'Hoskin offered Clement more money than he'd seen in years – if he did what he was told. Best part of three month's pay. To do nothing! No signals. And, yes, Clem accepted. He had no choice. Moyle would have snapped his arms and legs like a twig if he'd refused.'

'And Hoskin did all this just so the fleet would put to sea?'

Nessa nods. 'It'd been a lean time. It weren't only Clem. Hoskin was pushing his skippers to catch fish any way they could.'

Maggie sits in silence, letting the old woman talk. 'Babbling like a moorland brook at Dozmary Pool,' her dear departed mother would have said, meandering at times but always coming back to her main course.

'Clem was mortified when he heard about the disaster

and the men lost. Felt he'd betrayed them, that he was worse than Judas Iscariot in this here Bible.' She snatches up a well-thumbed copy from a side table. 'People began pointing fingers at him, blaming him. And then George Moyle turns up here. Says Mr Hoskin has found a place where Clem can lie low until the hue and cry has died down. Moyle whisked him away in the middle of the night.' She pauses, bites her lip. Tears well in her creased eyes. 'I never saw him again.'

Maggie breaks her silence at last to ask a question. 'Do you have any idea where he might have been taken?'

'I went up to that bastard Moyle in town and asked where my husband was. He wouldn't tell me. Said Hoskin arranged everything. Then he walked away with that horrible laugh of his that ain't a laugh at all.'

Maggie grinds her teeth. 'Hoskin is a plague on this town. Mark my words there'll be a reckoning.' She stands. 'You've been wonderfully helpful, Nessa. I see who the real culprit is.'

The old woman blinks at her, resigned. 'There be nothing a young girl like you can do. Mr Hoskin is a powerful man with powerful friends.'

A few final warm words are exchanged and then Maggie strides with a new purpose to a waiting Jack who is shooing away a few cheeky boys.

'Did you learn anything of value from the old crone?' he asks.

'I learned plenty. And she's not an old crone. She's a widow who has lost everything.'

Jack's cheeks colour. 'Yes, yes, of course…'

Maggie gazes down the length of the potholed road leading back to St Branok. 'Where will Hoskin be at this time of day?'

'On the quayside, I believe.'

'Will you take me to him?'

Jack looks alarmed. 'That's not a good idea with Jed in his present foul mood. It would be downright dangerous –'

Maggie cuts him off, her tone impatient. 'Will you take me to him?'

'Why? What are you planning?'

'I'm going to confront him.'

'No. Maggie, this is madness.'

'If you are unwilling to help, I will walk.' She storms down the road, heading into an onshore breeze, her patience exhausted.

'Wait!' Jack gees up Betsy and follows until he is keeping pace alongside. 'Maggie, will you stop for one single moment so we can talk properly?'

She glares up at him. 'Will you take me to him or not?'

'Of course, I will take you. But tell me what …Mrs Thomas said.'

'Everything. She told me everything.'

Jack mutters an oath in exasperation. 'I haven't the slightest idea what you mean by that, but I can see there is no turning you.' He adds in a resigned tone, 'As usual.' He reaches down and with a firm hand helps her on to the seat next to him.

A confrontation with Hoskin is looming.

# CHAPTER FORTY-THREE

Maggie recounts the full story as they clatter down the hill to the quayside where the usual hustle and bustle prevails. Jack asks a few questions though he appears to have given up on any notion of persuading Maggie to alter course. On the quay, tradesmen and labourers are busy going back and forth, making deliveries, heaving supplies here and there. But, among the mass of purposeful humanity, of Jed Hoskin there is no sign.

'Wait here,' says Jack. 'I'll make enquiries.' He climbs down.

'Jack…' Maggie calls out.

'Yes?'

'Thank you.' Her tone is soft.

He smiles through his anxiety. 'This is…this is…' He stumbles on his words and gives up, disappearing into the crowd. A few minutes later, he returns with news but looking no happier. 'He's in The Mermaid. For a meeting.' He makes a last attempt to dissuade her. 'Maggie, this is wild… dangerous.'

Lips pursed, Maggie climbs down and sets off in the direction of the inn at a brisk pace, leaving Jack staring after her with Betsy's reins in his hand.

He slips a coin to a boy to mind the sometimes

recalcitrant horse and takes off in pursuit. By the time he catches up, he is out of breath. 'Maggie…Maggie, listen to me. Please. Hoskin will have his bruisers around him, Moyle and the rest, and they've all have downed a drink or two. It would be better if –'

'I'll confront him wherever I choose,' Maggie says, without so much as a sideways glance.

The Mermaid hoves into view in all its shabby glory. It's mid-afternoon, so it is quieter than usual. One of Hoskin's cronies is hanging around outside – a short, rotund man sitting on a beer barrel. He pulls himself to his feet when he sees Maggie and Jack.

Jack greets him warmly. 'Nate, we've come to see Mr Hoskin.'

The man's stare is cold. 'He's busy. Not to be disturbed.' He points a stubby, accusing finger at Maggie. 'Least of all by her.'

Maggie marches straight past him.

Nate twists and stumbles to block her way. 'Hey, wait! Are you deaf or summat, woman?'

Jack halts him with a firm hand on his shoulder. 'It's an urgent matter, Nate. I'll explain it to Mr Hoskin.'

The crony brushes Jack's hand away. 'She can't barge in.'

As the two exchange heated words, Maggie slips into the drinking house, blinking as her eyes adjust to the gloomy interior. To her right a few wrinkly old salts are at a table, shirt sleeves rolled up, playing cribbage and nursing pints which they will make last until early evening.

At the far end of the bar, George Moyle is slouched against a wall beside a closed door. Where Moyle is, Hoskin is rarely far away. Maggie strides towards him, her stomach churning.

Moyle straightens up, his dead eyes flickering. 'Look who we have here. Anything I can do you for, luv?' He makes a lewd gesture that provokes a snigger from the man standing next to him.

'I want to see Hoskin.'

'You might want to see him, but he won't want to waste his time with scum like you.'

She reaches for the door. 'I *will* see him.'

Moyle reaches out and wraps a muscular arm around Maggie's waist and pulls her towards him. 'Hold hard there, girl. You ain't going nowhere without my say-so. I said Mr 'oskin is busy. Now be a good girlie and do what I say.'

'Let go of me!' Her voice emerges as a shriek. Faces turn in their direction and then look away.

Maggie wriggles to get free, but a snickering Moyle holds her with ease.

A shout rings out. 'George, what the hell are you doing?' Jack runs towards them.

Moyle snarls. 'What's your problem, Jack?'

'Leave her alone!'

Moyle juts out his massive jaw in defiance but his grip on Maggie loosens. 'Have you lost your head for a bit of scrag end? Is that it?'

Maggie slips out of Moyle's grip and flings open the closed door, expecting to see Jed Hoskin in a smoky room, plotting dark deeds with dubious associates, but the only other occupant is Norah. She and Hoskin are deep in conversation sitting at a table but look up in shock when the door swings open and bangs against the wall.

Hoskin's eyes blaze. 'You? What the hell are you doing here? Get out.'

Norah's mouth slackens in surprise. 'Maggie…'

Maggie places her hands on the table and fixes Hoskin with an expression full of hate. 'I've come to speak to you about Clement Thomas.'

Hoskin stands and gestures to the door. 'Get out, damn you!'

Maggie stays right where she is, not moving an inch. 'I've just been to see Clement's widow.'

Hoskin steps out from behind the table. 'I'm not the sort of man who roughs up women but so help me I'll turf you out myself if I have to.'

Norah clutches his arm. 'Wait, Jed. Please. Maggie, what do you want to say?'

Hoskin snorts. 'She's ranting. Can't you see? She's a mad woman. An asylum's the best place for her.'

Outside the room, there's the sound of angry exclamations and a scuffle. Maggie turns to see Moyle swing a punch at Jack who ducks, leaving the blow to whistle over his head, and then thwacks the giant in the midriff. He might as well thump a lump of Cornish granite. Moyle's huge hands close on Jack's neck. Jack coughs and splutters, his face turning puce.

'Jed, stop them please.' Norah looks distraught.

'Moyle, let him go,' says Hoskin.

The stranglehold is released. Jack slides to the floor.

Maggie runs to Jack. His eyes flicker. He groans. .

She rounds on Hoskin. 'You brute.' And then turns to Norah, her mind suddenly clear on what to say. 'Your son is dead not because of Clem Thomas or because of me or my family.' She points a shaky figure at Hoskin. 'He's the one. He's responsible for the deaths of all who drowned that day.'

Hoskin barges forward. 'Don't listen to her. She's a liar. She'll say anything.' He raises his voice. 'Moyle! Get this stupid wench out of here.'

The giant reaches for Maggie.

'No! Wait!' Norah cries. 'Hear her out.'

Her shout halts even Moyle in his tracks. She gives Maggie the most penetrating of stares. 'What do you mean?'

Electricity sparks between the two women. Maggie nods at Hoskin. 'Old Clem didn't put out the storm signs because he stopped him. He was willing to do anything, take any risk, to make sure the fishing fleet put to sea. Old Clem was threatened and bribed not to do his duty.'

Hoskin finds his voice again. 'This is malicious Pascoe shit. They're a family of liars and cheats. I've never had anything but the best interests of the fishermen at heart. They're my people. I grew up with them.'

Maggie scowls at him. 'Yes, *your* people to do what you like with. Why, Jed, why? Was it all about the money? Were you that desperate? How can you live with yourself?' She turns back to Norah. 'If you don't believe me, speak with Clement Thomas's widow. She'll tell you everything.'

'Get her out!' Hoskin shouts – a raw, guttural shriek.

Moyle drags Maggie across the grimy, slate floor of The Mermaid, knocking aside a chair which is sent spinning across the floor. Something rips.

'Let go of me. My dress!'

'Where you're going you won't need no dress,' Moyle hisses through gritted teeth. 'You're coming with me. To get the lesson I've been aching to thump into you for a long time.'

Maggie screams. Nobody shows any sign of coming to her aid.

'Get off me!' Maggie twists and turns. The sharp sound of more ripping silences the murmurs of those watching. A gap has been torn in the back of her dress. Moyle chortles. He pulls harder. The gap grows.

'You've had this coming for a long time. This dress is coming off, luv. Might as well be here as upstairs. We'll all enjoy the sight of a bit of white flesh.'

Norah jumps forward. 'Jed, stop him! Stop him!'

The veneer of civility that Hoskin has cultivated with Norah is shattered. He shoves her into the back room. Norah saves herself from falling over by grabbing hold of the table. 'You'll not order me around, woman. Get back in there and stay there until I say otherwise. This is not for the likes of you to see. She's got it coming.' He slams the door and locks it.

Moyle is tugging Maggie like a rag doll towards a staircase, sniggering as he goes. 'What do you want me to do with her?'

'Do as you please,' says Hoskin.

There is a blur of movement and Moyle is knocked sideways by a hurtling body. The big man drops to one knee and releases Maggie. She twists away to see Jack grappling on the floor with Moyle.

'Get out of here. Run! I can't hold him for long,' he croaks to Maggie. Tendons and arteries bulge in his neck. He's straining to the limit. 'Go!' he screams.

Maggie seizes a copper flagon from a corner of the bar. It's empty but heavy enough. She smashes it across the back of Moyle's head. The giant drops like a stone.

Hoskin strides forwards. There is spittle in his thick beard. 'Whose blamed side are you on, Jack? I thought you were one of us, a fisherman through and through.'

Jack clambers to his feet. 'You're not a fisherman, Jed. You're a man who lives off fishermen. Who breaks and bends the rules. You're in it for the money. How many fishermen's lives have you sacrificed to get where you are?'

Hoskin's voice is cold. 'You're either for me or agin me,

Jack. Decide now. You've done well over the years, thanks in no small part to me.'

'Aye, I've done well but you've done well too. You've helped me to help yourself.'

'You owe me everything, Jack. Not least a tidy sum of money. Don't ever forget it. I'll bring you down if you go against me.'

'Damn you! Damn the money!'

There is movement on the floor. Moyle is starting to stir. His dull eyes flutter into life.

Jack reaches for Maggie's hand. 'Let's get out of here.'

Hoskin is apoplectic. 'You're finished in this town, Jack.' He's still ranting, his voice fading into the distance as they run out into the street.

From a girl selling flowers, Jack buys a woollen shawl for twice what it's worth. It is filthy and frayed but Maggie is nevertheless grateful when she wraps it over her shoulders to hide the white skin of her back exposed by the rip in her dress.

Jack leads the way down the street to his buggy. Thank heavens, it is where they left it, still tended by the lad. Jack gives him another coin and they climb aboard. He gees up Betsy and they trot away at a fast clip.

Maggie braces herself against the sway of the buggy with a firm hand on a rail. 'Where are we going?'

'We need to get away. Hoskin will gather his bruisers quickly enough and he'll be out for us. Our fight with him and Moyle will be the talk of St Branok by sunset. They'll be set on revenge. And God help us if they catch us.'

'Where can we go? Where can we hide?'

Jack shakes his head. 'We might as well have the plague. Nobody in St Branok will want anything to do with us.

Nobody's going to go against Hoskin. We will need to go further. I have some money.'

Maggie glances over her shoulder. There is no sign of pursuit. 'The parson. He's our best hope.'

# CHAPTER FORTY-FOUR

The buggy lurches around a bend at speed, its right-side wheels skittering across the muddy ground. Betsy is being pushed to the limit, but on this occasion she is game enough, having sensed her master's urgency. The elegant shape of The Vicarage appears between trees.

Jack hauls on the reins to halt his snorting horse. He glances at Maggie. 'You truly believe the parson will help us after all that has happened?'

Maggie feigns confidence. 'Yes, Parson Kellow is a good man. And, anyway, at the very least I need fresh clothes. I cannot spend my days in this.' She gestures at her ruined dress, smeared with the filth of The Mermaid's floor.

Mrs Ellis flings open the door and throws up her hands on seeing their dishevelment. 'Oh, my Lord, what happened? Have you been in an accident?'

Maggie ignores the question. 'Is the parson at home?'

'He's up at the headland, spending a quiet few hours at his hut. He had his painting instruments with him.'

Maggie performs a quick change into clean clothes and she and Jack set off to negotiate the muddy path to the headland. A blustery wind caresses their faces. When skittish clouds aren't concealing the sun there is a welcome warmth on their backs.

Jack glances at the patchy sky. 'The weather is brewing up again. It could be a rough night, not one for spending in a ditch. We will need shelter.'

A familiar lanky frame is perched on a stool outside the hut, a paint brush in hand and an easel in front of him. Kellow greets them with a smile. 'A fine day for creation,' he says. 'I couldn't resist seeking respite from my many duties to – '

Maggie butts in. 'Father, we need your help.'

Kellow's smile dies. 'How?'

'There has been a big falling out with Jed Hoskin,' says Jack. 'A fight in The Mermaid. Maggie was attacked by George Moyle.'

'Oh, my goodness!' Kellow examines Maggie with a troubled stare.

'We need shelter for a few days,' says Maggie. 'To make plans. And then we will be on our way and trouble you no further.'

Kellow's forehead creases. 'I expect it will all blow over in a couple of days. Hoskin is famous for blowing hot and cold.'

'Not this time,' says Jack. 'There's no future for us in St Branok while Hoskin is here. We will need to make a new life elsewhere, out of his clutches.'

The parson puts down his paintbrush. 'There is space for you at The Vicarage in the short term. And I have many contacts around the county who will be able to help.'

'Hoskin is intent on exacting revenge not only on us but anybody who helps us,' says Maggie. 'There will be a risk.'

Kellow waves a dismissive hand. 'He won't find out. Mr and Mrs Ellis are the souls of discretion.' He starts to put away his painting instruments. 'In any event, I doubt he would seek to exact revenge on a man of the cloth. Even his power has its earthly limitations.' He picks up the easel. 'Besides, I have heard it said that Hoskin has his own problems. Avenging an incident in The Mermaid is unlikely to be at the top of his priorities.'

'What problems?' says Maggie.

The parson taps his nose. 'I have my sources. Hoskin is not as rock solid as he might appear. There is talk of him owing substantial amounts to creditors. He is reverting to his old ways of smuggling to make ends meet, hence the ill-fated sailing of the good ship *Endeavour*.' He lowers his voice, though there is no one else to hear. 'And there are whispers of further expeditions.'

Jack nods. 'I had heard of a forthcoming venture. Do you have any knowledge as to what kind?'

'Little more than murmurs though I believe them to be sound. Whisky and rum are his preferred contraband. He has contacts to get it to London. It will fetch a small fortune on the streets of Whitechapel.'

The parson takes a wistful gaze at the landscape . 'The best light of the day has passed for painting. I will accompany you down to The Vicarage and make arrangements with Mr and Mrs Ellis for your stay.'

'You are more than generous,' says Maggie. 'How can I ever thank you enough?'

Kellow waves dismissively. 'It is the least I can do in the circumstances. I pray that, in time, you'll be free to return to St Branok.'

At The Vicarage, the parson has a whispered word with Mr and Mrs Ellis in the kitchen. He emerges a few minutes later with assurances that all is well.

'Mr Ellis suggested that we accommodate you in bedrooms at the back,' says Kellow. 'It is quieter there and you are less likely to attract the attention of any of my regular visitors. Please excuse me. I have evensong to prepare for at the church.' He limps up a few stairs before pausing to add, 'When I return, I'd be delighted if you could join me for supper.'

Mr Ellis shows Jack to a small box room and then helps Maggie move her few possessions from the much larger, bright bedroom she previously occupied to another small room, which is close but, for propriety's sake, not too close to Jack's. A line of pine trees outside means that both rooms remain dark and gloomy, whatever the time of day.

By the time they return to the hallway, the parson is preparing to leave in his buggy. He pulls a rueful smile. 'Your rooms are less opulent than I'd hope for valued guests, but they have the benefit of not being overlooked.'

'Would you prefer that we remain in our rooms during our stay?' says Maggie.

'That shouldn't be necessary. Please leave Mr and Mrs Ellis to deal with any callers and stay out of sight though I'm not expecting anybody today.'

Maggie rests a grateful hand on his arm. 'I don't know where we'd be without you.'

'A friend loveth at all times,' Kellow says giving her a wry grin and then, with a flick of the reins, setting off at a lazy trot.

# CHAPTER FORTY-FIVE

Kellow returns several hours later at a more frenetic pace. Maggie, who is in the sitting room with Jack, looks out to see Kellow clambering down from the buggy as fast as his bad leg will allow and then limp at speed towards the house. The horse is blowing hard with froth at her nostrils.

'Uh-ho, something's up,' says Jack. They pace out into the hallway to find a troubled Kellow. 'We need to talk,' he says and ushers them back into the sitting room. Once inside, he is careful to close the door.

He turns to them. 'I had somewhat underestimated the impact of your *incident* at The Mermaid. Hoskin's men are scouring the town for you both. Woe betide anyone who gets in their way.'

Jack steps forward. 'We have no wish to put you at risk. We should leave immediately.'

Kellow holds up a restraining hand. 'Do not worry on my account. My offer of a refuge remains but it might be best, for the sake of us all, if you stay in your rooms as you suggested.'

Jack shakes his head. 'No, no, we will have a few hours rest and then be away in the early hours.'

Kellow points to the window where the flecks of rain drizzle down the glass. 'It's not a night for travel. I have contacts away from here who will be able to help you on your journey if I can get word to them.'

Jack will have none of it. 'If the weather is bad, it will be the perfect time for leaving St Branok unobserved. Nobody in their right senses will be out on such a night. I will need to return to my home for money and a few possessions. But on a God-forsaken night such as this I should be able to slip in there without attracting attention.'

Parson Kellow interjects. 'Hoskin's men are everywhere in St Branok tonight, regardless of the weather. If he's half as cunning as I give him credit for, your home will be under watch. Hoskin's bullyboys will be waiting.'

'The parson's right,' says Maggie. 'See sense, Jack. Things should have quietened down if we wait a few days.'

At last, Jack nods in grudging acceptance. 'Very well, we will wait.' He takes hold of Kellow's hand in both of his own. 'We will cause you the minimum of fuss, sir. I cannot thank you enough.'

A shiver runs down Maggie's spine as she stares out into the darkness, imagining men turning St Branok upside down to find them and their grisly fate if they fall into Hoskin and Moyle's clutches. Death would be the least of their worries.

# CHAPTER FORTY-SIX

Days pass. Christmas and the New Year come and go. The weather remains foul. Maggie and Jack wait in the gloomy light of their tiny box rooms for Parson Kellow to bring them better news. Their days are broken by meals delivered by Mrs Ellis. She is scrupulous with her timing. Breakfast is at nine prompt, lunch at one and supper, usually taken with Kellow in the parlour, is at ten. The parson has a liking for staying up late and then, when duties allow, sleeping in until mid-morning. The waiting frays their nerves. Their impatience grows, especially for Jack who is unable to share Maggie's love of books. Propriety ensures that time spent in the intimacy of each other's rooms is short and any discussion conducted at a distance. A splendid Christmas Day meal prepared by Mrs Ellis with all the trimmings, taken with Kellow and the housekeepers, is one of the few brighter moments of their confinement.

After almost two weeks of persistent winds and rain, the sun makes a most welcome reappearance. Parson Kellow returns late afternoon from his rounds, bright-eyed with better news. 'Hoskin is out of town for a few days with Moyle and a few other bully boys,' he says. 'It looks like they've given up the search for you.'

Maggie tears herself away from *Great Expectations*, the

most recent work of the celebrated Charles Dickens. 'Where have they gone?'

Kellow shrugs. 'Nobody knows. Or, at least, they claim ignorance. It'll be another of Hoskin's smuggling expeditions, I'll be bound – a big one to make up for his losses with the *Endeavour*. In any event, I have been assured that they won't be back until tomorrow at the earliest.'

'So tonight's the night,' says Jack rubbing his hands together, his usual buoyancy restored. 'We can make good our escape long before Hoskin sets foot back in St Branok.'

'There might still be some of Hoskin's bullies on the lookout,' says Kellow. 'Borrow some of my clothes. With a little adjustment we are not too dissimilar in size. A casual passer-by will assume I am out on my rounds, visiting a needy parishioner.'

'We'll be forever in your debt, Father,' says Jack.

They fall silent as a gust of wind and a smattering of rain rattles The Vicarage's windows. Kellow stares out. 'It looks like the better weather was a brief interlude.'

'All to the good,' insists Jack. 'The streets will be deserted. We'll have a clear run.'

And so it is that, as the clock in Kellow's hallway chimes midnight, Maggie and Jack say the fondest of farewells to the parson.

'On a dark night, you would pass for me to a casual glance,' says the parson with satisfaction as he surveys Jack in the familiar Kellow attire of a claret-coloured coat, blue fisherman's jersey, sea boots and a pink brimless hat. He hands Maggie, who has a shawl draped over her head as a rudimentary disguise, a scrap of paper. It contains a list of Cornish households who will offer them shelter. 'Tell them Parson Kellow sent you. It will be enough.' He points to a name at the top of the list. 'I have managed to get word to these people confirming your worthy nature. I'd advise going there first. They are fine, God-fearing folk.'

He grasps Maggie's hand in both of his own. 'I almost forgot to tell you, in the heat of the moment. Lady Kendall told me today that she has made her own enquiries regarding the theft allegations levelled against you and decided they are malicious and false. She would like to see you again when you are next available.' He turns to Jack. 'May God go with you and guide your hand.'

They depart into the turbulent night with a final wave and the crack of a whip. The hood of the buggy is scant protection against the torrential rain as Maggie and Jack negotiate the pockmarked road back to St Branok.

At last they reach the outskirts. The town seems dead with only an occasional light at a window breaking the darkness. Through empty, soaking streets they trot at a pace brisk but steady enough not to attract unwanted attention. Above the rush of the gale comes the roar of waves crashing against the coast. The few people they see take no interest in them, being more concerned about sheltering from the wind and rain.

Jack brings a snorting Betsy to a halt in a storehouse behind his home used for fishing gear. 'It's safest for you to wait here,' he says to Maggie. 'Hoskin might have left a lookout. I'll be as quick as I can.'

Maggie jumps down. 'I'm coming with you. If there is anybody waiting, then it is best that two of us face him together.'

'I refuse to put you at risk – '

'I am already at risk. What will become of me if something happens to you?'

Jack puffs. 'I must insist…'

Maggie squares up to him. 'You may insist as much as you like, but I am coming.' There is a pause and then she says, 'We are wasting time.'

She follows a crouching Jack along an alleyway to a rear door, partially hidden by a scraggy gorse bush. He uses his shoulder to heave it open. It gives way suddenly and bangs back against the wall. Jack lurches forward with Maggie close behind. They are in the walled back yard of his house.

Jack again applies his strength and weight, this time to force a rickety window. He strains. There is the crack of wood snapping and the window creaks open. More unwanted noise. They wait, hold their breath listening. Have they been heard?

Mercifully, the house remains silent and dark.

Jack climbs inside and offers a helping hand to Maggie. She negotiates the window ledge by hitching up her skirts in a manner which in any other circumstances would be considered most unbecoming.

'The housekeeper is a deep sleeper and her bedroom is at the far end of the house,' Jack whispers. 'We should be able to get what we need and be on our way without disturbing her.'

His assurances prove optimistic. A croaky voice shouts from upstairs. 'Who's there? Who's there?'

'Mrs Madison, it's me. Jack.'

'Mr Treloare? What in heaven's name are you doing here in the dead of night? Any number of men have been round here asking after you, sir.'

They slip into the hallway to see an older woman dressed in a white nightgown bent almost double at the top of the stairs, staring with weak eyes into the darkness. She is clutching a candle with a flickering flame, casting long shadows.

Jack talks in calm, measured tones. 'I have to leave St Branok for a time. I have come for a few belongings and will then be on my way. I apologise for frightening you.'

'You're going away? At this dead hour?'

'Unfortunately, circumstances forced a clandestine visit at night. I'll be relying on your good self to ensure the house remains in good order whilst I'm away.' He takes a deep breath. 'Rest assured, I will return.'

Mrs Madison steadies herself with the help of the bannister. 'When Mr Treloare? When?'

'When the time is right. I have no other choice.'

Her rounded shoulders sag in acceptance. 'May God go with you, sir – '

Her well wishes are cut short by banging on the front door.

Maggie grabs Jack's sleeve. 'They've found us.'

# CHAPTER FORTY-SEVEN

They strain their ears, listening. How many? Outside, there is a murmuring exchange between two men. The voices are too faint to hear what is being said, though the urgency of tone is unmistakable.

The hammering on the front door is repeated, echoing through the house. At the top of the stairs, old Mrs Madison is shaking.

'We need to get out the back way,' says Maggie.

Jack shakes his head. 'Hoskin's men will have surrounded the place. We're going to have to fight our way out. I have a pistol upstairs. George Moyle will think again when he's staring down the barrel of a firearm.'

He races up the stairs, ushers the elderly housekeeper back to her bedroom with soothing words and then disappears down a corridor. Maggie waits whilst he rummages in an upstairs room, flinching when there is yet more hammering on the door. Will they try to break it down? It looks sturdy enough to withstand most assaults, though maybe not from the battering ram which is George Moyle. He could no doubt tear the wood apart with his shovel-sized hands.

The banging stops. To be replaced by a raised voice. This time Maggie catches the fragments of a sentence. A name. 'Jack, Jack…' It sounds nothing like the demanding tone of

Hoskin or any of his cronies. Keeping to the shadows, Maggie sidles to a window in the sitting room which looks out on the front door. She sees two dark shadows. Men. Average height. One of them speaks and for the first time she hears a complete sentence. 'I told you he wasn't here. We best be going.' At last, she puts a name to the voice.

She runs back to the front door and opens it wide. 'Goron, what brings you here at this hour?'

'Is Jack at home? There's bin a shout. A clipper's in trouble. There ain't much time. It might already be too late.'

Jack appears behind her, clutching the pistol and having changed into his own clothes. 'Goron, I'm here. How bad is it?'

'Bad as it gets. She be on a leeward tide out beyond Silvery Cove. The rocks might already have claimed her.'

'What in God's name is a clipper doing out there in this weather?'

'It's the *Rarotonga*, sir,' he says, as if that explains everything.

'Another of Jed Hoskin's vessels?' Jack says, his voice edged with disbelief.

'Aye.'

'The damned fool,' mutters Jack. 'Do we have a full crew to launch the lifeboat?'

'Everybody's out gathering as many as they can.'

'Get back to the boathouse, Goron, and get everything ready. I'll join you as soon as I can.'

'Aye, sir.' The tap of their footsteps on the cobbled streets fades into the night.

Jack turns to Maggie. 'Stay with Mrs Madison until I've returned from the rescue. She's had a terrible fright. She'll welcome your company.'

Maggie faces him with hands on hips. 'I'm not going to

cower in your home in a warm bed while brave souls risk their lives at sea. You'll need every pair of hands you can get to launch the lifeboat in this weather.'

'There is no time to argue. I implore you, just this once do what I ask.'

'I'm coming.'

Jack shakes his head. 'Your bravery is bordering on rank foolishness.'

They run through the darkened streets past sleeping households and arrive at the boathouse, breathless and soaked to the skin. A cluster of men and women are waiting, uncaring of the wind and rain. Goron hands Jack a cork lifejacket. 'Thank the Lord you're here. We've got together as many as we can.'

Jack glances around. 'I'd expected more. Where is everybody?'

'Some boats went to sea this morning when it was calmer. They were desperate but when it turned bad again, many of 'em ran for cover in nearby ports and coves.'

'Do we have enough to launch?' says Jack.

Goron hesitates. 'It's a scratch crew but I think we can manage.' He reels off a list of names. Maggie stops him at one name. 'Young Curnow Hawkins? Curnow's little more than a boy.'

'He's a big, strong lad,' insists Goron. 'Reached his sixteenth-year last month. He's a regular hand aboard the *Neptune*.'

A hollow dread sparks in Maggie's gut. The death of young Jowan Bray still haunts her. 'Jack, you can't allow – '

A muscle tightens in Jack's jaw. 'Goron's right. Curnow knows the sea. He's been out in high seas many a time.'

'This is more than high seas.'

Jack waves a hand to fend off Maggie's concerns. 'We don't have time for talk. Curnow is able and willing. We need him and he understands the risks as well as any man. There are souls out there desperate for help.' He strides to the boat. 'Let's get her down to the water.'

Clenching teeth, blowing hard, the men and women begin the gruelling job of hauling the *Jowan Bray* out of the boathouse down the slipway and over the wooden skids. They are soon soaked to the skin from rain and sweat. Feet slip and slide in the soft sand at the top of the beach.

'Heave! Heave! Keep going,' shouts Jack.

His words are eclipsed by the hiss and thunder of crashing breakers as the boat edges closer to the water.

On they go. On and on. Puffing. Gasping.

Ahead, a wave, flecked with froth, towers above them before crashing down on the rippled sand. Maggie licks her lips and tastes the salt of the Atlantic. They heave again and inch closer, their arms burning, their breaths coming in gasps. A surge of water rushes up the sands.

Jack calls them to a halt. 'We can't launch here.'

'There's no other way,' Goron shouts.

With the sleeve of his jacket, Jack wipes away the water streaming down his face. 'It's too dangerous. We won't help those poor souls on the *Rarotonga* by sacrificing ourselves.'

Maggie pushes forward. 'Trencreek Cove is the best sheltered when the wind is from the nor' west like now. My dad always said so.'

Goron shakes his head. 'That's three miles over Polgurrian Hill. We'd take half a night hauling her there.'

'With horses, the journey might be possible,' says Jack. 'Charlie Brough's beasts have the strength to do it. And they're calm and steady enough. Go and wake him. Tell him it's a matter of life or death.'

Goron sets off at a pace remarkable for a man of his years. The others haul the lifeboat back up the beach and onto its carriage. A small figure rushes into the boathouse, wrapped in a heavy shawl. Norah. Sucking air, a picture of distress.

'Why haven't you launched?'

'We can't, not here,' says Jack. 'Tide and wind are all wrong. If we're going to launch, it will need to be at Trencreek.'

'That's impossible.'

Maggie grips Norah's shaking shoulder. 'It can be done. Charlie Brough's horses have been sent for.'

'The ship in trouble…which is it?

'The *Rarotonga*,' says Jack. 'She's owned by Jed.'

Norah gasps. 'He's aboard.'

'What in God's name is he doing out there?'

'He said he had to personally oversee the safe delivery of an important cargo. George Moyle is with him.'

The clip-clop of hooves halts the conversation. Goron appears with Charlie Brough and his eldest son, Kenwyn, leading two muscular beasts. They look in fine condition with powerful limbs and gleaming hides.

'My horses can be of service, I understand,' Charlie says to Jack. 'You'll not find a stronger team this side of the Tamar. They'll move heaven and earth if we need 'em to.'

The mighty animals are hitched up to the lifeboat's carriage, the milling crowd organised into a semblance of a team. Near enough three dozen men and women take their places on two ropes either side of the whinnying horses.

At a final nod from Jack, Charlie shouts above the wind,

'Go!' and then cracks his whip. The slack is taken up, leathers squeak and groan. 'Go!' Charlie shouts again, louder.

At last, with a snort, they begin moving, slowly at first, gathering momentum. The procession eases past the boathouse with carriage wheels creaking to join the pale ribbon of road leading out along the coast. The sharp summit of Polgurrian Hill looms up when the scudding clouds part to reveal a half-moon. The incline steepens. The pace slows to a crawl. Maggie, hauling on the right-side rope, struggles for breath, her legs and arms shaking with fatigue. The road ahead stretches endlessly upwards.

The volunteers are weakening and Jack must call a halt despite knowing that starting again on a hill will be doubly difficult. Wooden chocks are placed under the trailer's wheels, stopping it from rolling backwards. Maggie and the men and women near her bend over in exhaustion, fighting to recover their strength and their breath.

'We need to get going again,' Maggie gasps to Jack.

'Let's give everybody a mite longer to gather themselves,' says Jack. 'The last bit is steepest and narrowest.' He looks over at Charlie, who is calming his two horses. There is spittle and snot at their noses and mouths. 'Can they do it?' Jack asks.

'There's life in 'em yet,' mutters Charlie.

A few minutes pass. The wind continues to rise. The rain intensifies. The volunteers find fresh vigour. At last, they are ready to go again.

'Heave!' Jack screams. Backs are bent to take up the strain. Feet scrabble for grip on the streaming, muddy road. 'Heave!' he shouts again. At first there is no movement but then the crack of Charlie's whip again rings out. The horses strain and the wheels of the trailer turn grudgingly. They edge forward, every yard a gasping torture.

On they go. On and on and on. Inch by inch.

Just short of the summit they are forced to stop once more. At a signal from Jack, men and women flop to the ground. The gale is strongest here, billowing their sopping clothes but the wind is now at their backs and, for once, is a friend rather than an enemy.

The rest is all too brief. In no time Jack is calling them into line again. The response is slow, reluctant. Some rise but a few remain sprawled on the ground. Jack calls out again, more harshly. And this time even the most knackered souls drag themselves to their feet.

The load is taken up. They push forward. As the incline eases so does the effort and the breathing.

Nearly there! Nearly there! Maggie grits her teeth and renews her efforts to get this accursed load up and over the hill.

At last, they crest the rise. Jack calls out, this time with a ring of triumph, and every man and woman again sags to the ground, exhausted and ecstatic in equal measure.

Jack wipes spittle and rain away from his mouth. 'We still need to get down there.' He points at the pale horseshoe-shaped cove far below, flanked by dark cliffs. Trencreek Cove, bordered by a mercifully calm sea, is visible until the driving rain closes in again.

Jack claps Charlie Brough on the shoulder. 'Your horses have been a Godsend. You'll not want to keep them out in these conditions any longer than is necessary. We can take it from here.'

Charlie rubs a hand over his wet face. 'Men's lives are at stake. Glad to help.'

The horses are unhitched from the carriage and men and women take their places on the ropes once more. 'One more effort,' Jack calls out. 'Take the strain. It's downhill all the way.'

The lifeboat sets off down the gathering slope, held back by exhausted souls many of whom are calling on their last reserves. There are grunts. There are curses. There are cries of fear as feet slip and slide and hands, already raw from hauling the boat up the hill, grip the ropes, this time to prevent the boat careering downhill, out of control.

A woman falls. A man behind her trips. The boat gathers speed. 'Hold her! Hold her!' Jack shouts as they fight against the pull of a steep section. The boat slews sideways across the lane. A sturdy oak tree brings it to a shuddering halt. A scream of pain goes up. Maggie runs forward to find the youngster Curnow Hawkins lying near the bow, clutching his leg, his face deathly pale.

Maggie bends down. 'Stay still. Let me have a look.' The leg is at an unnatural angle and clearly broken.

Jack hastens over. 'We are almost down.' Trencreek Cove is little more than a stone's throw away.

'Who can take his place on the boat?' Maggie asks.

Jack surveys the people pulling themselves upright after the fall. 'We'll find a willing hand, I'm sure.'

Maggie stares at him aghast. 'Send somebody out with no experience? In this weather? Be sensible, Jack.'

'We cannot stay kicking our heels here while the crew of the *Rarotonga* die at sea.'

'Let me take Curnow's place.'

Jack regards her with scepticism. 'You?'

'Haven't I proved my worth?'

Jack sucks his lower lip. 'I…I don't know.'

'Trust me, Jack. Please. I can do this.'

Jack contemplates the darkness of the ocean and shakes

his head. 'Let's get her down to the water and then we'll decide.'

An older woman is left to stay with Curnow and a boy is sent back to St Branok so that transport can be arranged to carry the injured lad to Dr Lander.

The final part of the journey is completed without further mishap and soon the *Jowan Bray* is riding in knee-deep water on the shoreline. Such is the shelter provided by the formidable Polgurrian Hill, the waters close to the shore are as placid as a lake, the gale no longer snatching at the rescuers' hair and clothes.

Jack turns to his scratch crew. 'Take your positions, lads. It's going to be a rough ride and there's no time to waste.'

Maggie touches him on the shoulder. 'Well?'

Jack turns. 'Well what?'

'Am I coming or not?'

He stares at her, flushed with exertion. 'I'm not prepared to risk the life of a young woman on such a dangerous expedition.'

'Who then? I am a better swimmer than many of your crew.' She leans inside the lifeboat to take the cork life jacket intended for young Curnow Hawkins and, undaunted by Jack's objections, proceeds to put it on. To looks of disbelief from the crew, she clambers aboard.

# CHAPTER FORTY-EIGHT

Goron hastens over. 'Jack, what's going on? A woman aboard again? You saw what bad luck she brought us last time – all those poor souls from the *Endeavour* taken by the depths.'

'We need an extra pair of hands, Goron, and Maggie is as capable at sea as any man here.'

'Jack, this be madness, it be wrong.'

'I'm coxswain. It's my decision. I'll account for it later if need be.'

'Jack, please –'

'There are lives to be saved and not a moment to waste. Let's get her out on the water,' Jack growls.

The difficult conversation stutters to a halt. A muttering Goron takes his place at the bow.

A group of women, including Norah, ease the boat out further. She looks up at Maggie, her eyebrows furrowed. 'Be careful,' she says, her voice firm but low.

Maggie manages a grim smile. 'I will.'

'We have wronged you, Maggie. I have wronged you. Come back. I will do everything I can to make it up to you.' Norah's voice cracks. A shaft of moonlight lights up the tears streaming down her face.

The crew bend their backs to their oars and the boat slips out of the cove, bobbing easily on a smooth sea. Maggie hauls her own oar as hard as she can, trying to ignore the pulsing agony from palms and fingers rubbed raw afresh by the coarse rope used to pull the lifeboat up and over Polgurrian Hill. Recent wounds have opened up again and are oozing with blood and pus.

The first snatching gusts of wind hit them as the *Jowan Bray* surges out of the shelter of the cove into the turbulent open sea. But the wind is blowing from behind them for the most part and they make good headway, the lifeboat riding easily on the heaving ocean.

They cross the bay and glimpse a rocky headland, visible in the darkness because of the white surf breaking at its base. Of the clipper, there is no sign. Where is it? On they row. Jack turns the boat into the wind to round the headland and they are hammered by the full force of the gale and the spray.

Jack, searching the darkness with eyes screwed half closed, urges them onward. 'Keep going, lads. Pull strong. Pull hard. Let's keep a good speed.'

Maggie struggles to grip an oar made slippery by sea froth and the ooze seeping from her broken hands.

A flash of lightning reveals mountainous waves and treacherous rocks. They battle on, the hiss and wash of the ocean now broken by the sound of rolling thunder reminiscent of artillery on a battlefield as waves expend their power and fury on cliffs and beaches.

Another strike of lightning splits the night sky. Jack calls out at the tiller. 'I saw her…the *Rarotonga*…her masts…up ahead. Keep going!'

Weary limbs push and pull. Another wave, the biggest so far, crashes over them. And then another. A rearing swell of water hits from the port side. The boat heels over, the gunwale dipping to within an inch of the water.

They're going over!

But no.

The boat recovers, rights herself.

They push onwards.

Jack points. 'I see men on deck.' He squints. 'Nearly there, lads. We're going to leeward of her. It'll be easier –'

His words are interrupted by a new sound – the screech of tortured timber breaking on rocks.

'There isn't much time,' yells Jack. 'I'll bring us in as close as I can…'

They turn to starboard. Maggie twists to see the *Rarotonga* for the first time. The clipper is bigger than she expected, much bigger than the *Endeavour*. It towers over them, a stricken giant, impaled on rocks. A cluster of souls are gathered on deck.

In the lee of the great vessel, the sea is calmer, the wind muted.

'Easy…easy,' Jack yells.

The lifeboat edges in closer, rising and falling in the swell while the dying *Rarotonga* sits there, barely moving. The two vessels are close enough for the terrified faces on board to be visible. Maggie looks for Jed Hoskin and George Moyle but there is no sign of either of them. Perhaps they aren't aboard, after all, and the two of them are safely sozzled in a distant inn waiting for news of this most important cargo.

'Get ready. We're going in!' shouts Jack. 'Prepare to receive –'

More shrieks of timber and metal rent the night air. The *Rarotonga* is raised from her resting place and then crashes down again. The vessel heels over. The men on board are thrown off their feet and slide down the sloping deck. Some save themselves by clinging on to any solid object they can lay their hands on. A small figure is hurled overboard and disappears beneath the waves. A head pops up.

'A boy…in the water,' screams Jack. 'Haul hard, lads.'

Goron is bracing himself at the bow with a coil of rope which he hurls into the sea. It falls short. He tries again. Pulls it back. Nothing. He waits at the bow, scanning the water for long seconds. 'He's gone,' he says. 'The boy's gone. God rest 'is soul.'

The *Rarotonga* leans over at an absurd angle, on the brink of rolling over and crashing down on the tiny lifeboat.

Cupping his hands, Jack screams at the top of his voice to the men of the *Rarotonga*. 'We'll throw you a line. Get ready.'

There is an answering shout and Goron, bracing himself against the surge and swell of the ocean, hurls his coil of rope again. Miraculously, it lands on the deck of the stricken vessel and is secured by frantic hands.

Jack yells out, 'Jump for it and swim to us. One by one. We can't get in closer.'

A man hurls himself into the water. With flailing arms and legs, he thrashes his way over to the lifeboat. Waves wash over him again and again but each time they think he is lost, his head bobs clear. The man grabs hold of Goron's outstretched hand and is hauled aboard to lie face down on the deck of the lifeboat, gasping air. One saved at least.

Maggie helps the man into a seating position. In the pale light of dawn, his face is a ghostly white. Jack bends down. 'How many aboard?'

The crewman slumps there, shaking, head bowed, unable to speak.

Maggie addresses him in softer tones. 'How many crewmen?'

'Maybe twenty left,' the man mutters at last and then stops to puke a lungful of sea water. She wraps a woollen blanket around his shoulders and he sits there, shivering, his teeth chattering.

'Twenty…that's a hefty load to take,' Goron yells.

'We can do it,' says Jack before murmuring, 'And, in truth, I doubt we'll need to.'

More crewmen attempt the desperate journey. Ten more make it. Eight are washed away, never to be seen again.

Maggie surveys the *Rarotonga*'s empty deck for long seconds. She screams out and points. 'There!'

A giant figure clambers out of a hatch and stumbles to the gunwale. Even at a distance in appalling weather, the man is unmistakable.

George Moyle.

'Jump for it!' shouts Jack.

Moyle's broad face has a bleak expression. 'I can't swim.'

'Use the line to haul yourself over to us. There's no other way.'

Moyle shakes his head and retreats a few steps. Something cracks and groans above him. He looks up. Too late. The mizzenmast crashes down onto the deck and across him.

A smaller figure, who has been crouching near the stern in the shadow of the deckhouse, races over to the fallen giant.

'It's Hoskin,' shouts Maggie. She points. 'Look. Jed Hoskin.'

'Jump, Jed, jump!' Jack screams into the wind.

Hoskin waves at them frantically. 'Get in closer. It's too far.'

Jack shakes his head. 'We're as close as we can get. You'll have to leap for it and trust to God. Is Moyle dead?'

'His legs are trapped.'

'Can you help him?'

'Ten men couldn't move that mast.'

The *Rarotonga* is like a rearing cliff above them, creaking in the surge and swell of the ocean. If the clipper capsizes, they are all lost.

Hoskin leaps. He disappears into the water.

Jack points. 'There! He's there!'

High above them, the *Rarotonga* leans over to an angle that defies gravity. 'She's going over,' yells Goron. 'We need to pull back, Jack. She'll take us with her.'

'Wait.'

Hoskin's balding head bursts clear of the sea a handful of yards away. He reaches out with a desperate hand but is pushed sideways away from the rope connecting the lifeboat to the *Rarotonga*. 'Don't…don't leave me!' he splutters. Goron hurls another rope towards him. It falls short.

A wave catches Hoskin, sucks him under. He doesn't reappear.

'He's gone,' says Goron, staring at empty water. He glances upwards at the dying Rarotonga. 'We need to get out of here.'

The crew get ready to haul on their oars. Jack holds up a restraining hand. 'A moment more…we need to be sure there are no others.'

'Jack, we can't wait no more.' The hulk of the *Rarotonga* creaks and shifts again.

At last, Jack accepts the inevitable. He nods. 'Let's get home, lads.'

Goron cuts the lifeline connecting the *Jowan Bray* to the *Rarotonga*. Legs are braced. Backs are bent. A pull on the oars starts to carry them clear.

A grey dawn is breaking, revealing the full horror of the

plight of the shattered clipper, eviscerated by rocks. The lifeboat builds momentum. Something catches Maggie's eye, a movement. Not the surge and swell of the restless ocean. Something else.

She jumps up and comes close to pitching herself in the sea. 'Stop! I saw him.'

The lifeboat crew freeze as if caught in a photograph. 'What?' says Jack.

'Hoskin. He's still alive.' She points. 'Over there! Over there!'

'He can't be,' yells Goron.

'We're going about,' yells Jack.

The lifeboat turns. Ahead, a head bobs up and then disappears again. 'There! There!' Maggie screams.

The ocean froth parts to reveal the face of Jed Hoskin a few inches below the surface. His eyes are wide open, staring at Maggie. Can he still be alive? Yes. He blinks and reaches out with a clutching hand. Maggie thrusts her hand into the water. Hoskin's outstretched hand locks onto hers. She braces herself and pulls. Hoskin's head and shoulders burst clear. A long-held breath erupts from his mouth in an explosion of spit and sea water.

He uses his free hand to grab hold of the side of the lifeboat and pulls himself up. They lock gazes. His jaw drops.

'You…' he gasps.

Maggie extricates her hand from his frantic grip and thrusts her arms under his shoulders to take him in a desperate embrace and heave him aboard but he's too heavy.

'Help her!' shouts Jack.

Hands reach down. One grabs Hoskin by the collar and pulls.

A mighty swell takes the lifeboat by the stern. The boat

is upended, her bow dips. Maggie is thrown off balance. Her head hammers against something sharp. She lies dazed in the bottom of the boat, vaguely aware of bilge water sloshing around her. The *Jowan Bray* rights herself thanks to a combination of robust engineering and fine seamanship. Two of the *Rarotonga*'s crew place Maggie back on a seat, steadying her until she recovers her senses.

'Where's Hoskin?' she says when her vision clears.

Jack, clutching the tiller, shrugs. 'Gone.'

'He was almost aboard.'

'Swept away. There was no saving him. Goron threw him a line but couldn't hold him.'

Maggie glances over at Goron who is staring out into the bleak seascape, his ruddy face unreadable.

A squealing sound, like a dying animal, causes them to look up at the once-fine ship being pulled apart on the rocks. 'She'll be firewood by nightfall,' Jack mutters. 'Let's get out of here.'

With a will, the crew pulls hard, desperate to put distance between themselves and the *Rarotonga*. The clipper is in her death throes, grinding and smashing herself to pieces. And then there is movement on deck. A giant staggers clear, having somehow extricated himself from the mess of broken mast and rigging.

Maggie screams out. 'It's Moyle. He's free.' But even as she says this, the Rarotonga shudders and then crashes down on her side. When the spray clears, there is no sign of him.

The lifeboat crew scan the waves for long seconds until Jack declares, 'There's nothing more we can do. Let's get home, boys.'

Oars dip into the turbulent water and they head for safety. In his rich tone, Goron starts a Cornish folk song. 'As

I was a-walking down by the seashore, where the wind and the waves and the billows do roar…'

And every voice joins in.

# CHAPTER FORTY-NINE

Dusk has fallen. Piles of driftwood from the wreckage of the *Rarotonga* have been collected for a bonfire at Silvery Cove. Flames cast long shadows on the teeming figures on the beach as they hurry back and forth like ants. Excited voices ring out, many of them slurred by drink. Rich pickings are there for the taking and every able-bodied man, woman and child in St Branok has turned out to scour the beach. The wind has subsided to a breeze.

A small group of people watch from the cliffs above. 'The bounty of the sea,' Jack says. 'The *Rarotonga* has already yielded more than twenty crates of the best Irish whisky, so I'm told.' He licks his lips as if savouring a dram. 'Half of St Branok will be three sheets to the wind for the next few days.'

'They sound so happy,' says Maggie, puzzled. 'But men have died. And a fine ship has been destroyed.'

Norah stands beside her, her head bowed. 'They've learned to take whatever windfalls the Atlantic offers.' She adds, as if it makes the drunken celebrations more palatable, 'Most of the men lost weren't St Branok folk.'

Maggie turns to stare at her. 'What about Jed Hoskin and George Moyle?'

'There was no love for Moyle in this town. He was a bully, as you know better than most.'

'And Jed?'

Norah shrugs. 'He was a liar and a murderer. It just took longer for people to realise it.' She pauses and then murmurs, 'Me included.'

'What will happen to his businesses? St Branok relies on them.'

'They were already on the rocks, like the *Rarotonga*,' says Jack. 'Rest assured, there's no shortage of ambitious people ready to take Hoskin's place. St Branok will survive without Jed Hoskin. The pilchards will come again and we'll be ready to catch them.'

'And what about you? What will you do?' Maggie asks Norah.

'I have some gifts from Jed which I can sell. That will keep me going for a while.'

'And when those run out?'

'I managed without Jed Hoskin before, and I'll do so again.' She clutches Maggie's hand and gazes into her eyes with a solemn expression. 'I want us to be friends. We were once great friends, and we can be so again.

Maggie can offer an assurance no firmer than 'I hope so.' Can she ever forgive Norah for the treatment she received in her darkest hours? Time and tide will tell. She adds in a firmer tone, 'I've made a decision about my own future – I want to become a teacher. It's a rewarding profession for which I seem to have a small talent.'

When they have watched the riotous antics at Silvery Cove long enough, Jack and Maggie stroll back into town, leaving Norah to head down to the beach for her own pickings. She will need everything she can find. For once, Maggie and Jack's conversation turns to happy chatter about dances, afternoon tea at the Regent – and something more lasting and much stronger.

When the path widens enough to allow Maggie to walk beside Jack, she takes his hand.

## THE END

# MESSAGE FROM THE AUTHOR

While *The Silver Tide* is a fictional story, it was inspired by real-life events and people. Countless Cornish fishermen have been swept away to their deaths by the county's dangerous riptides and storms though my inspiration for Maggie Pascoe came from a woman who lived in the Northumberland fishing village of Cresswell. In 1874, Margaret Brown (later Armstrong) saw her father and three of her brothers die in a summer storm. She gathered with friends and neighbours on the beach hoping to see the fishermen make it to safety but was left with the heart-breaking task of pulling their bodies from the sea. That same year, the Royal National Lifeboat Institution established a local lifeboat station and Margaret threw herself into it fully, helping with the launching and recovery work and never missing a launch for more than fifty years. She also helped in other ways with hazardous rescues, one of which is especially remarkable. In the early hours of January 1876, the German ship *Gustaf* hit rocks in a gale. The lifeboat had difficulty launching and so the women of the village formed a human chain with Margaret at its head, often being swept off her feet by the surge of the ocean. Thankfully, the lifeboat did eventually manage to reach the *Gustaf* and all ten people aboard were saved. In 1922, Margaret was awarded the Gold Brooch by the institution for her long service.

Women have played a vital role in the institution from

the earliest days, often being responsible for hauling the boat down to the water's edge and a variety of other activities such as fund-raising. In 1969, Norwegian student Elizabeth Hostvedt, aged 18, became the first woman to command one of the institution's inshore lifeboats, though women had been recognised for their role in sea rescues long before then. Among the most remarkable was Grace Darling, the daughter of the Keeper at the Longstone Lighthouse. In 1838, Grace, aged twenty-three, joined her father, William, in a small open boat to row to the rescue of people aboard the *SS Forfarshire* which had broken in two on nearby rocks.

The attempt in chapter forty-seven to haul the lifeboat overland because of conditions preventing it from being launched from its usual site reflected real-life rescues. For example, in 1861, the lifeboat at Cullercoats, Tyne and Wear, was dragged by villagers for two miles in a gale to go to the rescue of the ship *Lovely Nelly*. The extraordinary feat was later depicted in a painting by John Charlton called *The Women*. In 1899, about one hundred volunteers from the Devon village of Lynmouth hauled their lifeboat overland for thirteen miles, including up a challenging climb called Countisbury Hill, to launch at Porlock Weir and go to the aid of the *Forrest Hall*.

The creation of the parson in my story, Hedrek Kellow, was also sparked by a real-life character – Robert Stephen Hawker, a celebrated clergyman and noted poet, who was parson of a remote parish on Cornwall's north coast for forty-one years. Hawker, who lived from 1803 to 1875, was an eccentric, often dressing in a claret-coloured coat, blue fisherman's jersey, long sea boots and a pink brimless hat. He had a hut made of driftwood much like Kellow's hut in this story. Hawker took the extraordinary step of excommunicating one of his many cats when it caught a mouse on Sunday.

I have taken a small liberty with Hedrek Kellow's successful use of sternal compression to resuscitate a drowned woman in chapter one. John Hill, of London's Royal Free Hospital, wrote about this method in 1868, a few years after the period in which my novel is set. But there is evidence of a rudimentary understanding of resuscitation much earlier. Breathing life into a person is mentioned in the Bible (though not as a medical procedure) and it is believed to have been used in the Middle Ages by physicians and peasant midwives. A learned man such as Kellow might well be aware of such methods and, in extremis, use them.

The vast shoals of pilchards that swept past Cornwall each summer and autumn were a source of great wealth. A twenty-eight-foot lugger of the type mentioned in this novel could catch up to thirty-thousand pilchards in a good night's fishing. Even more effective was seining which typically involved three boats working together with two large nets. In 1851, off the coast of St Ives, a pilchard seine-net was estimated to have captured sixteen and a half million fish, weighing in at eleven hundred tons. Improved communications allowed Cornish pilchards to be sold far and wide. Sadly, even the huge fish stocks of the Atlantic had their limits and by 1930 this once-great industry had all but vanished.

Rear-Admiral (later Vice-Admiral) Robert FitzRoy introduced a national Storm Warning Service in February 1861 after becoming convinced that storms and gales could be predicted. Between 1855 and 1860, 7,402 ships had been wrecked off the European coast, claiming 7,201 lives. FitzRoy believed that with forewarning, many of these people could have been saved. His daily reports attracted much praise but also criticism. The service was typically popular among coastal communities where lives were saved but, inevitably, there were errors with such a pioneering service that attracted criticism. Among FitzRoy's detractors were politicians, scientists, and fishing fleet owners who had a vested interest in the fleets putting to sea.

My thanks go to the many people and organisations who provided advice and information for this story, in particular Tony Pawlyn, of the National Maritime Museum Cornwall; the Reverend Geoff Andrews; Hayley Whiting, Heritage Archive and Research Manager for the Royal National Lifeboat Institution; and Mark Beswick of the National Meteorological Library and Archive – Met Office, UK. Any mistakes in this novel are my own.

Thank you so much for reading *The Silver Tide.* I hope you enjoyed reading it as much as I enjoyed writing about it. I am a shore-based volunteer for the Royal National Lifeboat Institution and have strong family connections with Cornwall's north coast. In fact, my father was one of the county's early lifeguards. The linking of arms to form a human chain to save a swimmer (as mentioned in chapter one of this story) was used by my father to try to save a man at Watergate Bay, Cornwall. My father was not on duty but there was no lifeguard on the beach at the time of the emergency.

If you wish to make contact or get updates, please go to my website www.jhmannauthor.com

I love to hear from readers.

# ALSO BY J.H.MANN

## THE ECHOING SHORE

A lifeboat is lost off Cornwall's wild Atlantic coast. All eight crewmen die. The cause is never fully explained.

Ten years later, Kate Tregillis, the editor of a small newspaper on the brink of closure, becomes obsessed with solving the longstanding mystery.

Her investigations provoke a backlash of threats and violence in the insular fishing community of St Branok. In exposing the truth, she risks the future of her newspaper and even her life – and learns that the man she loves has his own secrets.

## HIDDEN DEPTHS

On a wild Cornish headland, Catherine Carlyon takes a decision that will change her life forever.

She is facing the bleak prospect of years in prison after being sucked into a fraud by a man she thought loved her.

Catherine has found a possible way out – to disappear. But disappearing comes at a price. She must abandon her family and everything she holds dear.

The greatest challenge of her life is looming, an epic adventure in the North Atlantic which will take her to her limits and beyond…

Printed in Dunstable, United Kingdom